THE MIDNIGHT CALL

JODÉ MILLMAN

Appropriate for Teens, Intriguing to Adults

Immortal Works LLC
1505 Glenrose Drive
Salt Lake City, Utah 84104
Tel: (385) 202-0116

Cover Art by Ashley Literski
http://strangedevotion.wixsite.com/strangedesigns

ISBN 978-1-7324674-9-1 (Paperback)
ISBN 978-1-7923072-0-1 (Ebook)

For Mike, Love you always

DISCLAIMER

This is a work of fiction. While I have mentioned actual places and locations in the story, they are merely to introduce the reader to the beautiful setting of the Hudson Valley. All of the characters and events in my story are the products of my imagination, and any resemblance to actual people, living or dead, or actual events is coincidental.

CHAPTER
1

"I think I killed someone," the man's voice whispered across the phone lines.

"Terrence," Jessie Martin's voice croaked, husky with sleep. She'd know her mentor's voice anywhere, anytime, even in the middle of the night. In the pitch darkness Jessie bolted upright in bed and blinked the sleep out of her eyes. "What are you talking about?"

"I've done a terrible thing, committed a sin against God," he said.

The anguish in his voice made the fine hairs on her skin prickle with fear, and her hand flew up with a desire to protect the baby tumbling around inside her swollen belly. Yet, it was the slow, quiet monotone of his voice that frightened Jessie even more than his confession. Her mentor usually had a confident, intense voice that commanded attention. Tonight, it was flat, as if he were no longer aware of reality.

"There's blood everywhere." Terrence's hollow voice cracked. "He was just a boy...a boy. I don't know how it happened. Oh my God, what have I done?"

Nothing was making any sense. Terrence Butterfield. Her mentor. Her teacher. Her friend. A killer? Impossible. But if what he said was true, the only way for her to help him was to remain cool and calm. She inhaled deeply to repress the panic crushing her chest and blew it out in a slow, cleansing breath as she'd learned in Lamaze class.

She turned toward Kyle's side of the bed. Empty. She gripped his pillow in her fist. She'd find him in a moment.

"Terrence, how—what happened? Was there an accident?" She tried to control the tremor in her voice.

"No, it was not...an accident."

Jessie tried to get him to talk, pushed him for more details. It wasn't normal for Terrence to stay quiet for so long about anything. Ever. So his lengthy, heavy silence only intensified her unease over his vague confession about killing a kid. If she'd gone into criminal law instead of corporate law, the right questions would've rolled off her tongue. For now, she'd have to rely on the adrenaline rush and her instincts.

"Just tell me where you are," Jessie demanded. "Whatever's happened, I can help you."

"I'm at home and... I have a gun. I can't continue to live. I need to make peace with God."

"Listen to me. Put the gun down." Jessie's mind raced. If Terrence had intended to kill himself he wouldn't have called her. He wanted her to keep him alive. "There are people who love you. Your family, your students —we all love you."

"I don't know what to do. I'm so confused."

"This is what you are going to do." It felt odd commanding him, reversing the roles so that she was the mentor and he was the pupil. Hopefully, Terrence had enough wits about him to comply with her instructions, but there was no response except for the clicking of his tongue as he wheezed into the receiver. "Just put down the gun and call the police. Tell them there's been an accident. Don't say anything else. Are you with me? I'm on my way. I'll be there in a few minutes. Please don't do anything foolish. Promise me."

The cell phone hung like a dead weight in Jessie's hand as the line went dead. Moist palms stroked the curve of her child in a strong, circular motion. A tiny foot rose up to accept the caresses like a cat seeking to nuzzle, and once sated, the appendage receded into the depths of her womb.

Jessie thought there must be some mistake, but she knew what she'd heard. The stretched-thin quality of his voice convinced her that something was seriously wrong.

Kyle, her fiancé, hadn't returned to their room, so she called out his name. No answer. Flinging back the covers, Jessie set her bare feet on the cold wood floor and ran toward the dresser.

Get dressed. Find Kyle. Go to Terrence. Before — She didn't want to consider the possibilities.

"Kyle," Jessie called out again, rifling through the drawers. Three shirts spilled out onto her feet. She grabbed a striped t-shirt and wriggled into it. It was a bit snug over her belly, but there was no time. She had to go. "Kyle!"

The bedroom door flew open with a crash and Kyle burst into the room, wild-eyed. "Is it the baby?"

"No, no, it's not me. I'm fine, but we've got to go," Jessie said, yanking on her sweatpants. "Terrence said that he's killed someone and he's going to kill himself." She gathered her flyaway hair into a ponytail and hurried toward the bathroom door, but Kyle stepped in front of her blocking her path.

"You scared me half to death… and this is, yet again, about that old—I mean, about Terrence."

Jessie flinched and jerked back, glaring at him.

"Let's a take a second before you do anything crazy and discuss this." Kyle paused. "Babe, as odd as he is, you don't believe that Terrence killed anyone, do you?" He raised his eyebrows and cocked his head. When she didn't respond, he added, "Just in case, why don't we call the police and let them handle it?"

Jessie shook her head adamantly. "Kyle, there's no time to get into this right now so please, call my dad. Have him call Terrence." She shivered uncontrollably from the tension ricocheting through her body, her teeth chattering so violently she believed they'd shatter. "Ma-make him stay on the phone until we g-get there."

"Come 'ere." His tone softened. Kyle encircled her in his arms and a tender hand reached down to embrace their child. She trembled, immune to the warmth of his touch and his soft, cajoling whispers in her ear. "You shouldn't be running around in the middle of the night."

"Sweetie, look, I've got to go and I'd appreciate it if you came along," she said, disguising her fear with determination.

After four years together, Jessie knew that Kyle knew better than to argue with her; after all, she was a lawyer. A damn good one, and once she set her mind on something there was no stopping her. It was all part of her job. Her clients demanded it. But this was the first time the call had come before the arrest. And it was the first time the late night call had been from Terrence.

Kyle growled and released her, shaking his head in resignation. "I guess I can't stop you, can I?" He stepped into the crumpled jeans lying on the floor, then zipped them up and was tugging a Yankees sweatshirt over his head when she disappeared into the bathroom. When she returned to the bedroom, it was empty.

Jessie discovered Kyle downstairs in the kitchen. He shoved his phone into his jean's pocket and fiddled with her car keys with his free hand.

"Did you call my dad?"

Kyle nodded. "Ready? Come on, let's go."

She reached into the pocket of her hoodie and discovered her phone wasn't there. "Damn, I must have left my phone upstairs. I'll be right back."

He twisted his mouth in a soured expression. "Okay. I'll meet you in the car."

As she returned upstairs, she tried to remember where she'd last seen her phone. She'd been in such a rush to get ready that she could have set it down anywhere in the bedroom or bathroom. She couldn't believe she'd been so stupid, especially with Terrence's life at stake.

Jessie entered her bedroom and gave the room a quick once-over. Her phone was nowhere in sight.

Several minutes later, Jessie slipped into the Jeep that was idling in the driveway. Kyle was anxiously tapping his fingers on the steering wheel.

"Sorry I took so long. My phone was under the nightstand. I must have knocked it there when I was getting dressed."

Kyle grunted, threw the car into reverse, and backed out of the driveway.

Jessie's eyes were drawn to the keychain dangling from her Jeep's ignition. It contained the motley gray rabbit's foot that Terrence had bagged on one of the many hunting trips with her father. They'd made an odd couple, her father and the younger teacher, but they had a lot in common, and they'd always come home with a kill or two. After one trip, Terrence had presented the token to her with great flourish on the night before she'd left for law school, attaching it to a Black's Law Dictionary and a pound of Ethiopian coffee beans. Jessie had kept it with her always for good luck: during finals, the bar exam, and her job interviews. Whenever the fates needed an extra boost.

Now, the sight of the cherished charm made her shudder as it assumed a more grisly visage. She felt sorry for the little critter so brutally killed and felt a twinge of doubt as to whether she really knew the man who'd been on the other end of the line—the patient friend who'd spent his Saturday mornings laboring with her over her college admission essays, the charismatic bachelor who'd delivered yellow roses on her mother's birthday, the popular high school teacher who'd brought history to life by dressing as Genghis Khan, George Washington, and Gandhi. And who, ever since she was a teenager, had been the keeper of her deepest secrets and dreams.

For Terrence's sake, Jessie hoped that he'd been mistaken tonight. Otherwise, he'd need more than her rabbit's foot to protect him.

Kyle screeched to a halt at the curb in front of Terrence's home, and she glanced toward the small white clapboard ranch. While the neighboring houses were dark, Terrence's house shone like a beacon among the Cape Cod cottages nestled along the quiet, tree-lined boulevard in Poughkeepsie, New York. In the humid August night, hazy lights blazed from every window, illuminating the well-manicured lawn and beds of roses and daylilies that she'd helped him plant more than a decade ago.

Terrence's tall, lean silhouette was framed within the front bay window. He was speaking on the phone, presumably to her father. The front door stood ajar, inviting her to enter.

In the darkness, Jessie glimpsed two black and white cop cars creeping toward them from the opposite direction. With sirens silenced and headlights extinguished, the cars glided toward the far curb and parked. Bathed in the amber glow of the overhead street lamps, the officers were motionless inside their cars.

"Did you call the police?" Jessie asked.

Kyle didn't answer. "What are they doing?" he whispered, as though the cops could hear.

Jessie eyed Kyle, but there were more pressing matters. "They're probably waiting for back up. Come on. Let's go." She cocked the door handle, but Kyle grabbed her arm and squeezed. She glanced over at him, confused.

"You're not going out there, Jessie."

"This is Terrence's life, Kyle." Her voice trembled with conviction, fear, and the desire to help the one man she trusted and revered almost as much as her own father. Kyle never understood that before Terrence entered her life, she'd floundered in school. At best, she'd been a B student. Terrence's energy and enthusiasm had ignited a spark inside her, instilling knowledge, values, and moral lessons that had helped her achieve her goal of law school. She'd had many teachers and professors over the years, and recognized the rarity of such a man. She was deeply grateful to Terrence but Kyle insisted that the man was a fraud.

Jessie started at the sudden sound of the patrol cars' doors banging open like cannon fire. She blinked rapidly to dispel the horrible image unfolding in slow motion. A pair of officers emerged from each vehicle. They drew their guns and strode in the direction of Terrence's house. Her eyes tracked them through the pools of streetlight dotting the avenue, knowing they were on a collision course with Terrence. She felt paralyzed, like during the surreal seconds before an automobile accident, and the powerlessness of skidding toward the unavoidable impact.

"Come on, Kyle."

"Please stay in the car, at least until we know it's safe."

"Don't be ridiculous. Terrence won't shoot us." Instinctively, Jessie ran a hand over her belly, and in response to the baby's sharp jab to her ribs, she yanked her arm free from Kyle's hold. Opening the door, Jessie slid out of the Jeep and sprinted up the sidewalk toward the broad front steps with Kyle trailing on her heels.

"Stop! Police!" commanded a gravelly voice. "Hands up. Over your head, where we can see them."

Jessie gasped, stopping in mid-stride. She froze in place, the toes of her sneakers flirting with the bottom step of the porch. Fumbling through the pitch darkness, she threaded her fingers in her fiancé's. Kyle clasped them, tugged her close to his side, and slowly, they raised their joined hands into the air.

"Sir, I'm here to see Mr. Butterfield. I'm an attorney. He's expecting me," Jessie shouted. Judging from the cop's voice, he was still a good fifty feet away. Far enough for her to make a mad dash for the front door. The door was so close, but Kyle's grip tightened, digging her engagement ring into her flesh.

"Miss, don't move," the officer said. "Please remain where you are. For your own safety."

"It's all right, Jessica." Terrence leaned against the doorjamb, swinging the screen door open to the night air. His voice sounded distant, otherworldly, and his fine-boned features were obscured by the night's shadows. "Officers, please come in."

The four police officers swarmed past them with their pistols aimed at the waiting figure. Two officers inched their way up the steps onto the front porch, while a few yards away, the other two covered them from the bottom step. As the team passed, Kyle stepped forward, shielding her from danger and obstructing her path to Terrence.

Terrence might need her, she thought, so she skirted around Kyle and waited and listened. She needed to be ready.

"Sir, are you Terrence Butterfield?" an officer asked.

"Yes."

Jessie had instructed him to keep quiet and sensed that he was about to break the golden rule—never admit anything.

"We're investigating a report about the discharging of a firearm at this address. Sir, do you have a weapon? Please show me your hands," said an older officer with a pockmarked face, as he edged another step closer.

Terrence raised his hands over his head. In his right hand, he gripped an old-fashioned revolver, like Jessie had seen in the Westerns. "I think I have killed someone."

"Terrence, stop talking!" Jessie exclaimed.

As long as Terrence kept his mouth shut, maybe she could salvage the situation. There had to be a reasonable explanation. Maybe there had been some horrible accident. Maybe he'd stood his ground against an intruder. Maybe he was drunk or stoned or he was hallucinating. She needed to know. To hear the truth from him.

"Sir, I'm Sergeant Mike Rossi and this is my partner, Officer Jen Macy." Rossi crossed the threshold, while Macy signaled for the other team to spread out around the back of the house. Cautiously, Rossi inched his way toward Terrence. "Mr. Butterfield, please set the gun on the floor."

Terrence's trembling hand offered him the weapon.

Rossi stepped backward, looking startled by the movement, but keeping his gun steady, trained on his target. "Just do as I say. Put the gun down and place your hands on top of your head."

"Please take it. I don't want it."

On the bottom porch step, Jessie balanced on her tiptoes, craning her neck to spy on the action through the screen door and windows. She held her breath as Terrence and Rossi eyed each other across the barrel of the shiny gun aimed point-blank at Terrence's chest. Tension seized Terrence's muscles, accentuating the slight tic along his jaw that appeared only when he felt threatened. It was a sign that he could attack with little provocation, something she'd witnessed more than once when he'd fended off troublemakers in his classroom.

Locked in a stalemate, Terrence and Rossi continued to glare at each other. Time seemed to stand still, interrupted only by the echoes of the midnight freight trains snaking along the banks of the Hudson River.

Jessie's pulse thrummed in her ears as she watched, too terrified to move.

The seconds ticked by and then, suddenly as if his nerve had drained away, Terrence's jaw slackened. He lowered his hand and set the weapon on the coffee table to his right. Then, he hung his head and cradled his temples with his hands.

"Drop to your knees," Rossi shouted, backing Terrence away from the window so that both men vanished from sight.

Jessie inhaled, inviting humid, sweet air into her lungs, and steadied herself against the steps' banister. "I should really be in there." She edged her way up to the next step. "He needs me."

"Let the police do their job, babe." Kyle's fingers clamped around her wrist like a vice. His eyes darted to her baby bump, and then they shifted, staring directly into her eyes, concern crinkling his brow.

Jessie's gaze swung back toward the house, consumed with the frustration that a bizarre tableau was being played out only a few yards away. Helplessly, she listened to doors slamming, footsteps thundering through rooms, and snippets of conversations and commands drifting outside into the night. As hard as Jessie tried, she couldn't hear Terrence or see him, and she prayed that he was holding up under the pressure. At least Terrence knew that she and Kyle were there for him and had his back.

Relief flooded her when Rossi herded Terrence back into view in the front hallway, but her chest tightened when a voice crackled over the two-way radio dangling from the officer's belt.

"Sarge, can you read me? You need to see this… down here in the basement. Copy?"

A scowl hardened on Kyle's face, and his fingers turned to steel bands squeezing her wrist past the point of pain. Jessie flinched, and he released her.

"Keep your eye on Butterfield," Rossi said to Macy. "I'll be right back."

Jessie massaged the shelf of her belly as the baby's angular limb stabbed deep into her chest cavity. She lowered herself to the dew-covered steps to ease the wooziness engulfing her like fog. The hour. The heat. The rush. It was all catching up with her.

She needed to shake it off. Stay alert and focused for Terrence. He'd always been there for her—the proms, graduations, fender benders, and panic attacks before the bar exam. Now, it was Jessie's turn. She owed it to him, and herself, to unearth the truth.

"Terrence, we're still here. Just do as they say," Jessie blurted, hoping that the sound of her voice would give him the strength to carry on, although her grit was circling the drain.

"Let's go." Kyle loomed over her, his mouth pinched at the corners. "You can't even stay on your feet. You're tired and there's nothing more you can do for him. Not tonight." He offered her a hand.

Jessie glared at him with an anger that recharged her depleted battery. Kyle knew better. Once she committed to a cause, she never budged. "I've got to help him get this mess cleared up. There's been a mistake."

"A mistake? It looks to me like Terrence finally flipped out and killed somebody. But I can't expect you to be objective about him. You wanted him to be our kid's godfather." Kyle paused, clenching and unclenching his fists. "You know, sometimes Terrence seems like a third party to our relationship."

Kyle had a way of believing the worst whenever it came to Terrence. It never bothered her when Terrence called to chat about the latest movies or books he'd read or stopped by to watch a football game with Kyle. He was Terrence being Terrence, and she knew that there was no ulterior motive on his part. Ever since she'd been a kid, she and Terrence had been close, and over the years he'd done plenty for her. And she for him. He'd worn many hats in her life—friend, confidante, teacher, mentor, even an uncle—and Kyle had known that from the beginning but Kyle insisted that Terrence was taking advantage of their friendship by calling and popping in uninvited. Why couldn't he acknowledge that each man had a special place in her life?

Low voices discussed the need to secure the crime scene and call the paramedics, the forensic team, the district attorney, and the medical examiner. Although criminal law was outside her wheelhouse, Jessie knew the working parts of a homicide investigation, so these whisperings confirmed her worst suspicions. First, there was a dead body or bodies somewhere in the house—probably the basement. And second, Terrence was implicated in the homicide.

Suddenly, the screen door swung open, and the dark figure of Terrence Butterfield emerged from the house in handcuffs shepherded by Rossi and Macy. With his head drooped forward against his chest and his limp arms shackled at the wrist, he shuffled across the whitewashed porch and down the entry steps.

Terrence drew closer and the veil of night shadow enshrouding his face and body revealed something much more sinister. His handsome face was smeared with glossy red liquid and his dark brown hair was clumped into a tangled mess. A rank stench, like rotten cabbage boiled in sulfur, emanated from the tattered, bloody shirt clinging to his chest. The smell of death on him hit her like a slap and grew worse with every step he took toward her.

Stifling a gag, Jessie garnered her strength and stepped into their path. She double-checked the name on his silver badge. "Officer Rossi, I know that you've got a job to do, but I do, too. Before you take Mr. Butterfield anywhere, I'm putting you on notice that he is not to be interrogated without my being present." She cleared her throat. "And has he been read his rights?"

Rossi eyed her with contempt, as though insinuating that she had no right to question his actions or authority. "We can discuss that after Mr. Butterfield has been booked."

"I think that we should discuss it now." Jessie's tone was insistent, hard.

Before they could respond, Terrence spoke up, "I believe that I'm entitled to speak with my attorney."

"You can speak with her down at the station. Move along, Mr. Butterfield," Macy said, shoving the captive's shoulder. "Ma'am, please move out of the way."

For a long moment, Jessie remained stationary, considering how far she could push the cops before she crossed the line. Her heart urged her to defy Rossi and speak with Terrence right then and there, yet her head warned her to follow the protocol. Strategically, the latter would be best for both of them.

"Not a word," Jessie counseled him as she stepped aside. Terrence stopped before her and gently rested his cuffed hands on the round of her belly. She smiled and cupped her hands over his in reassurance. "Don't worry. We'll be right behind you."

Gazing into his eyes, she searched for the truth, but instead, found cold, dead-fish eyes, and his dry, cracked lips were curled in a crooked, haunting smile. She shrank away from him, huddling against Kyle to steady her buckling knees.

The officers grabbed Terrence's shoulder, ushered him toward their patrol car, and loaded him into the back seat. The engine started and with lights flashing and sirens blaring, the police car sped off into the night.

Nothing in her thirty years of life had prepared her for this moment. This tragedy.

Terrence's life was in her hands. And in that instant, Jessie realized that she must follow her heart. She knew the kind, caring friend, teacher, and confidante that he'd been to her. She needed to disregard the blood, the stench, and the nagging worry that he was a cold-blooded killer. She'd prove him innocent. She owed him that.

As the police car taillights disappeared into the darkness, an undeniable dampness seeped onto Jessie's abdomen. Her eyes widened in horror as she looked down at her sweatshirt. Beneath the Syracuse University logo, a grisly tattoo of handprints smeared across her belly. Jessie flipped over her quivering hands and stared at her palms, black and sticky with blood.

"Oh, my God."

CHAPTER
2

The heavy metal door of the City of Poughkeepsie Police Station slammed behind Jessie and Kyle, definite and final. Jessie shaded her eyes against the greenish fluorescent glare of the faded cinder block walls stretching down the hallway. At the end of the hall, the desk sergeant attended an army green metal desk, which, like the man, had seen better days.

She straightened her posture to appear taller than her 5'5" frame and informed him that they were there to see Terrence Butterfield. "I'm Jessica Martin, Esq., his—"

"We're his friends," Kyle interrupted. "We were at his house when he was arrested."

Jessie's eyes narrowed, and she stepped away from him, closer to the desk. "I'd like to speak with Mr. Butterfield as soon as possible."

The officer checked his computer and motioned toward the folding chairs lining the wall facing his desk. "Mr. Butterfield's in holding. Wait over there. I'll let you know when he's ready."

They settled into the cold metal chairs.

"You okay?" Kyle asked.

Jessie yawned, nodded, and traced the comforting flutter in her stomach with her bitten fingernails. The chair squeaked beneath her weight as she fidgeted, trying to get comfortable.

The door to the waiting room swung open. A plainclothes officer, Detective Ebony Jones, entered. Her black braids were pulled tight into a ponytail that trailed halfway down her back, accentuating her topaz eyes and her flawless tawny complexion. With each step, her silver shield and leather holster swayed from the belt slung low around her waist. Spotting Jessie, she said, "Hey, girl. What're you doing here at this ungodly hour?"

Jessie hadn't seen her friend in months. They'd frequently exchanged texts, made plans for lunch and dinner, but life always seemed to get in the way. She couldn't remember who was the last one who'd bailed.

"Ebbie, hey. I still can't believe that they let you carry a gun." Jessie heaved herself up and hugged Ebony. "If they only knew what a wild child you were in high school."

"And I can't believe that they let you practice law." Ebony grabbed Jessie by the shoulders, examining her at arm's length. "You're looking pretty good for having a bean in your belly. But what's the deal with the bloodstain on your sweatshirt? You okay?" Jessie nodded, but Ebony's brows knitted with concern. "The last time I saw you, you guys were out with Butterfield at the Bardavon Theater gala. He didn't try to suck you into his case, did he?"

"Not exactly," Jessie said, over her fiancé's grunt. She gave Ebony an edited version of the last hour's events. After all, a cop was first a cop so all statements were on the record, especially where homicide was concerned.

"I saw Mr. B. when they brought him in. He was a mess so they hauled him off to gather evidence and to the showers. Then, they'll take him to holding or interrogation. Stay put. I'll check and let you know." Ebony bounded halfway down the hall, stopped short and swiveled about to face her. "Who would've thought that our history teacher was capable of murder, huh? Not me, that's for sure." She walked a few steps further then halted in her tracks again. "I pity the unlucky shyster who's stuck representing him."

Shyster, huh. That's a cop for you, Jessie thought. Thinking that all lawyers are crooked. Soon enough Ebony would discover that Jessie was here to represent Terrence and get him off, scot-free.

Jessie crossed her arms across her chest and was settling back into her chair when her cell phone vibrated inside the pocket of her hoodie. She whipped it out and checked the incoming caller ID. It was her father.

"Jess, I've been waiting to hear back from you or Kyle. What's going on? Has Terry been arrested?" Edmund Martin's voice was strained with urgency.

"Dad, I can't talk right now. We're at the police station waiting to see him."

"Honey, if you want me to come down to the station, just say the word and I'm there." He paused. "I'll do anything I can for

Terry, so if he needs anything, please let me know." His voice sounded choked and he paused again, clearing his throat. "He's like family."

"I know, Dad. But we're good and I promise to call you when I have news." Somewhat appeased, he let her go and Jessie returned the phone to her pocket.

Her father was justifiably devastated by this turn of events. As Poughkeepsie High School principal, he'd hired Terrence fresh out of Yale, almost twenty years ago, and since then, the two had developed a real bromance, as her mother had called it, despite their difference in ages. Ball games. Golf. Fishing. Guy stuff. Her dad had developed a tough hide—who wouldn't when one dealt with kids all day—but Terrence's arrest was hitting him hard.

Her gut warned her that Terrence could face manslaughter, or worse, murder charges, depending upon the circumstances or his intentions. Any scandal of this nature would not only rock her family but the community as well. Students, past and present. Parents. Faculty. The school administration. The eyes of the media and social media would be focused on the investigation unfolding in their small upstate New York community. Some would rush to judgment against Terrence while others, like herself, would believe in his innocence until the judgment by a jury of his peers.

Jessie's eyes shifted to her sweatshirt stained with blood, recalling Ebony's snippy remarks. *Shyster.*

Then her gaze settled on Kyle. Next to her, his head rested peacefully against the wall. His eyes were closed. His hands were folded across his broad chest, and his long legs protruded into the office pathway. She envied his ability to relax anywhere and admired his mane of wild black-Irish hair and the thick curves of his lips. This man had sacrificed so much to be with her, trading his marketing position at Madison Square Garden for a crappy one at the cash-strapped Mid-Hudson Civic Center. During the past four years, while her career blossomed, his had withered. Not once had he complained about his MBA gathering dust inside a cardboard box in their bedroom closet.

His eyes fluttered open as though sensing her scrutiny. He winked at her and a smile spread across his lips. His goofy, crooked smile said he was all in, no matter the circumstances. He was her guy.

Seriously, what was she thinking? What was she doing at the police station in the third trimester of her pregnancy? She was a corporate attorney, not a criminal attorney. During her brief career at the McMann and Curtis law firm, she'd paid her dues by handling a few drunk driving cases but knew nothing about felonies. Zip. Zero. Murder was way out of her league, as alien to her as aerospace law.

And there was no upside to her situation. On the one hand, her inexperience could land Terrence in prison for the rest of his life. On the other, if she remained his counsel, she could face censure or disbarment for misrepresenting her expertise. The last thing she wanted was to jeopardize his life or her license to practice law. Her life, family, and career were just beginning.

Without a doubt, she was in way over her head. Kyle would never mention his misgivings to her, he'd let her figure it out on her own. All it had taken was a wink and a smile for the realization to sink in.

Jessie fished around inside the hoodie pocket and dug out her phone. She scrolled through the contacts, mulling over whom she'd call if she were in trouble. After Kyle and her dad, of course. Who was the best criminal defense guy in town? Who could she trust with Terrence's life? Or her own?

"You're doing the right thing," Kyle said.

Sometimes it was spooky the way he knew what she was going to do, going to say, before she did. They may not be totally in sync about Terrence, but they were about their life together. Jessie rose from the chair and doubled back down into the entryway away from the prying ears of the police. On her screen, she stared at the name and certain of her decision, pressed the phone number. Cupping the phone to her ear, Jessie listened to the phone ring. The odds were fifty-fifty that he'd answer her predawn call for help.

CHAPTER
3

The time was well past midnight and Jeremy Kaplan was alone in his musty law office. He scratched his armpit through his undershirt and over-poured himself a glass of bourbon, topping it off since there were no witnesses.

The inner sanctum was dark except for the light of a lamp in the figure of Blind Lady Justice. At first, he'd detested the kitschy gift from his wife Gayle, but he'd grown to love the reminder of her thoughtfulness. Now, he and the Lady were sharing a smoke and drink, while his family slept two stories overhead. He sucked on a cigar stub and exhaled plumes of blue smoke, preparing to tackle the bills. On the last night of each month, Jeremy waited for Gayle to relax under the covers beside him, her breath rhythmically cresting and falling. Then, he'd slip from their bed and sneak downstairs to his office to attack the ledgers comprising his life.

The invoices were divided on his desk into three piles in priority of payment. The house. The office. The alimony. For the last couple of months, he'd slacked off, but now the creditors, especially his ex-wife Sheila, were threatening legal action.

"You're a cheap bastard," Sheila had shrieked during their most recent argument. They'd divorced fifteen years ago, but the woman continued to bust his chops. "You haven't sent me my check in three months. I know you have the money so send me my alimony or I'll contact the support collection unit."

Her kvetching played over and over in his mind as he contemplated the bills. With Sheila, nothing ever changed. If only she'd marry again, but Sheila was too smart. Ten years of alimony left to go.

Gayle was the polar opposite of Sheila. She was smart, even-tempered, frugal, and hot. Just thinking about her, asleep upstairs, made him want to forget the bills, crawl back into bed, and snuggle beside her, but the letter from the Hanover Life Insurance Company deflated his ardor. Out of desperation, he'd contacted them to withdraw the cash value from his whole life policy.

Fifty-thousand dollars. The windfall would satisfy his alimony arrears, his oldest daughter's Cornell tuition, plus the house expenses for the next few months. Jeremy had no choice. He'd held onto the paperwork for a few weeks, hoping that a large retainer would walk through the door. But no such luck. Only a few house closings and a small estate.

He sucked the glass dry, grabbed his pen, and prepared to sign his nest egg away. Jeremy paused, staring at a light blinking on the desk phone. Puzzled, he glanced at the clock—3 a.m., the witching hour when, in the good old days, his clients had made that one magic telephone call. And they'd always called him. Hookers. Pimps. Drunks. Pushers. Users. Wife beaters. Husband stabbers. Robbers. Rapists. Murderers. They'd all called him until the Great Recession of '08. These days, they contacted the public defender because they, too, were broke and unable to afford his hefty hourly fee. Apparently, the quality of the results was no longer important.

Although he figured that it was a wrong number and considered letting it go to voicemail, he picked up the handset.

"Jeremy? Jeremy Kaplan?" a young woman's anxious voice asked.

"Ah, yeah."

"Sorry to call so late, but this is Jessie Martin." Her voice squeaked like a teenager's. She cleared her throat and continued. "I need your help. Actually, Terrence Butterfield does."

Her name registered with him. She'd worked for him one summer when she was in high school—basic secretarial stuff—filing, running errands, and shadowing him at court. Smart kid. Her father was the PHS principal. She'd wanted to attend law school and to check out a criminal law practice. Back then, he'd been busy enough and had no problem with an eager, attractive teenager hanging around the office. He hadn't heard from her in years, though he remembered seeing the newspaper announcement when she'd joined up with Larry Curtis's firm.

The name Terrence Butterfield also rang a bell. His older kids had been Butterfield's students at PHS. He recalled the guy as a bit of a kooky character, dressing up like Robert E. Lee or somebody like that. The kids loved him.

Jeremy listened as Jessie rushed through her story, which grew more interesting by the second. A hasty brushstroke without any details, but he got the gist of it. This girl had been dragged into the teacher's dirty laundry and squeezed through the wringer. From what he gathered, she hadn't witnessed a murder or seen a dead body. She'd only observed Butterfield smothered in blood and the cops hauling him away after he'd admitted to killing someone. In his book, that scenario could be interpreted a thousand different ways. None of them good.

"This type of case, murder—alleged murder—is outside my area, so I don't feel comfortable representing Terrence. Ethically, I mean. I'm corporate, not criminal."

Jeremy gritted his teeth, waiting for the ask. The compliments. The groveling. He could hear them bubbling up in her throat.

"He's my friend and should be represented by the best. Someone I respect and trust. I know it's late, but could you please come down to the police station and speak with him? I'd appreciate it." And as if reading his mind, she added. "And the retainer's no issue."

There it was. The hook was set.

"Don't worry, Jessie," he said. "I'll be right there."

CHAPTER
4

The wall clock read 4:17 a.m. and Jessie wondered what could possibly be taking so long for her to see Terrence. For the fourth time in the two hours they'd been there, Kyle suggested that they go home, get some rest, and return later in the morning. His intentions were honorable, wanting to protect her, but she refused, although the uncomfortable chair, the glaring overhead lights, the grating unanswered ringing of the switchboard, and the endless waiting were wearing her down. Kyle couldn't understand that she needed to be here. Besides, Ebony might return with news at any moment.

Jeremy Kaplan burst through the precinct's door, his loud outfit—a wrinkled blue Hawaiian shirt, stained khakis, and topsiders—preceded his arrival. At the sight of him, Jessie's heart sank. The slick, Armani-clad genius she remembered had been replaced by a Jimmy Buffett Parrothead. She'd made a rookie mistake but there was no turning back.

"Where's Butterfield?" Kaplan asked, adjusting the wire-rim glasses on his beaky nose and smoothing the ruffled gray hair that reminded her of a pissed-off bird.

The desk sergeant swiveled his chair. "Kaplan, you here for Butterfield? I thought she was." He pointed his chin toward Jessie.

"We both are. Let us see him before I have to call and wake up Chief Shepardson." Jeremy smirked. "Then, it's on you."

"Yes, sir." The sergeant groaned as he rose from behind the console and disappeared down the corridor.

"Jeremy, thanks for coming," Jessie said, deciding that perhaps she'd misjudged him. She introduced Kyle, then said, "We've been sitting here since two o'clock. God only knows what they're doing to him."

"We'll get to the bottom of this, one way or another," Jeremy said, digging his hands into his pants pockets.

Moments later, Ebony Jones returned to the waiting area. "Jessie, sorry you had to wait, we've been swamped tonight. It took longer than I thought to collect evidence from Mr. B. and get him cleaned up. Someone was supposed to inform you that we're ready to take you down to see him." Her eyes shifted toward the sergeant standing beside her. "Please, come this way."

"Go ahead. I'll wait," Kyle said. He made no move to rise. It would be a solo trip on this leg of the night's journey.

Jessie nodded and squeezed his hand. She trailed behind Jeremy and Ebony toward the locked steel and glass door at the far end of the office. It dawned on her that she'd never been admitted into the jail annex before. She had no idea what to expect. Ebony swiped the lock with the identification card hanging from a lanyard around her neck. The door buzzed and clicked open. When Jessie stepped inside the door, she glanced back at Kyle, as though taking her last look at freedom. Stunned and a little anxious, she tottered along behind them like a colt testing out its footing.

On the way to the elevators, Jessie took quick notice of the doors flanking the corridor: Detective Division, Juvenile Division, Communications Center, Emergency Services Unit, and Evidence Room. The trio boarded the elevator and Ebony pushed the button for Lower Level Two. Jessie shuddered as the doors snapped shut, trapping her inside the polished steel tomb descending downward. The elevator jerked to a stop at LL2, the doors slid open, and they disembarked into a dark, deserted passageway. At the far end, the uniformed guard attending an iron security gate was bathed in a spotlight that dangled from the ceiling.

"Butterfield's in number two," the guard said, his foghorn voice echoing off the tiled walls. He unlocked the gate, permitting them entry.

Ebony motioned toward a cubicle on the right. She pointed at a small window in the center of the door. "I'll be watching in case you need anything."

The compartment was small, not much larger than the elevator, and was bare except for a small table and four chairs. Terrence sat at the table studying his fingernails, apparently unaware of the visitors entering the room until the door clicked closed. His eyes darted upward and tracked Jessie like radar until she sat down across from him.

At first glance, Terrence appeared to be in better physical condition than at their last meeting. His dark hair was slick wet from a shower and his skin flushed pink from the exfoliation of any evidence of the crime. To her relief, the cabbage scent was gone, and he smelled clean like deodorant soap. The sleeves of his oversized orange jumpsuit were folded back to compensate for the extra length, and white sneakers and rawhide bracelets and anklets completed the new prison ensemble.

Under closer scrutiny, metal chains connecting the bracelets and anklets to a stiff wide rawhide belt shackled him to the table like an animal. The table vibrated with the repetitive tapping of his foot against the table leg, rattling his chains.

"How are you holding up?" Jessie asked, masking her shock with an exaggerated cheerfulness. An unnerving silence hung between them. "This is Jeremy Kaplan. He's the top criminal defense attorney in the Hudson Valley. He's here to discuss representing you." Indecision continued to plague her because so far, Kaplan had remained silent. She'd expected him to jump right in to find out what had happened, but he sat there with his hands folded observing Terrence and Jessie.

Terrence narrowed his eyes, continuing to scrutinize them. When he finally spoke, his voice was barely audible. "None of this seems real. I feel like this is happening to someone else." He let out a deep sigh. "One minute I'm watching the late news, the next moment I'm waking up on my cellar floor covered in blood. Jessica, this can't be happening to me." He closed his eyes and rested his head in his hands. His shoulders shuddered as he sniffed. "God forgive me. What have I done?"

Kaplan caught her eye. *No,* he seemed to be warning her. *Don't. Do not help him. Show no signs of weakness. Remain strong. He needs a lawyer, not a friend.*

The pounding of her pulse filled her ears. What had happened? She'd never seen him cry, or come to think of it, display sadness or grief. Ever. Not even when his fiancée had ended their engagement years ago. In the wake of the breakup, just like at the crime scene, Terrence had been distant, detached, and completely removed from the situation. She'd pitied him, and his inability to emote or grieve.

His tears of remorse seemed heartfelt and genuine. It pained her to consider the atrocities that made him act so out of character, so emotional. She wanted to reach out, comfort him, and promise that his problems would vanish, but she couldn't. Not tonight.

"Mr. Butterfield, may I call you Terrence?" Not waiting for an answer, Kaplan proceeded. "Terrence, before we begin, I'd like your permission to record this conversation."

Kaplan withdrew a digital recorder from his pocket and placed it in the center of the table, just beyond Terrence's reach. Terrence looked up, wiped his cheeks with his sleeves, smoothed the wrinkles from his jumpsuit, and combed his stringy hair with his fingers as if preparing for a reporter's interview. He nodded his approval.

Kaplan pressed the record button and stated the perfunctory particulars; his name, occupation, and legal specialty as well as the date, time, and place of the interview. He obtained Terrence's verbal consent to the recording along with an acknowledgment of Jessie's presence. Kaplan rose from his chair and leaned his shoulders against the wall. His joints cracked as he rolled his stubbly chin down to his chest, then from side to side. "I know it's late and we're all dead tired but in order to defend you I need to know what occurred at your home this evening."

"Mr. Kaplan," Terrence said, "you don't know me but Jessica does. She will vouch for me. I'm not a liar. Or a killer. I say this as a preface to my next statement." He paused, clearing his throat. "Honestly and truly, I don't remember."

As Kaplan continued his stretching, Terrence sought out eye contact with Jessie. Deep crevices pinched the corners of his eyes and a malevolent grin settled across his face. His pointy nose wrinkled in what seemed to be delight. Then in a flash, the fiendishness vanished, causing her to question its appearance at all.

A frigid chill shot up her spine and her ragged fingernails scraped the sides of the chair as she steadied herself. This man sitting across from her looked like Terrence, spoke like Terrence, but she'd never seen the dark glint in his eyes before. It terrified her to think that he wasn't the kind, gentle soul who'd never hurt anyone, let alone kill someone. He loved his students, his community, and her family. He loved her, and she believed with all her heart that whatever had happened tonight must have been a horrible mistake. Terrence Butterfield could not possibly have committed murder. There had to be another explanation. He was innocent until proven guilty.

"You've got to believe me," Terrence continued. "I remember watching the weather report on the news. That was around eleven-thirty. There was some kind of commotion outside back by my garage. Then, I don't remember anything after that..." His long fingers inched across the surface like the spindly legs of a spider and snatched the recorder. He fondled the device and returned it to the table.

"Mr. Butterfield, please continue," Kaplan said.

Innocent until proven guilty, Jessie repeated over and over in her mind.

CHAPTER
5

J essie checked her watch. 5:30 a.m.

For the last hour, Terrence had recited the same sketchy details over and over again, like the loop of a soundtrack. She was beginning to worry that without more helpful information, Kaplan's hands would be tied and a defense would be impossible.

Her lids growing heavy, she half-listened as Terrence began his story. Again. She fantasized about crawling back into a bed with Kyle, curling up under the covers in their nice, comfy bed. Going to sleep.

"I was sitting in my living room watching the eleven o'clock news when I heard laughter and shouting outside. Garbage cans were being tossed around back by my garage." He tugged on the cuff of his sleeve. "I looked out my kitchen window and noticed a group of teenage boys, maybe five or six of them, loitering in my backyard." His brows furrowed, and his eyes were cold, dark, flinty.

"Naturally, I was perturbed. I yelled at them. Told them to get off of my lawn. One of the little brats had a spray can. The others called me obscene names. I was infuriated. Incensed."

Like all the previous times, Terrence stopped at this point, forgetting his train of thought. This time, he murmured, "Graffiti. On my walls. They yelled. Pervert. The boy. In my house. Drinking whiskey. I grabbed my gun. A kitchen knife." His attention flitted around the room and settled on his fingers knitted together as if in prayer. "What have I done?"

Having sat stone-still ever since entering the room, Jessie's body ached with tension. She jolted up at the mention of a boy, a knife, and a gun, and she leaned forward in her chair.

"The police... my gun..." Terrence trailed off. The manacle chains clattered when he folded his arms on the table and cradled his head within the nest.

Kaplan swiveled toward Jessie to speak. He hesitated when the door cracked open and Ebony beckoned him. He rose and joined the detective in the hallway.

Finally alone with Terrence, Jessie gently placed her hand on his elbow. She recalled a time, one of the lowest points of her life, when he'd been there for her. When she'd nowhere else to go and no one to turn to, he'd welcomed her into his home without judgment. Without questions. The confidence she'd placed in him all those years ago about what had happened with Robbie, her ex, had always remained. He'd kept it secret, just as she'd asked.

"I'm so sorry you have to go through this," Jessie whispered. "If you need anything at all, we'll be here, Kyle, Dad, me. All of us. You know that."

Terrence gave no indication that he'd heard her, just kept his head tucked in his arms.

Moments later, Kaplan stuck his head into the room and summoned her with a quick crook of his finger. His face no longer exuded confidence.

She joined him to find Ebony pacing along the hallway, wringing a document. The crumpled papers rustled within her fingers. "Forensics has identified the body based on a New York State driver's license inside the victim's wallet." Ebony's expression was blank as she delivered the horrible news. "Jessie, it was Ryan Paige."

The name hit like a bullet in the chest. Ryan Paige. Eighteen-year-old Ryan Paige. She couldn't believe it. Robbie's brother. Ryan had been like a kid brother to her, and had almost been her brother-in-law, if not for her broken engagement to Robbie. The same Robbie whom she'd confided in Terrence about all those years ago. A cruel coincidence.

"That can't be," Jessie said, "It's impossible."

"There was a wallet in the jeans pocket and we're waiting to confirm the dentals. Based on the evidence, we're pretty sure that the body is Ryan's."

"The Paiges? No, this isn't happening. They own half the commercial property in town," Kaplan said, ignoring Jessie's distress.

"Honey, are you ok?" Ebony reached out to embrace her, but Jessie pressed her palms outward and shied away down the hall. "I'm so sorry. What can I do?"

Jessie was at a complete loss for words. From head to toe, her body felt like she'd been mowed down by a freight train. Her arms cradled the swell of her baby, and she inhaled and exhaled deeply.

"Ebbie, give me a minute, please. Ryan? Are you sure?" Jessie swallowed hard.

Ebony nodded.

Kaplan's head flinched back slightly and he gave Jessie an odd look as if wondering why she should be so distraught by the news. Then he pursed his lips appearing to understand. "Weren't you dating a Paige boy when you worked for me?"

Jessie nodded. In the back of her throat, she tasted the sourness of the circular nature of the evening's events. She and Robbie Paige had met in Terrence's history class, and Robbie had been her first love. Now, a little more than a decade later, Terrence had allegedly killed Ryan, Robbie's brother and an heir to the Paige real estate fortune, her firm's largest client. With Ryan's death, Robbie Paige had returned to her life, and despite her determination to extricate herself, she was becoming tethered tighter to the crime with each passing minute.

"Mr. Kaplan, would you like to finish up with your client?" Ebony asked. He obeyed, leaving the two friends alone in the corridor. "Do you want me to go get Kyle?"

"No, just stay where you are. Please don't talk. Don't say anything." Jessie sniffled as tears stung her cheeks. She stared straight ahead unblinking, but in her peripheral vision, she spied Ebony inching her way along the wall toward her until their shoulders brushed against one another's. Her friend waited, comfortable with the silence between them.

A guard approached them and halted, shifting from foot to foot, as Ebony consoled her. After a few minutes, he cleared his throat and announced that the booking room was ready. Judge Hughes had arrived for the arraignment and was none too happy about being dragged into the city hall before sunrise.

"The Paiges. Have they been notified yet?" Jessie asked, wiping her burning cheeks on her sleeve.

Ebony shook her head. "Sergeant Rossi will head over right after the arraignment."

Her mind, her emotions, her actions melted into a state of shock. Emptiness. She wandered, trance-like, behind Ebony, Jeremy, and Terrence as the procession wound its way upstairs to the booking room. From the shadowy threshold, the shell of her body and mind observed Terrence roll each fingertip upon the scanner, his prints appearing on the electronic blotter.

When the lights flashed for his mugshot, Terrence's terror-stricken gaze sought her out, but she shunned him, turning away to avoid his gaze. Jessie slipped out into the dark, damp hallway and steadied her stiff back against the cold tiles. Her chest tightened.

Jessie loved Terrence. She'd loved Ryan. She hated Terrence for taking Ryan away. But Terrence needed her more than ever. She didn't know what to think, feel, or believe anymore. All she knew was that she'd lost them both in a millisecond.

CHAPTER
6

The Poughkeepsie City Court was Jeremy Kaplan's stomping ground. He was used to the airless, windowless courtroom attached to the ground level police station. He got his jollies strutting up to the defendant's table and slapping down his battered briefcase, just to make the point: Jeremy Kaplan was in the house.

Many of his infamous legal victories, the ones that had made him rich, famous, and sought after, had begun within these four walls. But that had been a while ago. A long while ago.

Out of habit, he usurped the middle seat at the defendant's table, motioning for Jessie to stand at his right, leaving the remaining spot for Butterfield.

He'd noticed Jessie's color drain at the mention of Ryan Paige. Clearly, his co-counsel had never experienced anything like this and was too emotionally involved in the situation. As sympathetic as he might be, he'd neither the time nor the inclination to offer her reassurance. She'd get over it. She was just getting her feet wet. Besides, there were more pressing concerns; namely, keeping their client out of jail.

Unlike her, he'd been through the drill a hundred times. Quick introductions. Abbreviated conversations. Arraignment. Not guilty plea. Grand jury. Indictment. Trial. Sentencing. He could do it in his sleep.

Across the room, the prosecutor's table and jury box remained empty, and at the front of the chambers, the mahogany judge's bench awaited the arrival of the Honorable J. J. Hughes. Behind them, plain-clothed and uniformed officers swarmed into the courtroom staking out their positions in the viewers' gallery. Local news stringers, tipped off by scanning the police transmissions, elbowed their way to the front row. The crowded courtroom buzzed with the electricity of cop gossip.

Jeremy ran a comb through his hair and tucked his colorful shirt into his slacks. He switched on his professional smile for the crowd and nodded to a few familiar faces. Through gritted teeth, he reminded Butterfield not to utter a word. He'd handle everything.

Judge John Jay Hughes marched into the courtroom tugging on a flowing black robe, which accentuated his girth like a circus tent. The uniformed officer pitch-hitting for the court clerk handed a cup of coffee to the judge as he scurried to the bench.

"Damn, I've burned my tongue," Judge Hughes snapped after taking a sip and wiping his lips on the wing-like sleeve. "Felony murder, huh? This must be a doozy to get me here at five-thirty in the morning. Where's the file? And the DA?"

The substitute clerk passed his boss a slender manila folder. Judge Hughes thumbed through the paperwork, his face pinching as though he'd bitten into a lemon.

"Sorry, Judge," a voice crooned from the rear of the courtroom. All eyes followed the woman striding down the center aisle. District Attorney Lauren Hollenbeck was in her mid-forties with the athletic figure of a woman a decade her junior. The casual khakis and navy cardigan draped across the shoulders of her creamy silk blouse neither diminished the District Attorney's stature nor softened the determination stamped on her face.

"Ah, Ms. Hollenbeck, nice of you to join us," Judge Hughes said.

The district attorney nodded politely to the judge, then turned her eyes to Jeremy. "Mr. Kaplan," Hollenbeck said. The slap of her briefcase on the tabletop heightened the tension of the room. Next to him, Jessie flinched.

Jeremy responded with a cursory smile. He gave little credence to her reputation as a legal vampire who sucked the lifeblood from every defense witness. He'd wrangled with her before and his record against her was 10-2. Without a doubt, Hollenbeck was a shark who possessed a talent for identifying and preying upon the weakest link. Hence, his two losses.

Hollenbeck approached the bench and, batting her dark blue eyes, requested a brief conference with the arresting officer. Appearing mesmerized, the judge assented. Sergeant Rossi offered Hollenbeck a package while they conversed in low, conspiring voices. Resuming her battle stance at the table, she said, "Ready, Your Honor."

The court stenographer, a girl in her late twenties, poised her indigo talons over her machine, ready for action. With a tilt of his head, the judge called the court to order. Silence blanketed the gallery.

"The first and only matter on the calendar is the *Matter of the People of the State of New York versus Terrence Butterfield.* Are all parties present?" the judge asked.

"Yes, Your Honor," sang the choir of Kaplan, Hollenbeck, and Jessie, who in turn identified themselves for the record.

The judge leaned forward, wagging his head between Jeremy and Jessie. "So, Miss Martin, are you appearing as co-counsel for the defendant?"

"No, Your Honor. As a friend of the court," Jessie replied.

Surprised, Kaplan snapped his head to her. He'd assumed she was going to take the case with him.

Satisfied with the response, Judge Hughes settled back in his chair, resting his double chin on his chest. The pseudo-clerk presented a copy of the complaint to Kaplan, who waived its reading on the record. Beside him, Jessie strained her neck to read the document over his shoulder: murder in the first degree, a class A-1 felony for causing the death of Ryan Paige by shooting him in the head and inflicting torture him before his death.

"How do you answer the charges of murder in the first degree?" Judge Hughes asked.

"Your Honor, with all due respect, I was retained by the defendant a little over an hour ago. We've only had a short conference, so I would request a recess of this arraignment until this afternoon for further discussion."

"Denied. Kaplan, cut to the chase. How does your client plead?" the judge interrupted.

"Not guilty, Your Honor." He proclaimed the plea as he had during every previous arraignment. He turned to Jessie, caught her eye and gave her a sly wink, indicating that's how the pros do it.

Jeremy couldn't be serious, could he? Jessie thought, trying to contain a gasp. She'd anticipated Jeremy's defense tactics, but hearing them announced in open court was another thing. After everything she'd witnessed and heard during the past several hours, she despised the legal lie, the charade of the not guilty plea. Terrence had admitted his guilt, so he should plead guilty and accept his punishment. Instead, there would be months of legal machinations when she, Kaplan, and Terrence knew the truth. What was there to gain, except pain and suffering for Terrence and the Paiges?

To her relief, the matter had been taken out of her hands and deposited into the legal system, which she trusted with an almost religious devotion. Ironically, it had been Terrence who introduced her to the principles of law. Through biographies of Thurgood Marshall, Sandra Day O'Connor, and Ruth Bader Ginsberg, she'd learned that the Truth was discovered, Justice was served, and Punishment was meted out. Thanks to him, she'd been set on her path to becoming a lawyer, and they'd become her role models.

As an officer of the court and protector of the life growing within her, Jessie believed in this paradigm with all of her heart, regardless of the outcome.

Justicia nemini neganda est. Justice is to be denied to none.

Jeremy continued the pretense by waiving Terrence's right to a preliminary hearing on the charges and requesting that the court set bail. It came as no surprise to her that Judge Hughes denied Jeremy's bail request and remanded Terrence into the custody of the Dutchess County Sheriff's Office Correction Division.

"Ms. Hollenbeck, do you have anything to add?" Judge Hughes said, grinning at the attractive gladiator.

"With all due respect, Your Honor, this is a class A felony committed in the most heinous fashion. I hereby serve defendant's counsel with a notice of intention to present the case to the grand jury. And we further request an indefinite adjournment for the purpose of further forensic investigation into this matter."

Voices humming in agreement filtered through the crowd. Terrence bore a glazed look as though he'd retreated inward as he rocked back and forth on his heels. He appeared oblivious to the sentiments of the gallery or, in fact, to the severity of the proceedings.

Jeremy, on the other hand, remained unruffled as he countered with a request for a grand jury, and seemed to be flying by the seat of his khakis. Surely he didn't intend to offer up Terrence to the grand jury. That would be legal suicide.

"Quiet in the court! Request for adjournment denied." The smashing of a gavel silenced the gallery. "Anything else counsel?

Nothing? Good. The court accepts the defendant's plea of not guilty. Remove the defendant at once. Court is adjourned."

Judge Hughes slammed his gavel one final time and vanished from the bench like a dark cloud in a thunderstorm. Within seconds, the county sheriffs seized Terrence by the shoulders and hustled him from the arena, leaving Jessie behind.

In a flash, the arraignment had sealed the fate of the players. She hoped that she wouldn't become a pawn in this deadly game of chess.

CHAPTER
7

Jessie and Kyle rode home from the arraignment in silence. She stared out the passenger's door window, surrendering to the exhaustion and grief of the past hours. The interview. Terrence admitting acts of unspeakable violence. Discovering the victim's identity. And finally, the arraignment.

Closing her eyes, she leaned her head back against the car's headrest. Ryan. She recalled a seven-year-old bouncing around in his Ninja Turtle Halloween costume, a voice-cracking twelve-year-old smashing a home run beneath hazy lights, and a high school senior soliciting college advice. Ryan Paige. He'd been like a puppy, all large paws and excited wagging tail.

Robbie Paige. His face and those of his family also flashed into her mind. Betty and Bill Paige presided over a family of survivors. They'd resisted the predatory challenges of the big box chain stores by remaining steadfast in their flagship appliance store in downtown Poughkeepsie. In a city where Main Street had become a shell of the past, when other family businesses had fled to the suburban malls, or worse yet, had shuttered their doors, Paige Appliance had persevered in the three-story brick building where it had operated for three generations. Since she'd known them, the Paige's brand had expanded into Middletown, Newburgh, Kingston, Rhinebeck, Saugerties, and Albany, becoming a household name in the Hudson Valley. While their business success was attributable to their customer service, their personal success was attributable to their devotion to church and community.

Although their smiling faces frequently graced the social and business pages of the local paper, the Paiges resided in the recesses of Jessie's mind. On occasion, she'd bump into Betty at the farmer's market or call Bill's shop to repair her washing machine, but they lived outside of her universe. About a year ago, her boss, Mr. McMann, had brought her in to assist with one of their zoning matters, her specialty, but generally, the senior partners handled the Paige account.

Ryan was another story. He'd been a fixture around their home, updating her laptop or assisting her domestically-challenged fiancé on household projects.

Yet she'd chosen to banish the painful memories of Robbie and their years together. She'd moved on. Now, with Ryan's death, Robbie would return. This time, she'd be prepared.

"Hon, we're home," Kyle said, gently nudging her shoulder. He held the car door open and offered her a hand out of the car. They crossed the new patio surrounded by flower beds and climbed the steps to the back door. Opening the door, Kyle stooped to pet their greeter cat patiently waiting inside. The tabby meowed a welcome and rubbed his sleek body against their legs as they entered their home. "Go on upstairs. I'll be up in a minute after I feed Bono."

Jessie dragged her aching body up the staircase, cleansed the jail grime from her face, and deposited her bloody sweatshirt and jeans into the hamper, making a mental note to pitch them into the garbage in the morning. Back in the bedroom, she crawled between the cool sheets and discovered Kyle already there, lying with his back toward her. She snuggled as close to him as her egg-shaped body allowed, her arms barely encircling him.

"I love you," she whispered, grateful that he'd indulged her exploits this evening.

Kyle pressed his cold feet against her shins, rocking with laughter at her awkward attempt to spoon. "Turn around."

She did as asked and he followed suit, tucking her close against him. They lay nestled together, like a lock and key.

"Isn't this better?" Kyle asked.

Inside her, a monarch butterfly flapped its wings. Her eyes fluttered shut and she inhaled his comforting, musty scent. Soft lips grazed her neck as sleep kissed her entire body. In the morning, she'd give him a proper thank you.

CHAPTER
8

Hal Samuels leaned against the doorjamb of Lauren Hollenbeck's office and watched his boss sitting at her desk staring into a steaming cup of coffee, appearing mesmerized. He raked his fingers through his auburn hair still damp from the quick shower, pushed aside a stack of files, old newspapers, and law journals, and settled into the leather couch that occupied the far wall of the district attorney's office. Draping his summer-tanned arm across the back of the sofa, he drummed his fingers along the well-worn surface. He eyed his boss and waited as her lips touched the rim of the coffee mug.

The demanding woman never called him on the weekends so something big must be up. As second in command, Chief Assistant District Attorney, he was game.

"I'd just finished the back nine when you called," he said. "Erin brought a change of clothes down to the club and here I am. What's the deal? Your text said it was urgent."

District Attorney Lauren Hollenbeck didn't lift her eyes in acknowledgement to his question. "Just before dawn there was a murder on the south side. The suspect's a teacher at Poughkeepsie High School and the victim was one of the Paige kids. I received a call around 3:00 a.m., so I dropped by the scene and we arraigned him in city court before Hughes. We need to act and issue a statement to the media. It's all in here." Her nail tips slid the file across the desk toward him.

She rose and in her stocking feet advanced to the window, turning her back to him. She gazed out on to the boulevard below and took another sip. It being Sunday, he knew that the delis, banks, and beauty parlors lining the street were shuttered, but something seemed to fascinate her, maybe the guests departing from the Grand Hotel next door.

Hal flipped through the incident report, criminal complaint, RAP sheet, and search warrant. "Terrence Butterfield? I know him. History teacher—ninth grade, right? On the Historic Commission? From what I know, he's an amiable guy, not at all the type I'd peg as a killer. And the victim is the Appliance King's eighteen-year-old son?" He paused to examine the preliminary crime scene photos. They were bad, really bad. There were several shots of the victim face down in a pool of blood and his hands were tied together with a rope. In Hal's book, that together with the bullet to the skull at close range spelled out murder in the first degree. "This is pretty brutal stuff. Do we know anything about the relationship between the two?"

"Not yet, but it's downright crazy the way he murdered that boy."

"I'm assuming that it's too soon for forensics. Are there any witnesses?"

Still looking out the window, Lauren spoke in her customary just-the-facts-no-commentary affectation, making every phrase sound like a command. "Two. An attorney and her boyfriend. I forget their names. They're listed in the incident report," she said, gesturing with the cup. "They arrived after the fact and are clean, or at least appear to be."

"Here it is...Jessica Martin?" Hal's pulse quickened at the sight of her name. Their romance during law school had been passionate and brief, and he hadn't heard her name in ages. Her association with her old mentor, Terrence Butterfield, didn't surprise him. It was her link to the murder that did.

Lauren pivoted about to face him. "Yes, that's her name. I'm not sure of their connection, but Jeremy Kaplan is representing Butterfield. They waived the preliminary hearing, so we'll impanel a grand jury. Pronto."

"So, you called me in because...?"

"This is one of those sexy cases that the press gobbles up. It's got all the angles—a popular, single male high school teacher, a small idyllic upstate town, a dead wealthy teenager. And the teen victim butchered by the teacher."

Hal nodded in agreement. "Plus, we'll probably have the school district and every parent in the city breathing down our necks.

School starts in a couple of days and they'll be worried that every teacher could potentially go bizarro and slaughter their kids."

"And the Paiges. They're a prominent family, and they'll press for life without parole."

"Well, wouldn't you?" he said, momentarily forgetting that Lauren was childless and lacked any maternal instinct.

"This can't become a Ringling Brothers Circus. We need to manage the flow of information. Control all of the competing interests. This can't become a runaway train," Lauren said.

"Got it…flow of information, competing interests. We'll call a press conference."

Lauren caught him glancing over at the half-empty fifth of vodka tilted sideways on her desk. Its contents had pooled on the Chippendale antique, which, as she'd often reminded him, had been bequeathed to her by her grandfather, State Senator Wallace Hollenbeck. Hal met her gaze and cleared his throat.

"I'll call Cindie and Leon and have them come in. We'll need time for the New York metro press to arrive. How about four o'clock? That'll meet the *Journal*'s deadline and the evening news." He waited for an immediate reaction but none came. She continued to glare at him, challenging him.

Finally, she said tersely, "That will work. Get on it, and I don't need to tell you that this prosecution is a priority. No plea bargaining. No offers. As I said, all eyes will be closely observing us." She turned her back to him and returned to the window, signaling his dismissal.

Hal knew what had to be done. Within the hour, his team assembled in the library, combed through the sparse paperwork, and prepared a concise statement for the media outlets. Hal signed off and presented the final draft to Lauren at three-thirty p.m.

At precisely four p.m., Hal, his assistant, Cindie Tarrico, Mayor Jason Meriden, Police Chief Matt Shepardson, and District Attorney Hollenbeck proceeded through the courthouse doors onto the temporary podium erected for the event. In the late afternoon haze, he squinted at the sea of journalists jostling for position in a feeding frenzy. Along Market Street, the logo-clad vans and trucks with satellites pointing into space idled, ready to beam the news to the rest of the world.

Hal tugged at his shirt collar, damp with perspiration. Lauren, dressed in the navy pantsuit stored in her office closet, seized command of the podium. Her demeanor remained as icy as a block of marble. Not a strand of her helmet of black hair was astray; her makeup was flawless, and her lips were stained a shade of spice. Hesitating a long moment for dramatic effect, the DA addressed the camera lenses with confidence.

Hal slipped on his sunglasses and closed his eyes, listening to her recite his words.

"On the early morning of August 31st, The City of Poughkeepsie Police Department responded to a call for emergency assistance at 327 Park Avenue. At that time, the mutilated body of a teen was found in the home belonging to Terrence Butterfield..."

Even though he performed most of the heavy lifting, he never minded that Lauren received the credit, glory, and political capital for his labors. It was his job to make her look good. As Chief Assistant, the various bureaus—Narcotics, DWI, Justice Court, Special Victims and Major Crimes—reported directly to him. Next to Lauren, his word was supreme and his power absolute. Sustaining her positive image was merely a byproduct of his getting the job done.

Not bad, he thought, hearing her conclude the speech with his favorite segment: "Although there is no immediate connection between the victim and the suspect, the suspect made incriminating admissions concerning the homicide to the police. In order to protect the integrity of these proceedings, we cannot speak to the particulars of the evidence recovered. However, we are confident that the evidence found at the crime scene will unequivocally tie the suspect to the crime.

"We thank the community for their cooperation and assistance during the investigation, and my staff and I would like to assure everyone that we are committed to holding the offender accountable for his criminal conduct. We are also committed to assuring that the voices of the victim and his family are heard and that their experiences with the criminal justice system justify their trust in our office. Thank you."

Hal stepped back and held the door open for Lauren who, without fielding any Q and A, led the procession back inside the courthouse.

"I think that went very well," Lauren said with a tone of self-satisfaction. Hal grinned at her as the elevator climbed to the fourth floor. "Before you go, can you stop by my office for a moment please?"

He returned to the sofa that still bore his indentation from hours ago, and she to the window. The shouts of reporters dismantling their circus tents and racing away to the next newsworthy scoop filtered into the office. Lauren turned toward him and removed her blazer. She deliberately, seductively eased each button through its hole and when she was done, flung it over the back of her desk chair. Sighing deeply, she kicked off her high heels.

"I need you to stay on top of this case. It's a real winner," she purred, like a cat licking its whiskers. "We have a confession and hard evidence. This should be an easy conviction and could be a tremendous feather in our cap."

"Knowing Kaplan, his client won't cop a plea. He'll drag this case out ad nauseam and motion us to death," Hal replied.

"He has a nasty habit of digging into his arsenal of legal tricks in these murder cases." She slinked toward him, a panther on the prowl. "He can be very creative."

"Kaplan's a pro. Juries love him."

"We need to find a connection. Between the kid and Butterfield. Between that attorney. What's her name? And Butterfield." Lauren advanced again. She poised over Hal, her hand on her hip. The ivory silk blouse clung to the curves of her body while her eyes bore through him. "There's more to this than meets the eye."

She'd made the moves on him before, and although he wasn't into playing her games, she still made him squirm. In the era of the

#MeToo movement, he thought that she'd be more careful about the way she treated her subordinates. Preferring to ignore her, Hal cleared his throat and rose to leave. "I'll get the investigators on it first thing in the morning. Anything else?"

"Watch the news," Lauren said. "Let me know how I look on camera."

CHAPTER
9

Jeremy Kaplan slammed the door of his office and his leaden feet clambered down the wooden stairway. After the arraignment and a shower, he'd hustled over to the Dutchess County Supreme Court to stave off a client's mortgage foreclosure by the Mutual Bank of New York. He was a warrior returning from battle, relishing the satisfaction of the win and desiring one simple reward: a decent cup of coffee.

He pitched his panama hat at the bench in the empty waiting room and, missing the mark, it landed on the floor. He bypassed it on his way to the coffee machine without a second glance and poured himself a cup. His secretary, Maureen Esposito, rolled her eyes at him, rose from her seat, sighed like a long-suffering wife, scooped up the hat, and hung it on a wall peg. After ten years together, Jeremy relied on her more than he cared to admit to himself and would never admit to her. Even on his deathbed.

"Any messages, Mo? Are we out of creamer again?" He rattled the empty container in his hand as if to make a point.

"They're in a folder on your desk and yes, we're out of creamer. Don't you remember the big yellow sticky note I left for you that said, 'WE ARE OUT OF CREAMER'?" Mo's nasal timbre sounded like cotton packing blocked up her nose. "And don't forget about your meeting with Butterfield at the jail. You've got an hour. There's a reminder note on your desk, too."

"You're as much of a nag as my wife."

"And don't you love it," she called after him as he vanished down the hall to his inner sanctum.

Jeremy sipped on the black coffee, pursing his lips at the bitterness on his tongue. He set the mug aside and surveyed his desk. It was clear except for a manila file marked "*People versus Terrence Butterfield.*" An acute heaviness settled onto his chest. His temples throbbed and he massaged them with his damp palms. The Recession. His finances. Terrence Butterfield. He refused to allow the pressure to plague him so early in the day.

Ever since his first job as a public defender almost thirty years ago, he'd represented killers but none like his newest client. From his prior experience, homicidal maniacs were motivated by greed, jealousy, or revenge, but Butterfield couldn't be pigeonholed into any of those categories. He was in a demented class by himself. Butterfield had admitted to both him and the police that he'd murdered an innocent teenager wandering into his yard late at night. As best as Jeremy could determine, the teacher had served a half-dozen toxic cocktails to the unfortunate Mr. Paige and then had shot him in the head. That didn't leave much to go on as far as a defense was concerned.

Jeremy pinched a contraband Cuban from the humidor and snipped off the cap with the stainless-steel cigar scissors. He balanced the cigar between his teeth and, steadying the tremor in his hand, lit a match to its foot. As he puffed away, he made a mental list of the case's highlights for the meeting at the county jail.

"Mo," he bellowed at the top of his voice, "Where's the PI report on Butterfield? Didn't you tell Carey it was a rush?"

"Here it is, his courier brought it by ten seconds ago," Mo said, handing him the delivery. The secretary wrinkled her nose, swatting away the fog encircling his head. "Does your wife know you're smoking those things again?"

"Nope, and nobody's gonna tell her, are they?" Jeremy puffed, ripped open the envelope marked URGENT and scanned the report scrawled in barely legible longhand. "For what I am paying him, you'd think he could at least type the damn thing."

"You told him you wanted it yesterday, so this is what you get. Remember you have to leave soon." With her arms akimbo, Mo glared at him over the leopard print reading specs perched on her nose and tapped her foot in disgust.

"Yeah, yeah, yeah." He flicked the cigar against the rim of an ashtray, its tube of ashes falling like grey snow. Unfolding the nail file tucked into the cigar scissors, he began digging out the black crud from underneath his nails while he studied the report.

The summary page read like a resume:

Terrence Eleazar Butterfield: DOB February 28, 1975, age: 44

Social Security Number: To be supplied

Place of Birth: Waterbury, Connecticut

Marital Status: Single

Parents: John T. Butterfield, age 72

Harriet Butterfield, age 70

Siblings: Arthur C. Butterfield, age 49

Clyde H. Butterfield, age 47

Education: Waterbury Public Schools

B.A. Yale: May 1996 (World History)

Merit Scholarship Recipient

M.S. School of Education, University at Albany, State University of New York: August 2002 (Curriculum Development and Instructional Technology)

Employment: City of Poughkeepsie School District, August 1996 to present

Class assignment: History - 9th and 10th Grades

Faculty Advisor: Foreign Exchange Program

Tenure: 2006

Awards: New York State Parent Teachers Association: 2011 Teacher of the Year

Community Service:

Historic Preservation Commission: Chairman (2005–present)

Bardavon 1869 Opera House: Board Member (2004–present)

Child Abuse Prevention Center: Board Member (2006–present)

Membership: Whortlekill Rod and Gun Club

Eastern Zone Amateur Trapshoot Association Champion (2015, 2016)

Candidate for NRA Institute Certification

Medical History: Asthma. No other conditions. No history of mental illness.

Criminal History: No previous arrests.

Remarks:

A favorite among the administration, faculty and students. Active on faculty committees.

Engaged to Cheryl Espinosa, Romance Languages teacher at Poughkeepsie High School, but the wedding was cancelled at the last minute. (December 1999–June 2003)

Jeremy flipped to the report, making margin notations in red pen as he went along. The spreadsheet of his client's financials looked decent. Butterfield was about midway through his thirty-year fixed mortgage and had nominal credit card debt. The checking and savings bank accounts were all local, no off-shore funny business. In fact, unlike most teachers, he had no side hustle or summer gig at all. His sole W-2 income was his teaching salary ($82,325.00), and dividend and interest income from a modest stock portfolio.

Besides the home at 327 Park Avenue, his client's major asset was a 1960 Porsche 356B. He could tell from the attached photo that it was a beaut. A flashy red convertible. Too bad Butterfield would have to hock it for the legal fees. There were no other collectables of value. No baseball cards, coins, or artwork. No handguns were registered in his name other than the alleged murder weapon, a 1978 .38 Special Smith and Wesson revolver, but he did own a Remington skeet gun, a Winchester shotgun, and an antique Berry shotgun that had been manufactured in

Poughkeepsie. He was Tier 4 in the New York State Teachers' Retirement Program and its value had rebounded satisfactorily after the 2009 crash. From what he saw, Butterfield didn't appear to be under the kind of financial pressure that would cause a guy to go nuts.

Jeremy rifled through the last three pages where he'd hoped to find Butterfield's personal and financial transactions, but the pages were blank. "Where's the rest of this?" he roared, more to himself than to anyone within earshot.

He thoughtfully inhaled on the cigar then smacked his lips to exhale smoke rings into the air. He was troubled. Something wasn't sitting right with him. His client was a melting pot of contradictions. Butterfield's rendition of last evening disturbed him. It had been sparse and inconsistent with the profile gleaned by his investigator. While Butterfield had spoken highly of his teaching abilities and his affinity for his students, he hadn't mentioned that he owned other guns, had been an amateur trap shoot champion or that he was in the process of getting certified to teach gun classes.

Terrence Butterfield struck him as a driven, calculating, and demanding individual, and Jeremy found it difficult to fathom that Butterfield had been as reckless as he purported. Butterfield had claimed that he'd gone out to chase the kids away and had invited Ryan into his home for a drink. He'd said that he'd blacked out after that and remembered nothing until he came to and had the wherewithal to call Jessie. If Butterfield was lying, as Jeremy suspected, he needed to win his trust and extract the true facts from him. Otherwise, the defense was like pissing in the wind. And his client might be looking at life without parole.

"Jeremy," called Mo, "it's time."

"Okay, okay, in a minute." Jeremy took one final hit of cigar and java. He scribbled a list of questions and expert witnesses on a yellow legal pad and chucked it into his briefcase. On his way past Mo's desk, he plopped down the half-full mug with the cigar stump bobbing around inside. "We need creamer."

Jeremy snatched his hat from the wall peg and with valise in hand, sprinted up the stairs two steps at a time.

J eremy closed his car door, pressed the lock on the key fob, and checked his watch. He dashed across the parking lot toward the modern yellow brick structure displaying the plaque that read "Dutchess County Jail." After bypassing security by flashing his attorney's ID, he paused at the large glass control booth to secure his credentials and meet the guard who would escort him up to the third floor where Butterfield was waiting. Again, he checked his watch.

When Jeremy was ushered into the conference room, Terrence Butterfield stood at the exterior window. His cheek was pressed against the screen of an open louver window sniffing at the cool breeze like a dog and basking in a stripe of sunlight like a cat. Butterfield shuffled his shackled feet across the floor to the table in the center of the compact room. "You're late, Mr. Kaplan."

"Terrence, give me a break. I'm only ten minutes late."

"Ten minutes is a lifetime in this place." Butterfield wrung his chained hands.

"We can expect the grand jury to begin proceedings within the next two weeks and we have a lot of ground to cover." Jeremy had no intention of being baited by the killer. He extracted the file and yellow legal pad from his briefcase and spread the documents across the tabletop between them. "Let's review the facts of your case and our trial strategy. First, we need to establish the timeline on the night—"

"Mr. Kaplan, I didn't mean to be obstreperous earlier this morning, but I didn't feel comfortable discussing any further details in the presence of Jessica Martin."

"Well, then," Jeremy interrupted, but Butterfield refused to yield the floor to his counsel.

"Last night, I heard noises outside and I saw Ryan, or whatever his name was, trespassing in my yard. I was afraid that he was going to vandalize my Porsche, so I called out to him from the kitchen door. Although he was not one of my students, I guess he recognized me from school and came over to speak with me."

"So, you didn't know who he was?" Jeremy asked, jotting along on a yellow pad.

"No, not until the arraignment. Anyway, we talked. He seemed like a nice kid and told me he was leaving for college soon. So, I figured that they all underage drank there anyway, so we did a few shots of whiskey."

"And?"

"That's it. That's all I remember…until afterward." Butterfield snatched Jeremy's silver ballpoint pen and yellow pad and clicked the pen with such rapidity that his hand appeared stationary.

"Had you ever partied like this before with other students?" Jeremy asked.

"No, never."

Jeremy narrowed his eyes, scrutinizing Butterfield. The guy was holding back. No doubt about it. Something about his speech pattern, the way he shifted his body in the chair, the sly expression on his face. What struck him most was the complete absence of light in the man's steel grey eyes. If, as Jeremy believed, the eyes were the windows into the soul, then Butterfield's soul had gone on permanent vacation leaving behind a shell devoid of any compassion or humanity. However, somehow, he had to draw him out.

"If we're to work together, you must trust me." He fixed Butterfield with a stern eye. "To mount a successful legal defense, I must know everything about your life. You have to answer all of my questions and give me the minutiae, everything." He paused. "You're paying me a small fortune to represent you and you must believe that I have your best interests at heart. If you have any qualms, you should tell me up front, or perhaps you should consider another attorney," Jeremy said, suppressing his anger.

Butterfield set pen to paper, feverishly decorating the tablet with arrows, loops, and scratch marks. Jeremy examined the scribbles and swirls scrawled on the yellow page. Jessica Martin's name was circled and slashed through with a thick black line.

"Dissuade her... do whatever is in your legal power, but just make sure that she is not involved in this."

"That may not be possible."

"Just do it." Butterfield's face hardened. The veins popped from his temples and he smashed his metal bracelets upon the table, sending the papers flying.

Surprised, Jeremy leaped from his seat, sending his chair toppling to the floor.

A sheriff darted into the room. "Is everything all right in here?"

"We're fine... aren't we, Terrence?"

CHAPTER
10

It was a longstanding policy of the DA's office that any contact with victims and their families was to occur within the confines of their office, the courthouse, or another appropriate venue, and Hal Samuels had always complied with that edict. Yet, it came as no surprise when Lauren requested that he serve as her ambassador and visit with the Paiges at their home on Yates Boulevard, an imposing Tudor-style manse. As he expected, their case would be filled with exceptions.

At the front door, he pushed aside the ivy to ring the doorbell, half-expecting to hear hounds baying in response. Instead, a solemn Latina housekeeper answered the door and escorted him through a foyer, its air heavily perfumed with the floral arrangements filling the center hall table and lining the marble floor. He stepped down into a large sunken living room. At the far end, Bill Paige, dressed for a day at the office, rested his elbow on the marble mantelpiece. Betty Paige, in designer jeans and a black cashmere sweater, poured coffee from a china coffee pot. Next to her sat another woman. From her identical blue eyes and delicate nose, he deduced that she was Betty's sister.

At first, it seemed odd that, in light of losing their son a few hours ago, Mr. and Mrs. Paige were conducting themselves with a relaxed civility. On second look, Bill's tie was askew beneath a curled shirt collar. His wife's triple strand of pearls clattered against her chest with the nervous movement of her fingers. When she paused midair to steady her hand, the sister tenderly assumed the coffee urn and seamlessly resumed pouring.

Bill Paige extended his hand in greeting, thanked him for stopping by, and suggested that Hal sit on the French gilt chair facing the settee occupied by his wife. "It's been a difficult night. With the autopsy, funeral arrangements, the telephone's nonstop ringing, and our son arriving in from the West Coast, we needed to stay close to home."

"Bill, Betty, I'm sorry for your loss and the intrusion at this difficult time. I wanted you to know that I'm personally heading the investigation and to assure you that this case is my priority." Hal hoped that he wasn't addressing them too casually by using their first names. After all, they socialized at the golf club.

"We appreciate that. How can we assist?" By "we" Hal assumed Bill meant "he." His wife appeared as brittle as a dead leaf scuttling in the wind.

"I realize that this is difficult, but can you tell me about Ryan, his friends, what was going on in his life?" Hal asked.

Bill heaved a sigh. At the mention of her son's name, Betty's hands flew up to her mouth to stifle a cry.

"It's okay, dear," Bill said softly. He sat down beside her on the armrest of the sofa and kissed her blonde curls, but the solace he offered her was insufficient. Her restrained veneer cracked wide open. She bent her head forward and her shoulders shuddered in rhythm with the uncontrollable tears. Betty's sister wrapped an arm around her, whispering words of strength that only a sibling can impart to another.

"Well, what can I say?" Bill paused, staring into the hearth. "You never expect your kid to go before you, that's not the natural order of things. Is it?" He returned his focus to Hal. "Sorry. To answer your question, Ryan was a great kid. He was popular, well-liked, no shortage of friends. They always hung around here like it was their second home. Called me Mr. P., which embarrassed Ryan when he was little. He was competitive with his older brother and adored by his sister. His brother's one of those whiz kids who scored twenty-four hundred on the SAT and won a full scholarship to Cornell for engineering." He rubbed at the back of his neck. "Ryan was never like that, more jock than scholar. Man, but that kid has some wise-cracking sense of humor. I tell him all the time that he should be a standup comedian. He drives Betty nuts sometimes, but he always eases the tension when Robbie and Brianne are at each other's throats. You know kids, right?"

Despite Bill's outward strength, Hal could tell he was devastated over his son's death. It was evident from the way he drifted between referring to Ryan in past and present tense, a sign of the freshness of the death and the shock.

"He's never been in trouble if that's what you're wondering. Only received detention once for some silly homecoming prank—painting the sidewalk blue and white, or something like that. He works on the sales floor at the store after school, weekends, and summers, when he isn't playing sports, but like Robbie, he has no interest in the family business. He wants to be a teacher, instead." Bill grew distracted again, examining his hands for a long moment. "We didn't see him much this past week. He was off with his friends for one final camping trip. If only we'd known…"

Hal felt like the biggest schmuck in the world, watching these people suffer and picking at their open wounds. The "victim" interview, as he called it, was the worst part of his job, especially when he knew the family. But it was a necessary evil and essential to the trial and conviction, which made it all worthwhile. "Did your son know Mr. Butterfield? Had he been one of his students?"

"No, but our older boy was. Years ago, though."

"Maybe they knew each other outside the classroom? Extra-curriculars? Clubs?"

Bill shook his head.

Now for the most difficult question. "When was the last time you saw Ryan?"

Bill slipped a reassuring hand on his wife's shoulder. "Last evening, Ryan left after dinner, around seven, with his buddies, Jeb Gordon, Billy Wright, and Ian Swift. They were meeting up with some of the girls to go to the movies, a late summer 3D superhero flick. The last time I saw him he was hopping into Ian's car." Bill paused and cleared his throat. "Ryan's going off to college next week, so we don't wait up for him anymore." Mr. Paige caught himself and corrected his error in almost a whisper. "Was going off to college."

Betty clutched her husband's hand. The grieving parents exchanged frazzled looks, making Hal squirm in his seat.

"We're both light sleepers and we usually hear him come in, but last night we fell asleep around eleven and heard nothing until the police woke us up around six," Betty said, her voice reedy. "We've already told them everything that we know."

"It's been a very trying day," the sister said. "We're all exhausted, so is there anything else?"

Taking the hint, Hal repeated his condolences and rose. "When you get a chance, could you please check Ryan's room? There might be something of assistance to us."

"I'll ask Robbie to do it when he arrives home," Bill said.

Hal nodded and his eyes drifted to a family portrait hanging over the mantle. From the looks of the hairstyles, clothing, and ages of the three children, it had been taken several years ago. Ryan appeared around ten, all freckles and sun-kissed blonde hair. The older boy was around eighteen with the daughter somewhere in between. Along the mantle, the family's photographic greatest hits were showcased, ranging from weddings to births, vacations, sports teams, dance recitals, and graduations.

To Hal's surprise, he recognized a young Jessie Martin in one of them. She wore a coral prom dress and her halo of auburn ringlets cascaded down the shoulder that she nestled against the older son. Even back then, the girl had been a stunner and he felt an unexpected twinge of jealousy that she'd loved someone else before she had loved him.

Bill noticed him admiring their gallery, wistfully shook his head, and then explained that the picture Hal was caught studying was Robbie with his old girlfriend. "We haven't had the heart to put it away. Once they go off to college, you have so few photos of them. Sometimes you wish you could turn back the clock. Hal, you have children, don't you?"

"Yes, a son. Six years old."

Although Bill looked him dead straight in the eye, Hal sensed that Bill was struggling to remain composed and strong for his fragile wife. He held himself rigid and erect, but the tremor in his voice was a giveaway. Bill Paige was ready to snap. "Well, then you'll understand. I want to make sure that Mr. Butterfield is punished for what he did to us. He stole our boy's life and though we don't know all of the details, we know that he tortured Ryan. Our son died in pain. We will never forgive or forget that. Please, promise us that Mr. Butterfield will pay for his sins."

Hal couldn't imagine what he or his wife Erin would do if anything happened to their son, Tyler. Waking up each day for the rest of his life knowing his child was gone. No longer being a parent. By nature, he wasn't a vengeful man but under similar circumstances, he knew that he'd react like Bill. Payback would be the only option. Hal swallowed the lump in his throat. "You have my word. As a public servant and a father, I'll do everything in my power to obtain a quick conviction."

Bill Paige extended his hand once more. "Thank you."

CHAPTER
11

A flock of mourning doves perched atop the sooty spires of the First Presbyterian Church on South Hamilton Street. It was an ominous sign, and reminded Jessie of the scene from Hitchcock's *The Birds*. She trod lightly along the sidewalk leading to the church so as not to disturb them. Above her, they cooed and preened each other as the weather threatened a heavy rain. At the sound of tires screeching in the distance, the birds startled and formed a tight brown-grey cloud streaking across the concrete sky. The din of their beating wings masked the sound of her heartbeat thrashing in her ears.

Inside the sanctuary, Jessie fidgeted in the last row of the cathedral's hard wooden pews nearest to the point of escape, the colossal oak doors. Consumed with dread, she found herself wishing rather than praying for Ryan. Wishing for seat cushions to ease her aching back. Wishing for fresh air to erase the mustiness of the vast cavern. Wishing for bright sunlight to replace the muted stained-glass chapel light. And being Jewish and a bit unnerved by the depictions of Christ's crucifixion and resurrection, she wished for Ryan's funeral to be over.

As a distraction, she watched the faithful and the faithless stream by filling the pews in search of a better view of God. They came to see and be seen. To honor and be honored. They were all there; the mayor, the state senator, the district attorney, and the partners from her law firm, McMann and Curtis.

Friends and associates greeted each other in respectful hushed tones as they maneuvered for the best seats. Teary teenage girls, classmates of Ryan's, shared their grief by falling into each other's arms. Ryan's baseball teammates suppressed anguish and guilt with silence, clasping their hands across their abdomens with heads bowed like monks.

Ryan's octogenarian grandparents led the family down the aisle. The patriarch, Randall Paige, hobbled along on a silver-tipped cane, and his wife, her translucent skin dewy with tears, clutched his bony hand in hers. Ryan's parents, Betty and Bill, and his siblings, Robbie and Brianne, followed close behind with their gazes averted to the ground, avoiding all human contact.

Ryan's sister cradled a box of tissues and camouflaged her distress behind oversized designer sunglasses. As the grieving family passed, each successive pew embraced their loss, plunging the cathedral into silent prayer and sorrow. Ryan's family settled into the first row, lifted their eyes to the pulpit, and waited.

In slow measured steps, six pallbearers ushered the polished black coffin, accented with brass handles and skirted with royal blue and white velvet, down the aisle. The procession halted before the pulpit adjacent to a makeshift altar displaying Ryan's baseball trophies, his electric guitar, and family photos.

Taking the cue from the family, the reverend commenced the service with W. H. Auden's "Funeral Blues."

The haunting poem washed over Jessie, reminding her of Kyle's pettiness as she prepared to leave for the service. They'd stood in the kitchen bickering. He'd argued that the Jewish religion forbade pregnant women from attending funerals. She'd replied that he was misquoting an old wives' tale that barred pregnant women from visiting cemeteries, not funerals.

"I don't want to jinx anything." Kyle placed his coffee mug in the sink and plucked a few cat hairs from his blazer.

"This isn't about the funeral, is it? It's about *who'll* be attending the funeral."

Kyle didn't reply. His jaw tightened and dark shadows flickered across his blue eyes. He was shutting down and crawling into his shell.

At first, she'd felt flattered that after four years of living together he still experienced jealousy. Yet, the more Jessie thought about it, the more surprised she became. Once a long time ago, she'd mentioned her engagement to Robbie Paige to clarify a comment that Ryan had made about the two of them. She'd believed that Kyle had forgotten the remark. Apparently, he hadn't.

More than anything, Jessie wanted to spare her fiancé's feelings, but she wasn't changing her mind. She'd asked him to come along but he'd begged off claiming yet another emergency board meeting at the civic center. They were caught in a stalemate and they both knew it, so she snatched her purse and car keys, and left him rummaging through his leather messenger bag. Embossed with the logo of Madison Square Garden, the emblem was a constant reminder of his sacrifice for her.

The deep vibrato of the pipe organ summoned her back to the present. The reverend invited Robbie to the pulpit to say a few words on behalf of his family. More scarecrow than she remembered, Robbie ascended the podium at the far corner of the pulpit. The heels of his pointy cowboy boots clicked along the wooden floor as he strutted with an exaggerated rock star swagger, so much so that Jessie half-expected him to whip out a harmonica and blow the blues. He withdrew a sheet of paper from his breast coat pocket, unfolded it, and flattened it against the lectern. Shifting uncomfortably in the suit and tie, he tugged at the starched shirt collar. After a long moment of staring at the written words before him, Robbie addressed the congregation in a low, raspy voice, which grew in volume with his confidence.

"During this difficult time, I am trying to maintain a positive attitude. My sister and I could never have asked for a more wonderful brother and my parents a more wonderful son. Everything Ryan did made us proud."

Jessie's eyes filled with tears. She listened to the heartfelt hymn from one brother to another, empathized with Robbie's grief and pitied him. Trying to forget who was speaking, she subdued the fear and regret he unsettled within her. That was the past. This was the present. She focused on his elegy to Ryan, on saying goodbye.

Robbie's voice cracked with emotion at the conclusion of his speech. "Ryan, we all love you and will miss you. You will be a constant in our thoughts and prayers. We will speak to you and laugh with you. Dad and Mom are so proud of you. You will always be in our hearts."

His strength depleted, Robbie returned to his place beside the family. The pastor chanted the Lord's Prayer in unison with the congregation and expressed thanks on behalf of the family by inviting them to the cemetery. In the background, the chords of the recessional organ blared. The Paiges rose and plodded toward the back of the sanctuary to prepare for the receiving line.

Determined to avoid eye contact with them, Jessie fixed her watery eyes straight ahead. She felt a cool hand graze hers. She recognized the touch, the fingers. Unable to ignore this bidding, she glanced up at Robbie and feigned a weak smile as he escorted his family past her.

Jessie navigated her way through the crowd, out the oak doors, and down the wide stone steps to the sidewalk. In relief, she inhaled the humid air filled with the sweetness of fresh cut lawns and the impending summer storm.

"Jessie. Jessie!"
Jessie had been walking toward her car in a numb daze. She became aware of Robbie's familiar insistent voice

repeatedly calling her name. Upon hearing it, the panic alarm sounded.

"Wait," he shouted.

Hoping to avoid him she quickened her pace, but she was no match for the rapid footsteps closing in on her. The hairs on her arm tingled warning that he was drawing uncomfortably close, and she froze in her tracks.

"Hi, Robbie," Jessie said, but before she could retreat, he'd bent his six-foot two frame down to brush his lips against her cheek. The redolent odor of a just-sneaked cigarette, leather, and cologne wafted in the air around him.

"Good to see you. It's been a while." Robbie's musician's hands, lacking any symbols of commitment, nervously twirled a tiny gold hoop earring piercing his left ear.

Jessie examined him. They hadn't seen each other since the autumn after her law school graduation, five years ago. Robbie's face appeared drawn, more angular than in her memories. His skin was the color of the ashen sky with darker crescents supporting his sleepless eyes. Shaggy brown hair skimmed his jacket collar but was slicked back to control its natural unruliness.

"I'm going to miss him," Jessie said. "I don't know if Ryan ever mentioned it, but he and I kept in touch after we…"

"Yeah, I know. He told me about the baby and Kyle. Said he's a great guy." A long silence hung in the charged air particles between them. Robbie's hand, tattooed with a python flicking its forked tongue toward the letters I-N-O etched below the knuckle of his ring finger, fiddled with his skinny black tie. "Coming to the cemetery?"

"Sorry, can't." She took a step backward, permitting him to absorb the image before him. "Tradition, you know how it is."

"Well, I'm going to be around for a few days so you should stop by, to catch up." He watched her expectantly as though offering a dinner invitation. "My parents would love to see you."

Stunned by his suggestion, her mind grappled to invent an excuse. "I wish I could, but I'm preparing for a shareholder's derivative trial starting next week in U.S. District Court in White Plains. There are depositions, corporate bylaws, and board meeting minutes to review plus conferences with top management." She figured that the legalese would sound impressive to a layperson and that he'd never discover her lie anyway.

"Maybe another time then." His voice failed to disguise the disappointment. Robbie leaned toward her as if to kiss her cheek but she drew back, and he awkwardly flipped down the sunglasses resting on his head. "Well, thanks for coming today."

"I wouldn't have missed it and please tell your parents…" she said choking back the words. A vice crushed her heart and the baby sharply stabbed her in the stomach.

"Sure, will do." He squeezed her hand, turned, and sprinted toward the stretch limousine waiting in front of the church. Robbie ducked his head and disappeared inside the car, which lurched forward, merging into the procession behind the hearse.

At that moment, nature fulfilled its earlier promise. The rain speckled her linen dress with polka dots and turned her bare arms into gooseflesh. Jessie reached her car, slid inside, and slammed the door just as the storm unleashed its full wrath. The deafening din of hail pelted the rooftop and wind-blown sheets of rain lashed the windshield. She shivered, unsure how long the storm would hold her hostage.

CHAPTER
12

The morning following Ryan's funeral, Jessie entered her office, flicked on the lights, and discovered a handwritten memo on the firm's letterhead taped to her phone. It read: "Jessica, please join me in the library upon your arrival. Signed, J.R. McMann."

There was nothing unusual about her boss's request. She'd recently completed the zoning board application for his client, the Hudson Valley Art Museum, so she was prepared for her next assignment. She grabbed a legal pad, pen, and her Lawyer's Diary from her desk, and padded in her ballet flats toward the elevator. She thought wistfully that it would probably be the last assignment before her due date, November 1st, which was circled in red in her diary.

"Morning, Albany," she said to Josh Spencer, a colleague catching a ride upstairs with her.

"Hey, Syracuse. The Orange still sucks." Josh, a junior partner and SUNY Albany alumni, never missed an opportunity for the friendly banter of collegiate rivalry.

"Not as bad as the Great Danes." Jessie exited the elevator but stopped in her tracks at the sight before her. Behind the glass walls of the enormous library, the senior partners argued boisterously with one another. Taking a quick headcount, she noted that all seven were present. This wasn't at all what she'd expected. It didn't appear to be a meeting about her assignments or caseload or even her partnership. She sensed that trouble was brewing and somehow she was involved.

She remained composed, pushed open the door and stepped inside. The partners fell silent but the air in the room was thick with interrupted tension.

Jefferson Roosevelt McMann III, the firm's senior managing partner and patriarch, rocked in a sleek white leather chair at the head of the polished zebrawood table. As the fourth generation of McMann barristers, he reigned over a legal empire which had counseled Vanderbilts, Vassars, Smith Brothers, and Morses, as well as his prestigious relations, two presidents of the country, and a governor of the state of New York. The silver-maned McMann convened the proceedings.

"Jessica. Good morning. Please take a seat." He signaled in the direction of the empty chair at the far end of the board table. His manner was polite, icy cool, unlike his usual warm and jovial behavior toward her.

Mr. McMann's sudden change in attitude confused her, but from the pinched faces of his partners, it was apparent that an explanation was imminent. Despite her eroding confidence, she slapped on a game face and resolved to keep her eyes and ears open for clues. Whatever was going on, she was determined to discuss it in a calm and professional manner.

Jessie had just taken the designated seat when Jonathan Lewis, one of the partners, sprang to his feet. He exploded, lashing out at her without preamble.

"The *Times*! The *New York Law Journal*! Our firm's name is smeared across the front pages," Lewis shouted. He brandished a copy of the *New York Times* and flung it onto the table. "You didn't even have the courtesy to call any of us or discuss your involvement in the crime. Running to assist a murderer, of all the foolishness—"

Her mouth went as dry as saltines and she felt a knot forming in her stomach.

"With all due respect," Jessie replied, her voice strong despite her nerves, "I was awakened in the middle of the night and I reacted as best I could under the emergency circumstances. I believe that I handled myself in a professional manner at all times, taking into consideration legal propriety, Mr. Butterfield and the firm. Even Jeremy Kaplan indicated that I acted properly."

"Jeremy Kaplan, that huckster," scoffed Lewis. "You may have acted within the boundaries of the law, but in my book, your actions were irresponsible and reflect poorly on your commitment to the firm."

"Jonathan, please, calm down. Let's discuss this rationally," McMann said.

Charlotte Perkins, the sole female partner, dabbed the temples above her wizened grey eyes with a lace handkerchief. "Jessica, unfortunately, this matter extends beyond Mr. Butterfield's predicament and the Paige's loss. We must consider our other clients. In this competitive legal environment, we must avoid any potential conflict of interest or implication of impropriety. Regrettably, action must be taken."

Jessie's vision turned white and heat flushed through her body, burning her cheeks red hot. She didn't care if they knew she was angry, because she was furious. After all she'd done, had sacrificed for the firm. For the past five years, she'd missed out on vacations, birthdays, holidays, weeknight dinners, and weekends whenever they'd asked her to work extra hours. She'd even assumed additional cases to prove she was worthy of a partnership. And this reprimand was how they repaid her.

"I have always made myself available to my clients 24-7 as the firm has required and that's what I was doing when Mr. Butterfield called. And I'm sure that none of you would have been too pleased to receive a call from me in the middle of the night. Contrary to Mr. Lewis, I thought I exercised good judgment."

"As you can see, we find ourselves in a difficult position, one which I trust that you can appreciate," McMann said. He went on to chronicle his family's long, intimate relationship with the Paiges. Even though she'd heard it a hundred times before, she listened patiently, keenly aware that all eyes were locked on her.

"As we hope you will never discover, it is every parent's nightmare to lose a child. But to lose a child in such a horrific fashion; needless to say, the Paiges are distraught beyond consolation. They are coming into the office today to consult with us regarding this situation and to explore their legal options," Mr. McMann continued. He picked up an errant paperclip lying on the desk, studied it for a second, and then began to deconstruct it until the thin metal wire snapped in half.

She empathized with the paperclip. Her life was being twisted and manipulated by the panel glaring at her from around the conference table. At any minute, her future could be snapped apart.

"I assure you, this is neither an easy nor unanimous decision amongst the managing partners. Jessica, you are an outstanding associate, one who shows great promise as a potential partner here at McMann and Curtis. We value your legal expertise and ability to generate new clients." He put his fingertips together and peered at her over the steeple. "However, we feel that at this delicate time, your continued association with the firm jeopardizes our relationship with the Paiges. Not because of any misconduct on your part, but because of your proximity to this terrible incident and Mr. Butterfield. Therefore, pending the investigation of the Paige boy's murder and the grand jury indictment, we are placing you on leave from the firm. Effective immediately," McMann stated unapologetically.

"What? Sir, aren't you going to permit me to explain?" Her heart raced and her knees reflexively knocked together beneath the table. It was no use. She was being prosecuted for following their rules. Apparently, one set applied to the wealthy clients like the Paiges, but not to the middle-class ones like Terrence. She stammered, barely able to muster the words, "I haven't done anything wrong."

"Jessica. There's nothing to explain. This isn't a termination. Please don't interpret our actions that way. Once the grand jury makes its determination and the dust settles, we'll revisit this matter. We hope that will be soon." McMann gestured his liver-spotted hand around the room at his partners in a show of solidarity.

"What about my clients, my pending litigations and scheduled trials?" Jessie asked.

"Arrangements have been made. The management committee will review your files and make the appropriate assignments to other members of the firm."

"What exactly will you tell my clients about my leave?"

"My dear," McMann said, "we are concerned about your health. You should be taking it easy and lightening your workload. You shouldn't be worrying about the demands of your clients, the non-stop emails and phone calls. The extraordinary stress is not good for you or your baby."

Jessie felt a tempest erupting within her and bit her lip to refocus her anger over his patronizing speech. "Sir, I've been with the firm for five years, and I deserve a chance to explain to you and my clients." She rested her palms on the table, her fingers widespread to stabilize her upended world. "I've earned the right to explain. Mr. McMann, Ms. Perkins, somebody, please let me explain," she pleaded, searching for sympathy in the expressionless faces staring at her.

"The decision has been made," McMann said. "The Paige family is expected here shortly, so we ask that you vacate the premises and deposit your keys with your assistant. Thank you, Jessica."

Mr. McMann's final, dismissive directive stung, suggesting that, despite his reassurances, what had just transpired was more in the nature of a termination than a maternity leave. She was no fool; their actions weren't motivated by concern for either her, her baby, or the Paiges. They were worried about the firm's bottom line, the lost revenue. Bad publicity. Alienating clients. The cutthroat poaching of clients by the competition. She was a scapegoat being sacrificed to protect the influential McMann dynasty.

Blindsided by McMann and the partners, Jessie stumbled back to her office, her head spinning in a panic. She had no Plan B. She'd been two years away from a junior partnership and had never thought that she'd need a backup plan. With the baby coming soon, it would be impossible to find a new job. Once word spread that she'd been fired from McMann's firm, who'd hire her anyway?

She froze in the doorway at the sight of a man sitting in the armchair facing her desk. When he reached up over his head, knitted his hands together and cracked his knuckles, she recognized the snake tattoo on the back of his left hand.

Damn. Dealing with Robbie was the last thing she needed right now, and she needed to get rid of him fast. She blew out a long, deep breath and proceeded inside. "Robbie, what are you doing here?"

Without a greeting, he blurted out, "Why didn't you tell me that you were at Butterfield's the night of Ryan's murder?" He hurled the *New York Post* on the floor at her feet. The headline blared, "School's Out for the Killer Teacher."

"There wasn't anything to tell. I wasn't there until afterward." Jessie skirted around him toward the credenza. "I didn't know it was Ryan. How could I?"

"You and Butterfield...I always knew there was something going on between the two of you."

She shook her head. He was the same old Robbie. The years hadn't changed him. Not one bit. He was still the jealous, possessive guy she'd dated in high school and college. In the beginning, he'd been all sweetness and light, but then his love had smothered her. She couldn't even go out with her girlfriends without having to call him a million times to check in.

"Your imagination is running away with you for a change." Jessie snatched her tote bag, crammed in her laptop, Rolodex, and a photo with Kyle, tanned and grinning on the beaches of Barbados. "Look, I don't know what you believe I've done, but I'm busy right now."

"Well, I think you owe me an explanation." He rose from the seat, his face reddened and his fists clenched tightly by his sides.

Jessie grabbed her Black's Law Dictionary from the bookshelf and shoved it, along with her diary, into a canvas tote. Robbie could threaten her all he wanted, but she wasn't afraid of him anymore. He may have remained the same, but she'd changed. She was stronger, confident, and ready to fight back this time. He was on her turf now. "I don't owe you anything so get out of my office. This conversation is over." She glared at him, cold as the tundra.

"It's not over until I say it's over."

When Jessie heard those words, she thought that her mind was playing a cruel trick on her. She held her breath, gulping down air to control the wave of alarm spreading throughout her body. Perhaps she'd overestimated herself.

Robbie Paige had first spoken those words to her a decade ago, on a blustery winter night during the Christmas recess of their junior year in college. Her parents had been out to dinner and she and Robbie had been alone in her house. She'd decided to broach the subject of his excessive drinking and partying, as well as his empty promises to seek help. Clearly, their relationship was strained by their constant bickering, his denials, her threats to break up, his desperate attempts to conciliate and ultimately, his reneging. Jessie felt beaten down by the endless merry-go-round and made the tough decision to jump off.

"Robbie, I've been giving this a lot of thought. Our relationship isn't working for me anymore," she said, choking on her words. "I'm not happy and when we go back to school, I think we should take some time apart from each other and concentrate on our studies for a while."

"You want to take a break?" Robbie said, agitation in his voice. "You're overreacting. I said that I'm sorry."

"We've been through this before. I've talked and talked but you won't listen to me." She shivered and crossed her arms to ward off the chill.

"Now I understand what's really going on." Robbie blinked his bloodshot eyes. A smirk crossed his face as if what Jessie had said struck him as a joke. "There's someone else, isn't there? It's him, isn't it?"

Jessie looked at him, wide-eyed. "No. There's no one else, I swear. I love you, but you need to get some help."

"You're going to throw away five years, just like that?" Robbie snapped his fingers. "We've made plans. We're getting married after graduation next year." Robbie reached out to clutch her around the waist, but she wriggled away from him and the stench of stale beer laced with pot that twisted her stomach. "I love you, we're meant to be together."

"I'm sorry, Robbie, but you're blowing your future and I don't want to be around to watch the crash. It's over." She walked toward the chair where his down jacket rested and picked it up, offering it to him. With her other hand, she reached for the handle of the front door. "Please go now before we say things we'll regret. Please get some help."

"It's not over until I say it's over." Robbie stumbled toward her, stopping within inches. The veins bulged from his temples and his pupils dilated, eclipsing his sky-blue irises. His normal calm demeanor had been replaced with that of a drunken monster that would do anything, say anything, to get his way. Fearfully, Jessie inched her way backward, but he cornered her against the front door, his palms imprisoning her.

"Come on, Robbie. You'd better go."

"What's the matter, Jessie? I thought that you loved me." Robbie stepped closer. Pinning her against the cold wooden door, he began to unbutton her flannel shirt, but she swatted his hand away.

"Leave me alone," she screamed, twisting and contorting her body to escape him and the sloppy kisses he forced on her mouth.

"Come on, baby. You know you want me. Stop fighting and chill out." Robbie reached up and grabbed a fistful of her long auburn hair and yanked her head back with such force that she thought it would snap off. "I said relax."

"Robbie, stop!" She thrashed about trying to dig her nails into his flesh to free herself, but his grip tightened. Her scalp burned as she felt strands of hair being wrenched out by their roots. "Let me go. You're hurting me."

"You belong to me and we're not over," he whispered in her ear. His hands tugged at the waistband of her lounge pants. Robbie's weight pressed against her chest like a boulder, squeezing the air from her lungs. Jessie tried to scream but terror had stolen her voice. She squeezed her eyes shut, surrendering to the white stars swirling around inside the blackness of her eyelids.

Robbie was going to kill her.

But he didn't. The crime he committed against her was far worse. In a single act of violence, he betrayed her trust and love. Robbie stole her dignity, her self-confidence, and her body.

When he was finished with her, Jessie drew her knees up to her chest and curled into a ball. The living room carpet was soft and warm, but she shivered uncontrollably.

"We're never going to be over until I say so," Robbie said, looming over her like a giant. He zipped up his jeans and snatched his parka from the floor. She blocked his access to the door so he shoved her aside, and stamped out, slamming the door behind him. Sobs of pain, humiliation, and helplessness mixed with the dry heaves that were strangling Jessie's throat. Her body burned from his unwanted touch, and she wished that she could shed her skin like a snake and start anew. She felt drained, empty. Twisted up inside.

Jessie couldn't understand why Robbie had been so cruel, attacking her that way. They'd had sex before, plenty of times, and Robbie had always been tender and loving. Each time she'd given herself to him because they loved each other, and she knew that he'd never hurt her. This time, while he'd repeatedly proclaimed his love, instead of showing kindness and affection, he'd brutally betrayed her trust and her body. He'd stolen a part of her heart that she could never reclaim and had branded her, making her feel like damaged goods. Trash.

If she reported his attack, it would be her word against his and those of his influential parents. They'd scrutinize each and every detail of her life and accuse her of instigating the assault. They'd say what had happened wasn't even an attack, that it had been consensual. And when she denied it, no one would believe her. No one would help her.

Outside, Robbie's Audi's tires whirled on the snow-covered driveway and then screeched into the street. Jessie leaned on an armchair and struggled to her feet. She pulled up the pants that were pooled at her ankles and looked out the window as the car's tail lights disappeared into the night.

The bastard. Jessie wasn't going to let him define her.

She needed time to think, to heal her bruised body and soul. She needed distance between herself, Robbie, and the prying of her well-meaning parents. One thing was certain: she never wanted to see him again.

The next morning a bouquet of pink stargazer lilies, her favorites, were delivered and Jessie promptly refused them at the door. Although her parents might have thought it strange, she announced that she was returning to Syracuse to finish a project due after the Christmas break. When her father asked whether there was trouble in paradise, as he put it, she lied, denying that anything was amiss with Robbie.

Meanwhile, she deleted Robbie's tearful, apologetic voice messages as well as his emails and texts begging her to call him. When they failed to cease, she grew more agitated with each new message. Her stomach swirled in a constant state of nausea. She could neither sleep nor eat.

As time passed, the secret of his attack continued to haunt her. Whenever she returned to her apartment, she feared that Robbie would be waiting on her doorstep, stalking her. But he never appeared. He just called, day and night. Begging forgiveness and mercy. As heartbreaking as it was, she banished him with the click of a button—or so she'd thought.

She had never wanted to be in the same space as Robbie again as long as she lived, but here he was, standing in her office, spewing his threats at her.

"You're still an unforgiving bitch, aren't you?" he sneered. "But I never thought that you'd become his accomplice to murder."

"Still jumping to conclusions, aren't you, Robbie? Always thinking the worst of people, especially me. And how do you think your family would feel about you if they knew you assaulted me?"

"You wouldn't," he warned, stepping toward her.

Only the desk separated them. Jessie measured the distance to the door and thought about whether she could make a run for it. If she hadn't been pregnant, she might have had a chance, but she was trapped.

In the midst of Jessie and Robbie glowering at one another like two boxers in the ring, Josh Spencer stuck his head into her office. "Hey man, I can hear your voice down the hall, maybe you'd better leave. Right now."

"He was just leaving," Jessie said, her pulse pounding.

"Jessie, this isn't over," Robbie said, shoulder-bumping Josh on his way out of the door.

"Are you alright?" Josh asked as Robbie tramped down the hall. "Who was that jerk?"

"I'm fine. Really. That's too long of a story." Her heart was still racing as she slipped the office keys from her keychain and handed them to Josh, who looked at her with disbelief. "You really need to watch your back around here. Remember that."

CHAPTER
13

Hal Samuels sipped on the cold coffee congealing inside "The World's Greatest Dad" mug. His chin rested on the heel of his hand and his fingertips massaged his graying temples. Before him, the contents of the *People vs. Terrence Butterfield* case file lay strewn across his office desk. He could barely bring himself to read the file, which contained the preliminary reports and photographs, but which would grow into a carton or two or three overflowing with ballistics, coroners and forensic reports, interviews, motions, demands for documents, and grand jury minutes and transcripts. It wasn't the potential magnitude of the case that he resented. It was the blood, sinew, and guts of this motiveless killing. And the photographs of the victim turned his stomach. The torment of Bill and Betty Paige's interview had made matters much worse.

An eight-by-ten glossy of Ryan Paige's high school graduation portrait was stapled inside the folder over the intake sheet. Dressed in a dark, nondescript V-neck sweater and open-collared white dress shirt, the kid's killer dimples and smoky blue eyes lit up the page. In contrast, the crime scene photographs depicted bullets and butchery rendering the boy as unidentifiable as roadkill. A naked torso bathed in a pool of dark, red blood. The left side of his head shattered by gunfire, exposing portions of the skull and spilling brain matter across the cement floor. A tangle of blood-soaked ropes wound around a steel foundation pole. Ryan's swollen flesh burned by the ropes that bound him. Unbelievably, the sum of the body parts had once been a vital, living being. Somebody's kid. The Paige's kid.

The autopsy and DNA results would confirm the victim's identity and ballistics would determine whether the slugs dislodged from Ryan's skull were fired from Butterfield's .38 Special. Fingerprints would further link the predator to his prey, altering the nature of the evidence from circumstantial to conclusive.

As a prosecutor, he was appalled, furious, and disgusted at the hideous murder committed within his community. As a father, he was horrified by the sadistic and torturous violence perpetrated upon Ryan. Through Bill's reminiscences, he'd sensed the deep connection between father and son, and the irreplaceable loss of his buddy, his dreams. If anything happened to his own son, to Tyler—he refused to permit his imagination to wander down that dark path.

Hal removed his bifocals and wiped their filmy lenses with the tongue of his tie. He replaced the glasses and studied the arresting officer's report. Jessica Martin's name in the report continued to trouble him. How was she connected to the murder?

He cupped the phone receiver in his hand and weighed calling her, fidgeting in his leather chair at the mere thought. They hadn't spoken in a long, long time, not since he'd announced his impulsive engagement to Erin and deserted New York City for upstate. Seven years ago. At the time, Jessie had been a third-year law student at NYU. A lifetime ago. In passing, he'd heard a rumor that she worked at McMann, but their paths had never intersected. There was no reason why they would. They operated in two different worlds—the criminal and the civil. Until yesterday. Until Butterfield.

If he contacted her now, out of the blue, what was he going to say? *Hey, Jess, this is your old pal, Hal Samuels from the DA's office. How's life been treating you? I hear that you're involved in the Butterfield murder. Anything I should know?*

He chuckled to himself. He was thinking like an idiotic schoolboy. Hal returned the handset to its cradle and took another sip of the cold java.

Or, perhaps he could call just to say hello. For old time's sake. Not even mention Butterfield. *Want to meet for a drink sometime soon?* Who was he kidding? He didn't want to go down that road either.

His mind churned, unable to let the thought go, unable to let Jessie go. He was the Chief ADA assigned to the most newsworthy case in the state and he had an obligation to interview any potential witness. After all, Jessie's name appeared in the police report. Contacting her was part of his job.

In any event, he thought, she'd probably hang up.

Screw it. He cleared his throat and dialed McMann and Curtis without any clear picture as to what he was going to say. On cue from the automated attendant, he punched in Jessie's extension and, hearing the familiar voice, he launched into a cheerful greeting, only to feel embarrassed when the recording requested that he leave a message at the tone.

"Jess, hi. This is Hal. Hal Samuels. It's been a while. When you receive this message, please give me a call." He mumbled his number and hung up.

"Hal?" Lauren Hollenbeck was situated in the doorway to his office. Her hand rested on one hip and her head was cocked in the opposite direction with one brow arched, her pose reminiscent of a question mark. "Meeting in my office in five minutes."

"Yeah, sure," he replied offhandedly. Hal wondered how long she'd been spying on him and what she'd observed. Lauren turned and left.

Hal returned the phone to his ear and hit the speed dial. His call went to voicemail. "Hey, honey, it's me. How about getting a sitter for Ty tonight? Let's go out to dinner. OK? Call me. Love you."

CHAPTER
14

Kyle's image reflected behind Jessie's in the bedroom dresser mirror. It was good to see him smile. Ever since the funeral yesterday, her fiancé had been bluer than an inkwell. Dinner last evening had been a complete bust. His conversation had consisted of a series of grunts and monosyllabic responses to Jessie's questions about his board meeting. The more she'd tried to pry him out of his shell, the more he'd withdrawn. She'd intended to tell him about her problems at work, but dinner hadn't seemed like the right time. She'd have to wait. Her thoughts bogged down with worry, she'd surrendered to his mood and they'd eaten in silence.

Tonight, Kyle was different. He proudly caressed her expanding waistline, his long fingers stroking the baby and his chin resting on her shoulder. She smiled back at him. They looked handsome. Right together. Their baby was going to be beautiful.

"I'm worried about you, the two of you," he said.

Jessie turned and buried her head against Kyle's chest. His concern enraptured her, reminding her that she need not be so ferocious and strong all the time. He'd catch her if she fell. She didn't want to break his good mood, but she had to. Keeping her news a secret was eating her up inside. Jessie breathed deeply, gathering her nerves, and told him about the maternity leave.

Kyle quietly listened to her describe the partners' ambush. The sharp shift in his mood was palpable, like falling off a cliff. His face grew red and his jaw tightened. "You know whose fault this is, don't you?"

She wasn't sure if he was blaming her or Terrence. She lowered her eyes to the floor, avoiding eye contact.

"What about the thousands of hours you've logged over the past five years? You've made them a fortune and helped expand their practice. Doesn't that count for something?"

Jessie shrugged and blew her runny nose. She walked over to their bed and sat down.

Kyle followed her and settled in beside her. "Should we be thinking about your recourse against the firm, like suing? Or consulting with an attorney? Why don't you pick Kaplan's brain? He owes you a favor."

Jessie's toes fiddled with the soft silk carpeting. She explained that since McMann had placed her on extended 'medical leave' and continued to cover her salary and benefits there was no legal recourse. "Hopefully, they'll reconsider my situation after the grand jury's decision."

"A lot could happen between now and then. And there may be some new opportunities, so let's keep our options open. That's all I'm suggesting."

She expected that both of them would be subpoenaed to testify before the grand jury and told him so. Jessie reasoned that her best course of action was to be prepared by researching the ramifications of appearing before the grand jury. "I'm not really familiar with the workings of the criminal justice system, you know what I mean."

"Give me a break, Jessie. Look at the mess we're in. None of this would be happening if you'd listened to me that night and contacted the police. I guess this is the thanks we get for our friendship with Terrence." Kyle's eyes narrowed into dark blue slits. "And your misplaced loyalty. You need to remember that it's not just about you anymore."

The sharp edge in his tone scared her. Kyle usually kept his snide remarks about Terrence to a minimum, yet she understood his irritation. By insinuating that Jessie had screwed up big time, he was making her second guess her actions on the night of Ryan's murder. When Terrence had called asking for her help, she'd been swept up in one goal, protecting him. There had been no way she could have ignored his plea and let the police handle the situation. Sure, she'd coerced Kyle into driving over to Terrence's house, offered Terrence legal assistance, and gone to the police station, but at the time it had seemed like the right thing to do. The more Jessie reexamined the chain of events, the more she became convinced that, practically speaking, Kyle might be correct. She could have allowed the incident to play itself out without her intervention.

However, her actions were clearly within the boundaries of the law and imperative to protect her friend and client.

Regardless, there was no rewind button in real life. No bringing Ryan back. No preventing Terrence from committing murder and no reversal of the impact upon her career.

Jessie raised her eyes to his. Kyle sighed in resignation, slipped his arm around her, and pulled her close. She melted against his shoulder as his soft lips touched her forehead. Within the comfort of Kyle's embrace, Jessie was able to briefly shake off the premonition that the horrible sequence of events might not have ended.

CHAPTER
15

Jessie pulled her Jeep into the Market Street parking lot and parked in the noon shadow of the court annex. Earlier that morning, she'd thrown on her robe and gone downstairs for a cup of tea and to check the email on her laptop. She'd planned to remain in her pajamas all day and work from home. Clicking on the firm's website icon on her dashboard, the logo vanished before her eyes. Sooner than anticipated, Jessica G. Martin, Esq. had been banned from the law office of McMann and Curtis. This would mean a trip downtown to the library on this very hot, sticky day.

The September sky was deepening from a crisp summer blue to the purplish hue of early autumn, but the relentless humidity still suffocated the valley in a haze. Departing her car, Jessie tugged on her straw hat and hoisted her canvas tote over her shoulder. The heat radiating off the asphalt scorched her swollen ankles as she walked toward the courthouse.

Once inside, the elevator carried her up to the fourth floor where she made her way down the hall to the Barnard Law Library. The faint odor of leather reminded her of law school, which seemed like a lifetime ago. She avoided the bank of computer terminals along the far wall and settled into a secluded table among the musty stacks. Barricaded by the piles of treatises and casebooks, she planned to figure out how long the grand jury deliberations would separate her from her clients. Without her work, she'd go stir crazy from boredom. She was driven to find an answer.

Jessie thumbed through the black and red leatherette volumes of "Criminal Procedure in New York," jotting notes about the various aspects of the grand jury, including its secrecy. The panel, consisting of twenty-three members, voted whether to direct the district attorney to charge the accused with a crime after the DA had presented evidence to the jurors. The defense attorney may only be present if the accused is going to testify before the grand jury. The entire proceeding occurred behind closed doors to encourage the cooperation of the witnesses, to protect the innocent who were being investigated, and to preserve the confidentiality of the deliberations.

That meant that Hollenbeck would present her evidence to the grand jury, and Kaplan could be present if Terrence was going to testify, which he'd indicated in court was going to occur. Terrence's mental stability was questionable, and it would be risky to subject him to the panel, but the decision was not hers to make. She had her own worries.

Tiny beads of perspiration dampened her forehead when she discovered that the panel could be extended indefinitely. In her mind, the pages of the calendar flipped from autumn to winter to spring to summer again.

Indefinitely, she thought, nibbling on the barrel of a plastic pen. There was little doubt that she would be subpoenaed but would her father? What about Kyle? Would she have a job to return to after the grand jury? Or even a legal career? The baby shifted, weighing in on the possibility that she may not be returning to McMann and Curtis anytime in the near future.

Kyle was right. She never should have answered the midnight call.

At the opposite end of the hall, Hal, Lauren, and Cindie were entering the glass corridor to the DA's office when he spotted Jessie, her face partially obscured by the brim of a straw hat. At the sight of her, his pulse quickened. Afraid of revealing his rekindled feelings, Hal excused himself from his colleagues and slipped into the library.

Jessie was settled at the rear of the room, and he sneaked in between the tall stacks of dusty treatises for a better view. From his place among the precedents and case law, he observed her unpacking her bottled water, arranging the legal pads and pens on the oak table before her and burying her nose into a book.

Moments passed, and his vigil continued. Deep in thought and oblivious to the audience, she chewed on a pen and swore under her breath. Multiple times. Hal chuckled to himself. This scene was not unfamiliar to him.

There was no other way to put it. Jessie was beautiful. More beautiful now as a woman than as the girl he'd loved so long ago.

As his vigil continued, he brushed away the memories of their time together as though they were butterflies alighting on his shoulder. The lavender scent of her skin. The curves of her hips against his. The golden sparkle in her eyes whenever she saw him.

While life had steered them along different paths, now their paths had intersected. Hal was tempted to return to his office and leave well enough alone. His reasons were evident. His wife. His son. His career as ADA.

And the Butterfield case. He recalled that once upon a time, Butterfield had been Jessie's mentor, and her potential involvement in the case could determine whether or not his murder one case would proceed to trial. There was too much at stake. Yet, as hard as he tried he couldn't resist the magnetic energy swirling around them. He was trapped in the inescapable field of their past which pulled him closer and closer to her.

He approached Jessie and slid into the seat across the table.

"Hey," Hal said.

She looked up at him and a generous smile lit up her face, plump with baby weight.

"Hal Samuels?" Jessie asked, surprise lilting her voice. "It's been a while, hasn't it?"

"Too long." He swallowed hard, clearing away the guilt choking his throat. His hand slid across to hers and gave it a squeeze. The warmth of her fingers intertwined in his was as sensuous as an embrace. "What brings you slumming in my neighborhood?"

"Haven't you heard? I'm an accessory to murder according to McMann and Curtis." Jessie moved to withdraw her hand but stopped. "Because of my friendship with Terrence, I'm guilty by association."

"What? Guilty until proven innocent?" Hal's eyes narrowed. "Did they fire you?"

She shrugged and explained that she'd been locked out of the firm under the guise of a medical leave pending Butterfield's grand jury hearing. "The partners are preempting the possibility of bad publicity about their precious firm. The bad part being me."

"That's a bit extreme, isn't it?"

Jessie's cheeks flushed and she turned her face away from him, hiding the tears he'd already seen welling in her eyes. It had been years since they'd seen each other, but he knew in his gut that Jessie couldn't be an accessory to murder. He recalled that she'd known Butterfield for years but even so, she wasn't the type of person who could have aided and abetted anyone, especially her mentor, in such a vile act. She'd simply been in the wrong place at the wrong time. This fact was apparent to him and her bosses at McMann should've given her the benefit of the doubt. But as she'd mentioned, there were other considerations in play. She deserved better from them. And from Hal himself.

He leaned across the table toward her and lowered his voice to a whisper. "Jess, I really can't discuss the Butterfield case with you, but just so you know, you've got no worries there."

Jessie met his gaze, wiping her cheeks with the back of her hand.

"Don't worry, just trust me," he said, "Please leave it at that."

"Are you the lead prosecutor? I thought that Hollenbeck was handling the case. Does that mean you won't be calling me before the grand jury as a witness?" Her watery eyes brightened to emerald and gold.

Hal squirmed uncomfortably and made a noncommittal sound in his throat. Under the guise of clearing his windpipe, he said, "Pregnancy agrees with you. You're feeling okay?" He raised his eyebrows and engaged his most charismatic grin hoping to change the subject.

"Great, until all this happened."

"Listen, Jess, don't let this situation mess with your head." Looking into her mesmerizing eyes, Hal momentarily lost himself and caught his thumb gently tracing the heart-shaped mole on the back of her hand. He stopped, but she didn't draw her hand away. "Relax. Trust me. In the scheme of things, this is just a temporary blip."

"I know, but it's difficult being bombarded from all angles." Jessie smiled weakly. "You know what I mean."

"Come on, let's get out of here. You look like you could use a good, stiff cup of coffee."

Jessie looked at him, pursing her lips to hold back a chuckle. She always used to enjoy his jokes and he liked making her laugh, but today his efforts were fruitless.

"Sorry, but I've got some research to do. Besides, you'd chance being seen with the Butterfield case pariah?"

He decided not to push her so he offered a rain check, but her acceptance sounded hollow, sad.

"I've already told you—no worries, but suit yourself. Most people would jump at the opportunity to chat me up." Hal shook his head and laughed. "Jessica Grace Martin, Esq., you were always so incredibly stubborn. I guess some things never change."

"Some things do," Jessie said wistfully, doodling circles on her legal pad. "I really have to get back to work; besides, you'd better get back before the dragon lady sends her troops looking for you."

"If you need to talk, call me." Hal pushed back his chair and stood to leave. She smiled at him and returned her attention to the books, dismissing him. Hal hesitated at the end of the stack before taking his leave. He considered returning to give her greater reassurance, but there was nothing more to say. Their conversation had already precipitated sufficient collateral damage to his heart.

Jessie glanced up, her eyes trailing Hal as he walked away. Unconsciously, she twirled the diamond engagement band around her moist ring finger.

Hal Samuels. Still unassumingly handsome and charming. His hair was styled shorter, sprinkled with gray. Not only was he still the cool guy who was comfortable in his own skin, but he also made her feel at ease just being in his company. The kind of comfort she felt in a well-worn pair of jeans. And when they spoke, he focused his full attention upon her as though she was the only person in his universe, the only person who mattered to him.

And that sexy smile. His golden-brown eyes sported a hint of crinkles furrowed by the trials of murderers, rapists, and thieves. Those eyes and his touch seduced her into believing and trusting him concerning Terrence's case. She longed to believe him, to trust him, but something restrained her.

And, even after all these years, how did he know her so well? His uncanny ability to worm inside her brain had been a maddening and endearing quality, which even now made the hairs on the back of her neck stand at attention. He'd always been able to read her, ever since their time together at NYU.

She had been a first-year law student when their paths had crossed for the first time. She'd been in the marble entry of Vanderbilt Hall, admiring the crystal chandelier glistening overhead in the morning sunlight. She'd been nervously huddled among the law school newbies comparing their schedules for the fall term. Like the rest of them, she was excited, yet terrified, about the intellectual and emotional challenges ahead.

From the corner of her eye, she spied a cluster of attractive, freshly barbered young men dressed in Oxford shirts and khakis leaning against the banister of the foyer's spiral staircase. Unlike the scruffy, tee-shirted, ripped-jeans boys of Syracuse University, these were men. Backpacks had been abandoned for leather briefcases. Buffed loafers replaced Converse All-Stars. In the center of the enclave, a tall man with dark ginger tousled hair threw back his head and laughed a deep, hearty laugh that emanated from his core. He was relaxed in his carriage and cool in his mannerisms—so cool that he would never break a sweat. Clearly, he was the alpha of the group.

She didn't mean to stare, but she couldn't help it; he was so unbelievably cute. He glanced over at her, caught her eye, and winked.

She'd been busted. Jessie looked away, feeling warmth rise to her cheeks. She was relieved when the first-year students were herded into the law library and divided alphabetically into study sections. She stood at the reference desk in the Lieberman Main Reading Room and appraised her surroundings in awe. The massive library was more than a century old and occupied the width of the entire block between West 3rd and 4th Streets. Ever since Terrence had sparked her interest in the law, she'd dreamed of being set free among the legal knowledge, precedents, and history bound together in the beautiful leather volumes. As she inhaled the heavy air, she silently thanked Terrence for his encouragement and hoped to make him and her parents proud.

"Come on, this way," said her friend Sarah Steinberg, tugging on the sleeve of Jessie's jacket. They brought up the tail of the students snaking into a classroom in the damp sub-basement level of Furman Hall. The section leader was making his introductions while the group filtered into the cramped space. From where she stood, she couldn't see the speaker but could hear him clearly.

"Good morning," he said. "I'm Hal Samuels, a third-year student, and I'll spend the next nine months attempting to teach you to research and write like a lawyer. Upstairs they teach theory, substance, and procedure. In a million years, you'll never be able to memorize everything you need to know. I'll teach you how to find the statutory and case law and how to cogently and persuasively present your arguments like a member of the bar. And maybe win a few cases." A chuckle filled the air.

He continued his spiel over the sliding and squeaking of metal chairs chafing across the floor. Sarah and Jessie snatched their seats in the back of the room and in the process, Jessie's backpack slid from her shoulder onto the floor with a crash that echoed off the cinder-block walls. She glanced up and recognized the hot auburn-haired guy from the hallway. He was sizing her up from across the room. Jessie's face flamed again.

"Oh crap, I mean, sorry," Jessie said, scrambling to pick up her bag.

"Anytime you're ready Miss…?" Hal said, pursing his lips to stifle a laugh.

"Martin."

He had flashed her a quick, disarming smile and returned to his lecture.

The slap of treatises being dropped on a neighboring library table drew Jessie back to the printed pages splayed open at her fingertips. How long had it been since law school? Too long. Ancient history. That Jessie Martin, the wide-eyed law student, naïvely believed in the principle that Truth and Justice always prevailed. She could never have imagined that one day her life would be tainted with the taste of blood and the shocking death of a friend. Or a scenario threatening her legal career and livelihood. This Jessie Martin, corporate attorney and mother-to-be, knew better.

CHAPTER
16

Hal returned to his office but his mind refused to focus on the Butterfield file. He felt a bit shaken knowing that Jessie was in the library a few feet down the hall. It bothered him that *she* still unnerved him. So he opted to establish some physical distance between them.

He wandered through the labyrinth that connected the courthouse to the office of the commissioner of jurors. The brick annex stood on the site of the original Poughkeepsie Courthouse where the likes of Alexander Hamilton, John Jay, and George Clinton had ratified the United States Constitution in 1788.

When Hal entered the central jury room, the commissioner, Tom Reese, was in his office mulling over the roster of potential jurors. Tom anxiously swiveled about in his chair like he was dancing the twist. Hal lifted his glasses and squinted at the photo collage of the little league teams that Tom had coached over the years. On the opposite wall, a large picture window afforded a view of the unsuspecting volunteers in the outer waiting area. Composed mostly of students, the unemployed, and senior citizens, this group had won the public service lottery of pocket change and free lunch. Some would serve on a petit jury impaneled for the mundane and banal: a dog bite, slip and fall, car crash, or a medical malpractice case. Civil cases were all about the bucks. Others would be assigned to the juicier criminal cases like larceny, shootings over gang turf, domestic violence, or embezzlement.

In the history of bucolic Dutchess County, the Butterfield case constituted a first. Never had a jury been confronted with a bloody dismemberment and torture case. Never had a teacher been accused of murdering a student. Never had the current of a case rippled through the community with such emotional charge. While Hal occupied himself with the hard facts, his staff fielded the barrage of calls from concerned parents, school administrators, and the press, of course. Behind closed doors, the grand jury would hear the police officers, the medical examiner, the parade of witnesses and reports, and they'd analyze the gruesome photos, the revolver, the bloody knife, and bullet casings.

They'd never experience the panicked voices that Hal had heard, but surely being on the grand jury and hearing all of the evidence would make them wonder whether anyone was safe. From all accounts, Butterfield was a good teacher, a bit unusual, but not someone that people thought of as a danger.

Surveying the jury pool, Hal observed the sea of tablets, laptops, and smartphones. Each juror appeared to be isolated in the solitary confinement of headphones and oblivious to their call to duty. A distinguished looking gentleman folded the *New York Times* lengthwise into a fan while intermittently checking his phone. A red silk handkerchief fluttered out from the breast pocket of his snappy navy pinstriped suit. Across the room, a brunette sipping coffee was absorbed in a mystery novel and two knitters chatted away, presumably exchanging tips of the trade.

"Quite a crowd out there in the pit. They have no clue what they may be in for, do they?"

"Nope," Reese said, scratching his bearded chin. "Otherwise, they'd be coming up with all kinds of cockamamie reasons to be excused."

"The guy with the *Times*. Isn't that Senator Stefan Hill?"

"Yeah, no one's exempt from service. You know that." Reese rocked back in his chair. "He's petit, but he'll get disqualified. Who wants a politico sitting on their panel, right?"

"Are ours ready to go?"

"Not yet. We have some civils to call first, so give me an hour or so. Once we clear them out, we'll run the orientation video. Then, we'll be good to go."

"Contact Cindie when you're ready and I'll send someone down to get them."

"You're scheduled for court room A. Judge Anthony will swear them in and then you can move back to the grand jury room. That works, right?"

Hal nodded.

Reese leaned forward in his chair, legs spread wide with elbows resting on his knees, as though he prepared to catch a pitch.

"Samuels, I don't envy you, but from what I know about the case it should be a slam dunk."

"You never know what the jury's going to do." Hal was certain, though, that the outcome of this trial would change his career—and maybe even his life.

The next morning before dawn, the Braxton Hicks contractions kicked in. Jessie's belly alternated between hardening into a basketball and releasing back to its normal pliable state. Weeks ago, these contractions had alarmed her but when her doctor said that they were merely nature's dress rehearsal for the big day, she'd relaxed. The spasms weren't painful, just weird and a bit disconcerting. Now, they were a matter of course, so she shifted her position and her muscles slackened and the spasms dissipated. The problem was that the hormonal contractions stimulated her emotions as well as her body.

As light filtered through the bedroom curtains, she lay beneath the covers listening to Kyle tiptoe away for an early meeting with desire smoldering in her belly. Her fiancé smacked his knee on the nightstand, swore under his breath, and, seeing her watching him, apologized for waking her. Kyle leaned over her, his breath minty fresh from mouthwash. "We're in the home stretch now, so relax and stay in bed," he said, gently.

"Care to join me?" She knotted her fingers into his wet curls, feeling the sudden overwhelming urge to grab him and pull him into bed. Yet, she wavered. Each day she became increasingly more insecure about his desire for her. Her rapidly blossoming waistline was as unattractive as a casaba melon with its pink fleshy valleys stretching outward from her navel. She was overwhelmed with exhaustion from toting the extra baby weight and so she couldn't blame him if she disgusted him.

"Call me after you see the doc today," Kyle said. He disengaged her hands and planted a peck on her cheek, which seemed to be the extent of their physical contact these days. He'd become a man of inconsistencies, mostly protective but increasingly distant, like a crab retracting into his shell. He seemed preoccupied with managing the struggling civic center and her recent problems added to his burden. His only joy appeared to be derived from the baby growing inside her.

Jessie touched his side of the bed. It was still warm. Sadness replaced desire because for whatever reason, they were out of sync and she missed him. His BMW sputtered out of the driveway and shifted gears down the street. She tugged the comforter over her head, turned to her side, and returned to sleep.

Mid-morning, Jessie awoke anxious and jittery with a splitting headache. She peeled back the sheets and discovered that a strange, alien body had been substituted for her own. The skin of her tanned legs was mottled like crackled rawhide, anchored to pink cocktail-wiener toes. She could barely flex her bloated fingers. She lost her footing as she rose from the bed, feeling as though she'd been tossed shipboard in a stormy sea. She braced herself against the bedroom wall and reminded herself that she was visiting her doctor shortly so there was no need to panic. She needed to take it easy for the next hour or so.

Jessie dressed, and then, clinging firmly to the banister, descended the stairs. Reaching the bottom rung, she sighed in relief and walked toward the kitchen. The saccharine odor of damp newsprint hit her, making her queasy stomach lurch. On the counter, the *Poughkeepsie Journal* lay open. Its headline grabbed her: "Grand Jury Selection to Begin in the Butterfield Case." In the accompanying headshot, Terrence wore a dark three-piece suit and a maroon medallion tie. His neat wavy hair framed his elegant features.

She recognized his faculty photo from this year's high school yearbook. When he'd shown it to her, his smirk had jumped off the page at her. It was a gloat of self-satisfaction that he reserved for outwitting her father in a so-called friendly game of chess or when reprimanding a recalcitrant student. She'd also noticed it flash across his face when he'd bragged about a joke he'd played on faculty members who he believed were inferior to him. Terrence's expression propelled a shiver up her spine when she considered that his prankish behavior may have been the symptom of a crueler, deeper, sadistic disease.

She quickly turned to the next page.

The article stated that Terrence Butterfield, a local high school teacher, had been charged with murdering a teenage boy trespassing through his yard. It alleged that he'd bound the boy in his basement and shot him point-blank. It went on to cite a brief chronology of Terrence's arrest, his denial of guilt, his incarceration without bail, and the impaneling of a grand jury to review the charges.

Jeremy Kaplan had issued a "no comment" regarding whether his client would testify on his own behalf before the grand jury. District Attorney Lauren Hollenbeck charged that the alleged perpetrator was "an animal who should not be allowed to wander free on the streets," and predicted an indictment and ultimate conviction on the crimes alleged.

The sensational news was one-sided, failing to mention Terrence's community service, his teaching awards, or his dedication to his students. In truth, his contributions hardly mattered. According to the news, the black-and-white facts were that the teacher in the photograph was a murderer.

Jessie struggled to reconcile the truth that Terrence Butterfield now represented the face of evil. He'd always been considerate, generous, and compassionate to her and her family. However, his aloofness, rigidness to routine, inability to express any emotion except anger, and cruel mischiefs could no longer be dismissed as idiosyncrasies. They'd been blinking neon lights spelling danger. They'd been signals that no one, including her, had seen. Now, in hindsight, she wondered how she could have been so blind.

Perhaps it was because Terrence had flawlessly juggled the various roles of teacher, mentor, friend, confidante, and community activist. For years, he'd deceived them all, but had he actually been a monster the entire time? Had his whole life in Poughkeepsie been a hoax? Or had he suddenly, unexpectedly cracked? Who or what had pushed him over the edge? She wondered whether she could have prevented this breakdown, or more horrific, whether she'd ever been in danger.

The chiming of the grandfather clock interrupted the internal debate and reminded her of the doctor's appointment. She grabbed her keys and purse from the foyer table as she left.

Cautiously, Jessie backed the Jeep out of the driveway, adjusting the rearview mirror. In her path, a burly man with a clean-shaven head stood on the sidewalk, blocking her access to the road. Reflexively, Jessie stamped on the brakes and the car jerked to a stop.

He approached her car and she rolled down the window, "Can I help you?"

"You, Jessica Martin, attorney-at-law?" he growled.

She nodded.

He pitched a stark, white envelope into the open car window. "You've been served." Two gnarled fingers snapped a Boy Scout salute and the process server lumbered away.

Jessie stared at the crinkled envelope in her lap. The return address and its threatening tidings, "Lauren Hollenbeck, Dutchess County District Attorney—PERSONAL—HAND DELIVER," glared at her.

Damn. This meant that she'd have to testify before the grand jury. Probably Kyle and her dad, too. Boy, they were going to be ticked off. Especially Kyle. He'd use it as more ammunition against Terrence, and she couldn't blame him. She blamed Hal. Once again, he'd lied to her.

She didn't have time to deal with this right now, and besides, there was nothing she could do at the moment. She crammed the envelope into her purse and sped off to the obstetrician.

CHAPTER
17

Merely thinking about the afternoon's conference with Butterfield drained the life out of him. Jeremy had yet to draw the ultimate conclusion that his client was out of his mind, but he was pretty darn close. One minute the guy was crisp and coherent discussing history, politics, and sports. The next, Butterfield babbled incoherently about the evening of the murder. Jeremy felt like he was on a seesaw with his client and the oscillations between reality and delusion were making him ill. Butterfield needed help. Jeremy needed help. Neither was able to help himself.

Jeremy flopped into his office chair, pushed his hat forward to shield his face, and closed his eyes. He needed to take a breather, a catnap, and then he'd tackle his work. The soft whooshing of the air conditioning relaxed him as he drifted off. Sooner than he would have liked, he heard his secretary's voice.

"Hey, sleeping beauty," Mo said, poking his shoulder with her sharp nails.

She'd startled him, sneaking up like that. Even in high heels, the woman was an office ninja, appearing out of thin air.

"There's a message from the DA's office on your desk."

He straightened up and slid the hat back on his forehead. "Do me a favor. Get me the Klein file out of the mothballs. Please."

"The Klein file? The storage unit? I'll pick it up on my way in the morning." Mo twisted her lips to one side and sighed resignedly. She tapped the pink message slip. "Don't forget the ADA. He called twice."

"Yeah, yeah. Hold up a sec, will you? I need you to drop something off for me on your way home tonight." Jeremy picked up the phone and dialed the extension on the message. Cradling the receiver against his ear, he jotted a quick note, placed it in an envelope, and handed it to a toe-tapping Mo. She stalked off and left him listening to the on-hold music.

"Well?" Lauren Hollenbeck squawked.

"As we expected," Hal said, hanging up the phone. "Kaplan won't be attending the grand jury. They're waiving their right to appear."

"He'd have to be an idiot to let his client testify." Lauren slouched in the chair opposite his desk, her legs seeming even longer and leaner in the four-inch black stilettos she was taking for a test drive. Her eyes darted past him to the window, her attention apparently distracted by the gulls on the ledge outside. "You know, I wish that I could be a fly on the wall in the deliberation room. This is going to be a spellbinding case. As prosecutors, we perceive the world through jaded lenses. Everybody's evil. Everybody's guilty until proven innocent. We're a callous lot. But lay people, they're a different breed. The world is all puppy dogs and rainbows. They abide by the opposite notion that everyone is innocent until proven guilty. How naive." Her voice was distant, faraway.

Hal scoffed, shaking his head as she continued with her musings.

"I miss that part of the job, hearing the way they kick around the evidence. The ballistics. The police photos. The autopsy and DNA results. And, of course, the witnesses. Be sure to dissect your witnesses. Especially Martin. Lawyers are a slippery lot, as you know."

Hal bolted upright in his chair and stared at her.

"Oh, didn't I mention it? I reviewed your list and assumed a clerical error, so I added her to the subpoena list," Lauren said, coyly.

"Lauren, she's a witness after the fact. You read the report. She won't have anything pertinent to add to the investigation. Let's not muddy the water with an unnecessary witness. If the panel believes that her testimony is relevant, they can let us know." He kept his tone flat.

"Well, it's too late, anyway. Jessica Martin was served this morning. There's no harm done. If she's only a witness and not an accessory after the fact, she's in no danger of prosecution. She can testify, say her piece, and be on her merry way." She waved her hand dismissively. "Anyway, Rossi's report suggests that she may have interfered with their collar and obstructed the investigation. It would be instructive for the grand jury to hear what she has to say for herself. Don't you agree?" Her full attention remained glued upon him.

They both knew that it wasn't too late. They could withdraw the subpoena anytime prior to Jessie's appearance, but Hal refused to argue with her. For some strange reason, Lauren was testing his loyalty. He selected his words slowly, carefully to quell his rising anger. "What about Emory? Was he served as well?"

"No, he wasn't necessary." Lauren tapped her fountain pen against her palm. "Butterfield made the initial contact with Ms. Martin. I'd like to determine the nature of their relationship. This should be interesting."

"I don't know what's going on in your perverse little mind, but I think you're barking up the wrong tree. This smells like harassment to me, but you're the boss."

"That's right. I am. And if I'm elected to the judgeship, I'll be the boss who'll create a vacancy and need to pick a successor. Just keep that in mind." Lauren stood up, resting her fuchsia lacquered nails on the edge of his desk. She leaned forward jutting her face so close to his that he could feel her hot breath on his lips, taste the jalapeños she'd eaten for lunch. "I think we understand each other. Don't we, Hal?"

Hal swallowed hard as she walked away, smoothing the wrinkles from her pencil skirt.

With the clicking of her high heels receding down the hallway, the lightness returned to Hal's office. The raven queen had flown. Like the large, sooty bird, Lauren was intelligent, intimidating, and the harbinger of doom and death. Having sworn an oath to protect the People of the State of New York, she executed her duties with a lethal severity and, unfortunately for the staff, without humor. She ruled her kingdom with absolute autonomy, terrorizing friends and foes, much like his father, Harold Samuels, Jr., had treated his own family.

As much as he admired Lauren, he played by a different set of rules, inspired by a passage that he'd read as a teenager, a quote attributed to Buddha: *Believe nothing, O monks, merely because you have been told it…or because it is traditional, or because you yourselves have imagined it. Do not believe what your teacher tells you merely out of respect for the teacher. But whatsoever, after due examination and analysis, you find to be conducive to the good, the benefit, the welfare of all beings—that doctrine believe and cling to, and take it as your guide.*

To the best of his ability, he sought to embody this philosophy in his life. Prior to law school, during a stint with Teach for America in Spanish Harlem, he'd explained Buddha's teachings to his students and, to his surprise, they'd remembered. On the day of his departure, he'd choked back the tears when they'd presented him with a cross-stitch plaque of the proverb, painstakingly embroidered by one of the mothers. The memento hung in his office next to the decorative wall scroll commemorating his admission to the New York bar as a reminder of the mantra guiding him into public service.

Occasionally, he ignored the adage, but not today. With the prospect of shepherding the grand jury through the evidence against Terrence Butterfield, Buddha's wisdom was reassuring. Doubtless, convicting Butterfield of his crimes would benefit all human beings and the community at large.

Hal grabbed his jacket and left for lunch, haunted by the nagging thought that he'd forgotten to resolve something urgent.

CHAPTER
18

The wafer-thin hospital gown that barely covered Jessie's round belly fluttered in the cool blast of air conditioning. Her exposed skin dimpled and she yanked the sheet tighter across her lower half. Laying back on the exam table, her bare legs dangled off the edge between the stirrups. In her mind, she composed a grocery list for tonight's dinner—chicken breasts, asparagus, rice pilaf, maybe Kyle's favorite wholegrain dinner rolls—distracting herself from the discomforts, indignities, and terror of the doctor's office.

Dr. Bakool Suryaprakash, or just "Dr. S." to his patients, approached the table. He was a peculiar amalgam of a man. His frame was so petite that he could have purchased his lab coat in the boys' department, while his hands were the size of catcher's mitts. But it was his pearly white, jack o'lantern smile that always put Jessie at ease.

"Jessie. Nice to see you. I understand that your blood pressure is a bit high. Let me take a listen, please. I see that there is some swelling in your hands and feet as well." His gentle voice rarely raised above a whisper, which required her to pay close attention. She pushed herself up into the sitting position and, for the fourth time in ten minutes, the cuff was clamped around her arm, then compressed and released. The doctor listened with the stethoscope and then asked her to lie down and place her feet in the stirrups.

Jessie hated this part of the exam, but she did as asked, flinching as Dr. S.'s blue latex covered hands patted her knees. Staring at the ceiling tiles, she expanded her list—paper towels, toilet paper, Kyle's deodorant, a bottle of acetaminophen—as he continued with the internal exam. She winced at the discomfort inside her abdomen, exhaling in relief when Dr. S. withdrew from down below. He then positioned the fetal heart monitor above her pubic bone and tilted its probe at various angles to locate the baby's heartbeat. The sound of a chugging freight train filled the room.

"A boy or girl?" Jessie asked, excitedly.

"Dear, that's an old wives' tale," the nurse said. "You'll either have to wait a while to find out or have another sonogram."

Jessie sighed. For the past several months she'd been clinging to old wives' tales like a life preserver. Kyle was old school and viewed the baby gender ordeal as the thrill of the unknown. A beautiful shared journey culminating at the moment of birth. Yet, she wanted to know pink or blue, whether to refer to her belly as "him" or "her" instead of "the baby," and she wanted to pick out names. The anticipation was one more thing driving her crazy. Considering that she'd convinced him to postpone their wedding after discovering she was pregnant, the least she could do for him was wait a little longer for the gender reveal.

"Perfect, a nice healthy sound. Please slide back and get dressed. We'll talk in my office," Dr. S. said, his words drowned out by the baby's heart thumping as loud as a washing machine on spin cycle.

Jessie hastily threw on her clothes and joined Dr. S. in his adjoining office. To her relief, he explained that the high blood pressure was of no great concern. A series of simple blood, urine, and glucose tests would rule out any serious conditions such as gestational diabetes.

"But I feel like something isn't right," she said. "I'm tired all the time, out of breath, light headed, everything's swollen."

Dr. S. appeared to notice her worried expression, so he continued. "Not to worry, Jessie. These symptoms are normal for the third trimester and the tests are only precautionary. You need to take it easy until I see you next week. If things haven't settled down by then, we'll discuss hypertension medication."

"Are you ordering me to stay in bed?"

"No, I'm urging you to take it easy. Please. Elevate your feet when you're sitting, drink plenty of fluids, and no salt. Relax. Your body is going through a lot of changes."

His soft voice was calm and reassuring, but Jessie sensed tightness in his tone. Was that her imagination or exhaustion? After all, a good night's sleep was becoming a luxury since the baby was awake dancing all night. And her professional life was a mess. She shook off her silliness.

"Jessie, get some rest. This may be your last opportunity for the next eighteen years."

She laughed a little as they shook hands. His were plump and soft. Hers were moist and clammy.

Back at home, Jessie flopped onto the soft leather couch in the den and clicked on the flat screen. A soap opera flickered on and she chuckled. Her life wasn't so different from the screwed-up lives presented on the television. Terrence. Ryan. Robbie. Hal. Kyle. Her "medical leave." No wonder her blood pressure had skyrocketed into the stratosphere.

She lay on her back watching the baby inside making waves in her belly and solidified a pact with him/her to re-prioritize her goals. One: forget other people's problems. Two: a healthy self. Three: a healthy baby. Four: a happy relationship. Five: plenty of mental and physical relaxation. Six: RELAX. But did she even know how?

Jessie followed the racket of pots and pans into the kitchen where she found Kyle flexing his culinary muscles. Surrounded by freshly diced oregano, basil, and tomatoes, he wasn't the guy obsessing about his job or her problems. He was completely absorbed in stirring the cauldrons simmering on the stove. Perspiration covered his brow, dampening his curls into tight ringlets and reddening his Fair Isle complexion as though he'd just stepped from the shower.

"Oh, no. I forgot to go the market," she said and yawned. "It must be my pregnancy brain."

"No problem, babe. I saw you sacked out on the couch and thought I'd surprise you."

She approached him and a heaping spoon of the Bolognese sauce found its way into her mouth. It tasted sweet and tangy, and she rewarded him with a basil-flavored kiss.

"Everything go okay at the doctor's?" he asked.

"Dr. S. says everything's fine, but he sounded concerned. He wants me to rest, have some additional tests, and see him next week." Kyle's face darkened and she added, "He says there's really nothing to worry about."

"If you're worried, then I'm worried, so call him. That's what he's there for." Kyle embraced her. She took one of his hands and placed it on her tummy shelf. A swift kick grazed their hands and Kyle's face broke into a broad grin. "Active little guy, isn't he?"

"Or she." Jessie feigned a smile to lessen his concern. "Enough about me. If you don't want to discuss it, I'll understand, but how are things going at work? You've been so quiet about it lately."

"It's the same old story. We're always one week away from bankruptcy and barely making payroll. It's tough with the bank breathing down our neck about the mortgage, but we'll make it. No worries," Kyle said. "Besides, you're much more interesting and I need you to set the table. Dinner's almost ready."

Jessie felt sorry for him, but there was no way to help other than to get the dinnerware. She turned toward the pantry, and, forgetting her girth, her bulge brushed up against the kitchen table. Her purse teetered over the edge and its contents scattered across the floor.

Kyle bent down and confiscated the white envelope lying amidst the rubble. He waved it inches from her nose. "What's this?" The thick, red sauce dripped from his ladle onto the floor.

She'd forgotten all about the envelope but knew what it contained. "Some goon served me this morning before I left for Dr. S.'s."

Kyle tore open the envelope and read the document aloud: "Judicial Subpoena Duces Tecum… Jessica Grace Martin set aside all business and appear before the Grand Jury of Dutchess County in the Matter of the *People of the State of New York versus Terrence Butterfield* on Thursday, September 10th, at 1:30 p.m. at the Dutchess County Courthouse, Poughkeepsie, New York."

Jessie shook her head, grumbling the name of Harold Samuels III. Once again, she'd believed him and once again she'd been betrayed. She had only herself to blame.

"Weren't you served?" she asked.

"No. I wasn't," he said sharply. "You're not going to risk your health or the baby's over this garbage." Kyle crumpled up the paper and dashed it at the can. "You don't know anything about the murder. And the doctor ordered you to rest. Besides, I forbid this."

"Hey, hold on one minute. *Forbid* me?" She pointed her finger at her chest. "I'm going to pretend that those words did not come out of your mouth. And whether you approve of my giving testimony or not is beside the point." The gears in her head fired up, shifting from pregnant mother to assertive attorney. Her manner was brusque, to the point. "Legally, I don't have a choice. If I refuse to appear, I could be held in contempt of court or be subjected to a censure, not to mention the further public and professional humiliation. I won't lose my license to practice law over this and I'm sure that you don't want our baby born in county lockup when I'm charged with contempt."

"Can't you get a note from the doctor? Wouldn't that make a difference?"

"Not really. If I can't attend, they'll come here to videotape my testimony. I don't want anyone invading our home." She eased herself into a chair at the kitchen table, her energy vanquished by the extra baby weight and the extraordinary events.

"Sorry, I didn't mean to snap at you," Kyle said, massaging her taut shoulders. The tremors in his hands and fingers revealed that he was out of his league. "This is all Butterfield's fault."

"Kyle, enough." Jessie raised both of her palms and pressed them against her temples to relieve the razor-sharp pain behind her eyeballs. She really needed something to take the edge off, and she'd read that one glass of wine wouldn't hurt her or the baby. "Let's enjoy your wonderful dinner. A glass of merlot, please?"

CHAPTER
19

Jeremy Kaplan's office phone rang. It was eight in the morning and the office was dark and empty except for the red light blinking on the phone console. He was surprised and slightly annoyed. He'd anticipated an hour of solitude before the onslaught of phone calls, faxes, emails, and the whirlwind of activity generated by his secretary. He reluctantly picked up the call.

"I need to see you," said a man's raspy voice.

"Good morning, Terrence. Nice to speak with you."

"Please. I must see you. This is a matter of life and death."

He noted the irony in Terrence's plea and the desperation in his tone. Paranoia was typical for first-timers and the guy had good reason to be concerned; the other inmates didn't take kindly to kid killers.

"Tell them to expect me around nine."

The line went dead.

Last night, Gayle had dragged him away from his study to their bed around midnight and he figured that he'd rise early to finish up in the morning. With Butterfield's unexpected summoning, his schedule had been sidetracked. This wasn't the way he'd planned his day.

This afternoon, he was scheduled to attend a deposition in a personal injury case against the town of Rhinebeck, which couldn't be adjourned. The town had postponed the interrogatories three times during the past two years, claiming the last-minute unavailability of their key witness. Kaplan had promised his client that there would be no further postponements, but his client was getting antsy. He could always tell when one was getting ready to ditch him like a lover refusing to return phone calls. When he got fired, case over. Fee gone. All his hard work down the drain. In the Rhinebeck case, Jeremy saw the signs. He couldn't afford to let either this lawsuit or the life and death of Terrence Butterfield slip through his fingers.

"Morning. Here's the Klein file." Mo trotted into his office on espadrilles and hoisted the moldy cardboard carton onto the credenza. Then, she tore open a lemon-scented towelette and wiped her hands. "It was stuffed in the back of the locker, of course. We should really think about purging some of those dead files. They go back to the Stone Age."

Jeremy thanked her, collected a cigar stub from the ashtray, and motioned toward the dusty crate. "You never know, do you?"

"Yeah, yeah. Mr. Pack Rat. Next time, it's your turn to go to the dungeon."

"Got the message." He lit the remnant and dismissed her with a wave of smoke. "I'm going to county to see Terrence in fifteen."

"Don't forget about the depo—"

"I know." He shoved the well-chewed stub back into his mouth. "I know."

Jeremy studied Terrence who was sitting across from him at the conference table. The wild eyes that resembled a sleep-deprived, basement-bound hacker stared back at him.

"You have to get me out of here. Everyone seems to know who I am and why I'm in here," Butterfield said. His feet pumped like those of a drummer on a kick pedal. "The other inmates watch me constantly. When I piss. When I'm in the yard. When I eat. I sit alone in the mess hall with my back against the wall so I can watch them. Jeremy, I'm scared. I don't feel safe."

Jeremy remained silent, his fingers fondling the cigar scissors in his jacket pocket. Loosening the knot in his tie, he slipped off his navy blazer, draped it over the back of the chair, and withdrew a stack of papers and pens from his briefcase.

"I can't sleep at night because they whisper things, awful things, in the dark. They're going to kill me in here."

For a brief moment, Jeremy violated the golden rule of lawyers—don't get emotionally involved in a case. He remembered how his older kids had idolized the teacher, constantly nagging him to invite Butterfield over for supper, like all the other families. But that was after Sheila and before Gayle. He was a lousy cook and it would've been excessive cruelty to force anyone to eat his cooking.

The sharp edge of pity stabbed at his conscience. His client was not thriving in the jail environment. Why should he? Up until a few days ago, Butterfield had been a pillar of the Poughkeepsie community. It must be a shock to the system to be, as Butterfield had been, the freest of men one minute and a prisoner the next. Or had he ever really been free? There must have been a virus festering inside driving him to act as he had. To go from being beloved to vehemently hated.

"I don't deserve this torture. These criminals have no right to judge me. They don't know me. And I have shamed the people who do—my family and friends… my students. Everyone has abandoned me. I feel so alone in here. Please, you've got to get me out of here. I can't live like this."

Jeremy tasted the compassion congeal into bitter disgust. As he listened, the blurry puzzle of his client's nature crystalized. His mind pieced together the various fragments of information, which his client failed, refused, or was incapable of providing. The ones that Jeremy obtained from his other sources via the furtive distribution of Reserve Macallan Scotch at the holidays, event sponsorships, and donations to benevolent causes, or by other random acts of kindness to well-placed sergeants, captains, or union officers. One never knew when such relationships would prove useful.

While these activities didn't guarantee an open-door policy, doors were never locked to Jeremy Kaplan. His eyes reviewed data available only to the District Attorney's Office, and then, only if their investigators asked the pertinent questions or knew whom to ask. Jeremy knew the right questions and people. He'd been in the criminal game longer than anyone else in Dutchess County, even the District Attorney, Lauren Hollenbeck, and her lapdog, Hal Samuels.

Butterfield continued to bemoan his situation. Jeremy bit his tongue at the gall of the self-absorbed whiner, who acted oblivious to the tragic consequences of his actions. He thought how odd that pity and revulsion both violated the golden rule of law. But, even dirtbags are entitled to representation. And those retainers were exactly what put food on his table.

The cell phone vibrated in his shirt pocket and he excused himself to answer the call outside in the hallway. He signaled to the door sentry, an Adonis flirting with a voluptuous co-worker, that he'd shortly return to his client. The guard nodded in distracted recognition.

"You're not going to believe this," Mo said and hesitated, "Banks just called and the Rhinebeck DPW Supervisor is unavailable this afternoon due to an emergency in the field."

A knot formed in his gut. He couldn't speak.

"Jeremy?"

Jeremy inhaled the recycled prison air. The antiseptic odor stung his nostrils like smelling salts, stimulating his thought processes. He should have known that the town would stick it to him again, playing their hand like a cardsharp. He'd abided by the rules for too long and now it was time to get tough. He ticked off instructions, racing through the words as fast as he could retrieve them from his brain.

"Don't worry. I've got everything under control," Mo said.

"I know." Beads of a cold sweat trickled along his hairline down his neck. He unbuttoned the damp shirt collar strangling him.

Alongside him in the narrow passageway, a uniformed guard tugged a handcuffed youth by the shoulder of his hoodie. The guard glanced at him. "You okay, man? You don't look so good."

"You a lawyer, dude?" the kid shouted. "Hey, I need a lawyer to get me outta here."

"Shut up and keep moving," the guard said, tightening his grip on the boy.

Jeremy turned and walked toward the men's room at the opposite end of the hall. The fluorescent light flickered overhead as he headed toward the urinal. Suddenly, a voice shouted his name and fists pounded on the restroom door. He zipped up and opened the door. An officer was already running back toward the log-jammed entrance of the conference room. Jeremy dashed out of the restroom on the officer's heels.

He wrestled his way into the room and stopped in shock. The furniture and his documents were strewn about as though the room had been destroyed by a tornado. Within a circle of spectators, a lifeless Butterfield lay pinned beneath the overturned conference table. One guard supported his client's head, while others unlocked the twisted manacles, lifted up the table, and dragged him out from under the wreckage. Butterfield's hands and clothing were coated in sticky crimson, and the Adonis bent over him, applying pressure to the severed wrists. Butterfield was alive, but his breathing was slow and shallow.

"What happened?" Jeremy shouted. He stood by helplessly watching the guards struggle to revive Butterfield.

"Sammy came in and found him," said the officer gesturing toward the Adonis.

The paramedic team arrived, assessed the situation, and hustled to address the prisoner's injuries. Within minutes, an oxygen mask was slipped over the blue lips, an IV was threaded into the severed veins, wounds were dressed, and the unconscious prisoner was gently lifted onboard the gurney.

"Fortunately, he didn't know what he was doing and the cuts are mostly superficial. Maybe he nicked a vein, but it's unlikely. We'll transport him over to Mid-Hudson Regional Hospital for stitching up and observation," the EMT said. She and her assistant wheeled the stretcher out the door to the waiting ambulance.

"Does anybody know how this happened?" Jeremy asked, his face as pale as his client's.

"Found this next to the body," said the Adonis. His gloved hands pinched the handles of Jeremy's bloodstained cigar scissors.

CHAPTER
20

Hal cleared his throat and stepped to the front of the grand jury chambers. He surveyed the two rows of jurors arranged in a semicircle around him. The intensity of the twenty-three faces eyeballing him pumped him up, making him feel like a prizefighter ready to battle his opponent. But there would be no mano a mano combat. Since he was presenting the evidence to the grand jury neatly tied up in a big red bow, he was playing against himself. The game was his to lose.

His palms grew clammy and his pen slipped from his grasp to the floor. It bothered him that he felt so uneasy. He'd been in this position dozens of times during his career. There was no question in his mind that the jurors staring at him were going to issue an indictment against Terrence Butterfield once they'd heard and seen all of the evidence. They'd be on his side, the side of justice. He only hoped that their stomachs were strong enough and that they didn't turn a deaf ear once the dark, grisly facts unfolded. His responsibility was as an advocate for the dead boy. He prayed that he was strong enough to fulfill that duty to Ryan Paige, his family, and the people of the state of New York.

Hal cleared his throat again.

"Good morning, ladies and gentlemen. My name is Hal Samuels, and I'm the Chief Assistant District Attorney here in Dutchess County. As you know, you have been impaneled to investigate the suspicious death of Ryan Paige, an eighteen-year-old boy, who was killed on August 31st. At present, Terrence Butterfield is incarcerated in the Dutchess County Jail, accused of the crime of felony murder in the first degree in the death of Ryan Paige, pursuant to New York Penal Law 125.27. It is your job to objectively listen to all of the evidence and make a determination whether Mr. Butterfield should be formally charged with that crime, or any other relevant or related charges, or whether those charges lack substantiation and he should be set free. In other words, whether there is legally sufficient evidence of the crime and whether there is reasonable cause to believe that Terrence Butterfield committed the crime of felony murder in the first degree."

He paced before the group and, in his trademark fashion, his eyes sought contact with as many jurors as possible. "We will undertake this journey together. My staff and I are available to answer any questions, bring in any witnesses, and assist you in any manner possible to help you reach an educated decision as to whether or not the charges have been established as a matter of law.

I need not remind you that a man's life is at stake. Not only do I mean that of the accused but of the deceased. I know that you will keep this in mind as we proceed over the next few days. Before we begin, are there any questions?"

The jury chamber was tense, silent.

"Fine, then, we will proceed. The prosecution's first witness is Dutchess County Medical Examiner, Dr. Frances Mailer."

Cindie departed the courtroom and returned with a stout, frog-like man in his mid-sixties. The man's steps were hurried, requiring Cindie to run alongside his athletic gait. Mailer's starched white lab coat covered green hospital scrubs, and his hair was buzzed close to his scalp, emphasizing his round, tan face.

Hal was well acquainted with his witness's grossly exaggerated ego. The guy wore scrubs everywhere, 24-7—to the market, to the gym, out to restaurants. He suspected that Mailer even wore the stupid things to bed. On the street, the doctor was more than happy to be called Frank, but in the courtroom, in the hospital, and on the job, he insisted on being called Dr. Mailer and refused to answer otherwise. Given the man's idiosyncrasies, Hal knew he could elicit the best results by employing a little flattery. He turned on his charm and extended his hand in greeting.

"Good morning, Dr. Mailer. District Attorney Lauren Hollenbeck sincerely appreciates your being here with us today. Are you ready to get started, sir?"

"Yes. Let's get going," Mailer replied brusquely.

The doctor hopped into the witness's chair and adjusted the microphone to a comfortable height. He grinned at Hal, indicating that he was ready to proceed. After the swearing in, Mailer's long-winded introduction detailed his medical qualifications as an expert witness, forensic pathologist, and his seven years as Dutchess County Medical Examiner. Hal noticed that some of the jurors were fiddling with their phones, but to his relief, they perked up when the doctor got into the meat of his testimony.

Dr. Mailer testified that at 2:30 a.m. on the morning of August 31st, the City of Poughkeepsie Police Department had contacted him regarding an alleged homicide at 327 Park Avenue. He'd arrived on the scene at approximately 3:00 a.m. and he'd examined the body of a male in his late teens who had been located on the basement floor.

"The victim, later identified as Ryan Paige, was naked. His feet and arms were bound with a half-inch thick braided cotton roping and his hands were secured behind his back. A portion of his skull was missing, and other parts of his body had been dismembered," Dr. Mailer said. His voice was a gravelly croak, as though he'd smoked a pack of cigarettes every day of his life.

At the front of the room, a flat screen television flickered to life. Ripples of gasps fanned through the men and women of the jury. The doctor aimed a laser pointer at the slideshow and spoke flatly as though presenting a dissertation at a medical convention. His tongue clicked along with the remote control and he aimed a red laser pointer at the screen to highlight the anatomy under discussion.

As ghoulish as it sounded, medical testimony intrigued Hal. He never tired of the nano-molecular operations of the human body. The severing of arterial veins, trauma to the ribs, the bloating of lungs, DNA. He thrilled at the blood-and-guts descriptions that he, along with the juries, heard in the prosecution of criminal justice. In the early years, he'd been squeamish, but as time passed he became hardened to the maiming and mutilation, instead viewing the courtroom as a classroom to master human biology. Which helped to make him a better prosecutor.

Watching Mailer's photostream, something was different this time. Hal was struck with sadness at the sight of Ryan's hands and feet posed as though sculpted in alabaster. Perfect in size, shape, and proportion. The bruised feet of an athlete had become cold as ice.

A slide appeared on the screen. A torso barely recognizable as human appeared, twisted like a pretzel on the cement floor surrounded by a pool of dark liquids and gelatins.

Although Hal had previewed the photos, he was shocked. He swallowed the bile rising in his throat. Ryan's body could have easily been mistaken for an animal carcass slaughtered in a butcher shop rather than a virile youngster walking on the path of a charmed life. A hot, vengeful anger colored his vision and his complexion.

He was going to get Butterfield if it was the last thing he did.

"Thank you, Doctor," Hal said, trying to regain his composure. "From your examination, can you conclude the time and cause of death?"

"The victim died between midnight and one-thirty in the morning from two bullet wounds to his head. Initial reports indicated that the bullets matched the .38 caliber Smith and Wesson obtained from the suspect on the scene."

Hal paused for a second and shot a quick glance at the jury to make sure they were still with him. They were. Since they were over their initial shock, it was time to build the record, a comprehensive transcript of the proceedings. The art of questioning required taking command of a witness like Mailer, one who had a tendency to go off on a tangent. This strategy required that Hal ask questions that allowed no leeway in the answers. Yes or no. He'd boxed Mailer into the corner before and it was imperative that Hal rope him in again.

Hal was prepared. He presented Mailer with a thick black binder that contained the organized reports and tests, which he intended to use as exhibits. Inside were the toxicology report, autopsy, and the analysis of the blood, tissue, hair, fibers, and bodily fluid samples found at the scene and on various articles of clothing and personal effects belonging to the suspect and the victim, as well as an inventory of the victim's personal items, and an analysis of the knife found in the kitchen.

"Doctor, could you please confirm that these official documents represent the forensic techniques used in the course of your investigation?"

Hal ignored the ME's contemptuous glare, which signaled, *how did you get your hands on these?* Mailer confirmed the paperwork and returned the binder to Hal, who passed it off to the court stenographer for cataloguing and adding to the official transcript.

"Ladies and gentleman, let's take a fifteen-minute recess. Please feel free to use the facilities, but please do not leave the annex," Hal said, returning to the prosecutor's table. A trail of hushed whispers followed the jurors into the hallway.

"You okay?" Cindie asked.

"It's unbelievable that Butterfield was surrounded by kids for so many years, and we have no reported incidents. You just don't explode like this out of the blue."

She shrugged. "He must've been a ticking time bomb."

"When he gets indicted, we're going to need a psych eval." Hal second-guessed that the same idea had already crossed Kaplan's mind.

The fifteen minutes flew by and the hearing reconvened.

"Dr. Mailer, before the break you confirmed the protocol used in this investigation. Can you determine with reasonable medical certainty whether the acts of the suspect, Terrence Butterfield, bear any causal relationship to the death of Ryan Paige?" Hal asked.

"Mr. Samuels, as you know I am a doctor, not a lawyer. I state conclusions based upon the medical evidence." As he counted off his deductions, Mailer held up a finger, starting with his thumb. "First, Mr. Paige was killed by two gunshot wounds thorough multiple lobes of the brain, inflicted at almost point-blank range and were not self-inflicted. Those gunshots caused massive cerebral hemorrhaging, fracture, and removal of portions of the skull. Second, the victim's blood and hair were found on both the person of the suspect, underneath his fingernails, and on his clothing." Up popped the middle finger. "Third, the blood alcohol level of both the victim and the alleged perpetrator was twice the legal limit. No other drugs were present. Fourth, other than as described, the organs, muscles, and skeleton were in excellent condition for an eighteen-year-old, without any signs of disease or degeneration, except for the usual minor sports injuries that all youth sustain."

He waved his five stubby fingers in the air. "Finally, the time of death was between 12:00 a.m. and 1:30 a.m. on the morning of August 31st, at the location of 327 Park Avenue, Poughkeepsie, New York. That is how I summarize my observations of the medical evidence."

"Did you prepare a death certificate in connection with the alleged murder of Ryan Andrew Paige?"

"Yes. A certified copy of the death certificate was in the binder," Mailer scoffed.

"Can you please advise the jury as to the legal cause of death stated on the form?"

"Homicide."

"Thank you, Dr. Mailer. I have no further questions."

Hal turned to the jury box. "Ladies and gentleman, you have heard the testimony of Dr. Mailer. Do you have any additional questions that you wish to ask him?"

In the back row, a young black man raised his hand. "Excuse me, Dr. Mailer, in layman's terms, how would you describe the condition of the body when you found it?"

The medical examiner grimaced, annoyed at the request to simplify his medical testimony. "I would say the body had been bound and tied, mutilated and murdered. Does that answer your question?"

"Yes," the man said, squeamishly. "Thank you."

"Dr. Mailer, thank you for your assistance this morning. You are excused," Hal said.

The doctor leaped out of his seat and gathered his belongings from the prosecutor's table. Hal extended his hand toward the doctor and was rebuffed again. He jovially slapped the good doctor on the back as the witness raced by.

CHAPTER
21

Jeremy shrank back into the corner of the cramped ambulance as it sped toward the Level II Trauma Center of Mid-Hudson Regional Hospital. His eyes remained glued on the EMTs as they monitored Terrence's vital signs during the ten-minute journey to the hospital. He felt as if there was a rock in his stomach, weighing him down and reminding him that this crisis was his fault.

Bringing the cigar cutter into the jail had been a simple oversight. Unthinking, he'd slipped it into his blazer pocket along with a pack of matches and the keys to his car.

He hadn't given the cutter a second thought when he'd breezed around the jail's metal detector, a perk of his legal credentials. Suppose his pistol had been in his pocket or briefcase? He shuddered to think of the consequences.

The ambulance wound its way up the hill to the hospital, which was perched atop one of the highest ledges overlooking the Hudson Valley. Upriver, there was a glimpse of the great lawn of the Vanderbilt mansion, and downriver, the fire tower guarding Mount Beacon. The approach by medevac helicopter was never an issue and for most of the year, the steep incline presented no obstacles to vehicular traffic. But during the winter's inclement weather, ambulances were often diverted through the quiet, winding residential neighborhoods behind the hospital's rear loading dock. In traumatic situations, the detour could be a matter of life and death.

Jeremy was grateful that it was summer because his unconscious client appeared to be delicately balancing between the two extremes. For the second time in a month, Butterfield was drenched in blood. This time it was his own.

The ambulance lurched backward into the hospital's trauma bay, tossing Jeremy onto the EMTs. They scowled at him and he apologized, unsure whether he meant it for them or Butterfield.

The navy uniforms hauled the stretcher out of the vehicle and transported it to the trauma unit, where the scrubs assumed responsibility. With lightning speed and precision, they surrounded Butterfield, inserting tubes, catheters, and IVs, and attaching monitoring wires. Bags of fluid and blood floated above him like balloons. Beeps recorded his heart and breath.

Jeremy hovered over the gurney in disbelief. In this sedated condition, his client's face appeared calm and angelic. It was difficult to reconcile this image with the monstrous acts that the man had committed. If Butterfield died from these self-inflicted wounds, Jeremy was responsible. If Butterfield was tried and found guilty of murder one, a prison sentence would follow. Either way, Terrence Butterfield's life remained in Jeremy's hands and his own negligence had nearly done him in. He'd never let this happen again.

Jittery, he reached into his empty jacket pocket.

"Stand aside, please," the staff nurse said, nudging Jeremy toward the waiting area. "We'll come get you when we've stabilized your friend."

My friend. My friend?

Jeremy backed out of the cubicle into the hallway, staring at his motionless client. His first instinct was to flee the hospital, but he had no idea where the exit was located. He stood at the busy crossroads of the T-shaped emergency room. He looked right. He looked left. Disorientated, he stumbled past more cubicles occupied by exhausted family members waiting in bedside vigils. He picked up speed and sprinted down the endless corridor, which branched out in all directions. At the far end, he spied a glowing red exit sign above a sliding glass door. Jeremy dashed toward it, dodging the oncoming pedestrians, and twisted his body sideways to squeeze through the narrow opening of the closing glass panels.

Once outside, Jeremy doubled over, taking in long, deep breaths of fresh air. The fear of what he'd done refused to release him. His chest tightened with the racing of his heart. Lightheaded, he leaned against the brick wall, waiting for the spell to pass. When it did, he realized he had two choices—return inside to the waiting room or leave. Jeremy wiped his moist brow on his shirtsleeve, stood up, and hiked down the steep hill.

An hour later, Jeremy lounged on a bar stool at the Brown Derby Bar and Grill, draining his second scotch on the rocks. Although the sun burned bright in the midday sky, the speakeasy was dark inside. The mahogany paneling, like a brown sponge, absorbed the natural light seeping through the stained-glass windows. The air conditioner must have been on the fritz, and the undulating bar top fans only exaggerated the heat and the stench of furniture polish, body odor, and stale beer.

Beads of perspiration dribbled down the back of his neck and pooled onto his shirt collar, but he didn't care about the sweat or that it was only noon. He didn't care about anything. He just wanted to get hammered. For the tenth time, his cell phone shimmied on the copper bar like a topless dancer. At the eleventh turn, he snatched the phone as it lurched close to the edge and answered it.

"Jeremy? I've been trying to reach you for hours. Where are you? Are you alright?" Mo asked, her voice thick with worry and desperation.

"I'm fine. I'm at the Derby." He slurred his words.

"The Brown Derby? Just stay there. I'm on my way." She hung up.

"No. I'm just having a few… Mo, are you there?" His blurry vision studied the phone as if searching for her inside the device. Jeremy slid his empty glass toward the young man cleaning the beer glasses with a tattered dishcloth.

Two scotches later, Mo rushed into the Derby like a truant officer on a bust. She marched toward him, her hips swaying in time to the Willie Nelson tune blaring on the jukebox.

Jeremy gulped down his refill. "Hit me again, please," he said, ignoring her.

"What do you think you are doing? I've been worried sick. Calling. Calling. Calling. What the heck happened? You were supposed to be back hours ago."

"Bartender?"

"Oh, no. You've had enough. Let's go," Mo said.

The youth froze with one hand on the glass. His eyes warily shifted back and forth between his patron and the loud woman, seemingly afraid to become involved in their domestic squabble.

"Come on," she snapped at the bartender, "give me a hand with him. It's the least you can do." Mo and the bartender scooped up Jeremy's rubbery body, guided him to her red Prius parked at the curb, and poured him into the front passenger seat. Turning a frigid stare toward the kid, she slipped him a Benjamin. She drove back to the office, and, upon arriving, grabbed Jeremy by the scruff of his shirt collar, dragged him out of the car and downstairs to the office, and deposited him on the reception bench.

"What were you thinking?" Mo thrust a mug of coffee into his hand. "There's no cream, remember, so drink it black."

Jeremy straddled the bench, his eyes lowered to the floor. He needed to confess his part in the tragedy to someone. Mo was the most convenient ear. "You wouldn't believe what happened this morning. Butterfield—"

"I know," she interrupted. "The sheriff's been calling. The hospital, too. It must've been awful, but the hospital said Butterfield's going to be fine. They've placed him on suicide watch."

"This is all my fault. I never should—" He closed his eyes and his head lolled forward in a sleepy haze. The full-body bliss that had been warming him evaporated with a sharp kick to his leg. He jerked upright, feeling the sting of a cold washcloth on his forehead.

"Hey, it's not your fault. The guy's crazy, remember? He slaughtered a kid like a pig. So you can either sit here and have a pity party or get to work."

Jeremy finished the coffee and wiped the dignity back onto his face with the wet cloth.

CHAPTER
22

Hal's cell phone, which was charging on the bathroom countertop, vibrated with an incoming text message. He stood naked before the bathroom's wall of mirrors, electric razor buzzing in circles over his morning stubble. His gaze shifted to the phone, but his eyes focused instead on the rich mocha granite, which was only one of the luxuries that this bathroom contained. Erin had appointed the master bath suite to perfection, with cream wooden cabinets, floor to ceiling travertine tiles, and an enormous steam shower encased in glass beneath twin skylights. It was attached to the bedroom by a passageway flanked by his and her walk-in closets. His wife considered it a retreat from the demands and insanity of work, family, and the world, but Hal found it a bit showy and wasteful.

Erin had no problem dipping into their trust funds for these extravagances, but Hal opposed it on principle. They should live within the means of his civil servant's salary. He preferred to pretend that their inheritances didn't exist. But their new five-acre country spread made Erin happy and kept her occupied, so he'd conceded. Making Erin and Tyler happy and safe mattered more to him than his contempt for the ill-gotten family fortune.

At that moment, Erin entered the room and hugged his muscular back, brushing her lips across his shoulders. "We were great last night," she said. "It's been a while."

His face twitched. He rotated away from his reflection, refusing to witness the guilt on his face. This feeling of betrayal wasn't new to him. He carried it around like a spare tire around the gut that couldn't be exercised away with crunches and free weights. Usually, the sensation festered inside, but this morning it bubbled to the surface. He enfolded his wife in his arms to hide it from her.

"You were great, as always," Hal lied.

Last evening when he'd stepped dripping wet from the shower, Erin had been waiting for him. In the dim candlelight, he could see she had slipped the blue satin nightgown from her shoulders, creating a shimmering pool around her feet. Shadows had danced across her goddess's body, but his mind had been elsewhere. He'd stepped toward her, gathering her in his arms. The warm softness of her skin had pressed against his cool wetness. He'd tasted the hint of chardonnay in her mouth, but his mind had been elsewhere. He'd carried her into the bedroom where they'd surrendered to base and instinctual desires not expressed for weeks, months, years, but his mind had been elsewhere. While his body had performed in the present, his mind had reenacted memories of another time, another place, and another woman.

It had been on the last night of the semester, during a downpour that hadn't drowned out any of the excitement that the end of finals brings.

Hal pushed open the door of Minetta's Tavern and shook the excess water from his jacket. The lenses of his wire-rim glasses fogged over with the body heat of the crowd of students celebrating the end of the first year of law school. He wiped the lenses on his damp shirttail and surveyed the crowd. Across the room, he spied the spring of auburn curls, the curve of her back, and her shoulders shaking as she laughed with her friend, Sarah, at the bar. Hal hadn't gone in search of Jessie, but there she sat, ordering what appeared to be her first round. He removed his coat and maneuvered his way toward the bar through the students high on freedom from torts, contracts, real estate law, and New York civil procedure.

He approached her and shouted in stiff competition with the jukebox. "So you made it through the year?"

"Harold Samuels III." She grinned at him. "One down, two more to go and presumably the one where they work me to death," Jessie said. "What about you? Donning the cap and gown next week? Got a job?"

"Bar review starts in two weeks. Then after the exam in July, I'll finally be raking in the big bucks at the New York City Law Department, probably after Labor Day," he said, wedging himself in next to her at the bustling bar.

"Congratulations and cheers." Jessie raised the pint glass, took a sip, and gave him a sexy smile. He watched with fascination as her tongue lapped the foam clinging to her upper lip.

Hal ordered himself a draft and two rounds of Stella and Corona for later. The two girls cackled at the barbs and jokes rolling off of his tongue. He was on fire, imitating the faculty and sharing gossip about the dean. He noticed Jessie elbow Sarah, responding to a wink from the muscular Latino server refreshing her beer. Scooting the stool closer to Jessie, he rested his arm around the back of her chair. Along the counter, other guys were checking her out and he figured that he'd better stake his claim before some other dude hit on her. He took a shot and asked her to dance.

"I really don't dance," Jessie said.

"Go on, I'm leaving anyway. I promised Kenny that we'd meet up at his place," Sarah said, grabbing her coat. As her friend started for the door she mouthed, *call me*, gesturing with an outstretched thumb and pinkie next to her chin. Before Jessie could beg Sarah to stay, her friend had disappeared.

"I'm not buying it," Hal said. "Everybody dances and you owe me for all the garbage you dished out all year." Sometimes Hal had thought that she'd stayed up all night conjuring ways to get under his skin.

"What are you talkin' about? I was the perfect student, always getting my work in on time, never cutting your class, hanging onto every syllable you uttered. You wish all your students were as attentive."

She was right. She'd been one of the brightest kids in the class. There'd been a sparkle in her eyes as she'd listened to him lecture, and he could always rely on her to have the correct answers. Not like the other students who were half asleep or texting in class. Jessie Martin had the ambition necessary to be a really good lawyer.

"But your attitude was pretty damn sassy."

"That's just me... being me."

It was time for him to turn up the heat. "We'll see how you are on the dance floor. Let's go, Ms. Martin. They're playing our song."

"Since when is this our song?" Jessie raised an eyebrow.

"Since now." Hal seized her hand and dragged her toward the dimmest corner of the dance floor. The singer's melodic runs poured from the speakers, drowning out the hum of the world. He slipped his hand around her waist, pulling her toward him, and firmly tucked her free hand close to his heart. Neither was shy to the touch of the other, swaying as one in rhythm to the music. Jessie's eyes fluttered shut and her head snuggled against his shoulder. His body trembled slightly as her breath tickled the skin exposed by the open collar of his shirt. The dreamy refrains of the music enveloped them.

She softly warbled along with the words, slightly out of tune.

The natural, easy feeling of Jessie within his embrace surprised him. The slow tempo segued into hot salsa beats growling with guitar licks. His hand trickled down her spine as he tucked her hips closer to him, grinding in tempo with the music. Jessie responded by rolling her hips and shoulders following his lead. Her head flicked from side to side, shaking her mass of curls as she danced with him.

When the last note ended, she whispered in his ear, "Where'd you learn to move like that? Ballroom lessons or *Dancing with the Stars?*"

"*El Barrio*, baby."

"Yeah, right."

"Seriously. Before law school, I taught in Spanish Harlem for a couple of years."

"I'm impressed. Nice moves."

"That's not all I learned uptown," Hal said, coyly. "Come on…one more dance?"

Jessie yawned, shook her head, and, acting like Cinderella leaving the ball before the stroke of midnight, she retrieved her jacket and bag from her barstool.

"Then, let me walk you home," he said. "Please?"

"I live in the neighborhood, so I think that I can make it back safely," Jessie said, stumbling into an ardently kissing couple. Hal gently held her elbow to steady her and they laughed as if sharing a private joke. She balanced on her toes and her soft lips brushed his cheek. "You're a good guy, Hal Samuels, even if you are a TA."

He smiled his Prince Charming smile, clasped her hand in his, and led her out of Minetta's into the spring night. The evening's storm had ceased, washing the city air fresh and clean. MacDougal Street was quiet. The only sound was the spattering of leftover rainwater as their shoes slapped upon the wet sidewalks. They slowly strolled the few short blocks toward her apartment building on Christopher Street, as though neither wanted the evening to end. With each step, Hal grew more anxious that soon they'd reach her doorstep and she'd send him on his way. He didn't want to leave her and he hoped that she didn't want to be left.

At her front door, Jessie extracted her keys from her bag, and when they slid through her fingers to the pavement, he retrieved them and slipped them into the door lock.

"Here you go, Jessica Martin. Home safe and sound." Hal dangled her keys in front of her and she snatched them.

They entered the foyer and hesitated at the bottom of the staircase leading up to Jessie's apartment. For an infinite moment, her hooded eyes probed his. She fisted his jacket's lapels and tugged him toward her. The warmth of her mouth, her lavender-scented skin, and the intensity of the kiss rocked him.

She grabbed his hand and they climbed the wooden staircase. They stopped on the fifth floor before a green door with crackled paint. Jessie handed him her keys and he unlocked the door, pushing it open. Inside, there was a small living room littered with empty pizza boxes and dirty dishes. Piles of clothes were draped across the overstuffed couch and chair.

"Sorry it's such a mess. Exams…and I wasn't exactly expecting company," she said.

"Counselor, under the circumstances you're entitled to a reprieve, a stay of execution," he whispered, brushing the stray wisp of hair from her face. Hal slipped his arms around Jessie's waist and stared into the glowing green and golden eyes. "From that very first day, I wondered what it would be like to kiss you. For the past nine months, you've been driving me crazy."

"Well, Mr. Teaching Assistant, any such actions on your part would've been totally in apropos." Jessie flashed a demur half-smile. "Perhaps even sexually harassing."

She threaded her hands around his neck, pulling his face toward hers. Their noses brushed against each other. With their deep kiss, their breaths intermingled.

"School's out, so with your permission, I request a closer examination of your corpus juris." His lips grazed beneath her ear and slid down her neck. Then, his lips found hers. Hal feared that if they didn't move their activities into the apartment there might be some indecent exposure occurring right there on the threshold. "Let's take this into chambers, shall we?"

Jessie broke away and, extending her hand to him, wordlessly guided him through the dark apartment into the bedroom at the end of the hall. An unmade bed was barely visible in the glow of the streetlights filtering in through the tall windows.

"Counselor, kindly approach the bench," he said, drawing her toward him. His lips slowly trailed down her neck toward her breasts as his fingers unbuttoned her blouse. "The court requires an inventory of your personal assets."

"Are you issuing a writ of habeas corpus?" Jessie asked, fumbling with removing his polo shirt.

"Hmm. I prefer a writ of mandamus. You must obey the order of the court." His khakis fell to the floor.

"Well, I pledge to serve at the pleasure of the court." She followed suit, wriggling out of her skinny jeans.

Hal had never been so moved by a woman. The way the light and shadows caressed Jessie, it was as if he was in the presence of Themis, the Goddess of Justice herself. He cupped her face in his hands and gently kissed the planes of her cheeks and forehead.

"With permission of the court," she sighed breathlessly, "let's dispense with the legal briefs."

Hal kissed her urgently, desperately, and, wrapped in each other's arms, they fell upon the bed.

Erin's hands sculpted their way down his bare back to his buttocks, bringing him back from the past. His body shuddered and he whispered into her pale hair, "Honey, I don't have time. Maybe tonight."

His wife had no idea that she'd already lost his attention. His eyes were focused on his cell phone, reading the text message: *MEET ME @ THE JAVA JOLT @ 8 am. URGENT.*

Hal finished dressing and a half-hour later he pulled into the parking lot of the Java Jolt.

The glossy cap of her dark head formed a crest above the back booth of Java's, a cheery-grab-and-go joint located on the north side of town. She must have picked the spot knowing that at breakfast time the booths were always empty. Java's steady stream of customers stayed only long enough to pick up their daily fix of bacon, egg, and cheese on a hard roll, homemade Danish, and coffee on the way to work.

But there she sat. Alone. Hal slid into the bench across from Lauren. Two cups of coffee and cherry Danishes had already arrived.

"I was surprised to get your message to meet here. We usually meet at Alex's."

"Too close to home." Lauren's face bore an air of excitement usually reserved for a kid on Christmas morning, unlike her customary scowl. Her hands fidgeted with a packet of sugar, her eyes anxious.

He waited.

"I received a call. An important call last night." Her clipped tone softened to a secretive whisper. "In a few days, news is going to break that a certain New York state senator representing our district is involved in one of those sexting Facebook scandals."

He raised his eyebrows. "Stefan Hill?"

Lauren nodded slightly. Her indigo eyes fine-tuned upon him. "The committee asked if I would be interested in filling his seat after he resigns."

"That's fantastic." Hal rewarded her with one of his generous smiles and listened while she explained, more like mused, aloud, that she wasn't the only candidate being considered. There were two others in contention. She felt that the committee was being cagey about the nominations, testing the political waters. With her usual confidence, she suspected that she would be hearing from them shortly with good news.

"What about the judgeship race? I thought you were interested."

"That's next year. I'd have to be nominated by the party. Raise money. Run an election campaign. All that junk." Lauren nibbled at her pastry, swiped the thick cherry drippings from her chin with her forefinger and sensuously licked the jelly. "This is now. Right now."

Hal nodded in agreement, trying to ignore the fingers lingering too long in between her blood red lips.

"Larry Murphy, head of the nominating committee, said I am the right demo. Female. Experienced. Tough on crime. A legacy. Hispanic."

He cocked his head. "Hispanic?"

"My maternal grandfather is Puerto Rican. He was mayor of San Juan in the seventies," she replied offhandedly. Lauren took another bite, repeating the routine.

"Lauren, no offense, but you're about as white bread as they come." He suppressed a chuckle, not wanting to insult his boss or his potential future predecessor. But that explained the straight midnight hair and the almond eyes, uncommon genetic traits for a WASP.

Lauren glared at him anyway, gritting her teeth. "Apparently not to the steering committee. The Hollenbeck family name still carries some weight in the state."

Her body had stiffened in the way that a cobra recoils when preparing to strike. Hal slid his hand across the linoleum table and touched the sleeve of her jacket to provide the reassurance she sought. He eyed her, judiciously selecting his next words. "Lauren, I'm happy for you. This is an extraordinary opportunity. There's always the judgeship if this doesn't pan out. And I'm sure you're their top candidate."

Her body relaxed. The toe of her stiletto nudged his pant leg. "This could work for both of us if we play our cards correctly. We must get an indictment and conviction in the Butterfield case." She arched her eyebrow, the devilish glint returned to her demeanor.

"I'm working on it. Frank Mailer testified yesterday. Today the arresting officers will be presenting."

"And tomorrow?" She watched his face, seeking a reaction.

He grinned at his boss. Her going behind his back and issuing the subpoena to Jessie made him long to place his hands around Lauren's slender throat and squeeze.

CHAPTER
23

Two days had passed since Jessie had been tagged with the subpoena and, in truth, the thought of testifying left her unfazed. As a litigator, she was prepared for the pitfalls of being a witness. She was anxious to tell her story about the night of the murder, such as it was, and to be exonerated in the eyes of her colleagues and clients. Although she fretted about losing her clients to her replacement, Jessie convinced herself that wouldn't happen. She itched to return to work—the depositions, hearings, briefs, conferences—the normalcy of routine. Hopefully, that would be soon.

Terrence's survival in the county jail also troubled her, but she made no effort to contact him, especially after her bosses' tongue lashing. Even her father avoided the subject of Terrence, though she read the pain in his slumped shoulders and observed the crescents beneath his eyes that suggested a string of sleepless nights.

Terrence's name had been banned from her household as well. Since the subpoena, Kyle had refused to speak his name, which made it impossible for them to discuss the topic. This was Kyle's gamesmanship at his best. Every time she mentioned the grand jury, he cleverly dodged the issue by cracking jokes about her voluptuous, milk-enhanced breasts or proposing a weekend getaway to the Berkshires. He meant well, but his distractions failed miserably. She refused to be tricked into shirking her legal duty.

She'd sensed coolness the prior evening when they'd kissed goodnight. Kyle had retreated to the far edge of the bed and she'd missed the comfort of his back pressing into hers. In the dead of the night, the mattress had shifted. The nasally sound of his breathing had ceased. Emptiness, hollowness, had engulfed the room as well as their bed. Jessie had tossed and turned as her mind churned with imaginary discussions between them.

Around seven in the morning, the baby began his/her somersaults. Jessie rose with a renewed sense of wellbeing. The prenatal aches and pains had melted away with the darkness. She went in search of Kyle, determined to make things right between them. To let him know she understood that he was considering her best interests. She'd make him appreciate her predicament and like always, they'd settle their disagreement.

Jessie followed the aroma of brewing coffee into the kitchen, expecting to find him there. The kitchen was empty, except for a hungry tabby and a note perched atop the morning newspapers.

Babe, Left early, see you later, K.

So much for reconciliation.

Revitalized by a good night's sleep, Jessie stepped out of her cool shower resolving to spend the morning attacking her neglected "to do" list. The bank. The market. The dry cleaners. Maybe sneak in a pedicure, although she could barely see her feet from a standing position.

After dressing, she snatched the bag that held the dry cleaning from the closet, and on her way out of the bedroom she noticed Kyle's navy blazer folded over the arm of her rocking chair. She picked up the jacket and, smelling a trace of stale cigarettes, she began to stuff it into the sack. A crinkling sound escaped from the inside breast pocket so she reached in and extracted a thick white envelope folded in half. The logo of a white eagle upon a field of sky-blue ribbons was unmistakable. It was the Barclays Center in Brooklyn, New York.

Jessie tore open the envelope and wrestled out a packet from their Director of Human Resources. Her hands trembled as she read of Kyle's appointment as Senior Vice President of Business Operation and Chief Financial Officer. The correspondence and the employment contract were dated August 15th, almost a month ago.

No, it couldn't be. That would mean Kyle must have been negotiating with Barclays since June or July, long before Ryan's murder and her suspension from McMann. The start date was set for September 15th. Five days from now.

The more she thought about Kyle, the angrier she became. Keeping the job search and offer a secret. Making life-altering plans without consulting her. Tearing her and the baby away from her family, friends, and job. From Terrence. Maybe that had been the end game all along.

Jessie sat down on the edge of the bed, fighting the morning sickness that had plagued her on and off during her pregnancy. The baby stirred and shifted unaware of his/her mother's turmoil. Love, betrayal, and hurt muddled Jessie's mind as she solved the riddle.

Kyle was planning to leave her. Soon.

At one o'clock, Jessie summoned the elevator that would take her up to the grand jury suite. As the wood-paneled cab crawled skyward, the baby pressed downward with gravity. She rubbed the bulge in her blue and white check dress for luck, as one would rub the protruding belly of a Buddha, and stepped out of the doors. A young man wearing an ID badge marked "Law Intern" greeted her and escorted her to the witness waiting room. Down the hallway were two imposing oak doors with "Grand Jury" affixed in brass letters, and above them, a white noise machine whirled to mask the inquisition occurring inside the chamber.

"They ran late this morning," the intern said, "so they're still on lunch break. It shouldn't be long though. Can I get you anything while you wait?" When she shook her head, he slipped out the door.

Jessie surveyed the nondescript room; Americana posters, a dusty rubber tree, cheap upholstered chairs, and a table offering sports and decorating magazines, some more than a year old.

Exterior light filtered in through a frosted glass window to preserve the privacy and ensure the claustrophobia of the occupants.

She squirmed to get comfortable on the itchy tweed seat, opened her bag, and withdrew the parenting magazine she'd stashed in case of a delay. A sharp knock on the door interrupted Jessie's skimming an article about exercises for your body after baby. She folded the periodical and rose in preparation to take the hot seat.

Hal opened the waiting room door and entered, closing the door behind him. He'd mentally practiced his apology to Jessie, but seeing her, he couldn't find the right words. "Before you say anything, I'm so sorry about this," he mumbled.

"You always convince me to trust you and when I do, I end up getting screwed," Jessie said, bitterly.

"I know you don't believe me, but I'd never hurt you again." He couldn't meet her eyes, so he stared at the floor. "There's been a crazy mix-up."

"Hal, you don't owe me any explanations. You're doing your job, so let's keep this professional. The sooner I testify the better, so I can resume mine. Does that work for you?"

He couldn't conceal the wince, the sting of her words, behind his glasses. He hesitated for a moment, summoning the courage to apologize again and explain. He'd make her understand that

Lauren, not he, had double-crossed her. But speech failed him and he sheepishly retreated from the room.

He returned to his office and slammed the door hard, rattling the diplomas on the walls. He felt like the lying bastard Jessie thought he was. The heel who'd said he'd love her forever, but who'd broadsided her by impulsively marrying Erin.

He should have rescinded Lauren's subpoena and taken the heat. He should have telephoned Jessie to explain. Instead, he'd followed the chief's order, as was his obligation. Or as Jessie had put it, he'd done his job. Once again, he'd proven that he was unworthy of her favor and more than deserving of her reproach.

Jessie felt shaken and lowered herself back into the chair. She'd surprised herself with her hostility toward Hal by dredging up the past, practically calling him a liar to his face and refusing his explanations. She considered the lovers in her life, Kyle, Hal, and even Robbie. There'd been a pattern. They were seemingly nice men who'd captured her heart and pledged theirs to her. Then, out of the blue, each had thrown her for a loop with their unexpected dishonesty and broken her heart.

A second rap on the door made her start and she steeled herself for a reprise. She shook her head. Hal Samuels never left well enough alone.

Instead, Lauren Hollenbeck sauntered into the room, slim and gamine as a racehorse. "I'd like to quickly review your testimony before we get started this afternoon. Why don't we start at the beginning?" The district attorney graced her with an over-solicitous smile.

Jessie eyed her with suspicion, but politely answered her questions about the events of August 31st. Yes, it was the first time Terrence contacted her at such a late hour. Yes, she sensed that it was an emergency and didn't think twice about helping him. No, she didn't meet privately with Terrence at the police station. Jeremy Kaplan had been present. Yes, she was shocked that Ryan Paige was the victim. Yes, she'd been close with Terrence and Ryan, and no, she was unaware whether the two had known each other.

"Perhaps, if you'd contacted me earlier, we could have informally discussed these details so as not to waste taxpayers' money." Jessie paused. "This situation hasn't been easy for me. I'm attending against the wishes of my physician and fiancé, but I'll honor my obligation." She rubbed her fertile belly for emphasis.

Hollenbeck's eyes flickered back and forth, revealing the speed of her inner thoughts. The accompanying scowl suggested the district attorney's displeasure with Jessie's responses. There'd been nothing sexy or exciting about Jessie's part in the crime. She'd been an innocent bystander. The prosecutor approached her and placed a finely manicured hand on Jessie's arm. "Dear, I'm going to get you out of here as soon as possible."

Hollenbeck left and the minutes dragged by. Jessie tried calling Kyle, but there was no answer. After five attempts, she decided, with mild annoyance, to keep her attendance as secret as his new job. Truth and honesty had vacated their premises, and she wondered when and where the foreclosure had occurred. How had she been so blind to overlook the warning signs? His moodiness. His withdrawal.

Without notice, the intern popped his head into the room and beckoned her to follow him. In the doorway of the grand jury chamber, she froze like an actor attacked by stage fright. It felt like she was entering a star chamber where she was no longer a witness but had become the accused. Her instincts urged her to flee, but her feet carried her into the silent, darkened room. In the shadows, she identified Hollenbeck and another female prosecutor at the table on the right, and on the left, the juror's chairs were configured into two semi-circular rows. From the silhouettes, she detected their genders, but their faces remained hidden by the dim lighting. In the center of the room, a bright spotlight flooded the witness's chair, alluding to an execution. Her eyes searched for Hal, but he was missing. It was no wonder after their earlier confrontation.

Hollenbeck motioned toward the hot seat and Jessie eased herself into the floodlight. She raised her right hand to shade her eyes, placed her left hand on the Bible, and swore to tell the truth and nothing but the truth. The DA's high heels clicked across the hardwood floor as she approached, and studying a legal pad, she began her inquiry without looking up.

In answer to the first question, Jessie stated, "Jessica Grace Martin, 59 Platt Street, Poughkeepsie, New York. My occupation is attorney-at-law."

The door opened and light spilled inside. All eyes shifted toward Hal, who entered with a folder tucked beneath his arm. He grabbed the seat next to the other prosecutor, nodded toward the panel, and then turned toward her, attentively.

"Ms. Martin, did you receive any phone calls on the morning of August 31st at approximately 1 a.m.?" Hollenbeck asked, following her script.

"Yes."

"From whom did you receive a call and what was the substance of the call?"

Jessie opened her mouth to speak but then hesitated. An alarm sounded in her brain, warning that she was on the slippery slope of an ethical dilemma. As a witness under the testimonial subpoena, she was obligated to divulge the truth. However, as a lawyer, she could not reveal any confidential conversations with clients, and couldn't be compelled to do so in a hearing. For the first time, Terrence's intentions in calling her that night came into question. Had he contacted her as a friend or as an attorney?

Her two identities had been so inseparable that she'd never before given it much thought. Over the years, she'd drafted his will, helped him refinance his home, and fixed a few speeding tickets. She tugged on her ear. "I really don't know how to answer that question."

"Ms. Martin, it's a pretty straightforward question. Would you like the question repeated?"

Jessie shook her head, considering her options and replied in measured sentences, measured thoughts. "On the morning of August 31st, I received a call from Terrence Butterfield. However, I am unable to divulge the contents of the conversation."

The muscles in Lauren Hollenbeck's jaw tightened. Jessie had struck a nerve. "You understand that you are under oath?" The DA hovered so close that her spit rained on Jessie's arm. The woman folded her arms across her chest, abruptly twisted away and marched to the frosted window on the opposite wall.

"As I stated, I'm an attorney." To conceal the clamminess in her hands and the pressure building in her chest, Jessie's gaze locked onto Hollenbeck, unwavering. "There may be a question regarding whether Mr. Butterfield contacted me in a personal or professional capacity. Therefore, I refuse to violate any potential attorney-client privilege at this time."

"Were you engaged by Mr. Butterfield on the night in question?" Hollenbeck leaned against the wall, balancing on her stiletto heels.

"Over the years, I've performed legal work for him."

"Are you currently representing him in connection with pending criminal charges?"

"No," Jessie said flatly.

In a graceful efficiency of movement, Hollenbeck returned to Jessie's side. "Well, then you should have no issue discussing any conversation which occurred that night."

Hate emanated from this woman. Jessie could smell it, a slight acid scent mixed with perfume. "Well, I do. I'm barred by the code of professional ethics to reveal any client confidences. However, I'm willing to answer any other questions which do not pertain to my conversations with Mr. Butterfield on the night of August 31st."

"Perhaps we should adjourn and present your concerns to the presiding justice." Hollenbeck smirked as though only she knew the punchline to the joke.

Jessie said nothing. Beneath the spotlight, she let the silence answer for her. Every passing second seemed to suck the oxygen from the room, igniting the veiled threat left dangling in the air.

The jurors shifted in their chairs, exchanged whispers and consulted with the jury foreperson, an Arabic woman wearing a black hijab. The jury-woman approached Hal and whispered in his ear.

"The forewoman recognizes Ms. Martin's potential ethical quandary. She asks that we honor her concerns and proceed with the appropriate questions," he said.

Hollenbeck clicked her tongue in apparent disgust. "Ms. Martin. I've only a few questions remaining."

A growing tightness inside Jessie's chest squeezed the air from her lungs. "May I have a glass of water, please?" She coughed to disguise a wheeze.

"In one moment." Hollenbeck issued a series of rapid-fire questions, implying a conspiracy in her tone. "You've stated that you have known Mr. Butterfield for almost twenty years. What is the nature of your personal relationship with him? Have you ever engaged in a sexual relationship with Mr. Butterfield? Is that why you're refusing to answer my questions? Are you protecting him? Are you protecting yourself against your participation in the crime? Didn't you prevent the police from investigating the murder? Didn't you—"

"Enough," Hal shouted, jumping to his feet.

A general confusion rippled through the chambers as the jurors began arguing among themselves. Within the heart of the chaos, Jessie's heart beat loudly in her ears and her hand gripped the armrests so tightly that its metal edges dug into her palms. She was stunned, left dumbfounded by the perverse cat-and-mouse game Hollenbeck was playing. Not only had the DA made this personal, but she'd also tested the boundaries of professional propriety. The chief prosecutor had accused her of committing a crime and had threatened her with obstruction of justice charges.

The way the light hit Hal's face she saw the tiny flicker of shock that widened his eyes, and the sudden panic that tightened the corners of his mouth. It was more than Hollenbeck's assault, more than the commotion engulfing the room. It was then that a dull cramping gripped her abdomen and a warm wetness touched the skin of her thighs. Her hands flew to her stomach as if to defend it, or as if gathering something from it, warmth and strength. She crumbled to the floor as a crimson stain mushroomed across the front of her dress.

Hal rushed toward her, cradled her in his arms and regarded her with an emotion that anyone could understand. "Jess! Jess!"

"Hal. Help. Please."

"Jess, I'm right here. We'll get you to the hospital. Everything will be fine." He seemed to deflate a little with those words.

"What the hell's going on here?" Hollenbeck demanded.

"For God's sake, Cindie, somebody, call 911," Hal yelled. Beside him, the other prosecutor dialed her cell phone and placed it to her ear.

Within the safety of his arms, she surrendered to the contractions squeezing her baby. There was no pain, only fear. "Hal," she said, softly, "please don't leave me."

He pressed his lips to her ear. "Where else am I going to go?"

CHAPTER
24

Jeremy Kaplan recognized the battered cardboard carton sitting on his credenza without even reading its label. After years in storage, the remnants of *People vs. Klein* reeked of mildew and ammonia, but it represented his most victorious defense effort. His success had boiled down to a pre-trial court application known as the "kitchen sink motion." To dismiss the charges against his client, Rabbi Gelman Klein, for the manslaughter of his wife, Jeremy had concocted a list of every imaginable legal argument. Through either luck or genius, he'd argued that when the hospital had sampled the rabbi's blood and DNA on the Sabbath without his consent, those tests had violated the clergyman's rights protected by the First and Fourth Amendments of the U.S. Constitution.

In a case of first impression, the lower court ruled in Jeremy's favor, making Rabbi Klein a free man and Jeremy a celebrity.

Upheld by the New York State appellate courts, the United States Supreme Court denied certiorari but adopted the ruling as precedent to protect other religions and nationalities. The landmark case also established a strict chain of custody rule for evidence involving Orthodox Jews, and that failing to follow the procedures required the dismissal of any pending criminal charges.

The scrapbooks in his library memorialized the yellowed front pages of the *New York Law Journal*, the *New York Times*, and the profile piece from *Time* magazine, highlighting the case. He'd also kept the old VHS tapes of his interviews on the *Today Show*, *Good Morning America*, and *Sixty Minutes* that had propelled him into the ranks of Johnny Cochran, Gerry Spence, F. Lee Bailey, and Gloria Allred.

Clients. Money. Fame. He'd had it all.

Over time, the cops became smarter and their arrests became more challenging to set aside. Despite Jeremy's best efforts, the murder, prostitution, breaking and entering, and possession of illegal substances charges all stuck. The magic had faded, if not disappeared. Young legal lions lured away his stable of clients. The bench, the bar, and former clients accused him of becoming old and lazy. Too expensive. They said he'd lost his mojo and Jeremy began to accept that as the truth. He was Windows '95 in an IOS world.

Jeremy began enjoying the company of booze more than that of his wife, Sheila, their two kids, and even his remaining clients. Sequestered within his basement office, the glass bottles didn't whine or complain or make demands. Then, on the fourth anniversary of the Klein decision, Sheila served him with divorce papers. A hand well played by his conniving soon-to-be ex-wife. In his heart, there was only enough energy to salvage one aspect of his shredded existence. The decision was obvious to him.

He granted Sheila her divorce, settled for joint custody, and curtailed his drinking. Eventually, he met Gayle who loved him, warts and all, and these days his practice relied upon the pittance paid by the state for assigned counsel cases. He earned an honest living; however, the constant financial pressures reminded him of his blemished past. Bills. Alimony. College tuition.

Almost twenty years had passed since Klein, and he hoped to polish off the tarnish. Jeremy picked up the moldy carton and placed it on the conference room table. He unpacked the box and located the thick folder labeled "Omnibus Motion." It had been the unusual fact pattern and the well-researched law that had persuaded the court to rule in his favor. He inspected the empty carton. Ironically, he'd triumphed by thinking outside of the box.

Outside of the box, he thought. Unique. Extraordinary. Exemplar. What makes the Butterfield case distinctive? The facts, maybe. At the scene, Terrence had admitted the murder to the police and the evidence had been splattered all over his house. At first blush, the evidence appeared to have been legally obtained, which distinguished Butterfield from Klein. Unlike Rabbi Klein, there'd be little sympathy for the bloodthirsty teacher, and if he challenged the chain of custody, he'd lose. These days, the crime scene technicians were trained to document and preserve even the most insignificant fluff of dog fur.

He scratched the back of his neck. What made the Butterfield case sensational, dramatic, or precedent-setting? His mind attacked the question with philosophical reasoning. What was the logical consequence of facts? What was the truth?

Then, it struck him. Start with the end and work backward. How did the cops know to go to Terrence's home? Butterfield swore that he hadn't called the police. If Butterfield hadn't, then who had?

He grabbed a pen and pad and scratched out a list:

1. *Butterfield made one phone call that night at 1:15 a.m. to Jessica Martin.*

2. *Ed Martin phoned Butterfield around 1:20 a.m.*

3. *The police arrived at the scene at 1:30 a.m.*

4. *Jessica Martin arrived on the scene at 1:30 a.m.*

5. *Butterfield said he did not contact the police.*

Jeremy reviewed his notes. The answer was on the tip of his mind's tongue, just beyond his grasp. His fingers reached into his pocket, searching for his cigar cutter. Recalling Terrence on the hospital gurney, he shivered, but proceeded to the humidor on his credenza and selected a cigar. He lit its sheared end and greedily sucked until it smoldered blood red.

His thoughts returned to the list. Ed Martin called Terrence. Logically, that meant Jessica phoned her father, but what had she told him? He returned to the million-dollar question. Who had contacted the police? Ed Martin? Jessica Martin? Jeremy's heart began to hammer like a judge's gavel. He realized where he might find the answer to his questions.

He dashed past Mo's desk, snatched his hat from the hook, and bounded toward the stairs.

"Where are you going?" she asked.

"Downtown to the police station."

"Will I be receiving a call from The Derby in an hour?" Mo glanced at him over the top of her reading glasses.

"You'll just have to wait and see, now won't you?"

"Hey, I'm not your wife. Do as you please," she called after him.

"Hey, Russ, how's it going?" Jeremy asked the duty officer behind the desk. "I'm hoping you could help me with something?"

"Sorry, man, I can't help you kill your client. That's your job." The black man in the blue uniform snickered.

Joke all you want. We'll see who has the last laugh. "I need to see the call logs for August 31st, the time the call came in to report the Paige murder."

"Kappy, I can't," Russ said.

"You know that I'm entitled to the information so we can either do the dance where I get a subpoena or you can do me a solid…"

Russ rolled his eyes in surrender. He must have remembered the dozen boxes of Girl Scout cookies that Jeremy had bought from his daughter last year. The officer scanned the room to make sure that they were alone. He leaned forward and whispered, "Just the call log, right?"

Jeremy nodded in satisfaction.

Russ closed down the YouTube channel of stupid pet tricks on his phone and pulled up the data on the monitor. "Make it quick."

Jeremy craned his neck to view the screen. "Thanks, Russ. I owe you."

Outside in his Lexus, Jeremy rummaged through the glove compartment, found an old gas station receipt, and scribbled down the name. He tucked the paper into his shirt pocket.

CHAPTER
25

Jeremy threw the car into reverse, spraying pebbles over the police officers milling around the lot during the shift change. They halted their conversations and were glaring at him when his phone vibrated inside his jacket pocket. He slammed on the brakes, shifted the car into park, and checked the caller ID.

It was Mo.

"Checking up on me?" he asked sharply.

"No. I thought you'd want to know that Terrence has been moved back to the jail."

"Oh," he said, apologetically. "Sometimes I can be a jerk."

"You think?" She hung up.

The Lexus melted into the flow of traffic on Mansion Street, driving past the Greek-revival post office championed by local resident Franklin Delano Roosevelt during his presidency. Then,

Jeremy turned left onto Hamilton Street and drove the few blocks to the Dutchess County Jail complex. This was a six-minute drive he could make blindfolded.

Jeremy entered the jail and proceeded on his customary path around the metal detector, having flashed his attorney's ID at the attendant. A second guard blocked his path, stopping him.

"Excuse me, sir. I'm sorry, but you'll have to go through the scanner today." The man's tone and expression said it all. Jeremy had been blackballed.

Jeremy swore under his breath and faked a smile for the sake of expediency. He emptied the contents of his pockets into the plastic bin, slid his briefcase onto the conveyor belt, and joined the rank and file marching through the scanner.

"Butterfield's in the medical unit, arrived about an hour ago," the deputy sheriff said. Jeremy thought he heard a snicker when the deputy slid a name tag through a slot and pointed toward the infirmary at the rear of the facility.

A heavy, antiseptic odor permeated the long hallway leading to the medical unit. He entered the infirmary and its starkness stunned him. A dozen dormitory style beds lined the white walls and there were no divider curtains, nightstands, or televisions.

To Jeremy's further surprise, Butterfield was the sole patient. He lay back in bed with his eyes closed and wrists bandaged like white cuffs on his green hospital gown. Thick leather wristlets strapped his arms to the bed frame. At the foot of the bed, a sentry with the physique of a linebacker flipped through the *New York Post*. Jeremy had considered bringing him magazines as a peace offering but then remembered that only religious scriptures were

189

permitted as gifts for the inmates. He was sure that Terrence wouldn't appreciate a Bible.

"Is he asleep?" Jeremy asked the guard in a low voice. The man briefly looked up from the paper, shrugged, and returned his nose to the sports section.

"Please stop shouting," Terrence said angrily. "I'm trying to rest." Butterfield slit open his eyes. His cheeks puffed out and his slender body twitched from side to side as he struggled against the restraints. "Can somebody get these off me right away?"

Jeremy started backward, noticing the second set of restraints buckled around Butterfield's ankles.

The guard remained seated and didn't even bother glancing up. "The meds must be wearing off."

A perky young nurse in sky blue scrubs appeared at the bedside with a hypodermic needle. She swabbed Butterfield's arm with alcohol and injected the medicine into his shoulder. "Mr. Butterfield, this should take the edge off. Please calm yourself."

"Are the restraints really necessary?" Jeremy asked.

"Mr. Butterfield has been quite a handful since they brought him in. He's been extremely agitated. He punched one of the male nurses in the face and has been screaming obscenities at the top of his lungs. The doctor felt it was necessary for his protection, as well as ours, to restrain him," she said. "The Xanax should calm him down."

Jeremy scratched the scalp beneath his wispy hair. "Shouldn't he be in the psych ward at the hospital?"

"That's better now, isn't it, Mr. Butterfield?" The nurse patted her patient's forearm, wiped the spittle from his chin and swept back a stray lock of his hair. Butterfield's glassy eyes rolled back in his head and his body visibly relaxed. "I suppose the hospital discharged him because they felt he wasn't an immediate threat to himself." She shrugged. "We get these cases all the time. After a few days inside here, the new inmates freak out and do something stupid like hurt themselves, but they eventually calm down."

Her brown eyes twinkled at the excitement of the moment. Jeremy wondered if she was one of those pathetic women with low self-esteem who fell in love with guys behind bars. Hopefully, she was smart enough to recognize that Butterfield wasn't like the rest of them. He could actually be a lady-killer.

"He's going to be knocked out for a while. If I were you, I'd come back later," she said, straightening the bed linens and blankets and fluffing the pillow.

Jeremy left the medical unit feeling irritated. He'd been turned away without an answer to the six words necessary to assist with Butterfield's defense: Do you know anyone named Avery?

Instead of returning to the office, Jeremy indulged in a twenty-mile detour up Route Nine along the Hudson River to the Smoke Shoppe in Rhinebeck, New York. The crimson and golden veins of maple leaves fluttered in the bright sunlight of the day. The purple ridges of the Catskills reminded him about the beauty of life outside the gutter of his daily existence. He opened the sunroof and breathed in the fresh air, tasting autumn's arrival on his tongue.

Jeremy's arrival into the tobacconist was announced by the tinkling of a bell. While some people savored the hint of berries, oak, and chocolate tasted in wine, for him, the ecstasy belonged to the rich essence of tobacco. The sweet scents of espresso and vanilla welcomed him into the cozy shop. He drifted past the tins and apothecary jars chock-full of flavored tobaccos and entered the spacious walk-in humidor. He lingered inside, tempted by the exotic leaves begging to be sampled with a light and a puff. Then he made his selection.

A new cigar cutter was the true object of his desire, but as he neared the counter, anxiety seized him. His mind conjured the pleasure that lay within his grasp, and, shrugging off the ghost, Jeremy selected a handsome titanium guillotine. Cupped in his hand, the egg-shaped body felt lighter and sleeker than its predecessor. He stroked the object and smiled. This one belonged in his hands. This one made his worries, his guilt, and his responsibilities vanish.

He departed the shop two hundred dollars lighter, with a wooden box tucked beneath his arm and the new cutter safely stowed in his jacket pocket. The blue smoke of a Nicaraguan special trailed him down Main Street as he wandered along the storefronts that displayed trendy fashions, over-priced real estate listings, and handcrafted jewelry.

It dawned on him that Gayle's birthday was at the end of the month. She endured a lot from him and a few brownie points never hurt in the bedroom. Perhaps she'd like pearl earrings, a gold necklace, or a silver cuff bracelet as a gift. The trinkets in the jeweler's window were enticing but paled in comparison to the glittering diamond engagement rings. He and Gayle had been married for thirteen years and it was unbelievable how quickly the time had flown by.

Jeremy froze on the sidewalk as a spark shot through his mind. Jessie Martin was engaged. She'd introduced the guy at the police station, but for the life of him, Jeremy couldn't remember her fiancé's name. Was it Avery? Could the solution possibly be that simple?

Jeremy returned shortly after three o'clock and discovered that the office lights were off and the door had been bolted. He was pleased with his timing. Mo had cut out early and wasn't around to spoil his mood or pester him with questions. He unlocked the door, keyed the security code into the wall panel, and entered the basement.

A message was taped to his desk chair.

Called The Derby. They said you weren't there. Assumed they weren't lying. If you're reading this, you're still alive. See you in the AM. P.S. We still need cream for the coffee.

Mo was gone, but even in her absence, she had the knack of pushing his buttons. He couldn't figure out why she didn't go to the market, buy the creamer, and reimburse herself from the petty cash. Damn stubborn woman, that's why. He crumpled the note and pitched it into the trash.

Jeremy turned on the computer and searched the New York State public records for the last name Avery. To his disappointment, fifty-five people were listed with that surname, none of who satisfied the parameters in terms of address or age or sex. Even Google offered no assistance.

He reviewed the summary list, but always returned to number one: Jessica Martin. The online directories for the Dutchess County Bar Association, Martindale-Hubble, and attorney listing resources proved useless, supplying nothing except her affiliation with McMann and Curtis, and her graduations from Syracuse and NYU. He required deeper, more advanced information about her.

Digital stalking was not his métier, which was why he employed people who detected for a living. He picked up the phone and placed a call.

"Hey," he said, "I want to know everything there is about Jessica Martin. Middle name Grace. Approximate age 30. Yeah, that one. The attorney who lives in Poughkeepsie. I need this no later than tomorrow morning."

Jeremy hung up the phone. He was finished for the day.

As usual, chaos was the main course served at Jeremy's family dinner. The pair of overweight beagles begged for table scraps. Gayle dished out the baked ham, mashed potatoes, and green beans while *Sports Center* blared in the background. He attempted to engage their pre-teen twins, Jackson and Brandon, into a conversation, only to be met with grunts and groans. The NFL season was gearing up and the boys were absorbed in the latest statistics and scouting reports for their fantasy football teams. They finished dinner and, after coercing Brandon to humor the old man in a game of chess, the phone rang. Gayle answered the phone and frowned at the unwelcome interruption of their precious family time. She shoved the phone at him and slammed the kitchen door behind her.

Much to his relief, a quarter-hour later Jeremy was sitting in his office.

"I was surprised to hear from you so quickly. I didn't expect any news until the morning." He folded his hands behind his head and leaned back in the chair. "What do you have for me?"

With one hand, Carey Wentworth clutched the information Jeremy so urgently desired and with the other, he unsealed the treasure trove sitting on Jeremy's desk. He grimaced as the private detective snagged a stogie from the new box. "Thanks, Jer," the man said, "I don't mind if I do."

It wasn't only Wentworth's five o'clock shadow, hair stringy and oily enough to be wrung out for cooking grease, and his stained maroon polyester blazer that irked him. Jeremy always cringed when Wentworth called him "Jer," a throwback to their high school baseball days. He hated the intimacy the nickname implied but tolerated it for the sake of business.

Wentworth was as sleazy as they came but once set on an assignment, the guy had a knack for worming the most intimate whisperings out of his prey. Secrets so well buried that even his victim's relations were clueless. Jeremy doubted whether the investigator operated within the boundary of the law and he didn't dare to ask. His sole concern was the final product that, most of the time, exceeded his expectations.

Concealing his disdain behind a toothy grin, Jeremy extended a lighter. Wentworth squinted, waved the cigar beneath his flared nostrils, deposited the cigar into the jacket's breast pocket, and slid the folder across the desk. In exchange, Jeremy shoved an envelope toward the investigator, and then placed the report in his top drawer.

"I thought this was a rush job? Aren't you going to read it?"

"It'll wait until the morning. I know where to find you if I have any questions."

"Hey, it's your dime," Wentworth said, standing up to leave. It was evening, but he whipped on a pair of green-tinted aviator sunglasses. "As always, nice doing business with you."

"Carey, I appreciate your efficiency and your discretion, of course."

Before Wentworth had let himself out of the upstairs door, Jeremy retrieved the envelope from the drawer. Although he may be desperate, he never let anyone see it. It gave them the upper hand, he thought. He clutched the sealed document, but his mind drifted to Gayle's ornery reaction to Wentworth's call. He replaced the papers inside his desk, locked the drawer, and turned off the light.

CHAPTER
26

The grand jury chamber echoed with Jessie's cries. It was empty except for Jessie, Hal, and Cindie. Much to Hal's surprise, Lauren had evacuated the panel and stenographer and instructed them to call the next morning for an update. At his insistence, Cindie had left numerous messages on Kyle's cell and office phones. He felt his assistant's eyes on him, scrutinizing the hemorrhaging woman cradled within his arms, but he didn't give a damn.

Over and over again, Jessie's muscles stiffened with exertion, then slackened like she'd collapsed at the end of a marathon. Helplessly, he watched her eyes squeeze shut as if willing away the contractions. "Everything will be all right," he murmured, mopping her damp forehead with his handkerchief.

They both knew it was a bluff. The terror in Jessie's teary eyes said it all, but he was grateful that Lauren was occupied elsewhere. He couldn't deal with anymore probing, accusatory looks right now.

Just at that moment, Lauren burst into the room accompanied by the medics. The medical team raced toward Jessie while Hal brought them up to speed on her condition. Hesitant to leave her side, he helped them load her onto the gurney, fasten the straps, and secure the oxygen mask over her flushed face. Her trembling hands grasped his, digging her nails into his skin with each cramp.

"We're almost there," Hal said, jogging alongside the stretcher toward the waiting elevator.

Outside the gaping elevator doors, the team grounded to a halt.

"There's no way we can fit the stretcher back inside. It's too narrow," said a stocky, muscular EMT. "We're going to have to carry her down."

Jessie's eyes widened in acknowledgment and the bright pink color in her face drained away.

"You're right, Tuck. This place isn't built for medical emergencies," said his female counterpart. "The elevator's not an option and the main courthouse entrance is only accessible through a maze of stairways and corridors." Her mouth twisted as she thought over the various possibilities. "The only accessible exit is down the emergency stairwell, which empties out into the rear parking lot." Her partner radioed the ambulance to stand by.

"We can't stand around and debate this, let's get going. She needs to get to the hospital." Hal's words came out rude, but his patience was wearing thin. "Cindie, please go grab some of the guys on our floor to help. Get about six if you can."

Within moments, eight men joined Hal and the paramedics in the foyer. On his cue, the volunteers surrounded the gurney, gripped its steel railing, and advanced through the doorway designated as the emergency exit.

"Meet us around back and be ready to roll out. Over," radioed the woman medic to the driver. "Roger," was the crackly reply.

Upon entering the landing, the group stopped short on the ledge of the steep, rarely used stairwell. Its dangerously uneven stone steps and rusted iron railings spiraled like a corkscrew downward to the main floor four stories below. Constructed as part of the original nineteenth-century courthouse, its deteriorated condition looked like it violated every current building and fire code, but it was Jessie's only escape.

Hal grew light-headed as he examined the precipitous incline. It reminded him of the jagged summits of the Tetons that he used to ski, and like on those snowy cliffs, they had no choice but to proceed toward base camp. Jessie's eyes were shut, and he was glad that she was blind to the dizzying summit and the journey that lay ahead. Although fear nipped at him, he refused to reveal his fear to her.

Time was of the essence.

Following the EMTs' lead, Hal and his colleagues rolled the gurney off the top step, folded up its legs, locked them into place, and lifted her airborne. Realizing the fatality of a misstep, Hal guided the team with precision so as to keep the patient steady. Taut arms passed the stretcher from hand to hand, man to man, down the mountain of stairs. They maneuvered around the tight corners, down each narrow story, hoisting Jessie over the rickety railings along the obstacle course toward the ground level.

Where an elevator would have taken minutes to travel the four stories to the exit, their mission dragged on into five, ten, fifteen minutes. Jessie remained silent the entire time, not even a whimper.

Between the second and first floors, the group ground to a halt. The glowing red exit sign was close, maybe twenty yards away, but the stretcher had become lodged into the corner of the last landing.

"Lift the front up first, then the back when I give the signal," Hal commanded. He waited until the men looked at him, ready to move. "Now." Hal's foot slipped on the slick stone, but he steadied himself. Grunts and groans echoed throughout the stairwell as the men crushed shoulder to shoulder to jettison the stuck gurney. In one cohesive movement, the men dislodged the stretcher and continued down the stairs. Pivoting around the last turn, the driver greeted them and hustled them toward the ambulance positioned outside the doorway.

Hal sighed in relief when he jumped into the back of the ambulance alongside Jessie. With a round of applause, the doors shut behind them, the sirens rang out, and the ambulance raced to the hospital.

Oddly, Jessie felt no pain. With each spasm, Hal's warm hand squeezed hers as though absorbing them into himself. It had been years since they'd seen each other or connected so intimately. Jessie wanted to savor the sensations she remembered so well, but her eyes fluttered shut and her mind drifted off to another time and place, their first and only summer together.

It was after Jessie's first year of law school and she'd remained in the sweltering city to assist Professor Blackwell, her corporate law professor, on a treatise for publication. The hours had been good, the stipend generous; plus, she'd earned publication credit, independent study credit, and a personal recommendation to boot. Best of all, she'd spent time with Hal. Meanwhile, Hal had attended grueling bar review classes by day, and by night, they'd met up at either his place or hers where he'd studied for the exam. They'd engaged in mind-blowing, lustful, and tension-relieving study breaks.

"If I fail the bar and don't become a lawyer, it'll be your fault," Hal said. His fingers trailed along Jessie's naked back, triggering an ocean of goosebumps from her head to her toes.

"Well, then back to work with you. But, just like Portia in the *Merchant of Venice*, I'll bet you a pound of flesh that you crush this exam."

"Hmm," he said and licked his lips, considering the possibilities. "I'll take the flesh now. You can give me the pound later."

Despite the jokes, she was keenly aware that he needed to pass the bar the first time around. Hal didn't have the luxury of time or money for a second chance. He was paying his own way without support from his wealthy father, Harold Samuels, Jr., of the Wall Street investment firm of Samuels and Grovers.

Because of his experience with Teach for America, Hal had landed fellowships at NYU Law, and a permanent position awaited him at City Hall, provided he passed the Bar. She refused to be the reason he failed the exam. But they could never keep their hands off one another.

Finally, after months of worrying, Jessie's eyes filled with tears when he told her the news.

"I've passed the bar exam," he said, lifting her off her feet and spinning her around. "I love you." He kissed her deeply and his mouth was salty like he'd been crying, too.

As Jessie fitfully clung to consciousness inside the ambulance, Hal's fingers entwined with hers, and he smiled the smile reserved only for her. The magnetic pull that existed between them was undeniable. She'd been fooling herself to believe otherwise.

The ambulance lurched to a stop, backed into the emergency room bay, and the rear doors swung open wide. As they rushed Jessie into an open cubicle, her mind was so overtaken with fear, and her body racked with involuntarily shudders, that she was barely cognizant of the flurry of activity that surrounded her. All she could think about was the cramping in her abdomen and the fate of her baby.

"Miss, we've put a call into your OB, and he should be here soon," the ER nurse said, peeling back the bloody dress stuck to Jessie's abdomen. She checked Jessie's vitals and hustled around the cubicle, hooking her up to the various monitors as she spoke. "In the meantime, he's ordered an ultrasound exam. You're approximately thirty-two weeks, right? Besides the bleeding, are there cramps? How far apart are the contractions?"

Jessie's teeth were chattering so hard she could barely speak. "I-I-I'm about seven and a half months along." She blew out a long breath in a vain attempt to relax. "Yes, there's cramping. When will he be here?"

"He'll be here shortly." The nurse placed a heated blanket over Jessie and patted her arm. "Try to get some rest and I'll be back to check on you. There's a buzzer if you need anything." She placed the call button next to Jessie's head before she left.

"Thanks. We'll be fine," Hal said.

The warmth of the blanket eased the shivers surging through Jessie's body, and she felt her muscles begin to relax. Her mind continued to be gripped by the horrible possibility that her baby was in danger, and there was nothing that she could do to help. Her cheek grew wet as a solitary tear ran down her face.

Hal leaned his face close to hers and his hand gently stroked her forehead. Her stomach lurched at the intensity of his gaze, his golden eyes brimming with pain. She mustered a weak smile in hopes of comforting him, but they both knew it was a sham. Nothing would ease their worries until the doctor arrived.

"Jess, I..." he opened his mouth to speak but was interrupted by a technician rolling the portable trans-abdominal ultrasound unit alongside the bed. As though caught in an indiscretion, Jessie yanked her hand away from his.

The woman, barely as tall as the machine, shook a white plastic dispenser, squirted cold blue gel, and rolled the probe across Jessie's abdomen. "Is this your first?"

"Yes, this is my first, not our first," Jessie blurted. Her face warmed. "I mean, he's not my husband. I mean, he's not the father."

"What she's trying to say, somewhat clumsily, is that we're friends. I'm waiting with her until her fiancé arrives."

The sonographer raised her pencil thin eyebrows and studied the grainy black and white images on the screen. The machine ticked off bleeps and peeps as it recorded the measurements and images. The probe jutted into Jessie's right side and then along her pelvic bone. "You may feel some discomfort but don't be alarmed. Would you like to know the sex of the baby?"

Jessie understood the implications of her decision. Kyle would be furious, but this was a secret worth keeping. "Sure, I'll know in a few weeks anyway."

The tiny technician's eyes lit up with excitement and pointed at the head, eyes, nose, and lips floating on the screen. Jessie stared in amazement at the baby tumbling around inside her womb. She'd never seen anything so beautiful.

For months, the protrusions had pressed against her skin. Feet had danced along the surface. Sharp elbows had jabbed into her ribs. On the screen before her, a fully formed human appeared. A baby. Her baby. And the baby was fine, with a strong, fast heartbeat and sucking on its thumb. Soon she'd be cradling her tiny infant in her arms and the baby would never leave her. Jessie glanced at Hal and he, too, was swept up in a state of wonder.

"Look, there, it's a—" the woman said but stopped.

Kyle burst into the cubicle and rushed to her side. His eyes were wide with panic. "Jessie, I came as soon as I got the message.

Are you all right? And the baby?" He bent over and kissed her lightly on the forehead.

The technician held the probe in mid-air and gave Jessie a long, questioning glance. Hal slipped back, making room for Kyle at the bedside.

Jessie's body tensed at Kyle's kiss. "We're waiting to see the doctor."

"The message said that you were in labor at the district attorney's office and were being brought here. Babe, I don't really understand. What's going on?"

"I started bleeding, so they brought me here," she said, quietly.

"Who brought you here? Why weren't you home in bed? I thought we'd agreed that you'd stay home and rest. I never would've gone to Brooklyn, if I'd thought..." His voice trailed off as he caught himself uttering the admission. Kyle blinked rapidly and wiped the wetness from his eyes with his shirtsleeve. "We'll discuss that later, but right now let's see what the doctor says. If anything happens to you or the baby, I'll never forgive myself."

Jessie glanced at Hal over her fiancé's shoulders. His features were tight with discomfort, but then they relaxed into his cool, professional persona as Kyle took notice of him and he extended his hand in greeting. "I'm Hal Samuels, an old friend of Jess's... from law school."

A puzzled look flashed across Kyle's face as though trying to make sense of this stranger's presence at the hospital. It had been so fleeting that Jessie questioned whether it had ever been there at all. Her fiancé reached out, clasped Hal's hand, and then returned his attention back to her. Kyle leaned forward to kiss her again, but she turned away.

"I know that things have been a little crazy," Kyle said, "but you'll see. It's all good."

A nurse entered the cubicle and crossed her arms over her ample bosom. Her head swiveled back and forth between the two men suspiciously eyeing each other. "Gentlemen, I'm going to have to ask you to leave. Ms. Martin needs to rest. She's in the middle of an exam and it's getting a bit crowded in here, so, please, let's give her a little space." At first, neither man moved. "Do I need to call security?"

"I was just leaving," said Hal, "Jess, take care of yourself." On his way to the door, he patted her feet covered by the thin hospital blanket. She smiled and thanked him for his help. "Nice meeting you, Emory," he called back without turning around.

"Who was that guy again?" Kyle's eyebrows furrowed, then released. He turned to pursue Hal, but he appeared to change his mind and returned to Jessie's side. "Seriously, what's going on?"

"I could ask you the same thing," she said curtly.

"May I continue with the exam?" the sonographer asked.

"Yes, please, but only what the doctor ordered," Jessie said, nodding her head toward Kyle. The technician smirked, completed her task, and rolled the machine away.

CHAPTER
27

Dr. S. checked Jessie's chart in search of the current medical workup: the CBC blood test, the Wright stain seeking an anemic fetus, and the RH compatibility between the mother and the child. Terror swelled in Jessie's heart as the doctor's expression remained as blank as the reverse side of the sonogram paper unfurling through his fingers.

A heart beating. A mouth sucking a tiny thumb. Five wiggling toes. Those joyful images were forever marred by the concern lurking in Dr. S.'s eyes.

"Jessica, how are you feeling?" he asked, quietly. "Mr. Martin?"

"Emory, Kyle Emory."

"Sorry, sir," Dr. S. said. "You've had quite a scare today, Jessica. I would like to explain the situation we're facing with your pregnancy." He paused. "It's complicated but please bear with me.

After fertilization of the egg, the placenta grows wherever the embryo plants itself in the uterus. During a normal pregnancy, the placenta moves as the uterus stretches and grows, working its way to the top of the womb. In the third trimester, such as in your case, the placenta should be near the top getting ready for delivery." A small muscle twitched near the corner of his mouth. "However, your sonogram indicates the placenta is low lying, implanting itself near the mouth of the uterus and pressing against the edge of the cervix. Fortunately, it is not covering it. The reports indicate that you have a marginal case of placenta previa."

"How serious is this?" Jessie gulped. "Life-threatening?"

The worry lines around the doctor's brown eyes softened. She recognized the heartbreaking expression, one reminiscent of her delivering bad news to an anxious client. She focused hard to absorb the doctor's words as he explained that both she and her baby could suffer additional complications, such as continued or increased hemorrhaging, or the placenta could attach itself to the uterine muscles.

"Your baby's growth could be restricted and there's an increased risk of congenital abnormalities," Dr. S. said apologetically.

The maternal heart monitor on the wall screamed a high-pitched squeal, rivaling the beat of the fetal monitor. Jessie's words got hung up somewhere between her brain and her lips, but she choked out, "The baby?"

"The baby is fine, in good position. The sonogram shows no present abnormalities and the blood tests were normal. But should the bleeding persist, we may have to inject the baby with steroid shots to mature the lungs if we suspect an early delivery."

"Did this condition cause her bleeding?" Kyle asked.

"Yes, the placenta previa is the culprit. How long did you bleed?"

She held up one finger, managing to whisper, "... hour, but it stopped when I arrived here."

"Well, fortunately, you did not lose a great deal of blood. However, I would like to keep you in the hospital overnight for observation and to make sure the bleeding does not reoccur. Just as a precaution. We'll see how you are doing in the morning. Maybe we'll perform another ultrasound then. We'll see."

She gripped Kyle's hand. The physical weight of the baby was negligible compared to the emotional burden and fear creeping up on her.

"And as I have advised you before, you must cut back on your activities. Absolutely no sex or exercise of any kind and get plenty of bed rest. I am also going to prescribe blood pressure medication which should also prevent preterm labor. Let's try to keep the baby in there until thirty-six weeks. That's four more weeks. This will be better for you and especially the child."

"What caused the placenta previa?" Kyle asked.

The doctor explained that there was no known cause; however, there could be numerous contributing factors, such as an abnormally shaped uterus, scarring in the endometrial lining, uterine fibroids surgery, or a dilation and curettage procedure. "We really don't know. But, as long as Jessie takes care of herself, and you take care of her, everything should be fine."

"She's had none of those, so that's a huge relief. You hear that, sweetie? Everything will be fine." Kyle gave her a quick peck on the top of her head.

Jessie's mind swirled with the diagnosis that the doctor had given her. The last medical scare she'd had was a long, long time ago when she'd returned to Syracuse University for the spring semester of her junior year. Her email, text, and phone inboxes had been inundated with messages from Robbie, all of which she'd deleted. She had nothing to say to him and couldn't stomach his lame apologies and excuses. Robbie had crossed the line.

A few weeks into the semester, she could barely button her jeans. When she zipped up her ski parka, it pulled tight across her chest and hips. Her bras no longer fit her round, firm breasts, which ached as if she was getting her period, but she didn't start.

Six polar, snow-filled weeks had elapsed since her last period. She'd been anxious since the New Year, which could explain her irregularity. Plus, she'd been stuffing her face with cookies, chips, and soda. She'd convinced herself that stress was the culprit, but she had to be sure.

After her American Lit class, she hopped into her Jeep and headed for the local pharmacy. She trudged past the disposable diapers, baby wipes, and shampoo to the feminine products at the end of the aisle. In a cloud of confusion, Jessie examined the home pregnancy tests and purchased the one that promised results within minutes; two pretty pink lines would indicate a pregnancy.

Back at home, her trembling hands ripped open the box and she peed on the little white stick. The three-minute waiting time felt like twenty, and just to be sure, Jessie waited two extra minutes. Her heart pounded in her chest as she picked up the wand and inspected the results. One bright pink line and another faint line appeared in the results window.

Her knees buckled and she collapsed on the toilet. She stared at the wand again.

It couldn't be, but it was. She was pregnant.

Jessie's mind raced. Within minutes her plans, her dreams had evaporated. The course of her life had been irrevocably altered by a random act of violence that would haunt her forever.

Bitter bile burned the back of her throat as she considered what to do. Her initial response was to phone Robbie, call him every vile name she knew and inform him that he'd ruined her life by getting her pregnant.

Jessie snatched her cell phone from her bag and dialed, gathering her nerve as the phone rang. When the call was answered, she spoke in an even, unruffled tone. "Hey. It's me. I've got a big problem. I really need to see you. Will you be around tomorrow? No, I don't want to talk about it over the phone. We'll talk this weekend. I'll see you then." She hung up.

The following afternoon, Jessie packed up her car for spring break, maneuvered around the snow banks in her apartment's parking lot, and entered Exit 35 of the New York State Thruway, homeward. The tedious ride allowed her ample time to mull over how she was going to break the news. This wasn't something which was shared every day or with just anyone.

At twilight, Jessie parked her car in front of the little white house with the green shutters. Snow dotted the lawn and crocuses peeked out from the frozen ground. The front porch light was on and she climbed the stairs and rang the bell.

"You made it in great time. Did you break the speed limit to get here?" Terrence held the screen door open and admitted her inside. He enclosed her within an embrace and his kiss was warm on her cheek. He took her coat and offered her something to drink.

"Got any tea?" Jessie asked, depositing her backpack on the wingback chair in the foyer.

"Nothing stronger? How unlike you." Terrence fussed with the creases in his shirt. "Will orange zinger suit you?"

She followed him into the kitchen and watched him scurry around, selecting mugs, tea, spoons, the honey bear, and scones, then lined them up in a row before her on the butcher block island.

"It's been a long trip," she said nodding toward the powder room down the hallway. "I'll be right back."

When she discovered the bright red spots inside her panties, she sagged against the wall and closed her eyes in relief. She wasn't pregnant. It had been a false alarm. In her panic, she must have misread the tests results. Her body must have been reacting to the stress after all.

"Your call sounded serious. What's up?" Terrence asked when she returned to the kitchen.

Jessie wanted to run to Terrence, hug him and shout the news out loud, but she controlled the giddiness bubbling up inside. "I thought that I was pregnant, but I'm not," she said, quietly.

"What happened?" His smile vanished and he stared at her sternly.

"It was Robbie. He was drunk one night and I tried to fight him off, but you know—" She stretched the sleeves of her sweater over her hands and nervously chewed them.

"Jessica, you should report him. You can't let him get away with this."

She shook her head. "I can't. Just leave it at that. Anyway, it's over. He and I are over." She blinked back the tears welling in her eyes. "I'm okay now, but you can't tell my parents. You can't tell anyone. You're the only one who knows what he did to me."

Terrence approached her and rested his hands on her shoulders. His touch reassured her that she was safe and could let her guard down. Jessie buried her face against his chest and let the pent-up tears flow, saturating his cashmere sweater. He comforted her, as a parent would a child until her shuddering and sobbing ceased. He cupped his hand beneath her chin and tilted her wet, raw face up toward his. "This is our secret. I promise."

Before Dr. S. continued, he caught Jessie's eye and cleared his throat. "There's one thing you should plan on. I know this is going to disappoint you, Jessica." His voice oozed with remorse. "You'll probably deliver by cesarean to ensure your baby's safety."

"That's no big deal, right?" Kyle asked.

"Depending upon the severity of the placenta previa, a hysterectomy may be necessary. But we're getting ahead of ourselves."

"No more babies?" Jessie asked. "No, that can't happen."

A line of perspiration pooled across the fine hairs above her lip, but, suddenly, she was cold. Every sinew of her body shuddered as if she had a fever. The memory of one frozen winter's night, a decade ago, invaded the heat of the Indian summer. A secret, suppressed though not forgotten, stabbed at her. She'd been lucky, but she asked herself, what if? Was her innocent, unborn child paying the price of Robbie's uncontrollable wrath, just as she was paying the price of Terrence's? She'd never know.

"That would only be in an extreme, emergency situation. It is a potential risk, not inevitability. Just take care of yourself and take it one day at a time."

"It'll be okay. Listen to Dr. S. One day at a time," Kyle said. The vertical crease between his brows relaxed.

The following morning, Dr. S. arrived for his rounds shortly after six-thirty and Jessie was elated at the possibility of going home. Taking a shower. Changing her clothes. Sleeping without interruption. Even resolving the unsettled issues with Kyle.

"Your latest test results are fine," Dr. S. said, "and I'll discharge you only if you promise moderation in all things."

This was a vow she was more than willing to make.

"I've called the blood pressure prescription into your pharmacy. Please make sure to see me before the week's end." He signed the discharge instructions and handed them to her. "As soon as the nurse disconnects your tubes and wires, you're free to leave the hospital."

Jessie leaned back against the pillows, closed her teary eyes, and imagined her little stucco house on Platt Street. It seemed like a lifetime ago since she'd been home.

An eternity of minutes passed before a genial nurse arrived, removed the IVs, and unclipped the sensors that were strung along her body like marionette's strings.

Jessie was ready to go. Excited, she called home and the sound of her own voice requested a message at the sound of the beep. She called again. Same voice, same request. She tried Kyle's cell phone. His rich, baritone voice requested the leaving of a message at the tone.

"Do you have a ride home?" the nurse asked, "Isn't your fiancé picking you up?"

"I guess not," Jessie said. "I can manage by myself."

CHAPTER
28

Jeremy gently fondled the private investigator's report labeled, "Confidential—For Your Eyes Only," in black block letters.

The dossier consisted of a dozen pages, but Jeremy was interested in only one fact. The summary sheet listed the name of the subject: Jessica Grace Martin, DOB 11/10/88, Poughkeepsie, New York, and provided an extensive biographical history of Jessie's skills, interests, community involvement, personal history, education, family history, medical history, and employment. The details were enumerated on individual sheets accompanied by supporting documentation. His tar-stained nails scanned the list, seeking the information he paid dearly for—her marital status—and found it at the bottom of the first page: Single, cohabits with Kyle Jones Emory since June 2015, at 59 Platt Street, Poughkeepsie, Dutchess County, New York.

Emory. Jeremy scratched his head and studied the parking receipt where he'd scribbled the blotter information. He had no reason to doubt his transcribing the name Avery. The entry on the blotter must have been a typographical error. He ruffled through the attachments searching for the copy of the deed to verify the facts. In its place was a blank sheet marked *To Be Provided*.

He barked at Mo to get Carey Wentworth on the phone. Seconds later, the intercom buzzed and he picked up the flashing line on the phone console. "Hey, where's the deed for the Martin place?"

"You're joking, right? The deed? The county clerk's computers were down and my sources can only work so fast. What kind of nutso case are you working on, man?"

"That's none of your concern," Jeremy said. "I need that deed so you'd better tell your sources to hustle up. Do you think that you can handle that or do I need to hire someone else next time?"

"Hey, dude, dial down the crazy, will you? You'll have it by this afternoon," Wentworth whined, his voice rising in octaves to a pitchy squeal.

"I paid you a king's ransom for this job and I expect—" Jeremy caught himself, realizing that he was beginning to sound like Butterfield. "Carey, sorry, just get it here as soon as you can."

While killing time waiting for Wentworth, he returned to the summary page. The banal educational details, family, and professional history bored him. There was nothing that couldn't be unearthed through a simple Google search. The salacious details were always hidden within the personal history and medical data. With the eye of a voyeur, he scoured those entries hoping to discover whether any skeletons were hiding in Jessica Martin's youthful closet.

After lunch, Mo trotted into Jeremy's office, her reading glasses swaying on a chain around her neck like the tail wagging the dog, and she deposited a brown parcel amidst the debris on his desk.

"Did you threaten that man? You know that I'm not crazy about him, but Carey slunk in here like he was afraid for his life. He didn't ask to see you; he just dropped the package and split."

Jeremy sliced open the packet with a silver letter opener and extracted a stack of documents under her watchful eye. "Can I help you with something?"

She must have realized that he had no intention of carrying the conversation any further because she turned on her heels and departed in a huff.

He disregarded the dramatic exit and rifled through the papers. His sticky fingers grabbed the deed. It confirmed that the buyer's names as Kyle Edward Jones Emory and Jessica Grace Martin, the property address as 59 Platt Street, Poughkeepsie, New York, and the date of conveyance was June 13, 2015. They'd purchased the property as tenants in common, a legal indication that they were co-owners of the house, and not husband and wife.

Emory, not Avery. Possible, but not definitive.

He returned to the dossier, his intuition telling him that a clue was staring him in the face. Page by page, from cover to cover, he scoured the documents. Once. Twice. Three times. He studied the scratchy scrawl on the receipt, comparing the transcribed phone number contained in the police logs to the cell phone records attached to the report. He slammed his fist on the desk. A smirk of self-satisfaction returned. "I knew it."

CHAPTER
29

The taxi dropped Jessie off in front of her home on Platt Street. She walked up the driveway but stopped partway and appraised her yard. Along the fence, the edges of the hydrangea leaves were beginning to rust and their purple-blue heads were fading to green. Even the black-eyed Susans and herbs were turning to seed among the overgrown grasses. Upkeep of the flowerbeds was demanding and she wondered who would assist Kyle now that Ryan was gone. Kyle had relied on him. She'd relied on him, too. The simple chore of gardening symbolized Ryan's importance in their lives. Sadly, Ryan was like the autumn and she was like the spring, balancing each other out in a perverse cosmic tragedy.

She turned her face toward the early morning sun, absorbing its warmth into her cheeks. September's damp, earthy odor made her feel lightheaded, but in a good way. Jessie opened her eyes and noticed Kyle's BMW parked in the driveway. It was strange that he hadn't answered her phone calls. Maybe he was asleep or in the shower or had forsaken her and gone to Brooklyn. She chastised herself for being so negative, for not giving him the benefit of the doubt. Despite his recent deceptions, Kyle would never ditch her in her time of need.

She let herself inside. The house was quiet and she proceeded upstairs to shower away the residue of the past day. Kyle wasn't in their bedroom but the bed had been slept in. His phone lay charging on the dresser so she presumed that he'd turn up shortly.

After her shower, she returned to the kitchen to attack the dirty pans soaking in the sink and run the fully loaded dishwasher. That was definitely like Kyle, forgetting to turn the machine on. Jessie submerged her hands in the tepid, soapy water, fishing around for the glass top to the frying pan. She withdrew her hands, holding the lid in one and the sponge in the other, and scrubbed away at the greasy residue.

"Jessie?" Kyle asked, his face flushed with perspiration. He was dressed in running clothes and sneakers, and rock music blasted from the earbud dangling from his ear. "What are you doing home? Why didn't you call?"

He hovered so closely that she could feel his breath at the hairline on her neck. As if warning of danger, the fine hairs stood on end.

"I was discharged and wanted to come home," Jessie said. "I needed to get out of there."

"Here, sit down. You should be taking it easy. I was going to finish those after my run." He grabbed the lid and sponge from her hand and practically pushed her into the kitchen chair.

She stared at him feeling confused, torn. Jessie honestly believed that the love existing between them was something real. Solid enough to last a lifetime. This man did not wear the mask of dishonesty. He wore the smile of someone who genuinely loved and cherished her. Why had he hidden his new position at the Barclays Center?

Kyle must have read her thoughts because he said, "I wanted it to be a surprise. I wanted to tell you about the job offer weeks ago, but you were all swept up in Ryan's death, then the subpoena ordeal. There never seemed to be the right time. And then, I didn't know how to tell you. Don't you see? This comes at a perfect time for us, with the baby and your office situation."

"When were you going to tell me?"

Kyle ignored her question, suggesting that they try living in the city for a month or so before the baby arrived. "We can see how we like it. Or I can commute for a while. Whatever you want," he said, crouching beside her on one knee as though proposing marriage.

"I can't believe that you applied for a job without discussing it with me." Beyond the betrayal, she was plain freaked out. "How long have you been job hunting?"

"It wasn't like that. Remember Barry Levy, my old boss at the Garden? Well, he's the new GM at Barclays." He groaned as he rose and his knees cracked. "About a month and a half ago, he called, said there was a vacancy as the VP of Business Operations and asked if I was interested. It's almost three times my salary at the Civic Center, plus benefits, a signing bonus, relocation stipend, and pension, and there's growth potential. Who wouldn't be interested? Right?"

Kyle's enthusiasm was not contagious. The opportunity sounded too good to be true, and she didn't know how to respond. On one level, she understood the purity of his intentions. He wanted a better life for their family with financial and job security, everything the bankrupt civic center lacked. But on the other, without considering her feelings, he wanted to uproot her from the life they'd established in Poughkeepsie, not to mention her family, their friends, her law practice, her home. At the moment, their life might be rocky but she remained optimistic about living in the Hudson Valley.

"Besides, Jessica, isn't your life a bit out of control?"

Her breath hitched at the conversation's unexpected detour. Whenever he used her full name rather than calling her Jessie, there was an argument brewing. He was referring to Terrence but refusing to speak his name.

"I thought we were partners, but lately you've done whatever you wanted. Traipsing around in the middle of the night. Accepting subpoenas. Appearing before the grand jury. Disregarding doctor's orders. I don't know what's going through your mind. You're being just plain reckless." Kyle's expression grew darker with each accusation. He was playing dirty and they both knew it. Terrence had been a part of her family since she'd been a kid, and she couldn't have let him face a murder charge without her assistance.

"I've repeatedly warned you about his unhealthy attachment to you, but did you listen?" Kyle shrugged his shoulders and held up his hands in surrender. "No, of course not. You're blind when it comes to him and I don't understand it. Never have. I've tolerated him because I love you. But this time he's gone too far. And look where we are because of it. Your career…your health…the baby. Somebody had to step up to the plate when the opportunity presented itself. Leaving Poughkeepsie will be the best thing for us."

Kyle could be sulky, withdrawn, and even cranky when life disappointed him, but she'd never seen him this agitated and vicious. With each syllable, he slipped further away from her, shape-shifting from her mate into her adversary. While his lambasting was unnerving, she allowed him to ramble on, using the time to steel herself, remain calm and in control as though preparing for cross-examination. To obtain the litigator's advantage, she must listen with her mind, not her heart. Allow the accusations to bead up like an oil slick upon water and roll off her tough hide. Be on the offense, not the defense.

"You don't even realize it, but you're drowning in quicksand. You'd better stop and take a long hard look at what you're doing. Before it's too late."

"Kyle, first, you seem to be forgetting that you lied to me by accepting a position in New York City without considering my needs. I don't know how I can trust you anymore," Jessie said. The floodgates opened, refusing to be dammed. "Second, we may be engaged and you may have planted your seed inside of me, but that does *not* create ownership over me or give you the right to dictate how I live my life or who should be in my life."

Sure, she'd been swept up in the whirlwind circling Terrence and had been yanked in competing directions to her breaking point. However, she was trying her best to manage the events beyond her control and expected Kyle, above everyone else, to support her through this crisis. Not criticize and attack her. "Finally, let's be clear, Terrence has nothing to do with us or our baby."

"*Us?* Ever since he called that night there's been no us. It's been all about you." Kyle's hearing seemed to be selective. He towered over her with clenched fists and retreated to the far end of the kitchen. "I need to do what I think is right for our family. I love you, but I won't allow that murderer to destroy me, too."

Jessie studied him, unable to read his eyes. Regret? Anger? Sadness? "Apparently, I was wrong about a lot of things, including you. If it evades you that you and this child are the most important people in my life, if your petty jealousy of Terrence makes you incapable of appreciating our relationship, if your pursuit of this new opportunity is a priority to you, then perhaps we should re-examine whether our relationship is working anymore, or if it has played itself out."

"I love you, Jessie, and I'm not ready to give up on us."

"I'm not either, but you're putting me in a difficult position. I need some time to think." The words trickled out as a whisper, muffled by the lump in her throat.

There was a long silence before either of them spoke. Kyle stared out the kitchen window and her eyes scanned the room, the empty wine bottle on the counter, the dust bunnies collecting in the fridge grill, the mud Kyle had tracked in on his running shoes, and the pile of old newspapers discarded, like herself, in the corner.

"Maybe it's best if I spend a few nights in the city until I get settled into the job," he said finally. His voice was far away, like he was thinking out loud rather than speaking directly to her. Kyle snatched his windbreaker from the back of the chair and his hand briefly paused on the kitchen doorknob. Without turning back to look at her, he left her sitting alone in the kitchen.

Her heart raced. She felt the cold. What had just happened? Jessie attempted to calm herself by staring at the door, willing Kyle to return. She replayed the scene over and over again in her mind, questioning what had made him turn so intolerably selfish. And what had motivated her asking him to leave.

A few hours later, Kyle packed his duffle bag, suitcase, and laptop. From the den window, Jessie watched him load his car and debated whether to stop him. There was no retracting the awful things they'd said to one another so she let him go. No further words were exchanged between them. No goodbyes. No apologies. Just a silent tension between lovers, unsure what to say.

She hoped that she'd made it clear to him that, once again, he was being ridiculous about Terrence. More times than she could remember, she'd told him that she and Terrence had never been romantically involved. It was the truth. Even thinking of Terrence that way gave her the creeps.

When she was growing up, Terrence had been her teacher, and as an adult, he'd been her friend, part of her family. Plain and simple. Yet Kyle's refusal to accept the truth had foolishly, and literally, driven them apart.

Upstairs in the bedroom, Kyle's dresser drawers hung open and empty. Jessie ran her fingers through the lint that had accumulated during their four years together. Most of the time, it had been good, but the past few weeks had been jarring and surreal as though she'd been imprisoned inside someone else's life.

Just as she'd suspected, Kyle had abandoned her. Seven months pregnant. Alone. No job. She was going to have to figure out what to do.

Her muscles ached with the stress and exhaustion. She needed time to think, but more urgently, she needed rest.

The knock on Jessie's front door was as firm and calculated as a military drum roll. A demand for entrance, rather than a request. Jessie peeked out the sidelights hoping that Kyle had changed his mind, but the shiny black Mercedes S-class parked curbside baffled her. On the doorstep, her boss, James McMann, and her colleague, Josh Spencer, grinned at her. Their faces were partially obscured by an excessive, almost funereal, bouquet. Her nap would have to wait.

"Jessica, you're looking quite well," McMann said. "I've been meaning to stop around for a chat, so I asked Josh to drive me over this morning. I hope that you don't mind an unannounced visit." Mr. McMann waited for an invitation to enter.

"Mr. McMann, Josh, please come in." Jessie stepped aside as the men entered the foyer and she led them into the living room.

Josh scooted past her, setting the flowers in the crystal vase upon the coffee table. There had been minimal contact with her office since the imposition of the medical leave almost three weeks ago. Her salary had been electronically deposited into her bank and she'd fielded an occasional email about her clients. That was it. She was intrigued by this unexpected visit from the managing partner, a man notorious for avoiding house calls. James McMann restricted his socializing to his business partners and politicos, not the underlings, unless to pacify a client or woo a new one.

Jessie was no fool; she knew that despite his compliments she looked haggard, but she was curious. James McMann was a master spin-doctor who switched on the charm when he desired something. Even the most obstinate client became powerless to resist his artful persuasion. She'd witnessed the dance a hundred times.

"I hope you enjoy them, my dear. Please, Jessica, take a seat," McMann said. He posed before the mantle, his hands clasped behind his back, seizing command of the parlor. Jessie made herself comfortable in a tapestry armchair, while Josh settled into the velvet couch across from her, half-hidden behind the cascading flowers. "We've missed you around the office but I trust you're taking it easy."

Jessie smiled uncomfortably and lied in response to his inquiry about her health. "I'm doing great," she said.

"On behalf of the partners, I'm here to apologize. We'd like you to return to work. We severely misjudged your situation and should never have presumed your involvement in the Paige boy's murder. We value your contribution to our firm and would like to express our appreciation for your dedication."

"That's very kind of you, Mr. McMann." The firm's loss of her billable hours flashed through her mind.

"We've given your situation a great deal of deliberation and would like to make your position, how do I put this? More family-friendly. How does that sound to you?"

She shot Josh a questioning look, but he averted his eyes toward their superior.

"Once the baby arrives, you'll want a more flexible schedule. No weekend work, nine to five, less travel." He hesitated briefly, clapping his hands in joy. "We'd like to accommodate your needs and are prepared to offer you a position as a permanent associate."

Permanent associate? She'd been with the firm since her graduation from NYU. For five years, she'd slaved eighty hours a week, not to mention the evenings and weekends. Missing birthdays, canceling vacations, and sacrificing holidays for sake of the Holy Grail they'd dangled before her. "I'm up for partnership review in two years," she said, almost choking on the words.

Josh squirmed in his seat.

When she'd first joined the firm, McMann had taken her under his wing and introduced her to the nuances of corporate law and the art of negotiation. The art of the deal. True to form, he'd deflected their conversation toward the firm's mission to reward her with a better lifestyle. She'd control her work schedule and be home to tuck the kids into bed, yet be professionally fulfilled by performing challenging, quality work for McMann and Curtis.

"Quite an opportunity, isn't it?"

"Interesting, to say the least," Jessie said dryly, twirling a curl of her hair around her forefinger. Permanent associate? With this ridiculous scheme, they'd condemn her to legal limbo, stealing the fruits of the labor she'd sacrificed so much to achieve.

"I don't need to remind you that it's a tough job market out there and some firms may not be as generous as we are. You're a shrewd lawyer, and I'm sure you'll make the right decision after discussing this with Kyle. He'll agree that we have your family's best interests at heart."

"I'm sure that he will." She concentrated on the hair twirls to keep her rising anger in check.

"Aren't you glad we've had this little chat? It's been such a pleasure to see you. We've taken enough of your time and you need your rest." The old man approached Jessie, planted his cold lips on her cheek, and marched out into the foyer toward the door. "You're welcome back whenever you like."

"Sir, I can't tell you how enlightening this visit has been," she said. "I'll consider my options and get back to you."

She sensed Josh's eyes probing her, but she avoided them as she let him and Mr. McMann out the door.

Damn James McMann and Larry Curtis. Damn their demotion. Damn Kyle. Damn them all. She needed a nap before her head exploded.

CHAPTER
30

Testifying before the grand jury, Sergeant Michael Rossi proved to be Hal's dream witness. He followed the script they'd rehearsed verbatim. The sergeant confirmed receiving the dispatch call at 1:15 a.m. reporting an incident at 327 Park Avenue. Rossi, his partner Jennifer Macy, and officers Peter Ferris and Derek Newton had responded and arrived at the scene at 1:30 a.m. The suspect, Terrence Butterfield, invited the first responders into his home and admitted that he'd killed someone with a .38 caliber handgun.

"Officer Macy remained with the suspect while Newton, Ferris, and I performed a search and secured the premises." Sergeant Rossi paused. "We discovered a body in the basement."

For the second time, the grand jury was treated to a slideshow. This time, the crime scene presented was more palatable since Ryan's mangled body was noticeably absent.

"I've never seen such bloodletting. The cement floor and walls were splattered with blood that trailed up the stairs to the first floor. The kitchen, it was a mess. I don't mean with piles of dirty dishes and spoiled food." He hesitated and exhaled a windy breath, garnering his strength to proceed. "We found a butcher's knife covered with blood in the kitchen sink."

A wave of revulsion swept through the panel. Disgusted, twenty-three jurors averted their eyes from the flat screen, perhaps feeling survivor's guilt that while they were alive, Ryan Paige had been pointlessly butchered.

Yes. That's it, Hal thought with satisfaction. *We've got the bastard. If they voted now, we'd get an indictment.*

But there was more testimony to go. More nails to be hammered into the coffin. "Sergeant, what did you do next?"

"Macy and I cuffed Mr. Butterfield and read him his Miranda rights. I called HQ, told them we were bringing Mr. Butterfield in for questioning, and requested that the crime scene techs be dispatched to continue the investigation. Officer Macy and I transported Butterfield to the station."

Sergeant Rossi described the delivery of Butterfield to the city jail, and since there were no questions from the panel, he was excused.

Hal called Jennifer Macy to the stand. She wriggled in the chair and played with the wedding ring on her finger. Macy corroborated her partner's testimony; however, she added that the suspect had been under her surveillance upstairs in the living room for almost ten minutes.

"Although Mr. Butterfield was polite and cooperative, my gun was drawn the entire time," Macy said. "He asked me for a towel to wipe the blood off his hands and he became agitated when I refused his request. He startled me when he began rubbing his hands on the sofa, so I ordered him to return his hands to his head and stand with his back against the wall." She also testified that there were no witnesses at the scene. "However, a man and woman arrived simultaneously with our team. They remained outside the house and I don't recall them interacting with Mr. Butterfield."

Hal's final nail in the coffin was Sean Williams, the crime scene technician, who, in a no-nonsense manner, explained the procedures followed to ensure the proper collection and chain of custody of the evidence at the crime scene.

"First, we took photographs of the entire home as we discovered it. A second set of photographs was taken after the removal of the victim and any evidence. We dusted the living room, kitchen, basement stairwell, basement, and other relevant areas of the suspect's home for fingerprints. DNA samples were collected from the victim and his clothing, as well as the suspect's person and clothing." Perkins stopped and looked at Hal, double-checking whether to proceed, and, at Hal's nod, continued. "Samples of bodily fluids were also collected. Forensic UV lights were used throughout the basement and first floor to determine the blood splatter. And we thoroughly examined the exterior of the suspect's premise as well as the garage. The knife, handgun, spent cartridges, and bullet fragments were bagged and marked for identification. They have all been sent off to the lab but, unfortunately, the ballistics are not available yet. However, we have identified the victim's blood and body fluids on the person and clothing and in the premises of Terrence Butterfield."

At four o'clock in the afternoon, the grand jury voted to deliberate without further forensic or witness testimony. This signaled that they'd been persuaded by his witnesses: Dr. Frank Mailer, Sergeant Michael Rossi, Officer Jennifer Macy, and Sean Williams.

Before the jurors recessed into their chambers, Hal presented his closing remarks to the panel.

"Members of the grand jury, now that the witness testimony, documents, and other items received as exhibits have been presented, I will give you instructions to guide you in reaching your decision as to whether or not to issue an indictment in this case," he said sternly. "It will be your duty to determine the facts and whether the accused, Terrence Butterfield, should stand trial for the count of Murder in the First Degree of Ryan Paige. Under New York law, a suspect can be charged with Murder in the First Degree under Penal Law 125.27 when, with the intent to cause the death of another person, the suspect causes the death and acted in an especially cruel and wanton manner by inflicting torture upon the victim prior to the victim's death."

After reading the applicable provisions of the penal law and the definitions of the relevant legal terms such as intent, depraved, and torture, he continued. "It is your job to determine whether there is legally sufficient and reasonable cause to believe that the accused, Terrence Butterfield, committed the crime of Murder in the First Degree and should be formally charged with that offense, with any other crime, or whether the charges before you must be dismissed.

If you have any questions during your deliberations, please let me know. Good luck, and we await your decision."

Within an hour, Hal received a call from the foreperson. A decision had been reached. He hid his excitement as he appeared before the panel and the foreperson presented him with the tally. The vote was unanimous. Terrence Butterfield would be indicted for the murder of Ryan Paige.

He'd never doubted the strength of the evidence against Butterfield, but it was a relief to be on the path to a full-blown trial. There was plenty of work to be done to obtain a conviction and his first step was presenting the indictment to the judge.

After the hasty transcription of the findings, the courier rushed the five-page indictment to Judge Perry Hamilton's chambers, only to discover the chamber doors were locked. The judge had left for the day.

The next morning Hal sat in his office reading the newspaper. It was early, around eight o'clock, and he hadn't had his first cup of coffee yet. He removed the blue wrapper from the *Poughkeepsie Journal* and his eyes fell upon the headline, "Poughkeepsie Teacher Indicted for Murder." The paper reported the impending indictment of Terrence Butterfield for the murder of Ryan Paige. He was befuddled as to how the news had spread. The court didn't open for another hour, and the only copy of the indictment sat on his desk, ready to go. What happened in the grand jury room was supposed to stay within the grand jury annex, just like Vegas. But for the first time, there'd been a breach in his office.

He decided to take no chances, and precisely at nine, he personally delivered the indictment to Judge Hamilton. The judge's secretary time-stamped Hal's copy of the indictment and said she'd call him later to schedule the arraignment.

Hal waited all morning for Lauren to burst into his office, hurling accusations at him about the news leak, but when she strutted into his office at noon, clutching a copy of the formal indictment she didn't mention the leak.

She convened her troops in the conference room for a celebratory pizza luncheon and toasted her team with a paper cup of diet cola. The chief glowed like Saint Joan of Arc. "I want to thank everyone for their hard work in obtaining this indictment against Terrence Butterfield. His prosecution for this heinous crime will serve justice and honor the memory of Ryan Paige. Special kudos to Hal and Cindie. I know they'll undertake whatever is necessary to obtain a conviction at trial. Everybody, enjoy our success and the lunch."

As cheers burst out around the room, Cindie's foot gave Hal a swift kick beneath the table, signaling Lauren's rapid approach. Moments later, his boss's hot breath whispered in his ear. Being the obedient soldier, he snatched his plate from the table and wolfed down the slice as he accompanied her to her office. Inside her lair, Lauren deposited her lunch into the trash, wiping her hands in disgust as though she'd touched a toxic substance.

"Call Sheriff Stone. Tell him that I need a favor. Ask him to bring Mr. Butterfield over to court immediately for arraignment because I'd like to announce the indictment at a press conference this afternoon," Lauren said, slipping off her stilettos. She grimaced as she massaged the balls of her feet. "These shoes make my legs look terrific, but my feet hurt like mad."

"Erin says the same thing," he said, eyes crinkling in laughter. "The press release is already on your desk. I'll check to see if Judge Hamilton can schedule us for three o'clock since I've already set the press conference down for four. We'll be cutting it close for coverage in the evening newscasts." He paused. "It should work out, but it might take some begging. It's nothing I can't handle."

Lauren padded across the carpet and reached into the credenza, drawing out a silver flask. She uncorked the stopper, pressed her lips around the wide mouth, and swallowed a swig. She offered him the carafe but he declined. "We make a good team, Hal. I'll know within the next few days about the senate, and then we'll have a great deal more to discuss. You'll have options. You could lead my team in Albany or the one I'll leave behind. The choice is yours, but you're extremely valuable to me in a variety of ways."

She waited for a response, one that he vowed would never be forthcoming, not in a million years.

"I'd better get back to work," he said. "We have to serve a copy of the indictment on Kaplan and inform him about the court appearance. The poor guy probably read about the indictment in the morning paper. Any idea how the story got leaked?"

Lauren sucked on the flask once more, languidly swishing the liquid around in her mouth before swallowing. "None. You?"

From her smug expression, it was obvious she was lying.

On the other end of the phone, Jeremy Kaplan spewed a string of expletives at Hal with the fervor of a drunken sailor. The guy deserved to be pissed off about his client's indictment. As Chief ADA, Hal managed the district attorney's office with the highest degree of professional ethics. He believed in his oath to serve the people. No backroom deals. No quid pro quo. He operated his division above reproach as well as transparent to even the most arbitrary and capricious scrutiny. Therefore, this breach of confidentiality gnawed at him more than he was letting on.

"Your boss gets her kicks rolling in the mud with the pigs and I'd like to think that's not true about you, Samuels. I've known her much longer than you, so a word to the wise—watch your back and do some housekeeping over there. The law is a gentleman's sport, not one played in the barnyard," Kaplan said flippantly. "In the meantime, when can I expect a copy of the indictment, bill of particulars, and the transcript of the minutes? I suppose we'll schedule the arraignment for sometime next week."

Kaplan was entitled to any information used by the grand jury to make their decision, including all documents, exhibits, and testimony. As a matter of course, the defense required these materials to prepare for trial and, naturally, Kaplan was anxious to get his hands on them. Further, Kaplan wasn't going to be happy about Butterfield's immediate arraignment, but he had to break the news to him about that, too.

"We're making arrangements to have Butterfield transported to court for immediate arraignment. There's a court appearance scheduled before Judge Hamilton at three, so I'll give you the papers then," Hal said.

"Three?" Jeremy asked. "As in two hours from now? That's absurd. It doesn't give me much time to prepare."

"You'll be able to meet with your client at the courthouse beforehand, but what are you going to prepare? We both know that you're going to be pleading not guilty," he said, trying to sound nonchalant.

"That's beside the point and you know it, Samuels. This is no way to run an office."

Hal didn't want to get into a pissing match with him over Lauren's unorthodox strategies. He needed to circle back to Kaplan's original complaint about the newspaper article. "Again, Jeremy, I don't know how the press found out about the grand jury, but we'll investigate and take the appropriate steps."

"Sure you will. And like I said, housekeeping, Samuels, housekeeping." Kaplan hung up.

Leave it to Lauren to incite another incident requiring immediate triage. Ryan Paige's murder had already created a logjam of the domestic violence, drug, rape, and assault investigations deserving attention. Thanks to her reckless pursuit of publicity, his limited staff would be further strained to address the alleged mole in the office. The last thing the district attorney's office needed was the specter of a scandal. The very last thing Hal needed was another demand straining his already tenuous personal life.

He'd deal with Lauren later. In the meantime, he had another fire to extinguish—the arraignment.

There was a hushed respectful silence in Judge Hamilton's cavernous courtroom on the second floor of the Dutchess County Courthouse. The judge's bench was empty, and the small group in attendance was waiting for the judge to appear. The hearing was closed to the public, so besides Hal, the Butterfield arraignment was restricted to the necessary personnel: Cindie, Kaplan, Butterfield, the two deputy sheriffs who'd accompanied Butterfield from the jail, and the court reporter.

It seemed to Hal that he was part of a secret proceeding engineered by Lauren at her whim. The two hours' notice hadn't allowed him a great deal of time to prepare, but he'd done his best to bring Cindie up to speed. With Cindie in tow, it would be the two prosecutors against one defense attorney and their message would be clear. They were ready to fight. And win.

Butterfield had been hustled up the back stairs without ceremony and would be whisked away as soon as the appearance was concluded. Perry Hamilton wasn't a long-winded judge, and since he'd been tipped off that the district attorney was under a deadline, Hal anticipated his time in court would be brief and to the point.

At the prosecutor's table, Hal drummed his fingers on his file, ignoring the daggers being thrust at him by Kaplan from the defendant's side of the room. Kaplan's bedraggled appearance — mussed hair, a shabby, outdated brown suit and scuffed loafers— matched his weary expression. There was a sudden rustling as the judge's chamber door opened and Judge Hamilton entered the room. The group rose and the judge gestured for everyone to be seated.

"Ladies and gentleman, good afternoon," Judge Hamilton said, after signaling for the stenographer to commence. "I appreciate your gathering here on such short notice. We have a pressing matter before the bench. There has been an indictment handed down in the matter of the *People of the State of New York vs. Terrence Butterfield.* The indictment, which has been signed by the jury foreperson and the district attorney, charges that Terrence Butterfield should stand trial for the murder of Ryan Paige under Penal Law 125.27 as he not only caused Mr. Paige's death, but inflicted torture on the victim prior to his death." The judge paused and flipped through the pages of the documents.

Hal's eyes shifted to Butterfield. This was the first time he'd been in the killer's presence because Lauren had attended the city court appearance on the night of the murder. The file contained photographs of Butterfield, but here he was in the flesh. Butterfield's dark, longish hair was tidy and he was clean-shaven, but there was something off-kilter about him, besides the fact he swayed on his feet like a drunkard. Sheriff Stone had informed Hal about Butterfield's troublesome behavior in prison and the botched suicide attempt. The white bandages around his wrists were evidence of the latter. Hal had no sympathy for whatever was making the murderer act lethargic today, but he assumed it was the pain meds or sedatives prescribed for the injuries.

The handcuffed killer standing next to Kaplan was difficult to reconcile with Jessie's glowing, almost saintly, descriptions of Terrence Butterfield. He'd expected a charismatic, swashbuckling champion with a golden halo hovering over his head. Not a puffy-eyed, round-shouldered weakling who'd tried to off himself because he couldn't handle the pressure of jail. The fact that she'd had a close friendship with this man, and that she'd trusted him, seemed unfathomable. She'd witnessed his brutality at the crime scene and Hal hoped that she now realized Butterfield's true nature. She'd have to be crazy to continue any relationship with this madman. And although Jessie might be many things, she definitely was not crazy.

Hal's attention returned to the proceedings when Judge Hamilton coughed.

"Mr. Kaplan, I believe that Mr. Samuels has a copy of the indictment for you."

Hal passed a copy to Cindie, who presented it to Kaplan at the defendant's table.

"As you can see," Judge Hamilton continued, "the document is rather lengthy. Does your client waive the reading of the indictment, or would you like me to proceed? This is your client's day in court, so it's your call."

"Your Honor, we'll waive the reading," Kaplan said solemnly, without consulting with his client.

"Then, sir, how does your client plead?"

"Not guilty."

Cindie snorted out loud at the plea, and Hal shot her a chastising look. He wasn't worried about obtaining a guilty verdict at trial. He'd make sure that this pathetic loser received the maximum punishment under the law, life without parole, and that justice would be served.

"So entered," Judge Hamilton said, "and the court will issue an order continuing the defendant's commitment in the custody of the sheriff, pending his further appearance in this action."

"Your Honor, what about bail?" Kaplan demanded.

"Judge," Hal said, "Mr. Kaplan can't be serious. Given the heinous crime committed by the defendant—"

"Mr. Kaplan, request denied. So ordered. Remand the defendant to the Dutchess County Jail." The judge banged his gavel. "Court is adjourned."

Kaplan barely had enough time to whisper into Butterfield's ear before the sheriffs grabbed the defendant's shoulders and hustled him away. Kaplan pursed his lips, squared his shoulders, and marched across the room toward Hal and Cindie. He slammed his briefcase on the floor as though he was throwing down the gauntlet. "I believe you have some additional documents for me," he said.

"Here you go, Mr. Kaplan." Cindie smiled politely and handed him a carton marked, "*People versus Butterfield*—Defendant's Copy," with two yellow slips of paper attached. "Sign here," she said.

Kaplan scrawled his initials on the two receipts. He returned one to Cindie, and folded the other and slipped it inside his jacket pocket. "There have been reports that your office withholds exculpatory evidence, so let's make sure it doesn't happen here."

"I don't appreciate your insinuations, but that's not how I operate and you know it," Hal said.

"It's not you I'm talking about, Samuels. It's your boss." Kaplan's eyes flicked back and forth between Hal and Cindie, apparently for emphasis. "Just make sure there are no more screw ups."

"If I were you, *I'd* be more careful," Hal said. "I'd leave the sharp objects home the next time you visit your client in jail."

CHAPTER
31

Jeremy was pissed. Ever since Butterfield had retained him, the case had been a succession of slip-ups, miscalculations, and tactical errors on his part. Now, this. Reading about the indictment in the papers had been bad enough. Hal Samuels' snarky remarks that insinuated Terrence's suicide attempt was somehow Jeremy's fault had been the last straw. That, along with the judge's denial of bail without even blinking.

"No calls this afternoon," he said as he passed Mo's desk on the way into the inner sanctum. "I mean it; unless Gayle and the kids are taken hostage, no calls."

"If you don't want to talk about it, I'll understand, but you can't let Butterfield and his case get to you. He's only a client and you shouldn't get emotionally involved. You can only do so much." She paused. "You know that. I know things around here aren't great, but we'll get through it. We always do."

He gasped. A sharp pain ripped through his chest, knocking the wind out of him. The Butterfield file slipped from his grasp and scattered across the carpet. Jeremy collapsed onto the bench across from her desk, loosening his tie and unbuttoning his shirt down to his waist.

"Jeremy, are you alright? I'm calling 911." She grabbed his wrist and pressed her fingers on his racing pulse. "If you drop dead on my watch, I'll never forgive myself."

He shook his head in protest and waved her away. "Water, please, water." He choked out the words.

He was getting too old for this garbage. He considered himself to be in relatively good shape for a guy pushing sixty and, for the most part, major illness hadn't plagued him. For the past twenty-five years, he'd managed as a solo practitioner and the business had kept food on the table, the slate roof shingled, and paid the child support and alimony— mostly.

He'd never taken in an associate or a partner because he'd never found the right person, and he'd hoped that one of his older kids would follow him into the practice. But that dream had slipped away as they'd studied disciplines other than the law. Lately, Gayle had been nagging him about hiring help. He'd sworn to make a concerted effort once the Butterfield case was resolved. If he survived the ordeal.

Mo urged him to go upstairs to rest and placed the water glass in his hands.

"I'll be fine. Thanks. And remember, no calls," he said, shuffling into the sanctum.

"Whatever you say. But I'm leaving your door open so I can hear if you kick the bucket."

Jeremy dipped his cotton handkerchief into the glass, then wiped the frigid water on his forehead and the back of his neck. The water evaporated upon touch. From his desk drawer, he grabbed three aspirin from a bottle and swallowed them with a slug from the glass.

"Mo, coffee," he bellowed.

"No way" was the response, so he gulped down the entire glass of water, picked up the file, and buckled down to work. Jeremy switched on the digital voice recorder, and using the Klein documents as a template, dictated:

"Please take notice upon the annexed Affidavits of Terrence Butterfield and Jeremy Kaplan, Esq., each sworn on the 15th day of September, the Indictment herein and all prior proceedings had herein that the undersigned will move this court for an order granting the defendant, Terrence Butterfield, the following relief pursuant to the Criminal Procedure Law:

1.   Inspection of the Grand Jury minutes and a dismissal of the Indictment herein,

2.   A Bill of Particulars,

3.   Suppression of all physical evidence obtained in violation of the Defendant's Constitutional rights guaranteed by the United States and New York Constitutions;

4.   Suppression of the potential testimony describing the involuntary declarations or statement of the Defendant, Terrence Butterfield;

5. Delivery to the Defendant, Terrence Butterfield, of all evidence favorable to him,

6. And for such other and further relief to the court may seem just and proper.

Mo appeared in the doorway. He sighed.

"I thought you'd need this." She set the organized file down on his desk and tiptoed out of his office.

"Thanks." He continued the dictation. "I, Terrence Butterfield, being duly, sworn deposes and says ..."

For the first time in months, Jeremy was jazzed up about seeing a client, even though it was Terrence Butterfield. He was surprised at his level of excitement and energy, despite his exhaustion from dissecting the file and analyzing it from every conceivable angle. Just like in the Klein case. He was proposing a new spin on the old fruits of the poisonous tree theory, arguing that Butterfield's arrest was the direct result of a single unauthorized midnight call to the police. That phone call was a Pandora's box, setting into motion events that prejudiced the rights and liberties of Terrence Butterfield. If successful, the law would forever change and consequently, so would his life. He'd be back on top, no longer scraping the bottom of the barrel. It was time for him to be ruthless, fearless, and cunning.

Butterfield's cell was isolated at the end of the block, away from the general prison population. The cell, if it could be called that, was more akin to a college dormitory room than to a penal colony. His client enjoyed a large bay window overlooking the Hudson River, a single bed, and a private bath. No cellmate, no gang showers. No being jostled in the mess hall line since every meal was delivered right to his quarters. The downside was no privacy. Not a minute passed without surveillance by a closed-circuit camera.

Butterfield's guard, Bernard, was posted outside the door and he greeted Jeremy upon arrival. "Sorry, man, but you're wasting your time if you think you're going to get anything out of him today. He got real nasty and violent last night after they transferred him here. He was howling like a coyote and making such a racket that the doc gave him tranquilizers and pain meds," Bernard said. "If you ask me, they should've kept him in the infirmary for a few more days or shipped him over to the psych ward. I've seen this a dozen times. The county wants the state aid, so they keep the crazy ones."

Unbelievable, Jeremy thought. What a buzzkill. "I'll check back with you later," he growled. Fortunately, he'd made alternate arrangements for the afternoon. Just in case.

Outside the jail's main entrance, Jeremy shivered like a wet dog in the unseasonably arctic breeze reigning in from Canada. He took one last draw on his cigar and stubbed the butt out with the heel of his shoe as his guest approached from across the parking lot. The dark figure bobbed and weaved between the cars, and Jeremy questioned the wisdom of his selection.

He was tempted to fabricate an excuse and send her on her way, but as she glided toward him, Jeremy reassured himself. This decision hadn't been entered into in haste. Dr. Miri Shtern's impeccable medical credentials, superb record in lower and appellate courts, and her quiet, serene, no-nonsense manner propelled her to the top of his list of forensic psychiatrists. That the two enjoyed a warm, personal friendship was another story.

"Miri," Jeremy said, folding his tall frame to kiss the petite woman on the cheek. "Thanks for coming."

"Like old times, right, Jerry?" The soft roll of the double "r" in his name, like a purr, hinted at her Israeli heritage. "Besides, I'm intrigued by the file you sent over. I've followed the story in the news, but you know you never get the truth from the papers. And the television, *aach*, they whitewash everything. There are a few questions that I would like to discuss with you. Is there somewhere we can go to talk before I meet Mr. Butterfield?"

He took her elbow and escorted her across the street to a small eatery, where a red neon sign invited them into The Dutchess Diner. The bitter cloud of over-brewed coffee assaulted them as they pushed the door open. Grabbing a booth, they ordered from a waitress as stale as the lemon meringue pie beneath the glass dome on the counter. The server returned with coffee and served Jeremy's along with a wink from her droopy eyelids. He tipped her with a generous smile.

"Jerry, if you're done flirting, I have a few questions. First, where are the medical records? I'll need to review them for his medical history and meds." Miri shuddered, buttoning her cardigan sweater against the frigid diner air.

Beneath her reserved demeanor, Dr. Miri Shtern operated in a dangerous, darker arena. While rumors circulated about her involvement with the national intelligence agency of Israel, Mossad,

Jeremy knew the truth, or at least what she wanted him to know. She'd told him that she'd served as a major in the Israeli Defense Force, Infantry Division, but there was uncertainty in his mind. However, while her mind might function like a covert killer's, he'd witnessed her great compassion for those stricken with mental illness.

Jeremy felt her eyes drilling into him as he explained his client's situation. "I truly need your help with this one. To say that my client is uncooperative would be an understatement. He drifts in and out of reality. He acts completely disconnected to his crime. He's argumentative, almost unreachable." He leaned in closer and whispered across the table. "If, after meeting him, you agree to take on the case, I'll need a comprehensive psych work up, the usual, if we're to convince a jury of his incompetence. If it comes to that."

"Does your client have any idea about me? Or that you are considering this approach?" she asked.

"In his more surly lucid moments, he has insisted that I employ whatever steps, or as he puts it, 'tricks,' are necessary for a successful defense. Like it's magic or something. Need I say more?"

Miri asked for the mandate for today.

"You've read the file. I need to know if he's lying to me, or if he is certifiable under the mental hygiene law."

"There's more to Mr. Butterfield's situation than that, I'm afraid. What you're suggesting is too narrow a strategic plan and may not be in the best interests of your client. As a mental health professional, there are several possible ways to handle the matter. Three, actually." Miri spoke with authoritative intensity. "Is he certifiable as mentally ill in need of hospitalization and treatment as you suggest under the MHL? Will you just plead lack of criminal conduct as a defense? And finally, is he a con artist who is deceiving us all? Each of these avenues mandates different criteria, assessments, and protocols for treatment under the medical and the court systems. Only you as his attorney know what would be most persuasive to a judge and jury, and ultimately, what is in the best interests of Mr. Butterfield." She took a sip of coffee. "How would you like me to proceed?"

"It's premature to ask me that right now. Meet him. Talk to him, if that's possible. Tell me whether you're on board. Give me your impressions and then we can revisit the strategy if you're interested in working the case," Jeremy said. His hands trembled slightly, causing his coffee to splash over the rim. He steadied them, hoping that they didn't reveal his desperation.

Miri wore a blank, almost bored, expression, but the gold flecks in her dark eyes sparkled as she brushed a strand of flyaway hair from her teeth. He'd calculated correctly; she was drawn in by the complexity of Terrence Butterfield. That he defied the template of the casebook murderer, the randomness of the killing, the lack of motive, and the prior contact between the victim and the perpetrator were irresistible factors. Jeremy could sense that she itched to sit in a room with this man. Observe him. Speak with him. Treat and heal him.

Sitting across from him in the diner was a woman who could not resist guerrilla warfare.

When Jeremy and Miri arrived at Butterfield's cell, Bernard was still on vigil. The hulky guard grimaced at them, as though blaming them for his banishment to the prison's Siberian outlands. Away from his chums, the man's only diversion was a closed-circuit monitor running a marathon reality show starring a half-crazed inmate on suicide watch.

Jeremy saw Butterfield within the darkened cell, curled into a fetal position on the cot, his chest rising and falling in the solitude of sleep. Not very interesting; in fact, so boring that Jeremy empathized with the large man's disdain.

"As I said before, your man's had a rough night," Bernard said. Jeremy's eyes fell on the empty energy drink cans littering the vicinity of the trashcan. "No man, don't get any wrong ideas. I didn't give him any. But I need this stuff to keep me on my toes. You never know what he's going to do. I'm telling you, Butterfield's crazy, man, crazy."

Jeremy turned toward Miri. "Maybe today's not a good day. Sorry for wasting your time."

"It's as good a time as any. Just give me a few minutes. Sir, could you kindly open the door for me?"

"Lady, are you nuts? You want to awaken a sleeping hornet?" Bernard asked.

Miri Shtern folded her arms across her chest and, for the guard's benefit, flexed her well-defined biceps. Her accompanying expression was a cross between ferocity and determination. She gave clear instructions not to be interrupted and that she'd request assistance if it was necessary. Bernard unlocked the door and the tiny woman, barely as tall as his barrel chest, skirted around him into the room. She shut the door behind her.

"Mr. Kaplan, with all due respect, we shouldn't leave her alone with him. Mr. B. could beat the life out of her," Bernard said.

"Look," Jeremy said, pointing at the screen. He'd never observed Miri in action before and didn't know what to expect. He'd only viewed her end products, the diagnosis and psychological reports, written in medical gibberish that had baffled his legal mind. This peek behind the curtain fascinated him.

She crouched bedside and gently rocked the shoulders of the sleeping man. Butterfield stirred, blinked at the unfamiliar figure, rolled over to face the wall, and tugged the covers tighter around his frame. Miri leaned over him and whispered into his ear. Then, her lips chanted a series of mantras while she stroked Butterfield's hunched shoulders, bent arms, and contorted legs. The exact words were inaudible to Jeremy, but as she recited them, she appeared trance-like, unaware of her surroundings, the passage of time, or that she was being observed.

For more than an hour, Jeremy watched in amazement as the interaction between the doctor and patient transpired through whispers and pantomime. Jeremy focused on Butterfield as he huddled beneath the covers. What was going on in his mind? Was something frightening him? Was his present state spawned by guilt or denial, or was he proud of his kill? Could Dr. Shtern unlock Butterfield's mind so that he could assist in his own defense or had the man fallen into the abyss?

One thing was certain: without Miri's success, it would be impossible for him to defend Butterfield. He would never discover what had really happened that night or what that kid had been doing in Butterfield's backyard. Or why Ryan had so willingly entered Butterfield's home. Had they secretly known each other? What had prompted Butterfield's rampage? Worse yet, had there been others who'd escaped the teacher's clutches?

His attention returned to the monitor. From her slacks pockets, Miri extracted two brushed silver wands the size of ballpoint pens, which she rubbed together as though igniting sparks for fire. The two wands conjoined into a single cylinder as the doctor flourished them in wide circles over Butterfield. Eyes clamped tightly and lips chanting, the psychiatrist conducted an invisible orchestra inside the tiny cell. In a final crescendo, Miri's flat palms batted the air away, and it seemed, to Jeremy at least, that she was clearing the stale air above her patient, exorcising the foul with fresh, replacing the dark with light, and giving calm to the stressed.

Butterfield's body twitched and shuddered in response, then yielded to a state of absolute relaxation. Miri stepped back against the far cell wall, studied the body at rest, and cranked open the window blinds, admitting sunlight into the room. She returned to her crouching position beside Butterfield, and once more, pressed her full lips against his ear.

"Look, she's like the dog whisperer," Jeremy murmured in awe.

"The crazy person whisperer." Bernard chuckled at his own joke.

Butterfield accepted the petite hand offered to him and rose from the bed. Miri smiled, nodded at him, and slipped from the cell. "He's famished and I'm interested."

For the first time, Jeremy thought he detected contentment on his client's face. He sighed in relief. He opened his briefcase and withdrew a thick packet of papers stapled inside a blue legal backer and a pen. The day wouldn't be a complete waste of time at all.

CHAPTER
32

Hal stood at the back of the bustling crowd watching District Attorney Lauren Hollenbeck prepare to deliver her huge announcement. In the breezy afternoon, video cameras rolled, camera shutters snapped, and journalists thrust their microphones aloft to capture what they suspected would be sensational news.

"I'm pleased to announce that the grand jury voted to indict Terrence Butterfield in the death of Ryan Paige. The indictment has been filed with the Dutchess County Supreme Court and the defendant has been arraigned on the charge of murder in the first degree." Lauren spoke with ease and charisma, as though she was auditioning for the vacant Senate seat. Before continuing, she flashed a smile and laughed on cue in the triumph of public service and justice over evil.

"She's really got them all fooled," a man at Hal's shoulder remarked, "but we know better, don't we?"

A crumbled panama hat shrouded the speaker's gray, tired face. Hal started, a bit surprised at Kaplan's mingling at the media event.

"If you want equal airtime for your client, it can be arranged," Hal said.

"No, thanks. We'll get enough attention when my client is released from jail." Kaplan hoisted a hefty envelope from a briefcase and deposited into Hal's hands. "Just returning the favor, pal. Here's some interesting bedtime reading for you."

Without responding, Hal watched Kaplan vanish into the crowd.

From the looks of it, it didn't seem like Lauren would be relinquishing the podium in any short order. Hal had had enough of her posturing for one day, so he circumvented the gathering in search of peace and quiet. He sought a refuge away from the adrenaline buzz of the office, the press conference, and the small, hollow victory of the indictment; someplace where he could think in solitude and anonymity. He turned left down Market Street and walked past the Adriance Memorial Library, permitting his instincts to guide him away from the madness.

The warm, damp smell of autumn filled his nostrils. The rusty brown edges of the maple leaves and the oaks tinged with red and yellow gently rustled in the canopy over his head. The late afternoon sun warmed his face, beckoning him to continue on his journey. He rambled out of the business district into the residential south side neighborhoods where the manicured lawns grew large and lush.

Of their own volition, his feet guided him toward a destination where he'd never dared to wander. They halted before the broad front porch of a small Tudor-style house. Planters overflowing with geraniums and impatiens lined the walkway and a Jeep was parked in the gravel driveway. He heard the pounding of his feet climbing up the porch steps and felt his hand reach out to ring the bell. His heart raced as footsteps trod toward the front door. It nearly stopped when she opened it.

"Hi," Jessie said, her face showing amazement to see him standing on her porch. She cradled a stack of envelopes in her hand.

"Hi," he said, "if you're busy, I'll leave."

"No, no. It's nothing. I'm just looking over some bills. It'll wait," she said. "Come on in."

Hal crossed the threshold and peered around like a tourist examining a foreign world. He immediately noticed the scent of lemon furniture polish and the tidiness of the house. Straight ahead at the end of the hallway, he spied a modern kitchen and to his left, a cozy living room with a fireplace flanked by a cream-colored couch and tapestry armchairs. "This is nice. It looks like you."

"Thanks. I—we—like it."

His eyes fell on the gilded framed oil painting mounted over the fireplace mantle. In it, shepherds herded their flocks through a dreamy English countryside. He looked at her with a wan smile. "I see you kept it."

"Why wouldn't I? I love it." A broad grin lit up Jessie's face.

"I don't know…because…" he said, awkwardly shrugging his broad shoulders. "Well, I'm glad."

"Would you like something? A drink maybe?" Jessie cocked her head as though trying to read his mind. She waited for him to answer as they stood inside the archway opening into the living room. The curves of her figure mimicked the architecture.

If asked, he'd describe her as fertile, fecund, fruitful. Like the Madonna. She never looked more beautiful. He never felt more jealous. Jessie carried another man's child and had a life with someone else. A child and a contented existence that could've been his if he'd played his cards right. Her fiancé was a nice enough guy, but she deserved better. Someone who'd cherish her like he would have, had he not been diverted from the righteous path.

Hal declined. He stood frozen in the foyer, not knowing whether to proceed further or turn and bolt out the door. Inside her home, his manly courage dissolved into that of a shy schoolboy. He was speechless.

"Hal, is there something you want?"

He wouldn't answer that question because the answer was forbidden. He was married to Erin. She was engaged to Kyle. And they both had kids—well, almost. But the answer was that he wanted Jessie. He always had and he knew he always would. Not just in the visceral sense. In the—and he was reluctant to even use the word—soulmate sense. The absolutely, completely in love with her sense. It had been a major error in judgment to impulsively wed Erin Halstead, the daughter of his father's business partner. A woman he'd been bred to marry. Their merger of the real estate and investment worlds had saddled him with a life riddled with regret.

But he loved Jessie. His heart burned to explain. Explain the abrupt change in temperament toward her. The abandonment of promises they'd made to each other. To bear his soul, apologize for the wrongdoings, and rectify them.

But he was a man of honor and would fulfill his promises to his wife and his family.

"I wanted to make sure that you were doing okay. After, you know, the hospital," he said. "And to apologize for antagonizing your fiancé." A pause. "I should be going. Please give Kyle my sincere apologies."

Jessie hesitated. A sad, confused look flashed across her face as though deciding whether to breach a secret. She placed her hand on the edge of the foyer table, steadying herself. She took a deep breath and blew out a long one. "Kyle left. Yesterday morning. I asked him to leave."

"Jess, I'm sorry." He wasn't though, not really, and the news made his life infinitely more complicated. He wished he could reveal his true feelings to her, but he wasn't free to do so.

Tears welled up in her eyes and the pain in them seared him terribly. As hard as he tried, he couldn't resist and approached her. Her body stiffened as he enclosed her in his arms but relaxed as she leaned into him, releasing tears onto his blazer. He buried his face in her auburn curls and inhaled the familiar essence of lavender, the essence of Jessie.

"Oh, Jess," he murmured.

She pulled her face from his shoulder and turned her mossy-gold eyes toward him. His thumb brushed the tears from her cheek, resting her chin on his upturned palm. Tracing her full mouth with his moist finger, he tilted her face toward his and gently drew his lips to the soft pink mouth of his memory, his dreams. Her arms encircled his neck, pulling him closer, bridging the gap between the years. With pleasure and delight, he feasted on the salty lips, tongue, and mouth like a starving man. Consuming her breath and the heat of her pregnant body warming him.

She loosened herself from his embrace as the baby shifted inside her.

"I'm sorry, Jess. I didn't mean to—" Again, he wasn't sorry. He desired her more than ever.

She smiled, wound her fingers through his hair, and lured his lips back to hers.

The parking lot adjacent to the municipal offices was empty except for a sleek black Volvo and a white Cadillac. Across the river on the western bank, the black mountains cut the jagged silhouette of a sleeping dragon against the golden sunset. The lot's overhead security lights flickered on as Hal inserted his key into the Volvo's ignition. He flinched at the harsh sound of metal rapping on the window of the driver's door. Lauren's nose pressed against the glass as she slammed a large ruby ring onto the glass. He rolled the window down, in part to speak to her, but also to prevent any scratches to his new car.

"Where have you been? I've been looking for you," she asked.

"Went out for a long walk after the press conference. Nice job, by the way."

"Where did you walk to, China?" Lauren asked slyly.

"Our friend Kaplan served us with an omnibus motion, and I wanted to clear my head before I tackled it."

"What did it say?"

"Don't know." He motioned toward the unopened package occupying the passenger's seat. "I'll read it in the morning. Sorry, gotta go. Erin's got dinner ready."

Before Lauren could drag the conversation from twilight into night, he closed the window and sped off. In the rearview mirror, he watched as she turned toward her Caddy in disgust. He smiled and cranked up Aerosmith on the radio.

Hal greeted his wife in the kitchen with a kiss, not the customary slight brushing by each other kind of peck, but with a long, lingering meeting of the mouths. He measured the reactions of the two women to his advances, as well his own stirrings. One was boiling hot and desirous; the other was lukewarm and distracted.

"You're in an awfully good mood tonight," Erin said, pushing him away to finish setting the table for dinner.

"I got to piss off the chief," he said. "A nice ending to a very long day."

"The kiss or the kiss-off?"

He laughed a full body laugh, raising a mischievous eyebrow. "Both."

"You rascal."

After dinner and story time with Tyler, Hal tucked his son into bed and absconded to the living room to watch the ballgame. The

Yanks were leading in their division and faced the perennial rivals, Boston, in the last vestiges of the season. When he'd worked in New York City, one of the perks had been tickets to the stadium, but up in the hinterlands, he settled for the game and a frosty beer on his sofa.

The unsealed documents taunted him from the coffee table. He mulled over whether they were important enough to ruin his evening plans and decided they absolutely were not. It had been a rough couple of weeks, and he was entitled to relax with a brew, and after all, it was the Yankees versus Boston—home advantage. He picked up the remote, turned on the game, and popped open the Sam Adams.

Fatigue overtook him at the top of the ninth with the Yanks winning 10-1, so he clicked off the screen and dragged himself upstairs to bed. The nightstand lamps were burning in the bedroom, casting a warm glow out into the hallway. Erin was propped up in bed reading when he walked into the room and disrobed for bed. She glanced up, smiled, asked the score, and returned to her murder mystery. It was ironic that she loved murders, considering it was his line of work. The bookshelves were jammed with them: P.D. James, Lee Childs, Agatha Christie, James Lee Burke, and Louise Penny. They lined the shelves and were stacked in a tall queue on the night table. Sometimes he thought that the blood and gore was a turn-on for her, and he knew that a day in his office would cure her of any romantic illusions. But he figured that her literary appetite was an attempt to vicariously share in his career, and since the fictitious villains, detectives, and lawyers made her happy, he never made the offer to set her straight.

Erin set her novel aside. "You've had a lot going on lately at work. Is everything all right?"

"Yeah, Lauren has us chasing rabbits over the Paige boy's case, which is really open and shut, but it's high profile. You know how she is." He deposited his shirt into the laundry bag on his way into the bathroom for his nightly routine.

"Honey, maybe we should plan a vacation, a getaway. My parents can take Tyler. Maybe just a long weekend. You and me in Vermont or the Adirondacks? What do you think?"

The water was running and he hadn't heard her proposal in full. Hal entered the room and she asked again. "What do you think?"

"About what?"

"A getaway? My parents can take Tyler for a long weekend." She was moisturizing her hands with lavender scented lotion as she spoke. Her face sparkled electric. The aqua flecks in her eyes glimmered in anticipation of time alone together. Away. Just the two of them.

"You make the plans and we'll go," Hal said, sliding in between the crisp cotton sheets next to her. Her cold feet rubbed up against his warm legs. Erin leaned over and kissed him lightly, an exploratory kiss. Then, she snuggled closer, pressing her statuesque body against his. Her hands slinked downward across his naked chest, the ridges of his toned abs, and beneath the elastic band in his boxers. The scent of lavender sparked his senses. He moaned softly and reached over and extinguished the bedside lamp. It was time to go back to work.

CHAPTER
33

On Hal's first inspection, Jeremy Kaplan's notice of motion to dismiss the murder charges appeared benign. It struck him as being identical to the hundreds of requests he'd opposed over the past five years. Customarily, he sped through the cookie-cutter versions of the motions, all plagiarized from the form books. Being the bread and butter of the criminal defense trade, these voluminous applications were designed to impress upon the client that they were receiving the biggest bang for their legal buck, especially when their family had drained life savings, retirement plans, or hocked the jewels to pay the hefty retainer. The papers all deposited a bitter aftertaste in Hal's mouth and proved to be a waste of judicial time.

He expected more from Jeremy Kaplan. He expected an adversary worthy of his time and talents. The first page was so boilerplate that he considered pawning the motion off on Cindie or one of the rookie ADAs. He skipped past Jeremy's affirmation, placing a red sticky note on the top of the page as a reminder to return. He flipped ahead to the sworn statement of Terrence Butterfield, leaned back in his office chair, and rested his loafers on the desk drawer he used as a makeshift footrest. He began reading what he anticipated to be the incoherent ramblings of a lunatic.

Terrence Butterfield, being duly sworn, deposes and says:

1. I am the defendant in the above-captioned matter and make this affidavit in support of the present motion to dismiss the charges of murder in the first degree leveled against me.

2. On the night of August 31st, shortly after 1 a.m., I called my attorney, Jessica Martin, Esq., seeking advice regarding a serious legal matter which had just occurred at my home. During the past several years, Ms. Martin has represented me in several legal matters, so it was only natural that I would contact her in my time of need and distress.

Hal's feet flew to the floor as he sprang up in his seat. He leaned over the document, digesting it word by word.

3. I made the call from my home at 327 Park Avenue, Poughkeepsie, New York. For more than ten minutes, we discussed the facts and circumstances of my legal problem and she rendered legal advice regarding the same. Ms. Martin told me that she was on her way to assist me and to wait for her at my home. The events of that night had greatly upset me and I was not, and still am not, in the best state of mind. However, I do recall that shortly after speaking with Ms. Martin, I received a telephone call from her father, Ed Martin, who also resides in Poughkeepsie, New York. Ed Martin told me that Ms. Martin had contacted him and related the substance of our conversation. Mr. Martin accurately portrayed the content of the conversation that had taken place with my attorney, Jessica Martin. It was his intention to speak with me on the phone until she arrived, but we conversed for only a few minutes. I spoke candidly with him about my legal problems, but all the time I was anxious about Ms. Martin's arrival.

4. While we were speaking, I observed two police cars park down the street from my home. I heard footsteps on my front path and noticed my attorney, Jessica Martin, and her fiancé, Kyle Emory, approaching my house. At the same time, a team of police officers swarmed around my home. Suddenly, the officers were standing on my porch, with pistols aimed at me. They asked whether I had a gun, and I replied, "Yes. Please take it from me." They demanded that I place it upon the coffee table, but I attempted to hand it directly over to them. With their guns pointed at my chest, I deposited my gun on the coffee table in front of me. One of the officers knocked the gun from the table onto the floor and told me to place my hands on my head, which I did.

5. I believe that three officers searched my home, while one remained with me. One of the officers searched the basement and called out, "Come quick. I've found something,'" and two of the officers ran to join him. The one guarding me asked me if I had a lawyer. "Yes, she is outside," I pleaded, "Please let her in." Even though I was distraught, the officer refused my request to speak with Ms. Martin.

6. When the officers returned from the basement, I was informed that I was being arrested for murder. I was handcuffed, read my Miranda rights, and escorted out of my home to be placed in their vehicle for transportation to jail. As I was ushered past my attorney, Jessica Martin, I felt like I was in a stupor. She must have noticed my state of shock because she insisted upon speaking with me. She was not permitted to do so. Disregarding the police's orders she advised me "not to say anything." Sometime later at the police station, I conferred with Ms. Martin along with my other defense attorney, Jeremy Kaplan. At the time, I was still in shock and it was comforting to consult with Ms. Martin before being formally booked and arraigned in city court.

7. I do not know how the police knew to come to my home on the night of August 31st. I did not call the police. Nor did I authorize my attorney or her father to call the police.

8. I believe that my attorney, Jessica Martin, or an agent of hers, contacted the police against my wishes and without my knowledge and that my arrest was a direct result of this unauthorized call.

9. I believe that the actions of Jessica Martin violated the professional ethics and secrecy requirements of the attorney-client privilege due to me with respect to the events occurring on August 31st and in connection with the information disclosed to her at that time.

Accordingly, I respectfully request that the Court grant the relief requested herein by discharging the charges against me.

Signed,

Terrence Butterfield

Hal's heart leaped when he read Butterfield's skillfully deceptive allegations. They reeked of a different animal, of a new, undiscovered breed of predator. He continued on, flipping through the pages, noting the exhibits and the newspaper articles describing Ryan's murder. When he returned to the red sticky note marking Kaplan's affirmation, the vein in his neck throbbed. The assertions unhinged a floodgate of fury within him.

Jeremy Kaplan, Esq., affirms under the penalties of perjury, as follows:

1. I am the attorney for Terrence Butterfield and make this affirmation in support of the present motion.

Hal furiously scratched notes to himself as he proceeded.

2. On the morning of August 31st, at approximately 3:00 a.m., I received a telephone call from attorney Jessica Martin. She stated that her client, Terrence Butterfield, required my assistance regarding a criminal matter. Butterfield was incarcerated in the City of Poughkeepsie Jail, pending arraignment for homicide. She asked if I would assist in his representation.

3. I arrived at the police station at approximately four o'clock and was greeted by attorney Jessica Martin, who had been waiting there to see her client, along with her fiancé, Kyle Emory. Attorney Martin and I were taken to meet with our client, Terrence Butterfield, in one of the interrogation rooms. He was distraught and appeared confused about the arrest. Mr. Butterfield stated that he did not call the police and had no idea how they were called to come to his home.

4. After we concluded, Mr. Butterfield was taken to be booked. Attorney Martin and I then met him in the Poughkeepsie City Court courtroom, where he was arraigned before Judge Hughes. He was charged with felony murder in the first degree in the death of Ryan Paige and no bail was set.

5. Attorney Jessica Martin is no longer representing the defendant in this matter. I am his sole representative.

6. Attached is my brief which supports my client's position that his attorney, Jessica Martin, violated his constitutional rights, including the right to the attorney-client privilege, when either she or her authorized agent contacted the City of Poughkeepsie Police regarding this crime without the consent of the defendant.

Based upon the foregoing facts and the law of this case, I respectfully request that the present motion be granted in its entirety.

Signed,

Jeremy Kaplan, Esq.

Hal reviewed his notes. In addition to the constitutional arguments, unreasonable search and seizure, confrontation of witnesses, self-incrimination, and fair trial, the twenty-page brief elaborated the history and law of attorney-client privilege. An absolute privilege guaranteed by the New York Code of Professional Responsibility, the attorney is vested with the cloak of confidentiality concerning his client's secrets and confidences. Unless waived by the client, the secrets remain inviolate. Jeremy Kaplan further asserted that the rule of secrecy not only extends to the attorney, but her employees, or anyone who obtains the confidential information.

At the heart of his argument, Kaplan accused Jessie of willfully violating her attorney-client privilege by informing Kyle and her father about Terrence's admissions. He also stated that Butterfield never authorized Jessie to contact the police. Therefore, whoever contacted them could only have gained knowledge of the crime through her violation of the privilege, not from the defendant. All pending criminal charges against Butterfield stemmed from the "fruits from the poisonous tree," hence all evidence should be suppressed. And if all evidence is suppressed, the charges against Terrence Butterfield must be dismissed.

"Damn." He flung the papers from his desk. To protect his client, Kaplan had painted a barn-size bullseye on Jessie's back and pulled the trigger.

Jeremy believed he'd hear from the DA sooner than he did. He spent the morning pacing the office, chewing on a Habano and second-guessing his adversary. His strategy was the babble, baffle, and bargain tactic: intimidate with a wild, frivolous legal argument so the People would offer a deal. In this instance, he sought to save Butterfield's life with the slim possibility of parole sometime in the distant future. Most likely, Butterfield would be a septuagenarian by the time liberty came his way, but if the actuarial tables were correct, he'd die as a free man. For some strange reason, Jeremy believed that his bordering-on-the-psychotic client was entitled to die with dignity, not in an orange jumpsuit.

He took the delay as a positive sign and barreled ahead like a freight train of confidence, however misplaced. Cocksure he had a winner.

It was mid-morning when the call came.

"Kaplan, are you out of your freakin' mind?" Hal Samuels asked.

"You've read the motion," he said, rolling on the stub of the cigar around in his mouth.

"Breach of attorney-client privilege? Are you willing to jeopardize the reputation of a competent attorney for the sake of your maniac client?"

"That's what I get paid for." Jeremy spit a wad of tobacco into the trash basket. "Besides, your office pulled the same stunt, didn't it?"

Silence hung heavy on the other end of the line, then his tense adversary snapped, "Your argument will never work. You're grasping at straws."

"That's for the judge to decide, isn't it?" The match point belonged to him.

"I guess we will see. See you in court," Hal said.

"If you need an adjournment for more time to respond, let me know, Samuels," he said, pouring a whole bucket of sarcasm into the phrase and hung up the phone. His fingers twirled the shiny cigar cutter. He could feel it. He had them on the run.

"Jess, Hey. It's me."

Jessie had heard Hal use the solemn tone once before, at the end.

She figured that she'd save herself the embarrassment and told him that apologies about their kisses weren't necessary. "We're two consenting adults who got caught up in the heat of the moment, that's all, so there's nothing to be worried about."

"No, no. I'm not calling about that. We have a more serious problem." His voice softened.

She listened as he explained about Kaplan's omnibus motion. He offered to scan and send it over right away. "Once you're done, please call me. It's urgent."

She was caught off guard by this turn of events and how it related to her. Jessie had thought that after the grand jury, she was finished with the entire business. Except for Terrence. She knew that he needed her. She'd support him any way she could, as he'd always supported her. After all these years, she'd never forgotten Terrence's kindness after Robbie's assault or how he'd remained true to his word. The secret remained between them.

"You'd better take a look and call me back." His voice cracked, melting into an apology. "And Jess, we'll work this out, please remember that."

More confused than ever, Jessie dictated her email address and they hung up.

CHAPTER
34

Hal had read Kaplan's papers three times, each time supplementing his notes in the margin. He'd distributed copies to his assistants and asked for their comments by mid-afternoon. By the time the team convened in his office, the pages were covered with red pencil scribbles and underlines.

He set the three copies across the desk and compared them page-by-page like stacks of cards in a game of solitaire. His assistants sat quietly observing him as he developed his plan and allocated the projects based on their strengths. Cindie, with her eye for detail, would research the law and advisory opinions, and Tony, the people person, would interview the witnesses. Then, over the intercom, he requested that his secretary contact Steve Hutchins, the Attorney General for the State of New York, and buzz him when the AG was on the line.

Cindie and Tony rose to leave and exchanged looks.

"What about Ms. Martin, Mr. Emory, and Mr. Martin?" Tony asked, hesitant to mention the name everyone was skirting. "Do you want me to bring them in as well?"

"I've already spoken with Ms. Martin. She's been emailed the docs and we'll wait until after she and I speak."

All eyes shifted as Lauren entered Hal's office, wagging the papers in her hand. A frown revealed the fine lines that Botox had failed to smooth. She scrutinized Cindie from head to toe as she sidled up next to her.

"We'll get started on this," Cindie said, leaving the room with Tony following close behind.

"There's a strong possibility that your friend undermined our case. Did you know about this?" Lauren asked.

"Of course not. This is just Kaplan being a jackass. He's posturing."

"On my first read, he raises some substantial issues, especially on the question of attorney impropriety. This looks like a case of first impression." Lauren walked to Hal's desk and perched on its corner. "Does your wife know about you two?"

Hal looked at her, puzzled. "What are you talking about?"

A mean little smirk crossed her face. "You couldn't fool me with your little display the other day. Perhaps you should think about withdrawing from the case to avoid any potential conflict of interest. I could assign Tim Reynolds to handle it from here on out. He's got enough experience to lead your team."

"Don't be ridiculous. My loyalties are to this office, you know that. And I'm your most experienced litigator. So can you drop the red herring and concentrate on the facts?"

"I don't have to remind you that we're being closely watched. A great deal rides on the win." She opened her mouth to speak but was interrupted by the buzzing of the phone.

"Gotta take this, it's Hutchins," he said.

Lauren narrowed her eyes as he picked up the receiver. She hurled her copy of the motion on his desk and made a little huffing sound as she strutted out of his office. The trail of Chanel No. 5 left in her wake made Hal's stomach turn.

Jessie didn't believe that she was born under a bad sign. She was a Scorpio, after all. Intense, profound, self-controlled, and one of the most powerful signs of the zodiac. Generally, she wasn't superstitious or a devotee of her daily horoscope, tarot cards, or natal chart. She believed that she was the mistress of her own fate. There was no such thing as preordination. If she worked hard, she'd be rewarded with success in life. The corny adage that when you were dealt lemons you made lemonade had served her well, but now she truly believed that the universe conspired against her. She wanted to curl up into a ball and die.

She'd received Hal's fax and was horrified at the words jumping off the page. More than horrified—hurt. Deeply. How could Terrence make those awful accusations about her? How could he betray her? Against Kyle's objections, she'd gone to help Terrence but there had been no clear understanding as to her role that night. Besides, since murder was way out of her league, she'd retained the best criminal attorney in town to represent him. Apparently, he was too good. That ungrateful bastard, Jeremy Kaplan. The two of them were toying with her life. Gaining Terrence his freedom at her expense.

And if Terrence discarded their friendship in such a cavalier fashion, she could only imagine what else he'd freely divulge.

Fueled by rage, Jessie settled into the den sofa intending to address Terrence's venomous lies, but stopped. She could feel her blood pressure throbbing in her temples and knew that her present state was unhealthy for both herself and her child. She forced the anger to subside with a deep cleansing breath and softly hummed a lullaby to the baby growing inside her.

Hush little baby, don't say a word.

Mama's going to buy you a mockingbird.

Now, it was just the two of them against the world.

Jessie must have drifted off because daylight had faded when she awoke to her belly hardening into a rock and a pleasant tingling stimulating her groin. She rubbed the sleep from her eyes as the Braxton Hicks subsided and she ventured into the hallway. The front door knob jiggled and the door creaked open.

"What are you doing here?" she asked, startled by the unexpected visitor.

CHAPTER
35

Jeremy sat at the kitchen table listening to silence. He was eating a tuna fish sandwich, a late lunch borne from the boredom of waiting for the DA to make her next move in the life-and-death chess game they were playing. The house was quiet when the kids and Gayle weren't puttering around. Only the appliances whirled and hummed, making their presence known. It wasn't often that he had the place to himself and he relished the peace, the aloneness.

He unfolded the *Times*, spread it out on the kitchen table, and flipped to the Metropolitan Section. There were feature stories about a fire in a Yonkers warehouse, a veterinarian who was busted for giving pot to his furry patients, and a free film series at a park on the Hudson River in Poughkeepsie. There was no mention of the Paige boy's murder.

Jeremy was jealous. He craved publicity, and his case deserved more attention than a stoned animal doctor.

There's time. Plenty of time, he thought.

He rose and returned downstairs to the office. His gait was confident, smooth, and relaxed. One-hundred-and-eighty degrees from the tight rubber-band man of the morning. The lunch break had done him good.

"We've been busy," Mo said, with wide eyes and a frazzled expression. Her henna hair sprang up, giving a bedhead appearance. "Check out the messages on your desk. A couple of new clients made appointments, and the press has been calling for comments about Butterfield. Oh, and there's a packet from the DA."

He thanked her, grabbed a cup of coffee, and headed into his office. Two stacks of messages lay atop a large manila package. He read through the potential client messages first—a commercial real estate closing, an automobile accident, and an estate proceeding. Mo always vetted the cases and only scheduled those of value into his appointment calendar. Not bad for a day's work.

Next, he fanned out an even larger pile of inquiries—the local papers, the New York City metro television stations, NBC, CBS, ABC, CNN, HNN, FOX, the *Daily News*, and the *New York Post*. With Columbine copycat stories inundating the media, a teacher murdering and butchering a student was definitely fresh headline news. His heart lightened. They'd found him after all. Then it sank at the possibility that his new popularity was the work of a prankster.

Jeremy screamed for Mo and she popped her head into the doorway. "Is this some kind of a sick joke or something?"

"Jeremy, that's what I thought at first. But the phone's been ringing off the hook all afternoon. After a while, I was praying that Anderson Cooper would call. He's gorg-e-ous!" She mugged an exaggerated frown.

"I'm assuming that he didn't."

"Not yet. But you never know."

"I'll ask Gayle to help draft a press release. She's the wordsmith of the family," he said. "Knows how to massage a phrase and lick my unruly sentence structure into shape. She gets to the point in a hurry."

"I bet she does." Mo pursed her lips.

Jeremy felt his face warm. But really, he could care less about Mo's innuendos. He was back with a vengeance.

He decided that the media could wait for a formal statement, but the package from the district attorney could not. From beneath the twine binding the package, he retrieved a white envelope bearing his name and opened the note inside.

Jeremy:

Thought you would like to review your client's handiwork.

Truly,

Hal Samuels

He cut the string and unsealed the package. Inside were two folders marked, respectively, CRIME SCENE PHOTOS and PAIGE AUTOPSY. He opened the photo folder. As a defense attorney, he'd seen it all before. How bad could these be?

The first was a wide-angle view of a basement, an old-fashioned unfinished cellar with a concrete floor and steel columns supporting the overhead structure. In one corner sat a washer and dryer with baskets neatly stacked on top. He flipped to the next picture, which appeared to be the opposite side of the room, apparently the murder scene. There were pools of congealed blood spattering the concrete floor. He flipped to the next, which showed a human skull that was smashed like a melon with its pulp exposed. And to the next, a naked male torso. And the next, bruised black and blue hands and feet bound to their mates with rope soaked red with blood. Another showed bloody footprints climbing the basement stairs. On and on. Scarlet handprints smeared across kitchen walls. A bloody butcher's knife in the sink.

Jeremy dropped the folder as though it burned his fingertips. He couldn't take anymore. No crime scene photos he'd ever seen could compare to these. Nor could any feeling compare to the loathing he felt for Terrence Butterfield. He'd believed himself to be hardened to the sight of bodies marred by bullet holes and knife wounds, but none he'd seen matched this butchery.

Before the murder, he'd had a passing knowledge of Terrence Butterfield, of his reputation and involvement in the community. The guy was a high school history teacher, surrounded by kids every day. Including Jeremy's own kids, all four of them. Without a doubt, his client's recent demeanor hinted at a crazy man but not a sadistic slaughterer.

He prided himself on having honed his client radar. Generally, it took him less than ten minutes to read a person. Whenever he interviewed a potential client in his office or at the jailhouse, his senses engaged. He observed. He listened. When answering whether they committed the crime, did they look him straight in the eye? The flash of a nervous smile. The too-long pause of a beat.

The twitching of an eye. What was their body language whispering to or yelling at him? Were they a liar? Would they be a pain in the neck? Would they pay his fee? Their responses determined whether or not he'd represent them. Save their lives. Set them free. Expunge their record. Work a deal.

Apparently, his superpowers had failed him with Terrence Butterfield. Or had he been so desperate and financially strapped that he'd ignored the signs?

If the truth be told, he was a whore. Jeremy was no different from his crack-addicted streetwalker client turning tricks under the railroad bridges down by the river. His conscience had come to grips with that fact long ago. Unlike the hooker's cheap sequins and hot pants, his uniform was a finely tailored Armani suit. The legal tricks he performed were a sophisticated parlor game. The client, the prosecutor, and the judge all desired a piece of him. Sometimes, he performed for them and other times they drained him dry.

Like an addict, he was hooked on the high of playing God and Redeemer to the weak, the stupid, and the caught. Butterfield's case fed this addiction. And the addiction to win again.

Jeremy forced himself to study the photographs again, although the images were already branded into his brain. He'd never be able to shake them off. A cold shiver ran down his spine, confirming the new revelations about Terrence Butterfield.

An unfamiliar flutter invaded his chest. He placed his fingers on the vein throbbing in his wrist, measuring the rapid palpitations. He struggled for breath, fighting the lightheadedness, the weakness. His shaking hands scavenged the cluttered desk drawer, searching for the aspirin bottle. He popped the cap, spilling its contents across the desktop. He dry-swallowed two pills and waited for the chest pressure to dissipate and his heart to return to normal.

Relaxing back in his chair, Jeremy wiped the beads of sweat from his brow with his handkerchief. He felt drained, exhausted. He closed his eyes, his consciousness drifting off to a sunny beach. Crystalline waters tumbled against the shoreline. A cloudless sky extended as far as the eye could see. A gentle breeze kissed his face.

"Jeremy?" a voice said.

"I'll have a Corona," he murmured.

"Jeremy, wake up."

A hand nudged his shoulder. His eyes popped open.

"You must've fallen asleep," Mo said. "It's after five. I'm heading home."

"Yeah, sure. Okay," he mumbled, blinking his eyes. "See you tomorrow."

CHAPTER
36

J essie stared at her guest as though he was a mirage. He'd never barged in unannounced before, even though a spare key was safely tucked under the geranium pot next to the front door. A code existed between the father and daughter—he'd ring the bell and wait for her to answer. But not today. Ed Martin was standing in her foyer, his weathered face tense. At the sight of her, his shoulders dropped away from his ears to their normal position and she thought she heard a sigh escape from his parched lips.

"Honey, I didn't mean to wake you." Her father huffed, almost out of breath. "But when we called and there was no answer, your mother was frantic and refused to quit bugging me until I came over. Just in case there was a problem. You know how she is." Ed Martin slipped his arm around his daughter's shoulder and guided her into the kitchen.

For a split second, Jessie considered slapping on a mock smile to reassure her dad that everything was fine, that Kyle was away on a business trip, she and the baby were healthy, and she was enjoying the sabbatical from work. She'd try to evade his probing, but she'd always been a lousy liar, especially where her father was concerned. From his decades as the Poughkeepsie High School principal, Ed Martin had developed a keen sense about trouble, and an uncanny ability to unearth the pranks and shenanigans of his students. He could weasel a confession out of any reprobate. Ed's nose wrinkled as though sniffing the air.

"Dad...Kyle moved out yesterday," Jessie said. She told him about Kyle's new job, the lies of omission, and the ultimatum that she leave Poughkeepsie. She felt guilty about burdening him with her problems. He had enough on his mind with Terrence's arrest and Ryan's murder. His close friend and his pupil. Without him saying so, she knew that he'd taken it pretty hard. And she suspected that he felt somehow responsible since he'd hired Terrence almost twenty years ago.

His pale gray eyes softened, their bright twinkle replaced by cataract dullness. Her father had a soft spot for Kyle, and his frown indicated that the news had struck him completely out of the blue. The disappointment on his face smashed her heart like a sledgehammer.

"I should've known he was keeping something from me. You know, his mind always seemed to be off somewhere else. And he's been so annoyed about my being dragged into Ryan's case," Jessie said.

"Now, honey. Don't go blaming yourself. Do you want me to talk to him, you know, father-in-law to son-in-law?"

"No. No way. Let us work it out on our own. Please don't call him, or Mom either."

"One question." He looked her straight in the eye. "Would you move to Brooklyn?"

"I don't know what to do. You and Mom are here. My friends, my job. Our house. We're settled. At least I thought we were." She paused. "And there's something else." She recounted the details about Butterfield's tactic to dismiss the murder charges.

"That miserable son of a bitch. After everything this family has done for him." From the tone of his voice, it was difficult to figure out whether his rage was aimed at Terrence, Kyle, or both men. But it made no difference; they'd both betrayed her.

"Dad—please don't get upset that I'm asking—but did you call the police that night?"

"Certainly not. As soon as I got off the phone with you, I called Terry. I didn't want him blowing his brains out on my watch. Maybe I should've let him." Ed removed his frayed baseball cap, scratched his graying head, and opened the refrigerator door. He grabbed a beer and joined her at the kitchen table.

While he savored the IPA, she rewound the night of the murder frame-by-frame, scene-by-scene, in her head. The phone call, Kyle's insistence that the police handle the matter, the mad dash to Terrence's home, and each step culminating to the arrest. While her fiancé had been persistent in dissuading her from helping Terrence, as far as she could remember he'd remained by her side during the entire evening. From their bedroom to the car to

Terrence's porch steps. Had Kyle made the call? He was the only possible suspect.

"This doesn't make any sense at all," she muttered.

"Did you say something, honey?" Ed said, swigging the beer.

Jessie shook her head, not ready to share her suspicions with her father.

"Maybe you should call Kyle. Talk things out."

She met his suggestion with the look, *that* look. The one that he joked reminded him of her mother. The one that said I love you but if you know what is best for you, please leave well enough alone. Her dad understood.

The phone sounded down the hallway and she let it go unanswered. For the past several weeks, she'd given up answering the landline. If she wanted to speak with anyone, she'd contact them.

"Don't you need to get that? Kyle may be calling right now." Ed wiped the foam from his chin on his shirtsleeve.

"I'll deal with it later." It was time to deflect. "Dad, what's new with you?"

In between sips, Ed nervously picked at the beer label and revealed the present state of the fall term: the students' deteriorating respect for authority, the new faculty members, the worsening staff morale, and how Terrence's unexpected vacancy snowballed into issues and inconveniences. While the substitute teachers were covering the history classes, they were a temporary fix. Hiring a new faculty member under these bizarre circumstances was the last thing he'd expected to be dealing with, particularly when, despite the shortage of teaching positions, no one wanted to be Butterfield's successor.

"Like the job is cursed or something. Ridiculous," he said, peeling the remaining bits of label from the bottle. "I can't believe what a disloyal, ungrateful louse Terry turned out to be. You know, it's like when you read about these tragedies in the papers and the neighbors say that the guy was always so quiet and kept to himself. It's like that." Ed's eyes became teary and he crushed the paper pieces in his fist. "I saw Terry every single day and I never saw this coming, not in a million years. He always seemed normal and healthy to me. It's unfathomable." He let out a deep breath. "And the toll on your mother. It's a tough thing to realize that one of your closest friends and co-workers is Dr. Jekyll and Mr. Hyde."

Ed blotted his eyes with his sleeves and grabbed another bottle from the fridge. "You wouldn't believe the fallout from the parents and students. The petitions. The emails. The drop-ins. All claiming that I endangered the safety of my students. Their children. And the school board is breathing down my neck as though I orchestrated the murder myself."

Her father said that he was considering taking some public relations action, perhaps holding a town hall session to lessen everyone's fears. He asked for her thoughts on the subject and about whether he was subjecting the school to any liability.

"For what? About what?" She'd half-heard his chattering. Her mind was still mulling over the phone call to the police station. When he repeated his idea Jessie begged off. "You should contact the school district's attorney. They'll know how to proceed."

"The hardest thing is that I've put you in this horrible situation. Your job and now Kyle. Jess, sweetie, I'm so sorry. You're the last person that I want to hurt."

She gave him a light peck on the cheek and rubbed his shoulders. After hearing his problems, hers seemed minor in comparison. "Don't worry about me. I'll get through this. We both will. We Martins, we're tough, right?"

Her father smiled weakly. He drained the last sip from the second naked green bottle as she watched in silence. "One last thing," he said. "Humor the old man, will you? Give your guy a call. I'm sure you two can patch things up."

"I'll think about it," Jessie said, concealing the irritation in her voice, "but I can't make any promises."

After her father had gone, she pressed the button on the winking answering machine and discovered that there were ten new messages. She hit play. Kyle. Her mother. Kyle. Hal. Her mother. Her mother. Hal. Kyle. Robbie. She hit erase.

CHAPTER
37

Jessie tossed and turned in bed. Her temples throbbed with a pressure unlike she'd ever experienced. She rose, went to the bathroom, and returned with a cool washcloth. She placed it on her forehead and lay back on her pillow praying for a respite from the incessant pounding in her head. Although she'd felt relief during the daytime, now she feared the blood pressure medication wasn't working. Or was the pain of loneliness eating her up inside?

She reached out to Kyle's side of the bed searching for his warmth and comfort, but there was none. She missed him.

In the moonlight, her eyes made out a spider spinning its web on the ceiling. A housefly buzzed around and fell prey to the sticky fibers. Jessie empathized with the captured fly that struggled to be free but grew tired and weak in the process.

Lately, death seemed to be dangling over her like an anvil on a frayed cord. Death. Hers. The baby's. The worries haunted her mostly at night, in the darkness when she was alone.

Her eyelids refused to shut as her mind raced, keyed up with anger at the spider, the fly, Kyle, Terrence, Jeremy Kaplan, and Hal. The baby, reacting to her adrenal rush, refused to sleep as well. Jessie shifted onto her side, hummed softly, and stroked her belly. She felt exhausted while all the baby wanted to do was somersault.

Shortly after dawn, she abandoned any possibility of sleep. After throwing on a T-shirt and maternity jeans, she returned to the den, collected Kaplan's handiwork from the coffee table, and sat down at her desk, ready to attack the documents. She'd pretend that she was representing a client, objectively analyzing the accusations through her attorney's lens and keeping her emotions in check. Then, she'd hatch her plan.

When the grandfather clock struck eight, she secured the thick package with a rubber band, placed it inside her tote bag, and climbed into her Jeep. It was necessary to arrive at her destination by eight-thirty to complete the necessary paperwork for her nine o'clock appointment. This was to be her first visit to the Dutchess County Jail.

Jessie's knees trembled as she passed the security guards milling around the visitation hall. On the far wall, there were a half-dozen booths where thick glass partitions separated the inmates from their guests. While a few cubicles were already in use, the surveillance cameras affixed in each corner were of no comfort. Nothing about the drab, gray room made her feel safe or secure, but she was determined to confront Terrence, no matter the result.

On the drive over to the jail, she'd practiced her speech. She would control the conversation, reminding him about their long history together. She'd mention the family barbecues, holiday parties, fishing trips, and Yankee's games they'd shared as well as the discussions, often heated debates, over their opposing opinions about the school district, supreme court decisions, and the state of the union. She'd be forthright about how distressed her parents were by his actions. Destroyed, in fact.

She'd try to hide her fury from Terrence although her anger over his betrayals and lies equaled, if not surpassed, the pain of her broken heart. She'd calmly demand answers about the allegations put forth in Kaplan's documents and press him to recant and withdraw his papers for the sake of their friendship. She knew Terrence well enough to know that he'd cave if she preyed upon his affection for her. Well, she *thought* she knew Terrence. Maybe she'd be wrong in this instance, too.

Terrence was waiting in the cubicle at the far left-hand side. Jessie approached the glass partition, taking a seat in the visitor's chair. She was disconcerted by his condition; his face was drawn and sallow-skinned. He was a shadow of the handsome educator who'd made all the teenage girls swoon.

His nose twitched as though he smelled her coming toward him. He reached for the black phone receiver and signaled for her to do likewise. "Jessica," he said, "I'm surprised to see you here. When they said I had a visitor, I had no idea it was you. I'm delighted. You're looking well. A bit tired, but well. How's Kyle? Your father?" He smiled at her and she tasted the sour bile in her mouth.

"Terrence, cut the crap." Jessie was stunned at the vehemence of her rage, and that out of the gate, the conversation wasn't proceeding as it had inside her head. She reached into her bag, withdrew the packet, and slammed it on the ledge of the window separating them. "Where do you get off dragging me into your mess?"

"What are you talking about? I'm not doing anything. I'm in here." He mocked her naiveté and rattled his chains. Jessie just stared at him, so he continued, "Jessica, I sense from your bitterness that you're not in the mood for games, so I'll be straight with you. It all came down to the math. I'm relatively young, forty-four, and if I'm found guilty, I'll spend the rest of my life in prison. Assuming that I live to be eighty, that's thirty-six years. You haven't even been alive that long. Thirty-six years is an eternity. You know me; I'm not made for this. I've been inside less than a month and know that this is hell on earth." He hesitated and winced as he rubbed his bandaged wrists. "It was either you or me, I'm sorry to say. What's the worst that could happen to you if my charges are dismissed? Maybe you'd get censured. Or maybe you'd lose your license. Me, if I lose, I'm stuck in here forever. I made a choice and I picked me."

Jessie scrutinized the man who looked like Terrence and sounded like Terrence. It was as though an evil spirit possessed him, rendering him unrecognizable. He wasn't the same man who'd trudged through a thunderstorm with her dad to rescue her car from a ditch. Nor was he the kind, caring man who'd opened his home to her during her time of need. This man was selfish, arrogant, and malicious. He showed no remorse for Ryan's murder, and he assumed no responsibility for the harm he'd caused her. Nor did he acknowledge her loyalty to him.

"Why are you being so cruel?" she asked. "What's happened to you?"

The corners of his lips curled into a sinister smirk. "Whatever do you mean?"

All traces of her friend, mentor, and confidante, along with any sympathy she'd ever felt for him, were washed away with the tide. It was a soulless shell speaking to her. Her Terrence was dead, just like the cold marble eyes waiting for her response.

"You have no idea the damage you've wreaked. To the Paiges. To me and my family. I've worked hard on my career and my life, and there's no way I'm going to let a murderer like you drag me into the sewer with you."

"For god's sake, don't be so melodramatic. You've always been such a golden child. That's why I took an interest in you, my dear. You twinkled like a star, so full of promise." He fluttered his hands in the air rattling his chains. "And so impressionable. You were someone I could easily mold into a stellar student and jurist, who'd make me proud to be your teacher … your mentor." His lips turned downward momentarily. "What the teacher giveth, the teacher can taketh away."

She'd been anxiously chewing on the inside of her cheek and the metallic taste of blood mixed with disgust filled her mouth. Long ago, Terrence had inspired her, but he'd had nothing to do with her motivation, hard work, and success. It struck her that jealousy and insanity were fueling his revenge against her. He couldn't take credit for the life she'd made or the child she was about to bring into the world. Unfortunately, his delusions were as real as the threats against her.

"This isn't all about you, Terrence. You're screwing around with my life and it's having real consequences."

"Don't worry. People will forget about this little incident and you'll move on to another opportunity. You always do." He pressed his greasy forehead against the glass as though he was stepping through it to grab her. The legs of her chair screeched across the floor as she skidded backward. "Look at it this way—you're making a sacrifice to save me. Isn't that what true friends do for each other? Isn't that what I always have done for you?"

Her chest tightened as she gathered the strength to speak the truth that had been gnawing at her since she'd read his affidavit. "We're no longer friends. I don't know who you are. I guess I never did."

"Be that as it may, we've shared too many confidences with each other. Secrets better kept between the two of us. Don't you agree, my darling?" The phone slid from his hands and he smashed his palms against the partition with such force that it vibrated.

Jessie dropped the receiver and jumped from her chair as a guard rushed toward Terrence. The guard clasped a hand on his shoulder, signaling the end of their session. Angrily, Terrence brushed off the warning and planted his thick lips on the shiny surface of the plate glass window in a sloppy kiss. A pair of sheriffs rushed to reinforce their coworker while Terrence struggled, becoming an orange blur of arms and legs. The hall fell silent as all eyes inspected Jessie and the commotion in the far booth.

"I hope you get what you deserve," Jessie shouted, "and I'll make sure that you do." Sadly, she'd never meant anything so much in her life.

After she returned home, Jessie reexamined Kaplan's motion for a third time. Her pulse pounded in her temples, clouding her vision. Her trembling hands flung the document into the fireplace and its screen collapsed inward as though extinguishing its own embers. Her fingertips rubbed against her throbbing eye sockets, willing them to restore their blurry sight.

Jessie sank on the couch wondering how, in the short space of a month, her life had turned upside down. What had she done to deserve the bad karma being heaped upon her? Had she invited it upon herself? She cursed her stupid idea of visiting Terrence in jail. What had she hoped to accomplish, a grand reunion?

God, he pissed her off. She'd let Terrence bait her into losing control—a trick he'd pulled on others, but never before on her. At least she'd observed the devil first-hand and recognized that there was no restoring their friendship or her devotion to him. That was g-o-n-e. Forever.

At that moment, the baby kicked her in the ribs. Hard. Once. Twice. Three times. As though he/she were scolding her: *Stop feeling sorry for yourself. Get off your butt. Do something.*

Damn right, she thought. She retrieved the document from the ashes and set to work.

Kaplan and Terrence's affidavits were concise and biting. Their razor-sharp fangs gnawed through her thick lawyer's hide. At fifty pages, the accompanying legal brief was intimidating in its length and cogency. Kaplan's clever argument blamed her for the police intervention on the night of the murder, nullifying all evidence gathered on the scene, including Terrence's admissions of guilt.

By the fourth reading, the synapses in her attorney's brain burned white hot. She slaved away, documenting the fact and fiction of the night in question. Her hand cramped as it feverishly attempted to keep pace with her legal imagination. By midday, her task was complete.

"Are you all right? You sound strange," Hal said to Jessie over the phone. The tone in her voice rang with an icy edge. She spoke rapidly, countering Kaplan's allegations, almost too fast for him to follow. Bordering on hysterical.

"I'm merely stating the facts of the case. Don't you believe me?"

"Of course I do." He understood that she was upset. There was a great deal at stake.

Silence.

Something else was wrong. He could sense it. But time was of the essence. Court procedure required a response to the motion within three days, one of which had already slipped away. He refused to give Kaplan the satisfaction of granting him an extension. That would reflect a sign of weakness. So his staff was grinding away to meet the deadline.

"Can you come in for a meeting today?" As soon as the request slipped out, he regretted it. He should have offered to go over to her home, but that was complicated.

"Come on, Hal. I can't just hop on in. After my last trip to the hospital, I'm supposed to be on bed rest. Like I've had the chance with this frivolous paperwork, and I'm not sleeping very well."

Hal knew it. She was ill and wasn't telling him. As soon as he hung up, he'd surprise her and come over. They'd figure this situation out together. Then, Lauren's insinuations sounded an alarm in his brain, and he reconsidered. Better to keep a little distance. For now.

"How about a video conference?" he asked. "Let's plan on this afternoon around four o'clock. Cindie will call you with the details. Does that work for you?"

"Apparently, I don't have a choice, do I?"

"We both know that Kaplan is scraping the bottom of the barrel. So let's go through the motion papers and get this request denied. Look, I don't blame you for disbelieving anything I say, but I'll take care of you. Trust me." *Trust me.* He had no right to ask that of her again, but he was sincere. Just like he'd meant every previous time.

"Harold Samuels III, please don't ever use that phrase with me."

"I promise that I've got your back. Talk to you later." Hal hung up the phone, feeling like a complete schmuck. And regretting everything he'd ever done to disappoint her.

CHAPTER
38

The quality of the video on Jessie's laptop was less than perfect, but it sufficed. Occasionally, the images froze in mid-sentence, but the video conference proceeded as scheduled.

On the screen, Hal, with his shirtsleeves rolled up and tie loosened around his neck, patiently asked her questions, direct and on point, about Kaplan's statements. To his left, Cindie busily transcribed her responses on a computer. To his right, the district attorney observed the discussion, clucking her tongue just loud enough to be captured by the microphone. Hal's face tightened at his chief's childish behavior, especially when the puppet master interrupted him with a nudge to the shoulder or a word in the ear.

Following the advice that she gave to her clients— "just the facts, no commentary"—Jessie carefully reconstructed the timeline of August 31st. From Terrence's telephone call at 1:00 a.m., to her trip to his home around 1:20 a.m., to the jail interview and the court arraignment before Judge Hughes at 5:30 a.m. Every interaction and conversation with Terrence, Kyle, her father, Kaplan, and Ebony Jones was discussed and dissected for their potential impact upon Terrence's claims until she grew bored with the sound of her own voice.

"The key is to raise a legal issue, which requires Judge Hamilton to order a hearing and to prevent him from rendering a decision on the motion papers," Hal said. He absentmindedly twirled his pen between his fingers. "No judge is going to dismiss a murder one without hearing the testimony of the parties. Especially in this case. He'll meticulously draft his decision to thwart an appeal. And no judge relishes getting his decision appealed on a potential life sentence."

"You can philosophize all you like, Hal, but I have a few more questions for Ms. Martin if you don't mind?" Hollenbeck asked, impatiently. "Good. Let's cut to the chase, shall we? Where was your fiancé during the evening?"

"With me, the entire time," Jessie said. Realizing that she was nibbling on her nails, she promptly balled her hands into a fist and dropped them into her lap.

"Are you telling us that Mr. Emory was with you every second, from the time you hung up from the phone call with Mr. Butterfield, until your arrival at the police station? What about when you were freshening up in the bathroom? Was he with you then?"

"No, Kyle was getting dressed in the bedroom. It was pretty chaotic, but we were separated for a couple of minutes. That's all. We were in a hurry get to Terrence's house."

"So, long enough to make a phone call to the police." The DA pressed her angular face close to the monitor as if seeking Jessie on the opposite side.

"Is that a question or a statement?" Jessie felt herself on dangerous ground, less than an arm's length away from the silky web of the black widow.

"Have you asked Mr. Emory whether or not he contacted the police?" Hollenbeck persisted.

"No."

"Why not? Didn't you consider the answer significant to your exoneration? Are you afraid of the answer, Ms. Martin?"

"Kyle would never do anything like that, so it never crossed my mind," she replied sheepishly.

"Well, maybe it should have, Ms. Martin." Lauren's nostrils flared and Jessie could practically see steam streaming out of them. "Maybe he's not as honorable as you think."

"Lauren, come on. This isn't an interrogation. We're all working together here. Besides, we can follow up with Emory. At this point, I think we have sufficient information to draft Jessie's reply affidavit. Cindie, Lauren, can you give us a minute, please?" Hal asked.

The district attorney shoved her chair away from the conference table in a huff and left the room along with Cindie.

Hal looked over his shoulder, confirming their departure, and leaned closer toward the screen. "I know that this situation is uncomfortable for you and for some reason, you're not one of Lauren's favorite people. All I can do is apologize for her behavior. She's not as bad as she seems. A bit trying, that's all."

"Maybe for you. To me, she's the wicked witch."

He laughed. "We're all good for now. You can expect the draft of your affidavit in your inbox later this evening. And Jess, I don't mean to pry, but do you know how I can get in touch with Emory? He's not answering his cell."

It had been days since she and Kyle had argued and he'd moved out of their home. Since then, at her father's urging, she'd phoned him several times but had never spoken to him directly. Kyle was avoiding her by playing phone tag. He'd left messages on their home's answering machine, knowing that she rarely checked the machine and that the best way to reach her was her cell phone.

When she'd retrieved his messages, they'd been simple. *Got your call. Busy, can't talk. I'll talk to you later.* Not even an "I love you" or asking about the baby. She'd expected more from him after four years together, but his reaction left them no middle ground. She was willing to talk, to discuss their options. Not give up because he'd chosen Brooklyn and she'd chosen Poughkeepsie.

Kyle's radio silence could only signal one thing. Their relationship was over. Deal with it.

With Hal's question, a dozen emotions and fears flooded through Jessie, clouding her ability to maintain a thin veneer of pride. Anxiety. Grief. Self-Doubt. Humiliation. Abandonment. Anger. She struggled to concentrate on the life growing inside her, not the petty war waging outside the womb between the grownups.

"I'd try the Barclay's Center. If you speak with him, please tell him that the baby and I are fine. Just in case he's interested." Jessie swiveled her face away from the camera's eye to avoid it capturing her tears.

Jessie pulled the dove grey pashmina, a present from Kyle on their first anniversary, around her shoulders to ward off the evening chill. She loved the twilight, when day met night, when both the sun and the moon glowed in the sky. She especially loved their new bluestone patio, the one that Ryan had helped Kyle install. She padded barefoot across the cold stones toward the wicker rocker and sat down. Her tight shoulders relaxed as she rocked gently. Around her, the towering maples blended into the night.

After dinner, she'd tackled her reply affidavit and had been pleased that Hal's staff had captured the essence of her statement. She had not contacted the police on the night of Ryan's murder nor had she been retained as Terrence's attorney. Hopefully, these points raised sufficient issues to require Judge Hamilton to set a hearing.

At the moment, Terrence Butterfield was her least worry.

In the crisp evening air, the pregnancy symptoms that had plagued her all day melted away. Gone was the aching in her breasts and the arch of her back, the bloated ankles and fingers, and the mild throbbing in her temples. It was a miracle. Her head lolled to the side as she slipped into a light sleep.

Soft fur brushed against her bare legs, startling her awake. Jessie discovered that her cat was nuzzling her, announcing his stomach was empty. She shooed him away, disoriented by a disturbing dream—or was it a memory? Terrence, Robbie, Ryan, Hal, and Kyle were at a party where Robbie was playing Frisbee with Ryan. Terrence stood off in a corner eyeing her. She was late to meet Kyle for a dinner date, so she began to run toward her car. Hal chased her, while his pregnant wife conversed with a group of friends. When he caught her, a silence undulated between them like the breeze, pulling them together and blowing them apart. Then, she'd woken up.

Jessie shook it off, but a sense of guilt lingered. The dream made her feel like she'd somehow disappointed the men in her life, when in truth it had been the other way around. Except for Ryan. He'd been so sweet and kind and had never let her down. Yet, she couldn't escape the feeling that she should have protected him from Terrence. In her heart, she knew that her self-reproach was unfounded because Ryan's murder had been so horribly random. There was nothing she could have done to prevent it.

She lifted herself up from the rocker and followed the feline toward the kitchen door. The sound of footsteps crunching on the gravel driveway stopped her in her tracks. A shadowy figure turned the corner of the house and crossed the patio toward her.

"Hey, there," Kyle said, his voice was as chilly as the evening.

Jessie wobbled and steadied herself against the outdoor grill. "Kyle, you frightened me."

"I've received all of your messages, but I wasn't ready to talk. I can't believe that you had your boyfriend track me down at work." Kyle remained hidden in the darkness so she couldn't make out his expression, but his arms were folded tightly across his chest. "Our problems are for you and me to resolve. It's nobody else's business."

"Maybe we could work them out if you let go of your petty jealousies and communicated with me. And I'm comforted to see how concerned you are about me and the baby."

"Don't be ridiculous. Of course I've been worried sick about you. I love you, you know that…I want to spend the rest of my life with you, but your father suggested that I give you some time and space to get over—"

"Get over what, Kyle? That you lied to me? Accepted a job behind my back? That after all this time, I have no clue who you are? That I have no idea where in the world you are and that you're avoiding me?"

"I haven't been avoiding you. I just needed to get my head straight. After all, you've been the one calling all the shots around here lately."

"What's that supposed to mean?"

"We were supposed to be getting married two weeks from now, remember?" he asked. His tone was as sharp as the edges of his shadow that stretched across the lawn to her feet.

"I've been waiting for you to throw that back into my face. That's unfair and you know it. Between my morning sickness, and the exhaustion and stresses of our jobs, I couldn't handle it. We both agreed to wait until after the baby was born." She paused. "Given the circumstances, it was a blessing in disguise." She regretted her words the moment they'd slipped through her lips, but his twisting of the facts irked her.

"Jessie, let's not forget that you're the one who gave me the boot."

"That's untrue. This separation was mutual. You know that I love you, but you're making this so hard for me. Too hard." She sniffled back the tears. "So, why exactly are you here? Did you forget something?"

Kyle sighed deeply and shook his head. "I'm sorry for everything, for things getting so out of control. Really I am, but it's complicated. I thought I was making the right decision." His voice turned soft, gentle as if he, too, was choking back tears. "I didn't expect to argue with you tonight, I just wanted to stop by to make sure you were doing all right. And to let you know that my coming home is not an option. Not right away, but soon. Maybe when the baby comes." He extended his hand through the blackness toward her. "How are you feeling? And the baby? May I please, you know, touch...?"

"Don't come near me, Kyle," Jessie said, bitterly. She couldn't believe her ears. Not only was Kyle accusing her of being controlling and manipulative, he possessed the unmitigated gall to think he could simply return to their home, her life, and the baby's life on his own whim. As though nothing had happened.

"I'd better get going. I need to get back to the city." Kyle moved toward her again and she backed away, tugging the shawl tighter around her body. "I'll give you a call when work calms down a bit. Then, we'll talk." As quickly as Kyle had arrived, he was gone.

Jessie opened her mouth to call after the shadow, but her body shivered in the dusk's sudden dampness. The doorknob turned icy beneath her fingers and she entered the kitchen, wiping her tears with the shawl's fringe. She cursed herself for allowing wrath to gain the better of her, confusing her thoughts and the love she felt for Kyle. She'd always wondered about what reduced once-loving couples to enemies. But she'd never worried about Kyle or let doubt seep into her thoughts. She'd thought their relationship was mature and honest. In retrospect, she realized that she'd been guilty of hubris, struck blind by love and happiness.

She imagined herself running down the driveway to his BMW, him rolling down the window, and her asking him back inside to talk. The two of them sitting at the kitchen table with their hands clasped. His face buried in her breasts as she listened to his apologies and declarations of love. Working out their issues together, compromising and making plans. Then, flying to the bedroom for make-up sex, every kiss a promise of the future.

The sudden rock-hard Braxton-Hicks and the warmth of pee in her panties shocked Jessie back to reality.

CHAPTER
39

A young man shouted at Hal Samuels from the top of the courthouse stairs. He'd been unaware of the clerk's attempt to obtain his attention until he'd heard his name called twice. He turned around and stared at the out-of-breath boy who was bent at the waist, his bowtie bobbing up and down like a yo-yo. The clerk informed him that Judge Hamilton desired his presence in chambers, *in arbitrium judicis*—at the pleasure of the judge. Jeremy Kaplan was already waiting there.

Hal straightened his own tie and accompanied the clerk to see the judge. In the large anteroom, a silver-haired secretary smiled and requested that he take a seat on the wooden bench next to Jeremy Kaplan. The judge was finishing up on the phone and would see them momentarily. Kaplan, stationed mid-bench and balancing his briefcase on his lap, slid over to make room as the men exchanged last-name greetings. While it was not unusual to be summoned into the judge's chambers, it felt like he and Kaplan had been called into the principal's office for starting a fight. It was unclear who had thrown the first punch.

Judge Perry Hamilton welcomed the two attorneys into his office, gesturing toward the conference table that formed a T-shape with his large oak desk. He was a man in his early fifties who'd invested time and energy in maintaining the youthful appearance and physique of his college baseball years. Just as he'd wound his way through the line-up to the top of the pitching order, the man had worked his way through the court system. First, as a local magistrate, then, after one term in family court, he'd been elected to his present seat in county court where he presided over the criminal docket.

It sometimes annoyed Hal that despite Judge Hamilton's reputation for fairness, the judge preferred to referee disputes rather than rule on them. And when called upon to render a decision, Judge Hamilton practiced a strict, almost biblical dedication to precedent rather than to creating law. The judge played by the rules and didn't make them up as he dispensed justice.

Taking their designated slots, Hal and Jeremy waited for the judge to proceed.

"Gentleman," Hamilton began, "we have quite an interesting ballgame here. Mr. Kaplan, I have your motion kicking around on my desk and I can tell you right now, I'm setting the matter down for a hearing. There's no way I'm deciding a dismissal request of a felony murder on the papers. So, Mr. Samuels, I trust I'll be receiving your reply shortly, but I thought we should set the hearing date on my calendar. Unless there's an offer on the table?"

Hal felt like a major league pitcher, at the bottom of the ninth inning. It was his game to lose. "Judge, there's no offer in this case at the present time."

"I can understand that, it's early. Or perhaps, Mr. Kaplan, you'd like to save us all some time and withdraw the motion. I'm not suggesting that I've made a decision, but considering the gravity of the allegations made against a fellow barrister and the likelihood of your success on the merits, you may want to invest your time into alternative defenses for your client."

Strike one. Hal kept a straight face as Kaplan squirmed in his chair. The judge had done his homework and was clearly telegraphing his intentions. It was evident that the court viewed Kaplan's request as a complete waste of time. Since it looked like a win for the prosecution, Hal thought he'd throw his weight around a bit.

"Kaplan, your client may have nothing to lose, but what about the waste of judicial resources and my staff's time on this frivolous motion?" Hal asked. And the damage to Jessie Martin, he thought.

"Frivolous? Counselor, who are you to call it frivolous?" Kaplan asked.

Hal made another pitch and Kaplan had taken the swing. The judge's eyes fell on him eagerly waiting for a reply, but Hal remained silent and calculated his next move. He inched his way to the edge of the wooden chair, its sharp edge digging into his thighs. The pain urged him onward. "Your Honor, the rules of professional conduct specifically bar the theory asserted in the motion—his claim does not exist under the law. The defense is fabricating facts and stretching the law beyond the limit." He turned toward Kaplan. "I trust that clarifies my usage of the word 'frivolous.'"

Strike two.

"You'd better read the code again, my friend. Under your weak argument, the court could never make new law. Maybe you're just out of your league with this one, Samuels." A sly smile crossed Kaplan's face.

"Your assertion isn't making new law; you're only manipulating and twisting the facts that you damn well know are completely false." As far as he was concerned, Kaplan was a lying bastard, and he and his staff had invested too much time chasing after Kaplan's foul balls. "Not to mention the bloody trail of carnage you're leaving along the way."

"That's for the judge to decide, not you or your boss." Kaplan addressed Judge Hamilton as though Hal was in absentia. "We're within our rights to present this pre-trial motion and I certainly don't believe that the court or the district attorney's office would begrudge my client of his rights, especially when his freedom is at stake."

"You're no better than your client," Hal muttered under his breath.

"Gentlemen, let's reserve the verbal sparring for the courtroom, shall we? Luckily, time has opened up on my calendar for next week." Judge Hamilton stole a quick glance at his computer monitor, then back at the opposing counsel. "Today is Thursday. The hearing will begin on Monday at ten a.m. How many days do you anticipate we're going to need?"

Kaplan indicated about a half dozen witnesses as did Hal, so they agreed to designate Monday through Thursday for the hearing. They also agreed to establish the ground rules for hearing, to avoid the duplication of witnesses by exchanging rosters by the next afternoon, and to narrow the field of inquiry by stipulating key facts and exhibits in writing.

"And I warn you," Judge Hamilton said, "we all know this is a case of first impression, but let's not let the tail wag the dog. I don't want this becoming the trial of the century. I trust that we can also agree to a gag order until my decision?" The attorneys had no choice but to consent to this as well, and a stenographer was invited into the chambers to place their understandings on the record. The thought of the mole in his office crossed Hal's mind as he stated his final "agreed, Your Honor." To avoid censure, he'd have to be careful. His staff, too. Lauren would be the difficult one; she loved publicity.

The courteous smiles of deference to Judge Hamilton disintegrated into scowls the moment the two adversaries left the judge's office.

"Are you really willing to put your license on the line for this freak show you're running?" Hal asked.

"This is getting a little too personal, isn't it, Samuels? Both of us seem to have a great deal at stake in this case."

"What the hell are you talking about?"

"I'm not stupid. There's been talk." Kaplan's pause was pregnant with possibilities. "A certain state senator? It's amazing what my PI has been digging up."

Hal was surprised at the comment since the trials and errors of Senator Stefan Hill hadn't hit the papers yet. It was funny what money could buy. He knew how Kaplan liked to play the game and refused to give up anything that could be used against him. He recalled his own interest when Lauren had confided in him about the sex scandal, followed by the titillation of a potential fat promotion. He agreed with Kaplan on one thing, there was too much riding on the outcome so Hal refused to respond or take the bait.

"We want a deal…criminally negligent homicide," Kaplan stated bluntly. "Butterfield does some time, maybe one to four. You get the credit. I look like a miracle worker. It's win-win."

"Homicide? An E felony? You're out of your mind. This is a murder one. Even death by lethal injection would be too good for Butterfield."

"If you think there's carnage now, just wait, Samuels. It's all up to you." Jeremy slipped his hand into his blazer pocket and extracted a small cigar cutter, which he fondled in between his fingers. His eyes widened and stared at the opponent standing next to him. "I mean it. I'm not joking."

Hal chuckled and waved him away. The receding click of his shoes across the marble floors provided Kaplan with his response.

Strike three. You're out.

Jeremy and Miri Shtern sat in his conference room preparing to watch a video of the doctor's most recent jailhouse session with their mutual client. The session had occurred in the morning while Jeremy had been in court, and Miri appeared anxious for him to view it. Before he hit the play button on the player, the psychiatrist explained that she considered the recording to be her confidential work product so under the doctor-patient privilege, it didn't have to be revealed to the prosecution.

"The running time is about an hour, but I won't bore you with its entirety. You'll get the gist of our conversation from the highlights," Miri said. "I must warn you that what you're about to see could be upsetting, but we'll discuss that later. Let me set this up for you." She explained that she and Terrence had conferred in the employee's lounge of the Dutchess County Jail. At her request, Bernard had unfastened Terrence's handcuffs, and grudgingly, the guard agreed. "This is how I build trust with my patients. I need to make them feel comfortable with me. Okay, now you can start it."

Jeremy stabbed at the button and they watched the flat screen that was connected to her cell phone by a cable.

In the video, Miri's hands rested in her lap along with her notepad and pen, avoiding any unnecessary contact with the stained, frayed arms of the club chair where she sat. Across from her, Butterfield fidgeted on a Naugahyde sofa, which cracked with every breath he took. After almost three weeks inside, the guy looked emaciated. His cheekbones held up his sunken eyes and the shapeless jumpsuit hung on his frame like an old coat on a hanger. Birdlike, his eyes darted about the lounge searching through space, inattentive.

"Let's begin with something simple. Do you remember me? Do you know who I am?" she asked.

"Yes, you're the woman from the other day in the cell," Butterfield said.

She introduced herself. "I'm Miri Shtern, the psychiatrist engaged by your attorney, Jeremy Kaplan, to help you."

"Help? Does Kaplan think I need psychiatric treatment? What about you, Dr. Shtern? Do you also believe I need treatment? Therapy, drugs, or something more drastic?" Butterfield jutted his face toward her, haughty and testing.

Dr. Shtern threw back her dark head and laughed, her brown eyes sparkling. "At present, I don't honestly know what to think."

"What's so funny? Are you laughing at me?"

"I'm not laughing at you. What exactly do you mean? Therapy or 'something more drastic,' as you put it?"

"You know exactly what I mean. Will I be talking away my alleged mental illness in therapy, will I be drugged into oblivion, or will you be attempting to prove that I'm out of my mind?" His flat voice cracked when he uttered the last syllable.

"Well, are you? What do you think?"

There was no reply to either question.

Jeremy grew concerned at what he'd observed so far on the video. The more Butterfield spoke, the more cogent he presented himself to be, and the more Jeremy questioned his defense strategy. Was Butterfield crazy? If so, could they prove it?

"Can we speed this along?" he asked, impatiently.

"Ssh, just wait," Miri said, swatting him on the arm. She was engrossed, watching herself and Terrence discuss his family.

Terrence was neither smiling nor frowning. He'd shifted into neutral. He spoke in a low, detached monotone as though discussing someone other than himself. More machine than human.

"I was born in Tornado Alley, the lovely Elkhart, Indiana. The recreational vehicle capital of the world. When I was a child, we moved around a lot because my father, also a Yale man, was a consultant in the automotive industry. Name a car company— Ford, Toyota, Chrysler—and he consulted with them. Name a car city—Detroit, Baltimore, Mahwah—and we lived there. My mother was a severe, pious Christian who believed that the church would be a stabilizing force in our vagabond existence." He snorted, amused at the apparent inside joke.

"I have two older brothers who live outside of Boston. My eldest brother, Arthur, is a Senior VP for Goldman Sachs. Clyde, my middle brother, is in the IT industry. He's also a brilliant fellow."

"How's your relationship with your parents and siblings?"

"My parents are deceased. Growing up, my brothers and I were close. We were all each other had. Moving around didn't give us much of a chance to make real friends. Our parents were strict, demanded that we study hard. They made it clear that we were on our own for college. Artie and Clyde excelled in math, while my strengths lie in linguistics and logic. I'm able to recall the minutest details. I should've been on Jeopardy." He chuckled. "I could've followed their paths into business. However, I preferred more personal interaction. That's why I took up teaching."

"Have you heard from your brothers since your arrest?"

"No," he said, painfully. His mask began to crumble but he caught himself. The pace of his speech quickened as though trying to soften the reality of his last confession. "I have made a good life here in Poughkeepsie and I have no regrets. I consider myself an excellent teacher and role model for my students and peers. It's a gift, actually. Identifying the talented student, recognizing the untapped potential residing within that young person and providing the encouragement and opportunity to flourish. There's nothing more satisfying than that. That is my talent." He paused and licked his lips. "Of course, I have favorites. Who doesn't? Over the years, there have been a dozen or so special ones." He looked her straight in the eye. "No, I haven't heard from any of them either."

Miri reached out and pressed the fast-forward button. She sped through a segment where the two of them stared at each other in silence for what appeared to be quite a long time. Then, she hit play and stated in her singsong, soothing voice, "Terrence, if Jeremy and I are to help you, you must help us. We need to know what happened at your home on the night of August 31st. I know it is deeply disturbing, but you cannot withhold anything. Do you understand me?"

There was a sudden shift on the screen like a third person had joined them in the jail's lounge. A shadow crossed Butterfield's face and his body tightened. He clenched his fists in his lap. Death had imposed itself into the conversation.

Jeremy read the signals and wanted to call out to the woman on the screen. Warn her. But it was too late.

"Sometimes young boys do not respect authority. They believe that they are entitled to violate your personal property and vandalize your home. Are you supposed to grit your teeth and accept their actions? What are their parents teaching them? That it's permissible to spray paint someone's garage and rummage through the trash cans like raccoons? What are they looking for? And where are the police? When you call them and complain, they laugh at you. They're incompetent. It's their job to protect your property. You work hard to build a life filled with things that you love and there's no one to help you protect it. Sometimes you must take the law into your own hands to protect your property."

Butterfield sprang to his feet, his face turning beet red with cheeks puffing like a steam engine, startling Miri. She also rose, but tumbled backward, managing to catch her balance against the dirty brown chair. He approached her and hovered over her, pinning her against the chair. His wild eyes pierced through her.

"Isn't it your right? Isn't it their job? Why didn't they get those rotten boys? What's going on here? Where's my privacy?" he bellowed.

"Guard," Miri screamed, "Guard!"

Miri quickly pressed the stop button and the screen turned black.

"My god, are you alright? What happened in there?" Jeremy asked, aghast at what he'd seen.

"I'm fine. Nothing happened," she said. She massaged the swollen purple knuckles, gently flexing and testing them for injury.

Miri was lying to him. Something disturbing had transpired. Jeremy tried to read his old friend, but her cool veneer stymied him. He knew no matter how much he probed, her barricade of stubbornness and pride made her impenetrable. Unless she wanted to, she wouldn't reveal what had occurred.

The bruises on her hands told him more than he wanted to know. With her commando training, Miri could cause bodily, if not fatal, injury. He suspected that she could be savage when provoked within an inch of her life. Hopefully, that had not been the situation with Terrence.

In any event, he'd placed her in danger and he swore he'd never do it again.

CHAPTER
40

Jessie's pashmina lay crumpled up on the floor where she'd tossed it last night. Out of anger, she'd wadded it up into a ball and pitched it into the corner of the bedroom, yelling, "Take that, Kyle, you idiot!" That had sent the cat scampering beneath the bed. This morning, still seething and with nerves frayed to the point of snapping, she retrieved the shawl and shoved it into the closet. As Jessie slammed the closet door, she swore so frequently that she was certain her child's first word would be an expletive.

Her Friday morning was the harbinger of things to come, beginning with Dr. S. During her appointment, he poked and prodded her tender body like she was a tenderloin of beef. When the good doctor snapped the blue gloves into the wastebasket, he plastered on his crooked smile.

"Jessica," he said, "your blood pressure has spiked to 135/90, which gives me concern. However, your cervix has not dilated, which is good for 33 weeks. The baby is breech, which is unremarkable as he/she still has time to flip downward into the delivery position. All in all, things are on track for your November delivery."

"What about my vicious bouts of headaches, the intense dizziness and nausea? Isn't there anything that I can do about them?" she asked.

"Not to worry," Dr. S. reassured her, "the placenta has not shifted to block the entrance into the birth canal. All of your symptoms come with the territory of gestational hypertension. They'll resolve themselves upon delivery of your little one." In a stern, barely audible voice, he urged her to take it easy. "Please, rest and stay at home. No more running around. You'll have plenty of that after the baby arrives. In the meantime, I'd like to see you twice a week. Just to keep an eye on things."

Desperate, she informed her parents of the situation as soon as she returned home. That evening after work, the front door flew open and Ed and Lena Martin marched in, armed with sacks of groceries. The cavalry had arrived and with them the comfort of knowing that she'd be pampered to the extreme. Jessie gave herself permission to become the little girl who needed her parents to take care of her, at least for the weekend.

In the kitchen, she watched her parents unpack the canvas grocery bags. The twinkle in her father's eye was apparent whenever he looked at her mother. Not shy about public displays of affection, Ed gathered his wife in his arms and kissed her.

"Pretty sexy for a grandpa-to-be. Don't you think, honey?" her mother, Lena, asked, mussing Ed's hair. Seeing her parents fussing over one another made her miss Kyle, the pre-Barclays Kyle, more than ever.

On Saturday morning, the Barclays Kyle resumed phoning the house, hourly. Once he'd figured out that Lena was caretaking, he'd sidled up to his ally, much to Jessie's chagrin.

"Kyle really does love you," Lena said, serving it as a side dish with the sandwiches she set on the coffee table. The three of them were in the den watching a home improvement show on the flat screen. "When are you going to sit down with that poor man and work things out? He's terribly concerned about you. You know that he was just thinking about what's best for his family. Maybe you should hear him out."

"Thanks, but I'm not hungry," Jessie said, pushing the plate away. The dizziness had returned, rippling from the tip of her spine to the top of her cranium. She gripped the sofa cushions beneath her, fending off the earth-quaking bout of vertigo. She considered calling Dr. S., but, not wanting to alarm her guardians, she let the spell go unannounced. The storm quickly passed, leaving a dull headache in its wake.

"You've got to eat something. Think about the baby, honey, not just yourself. No wonder Kyle is so worried about you," Lena admonished.

Kyle and Lena. Jessie was annoyed at their alliance. Since the beginning, her mother had overly involved herself in the relationship between Jessie and her son-in-law-to-be; arranging dinners with Kyle's parents and conspiring with Beverly, Kyle's mother, about the wedding venue, caterer, and music. Lena had taken it particularly hard when Jessie postponed the wedding after learning she was pregnant. Both mothers had offered to handle all of the wedding arrangements, but there was no way that Jessie was going to let that happen. She wanted it to be her day, not theirs. Lena and Beverly would just have to wait. And now with the impending arrival of Lena's first grandchild, her mother believed that she was entitled to greater access into their private lives as compensation for the delay in the nuptials.

"Come on, dear," Ed said. "Let her be. She'll eat when she's ready."

Lena sighed dramatically. Jessie imagined her mother rolling her eyes as her clipped footsteps trailed out of the den and down the hall toward the kitchen.

"If you don't eat, she'll just keep nagging you until you surrender," Ed said, sympathetically rubbing her shoulder. "She means well, you know."

"I know. I'm just a bit on edge about everything."

And, Jessie thought, so was her father. Terrence Butterfield's name remained unspoken between them, but the wrinkles in her father's forehead had deepened since the murder and his brilliant smile had become tarnished. But he valiantly tried to smile at his daughter anyway.

"I know, kiddo. Come on. Try. Take a bite."

Jessie nibbled the hot roast turkey with cranberry sauce on rye set before her on the coffee table. To her delight, the comfort food warmed her. With each bite, she grew more embarrassed about her impatience with the two people who unconditionally loved her, who'd do anything to keep her safe, and who demanded nothing in return but to share in the joy of the birth of their first grandchild. She blamed the runaway hormones making her into a crazy pregnant lady.

Under Ed's adoring eyes, she devoured her meal and half of his. The doorbell rang as her father carried the dirty dishes into the kitchen.

"Hold on," Ed called out, "I'm coming." The doorbell buzzed again.

Kyle, she thought. She wished they could return to the way things used to be. Before the murder. Before Barclays. A slideshow flashed in her mind: Kyle asking her out within minutes of their meeting at an entertainment law conference, popping the question at center court during halftime at a Knicks game, carrying her across the threshold of their new home on Platt Street, and tearing up at the sight of their baby on their first sonogram.

Jessie spread her moist palms across her belly, inhaled deeply, and made large circular motions across the wiggling bump. She breathed in and out. She blinked back the tears.

Her pregnancy hormones were not clouding her judgment where Kyle was concerned. He'd broken her heart into a thousand slivers that couldn't be put back together again.

Minutes passed and she remained alone in the den, the silence suffocating her. No one entered the room, but there were whispers out in the hallway. Her heart raced, her pulse pounding against her eardrums. She wondered what was happening.

Finally, her father returned. His gaze cast was downward and he anxiously kneaded his clenched knuckles. "Honey?"

"Dad, tell Kyle to go away, please."

"Jess, sweetie. We've been served," Ed said, barely audible.

Hal felt a gentle poke at his shoulder, but he ignored it. He was busy, concentrating on tapping out an email on his tablet.

"Dad, you said you'd play a game with me a half hour ago. Come on, Dad. You promised."

"Uh-huh," Hal mumbled, half-hearing his son's voice as he pressed the send button.

"Daaad?" The sweet voice rose in pitch, becoming more insistent.

Something in Tyler's pleading caught his attention. Hal glanced up from the tablet and the documents strewn across the dining room table. At his elbow, his six-year-old son waved two video game controllers and fidgeted from one bare foot to the other.

Tyler was correct. A promise was a promise. Besides, he couldn't resist the kid's smile, with his small pink tongue wiggling in between the gap where the baby teeth used to be. That crooked smile knocked him dead.

"Okay, bud. One game, then off to bed. I call the Yankees."

"Jeez, Daaad," Tyler said, disappointed.

"Just kidding. They're all yours. I'll be—" Hal cocked his head in mock thought, drumming his long fingers across his five o'clock shadow.

"De-troit!" Tyler shouted. With a high-pitched squeal of glee, he bounced away like the superhero on his pajamas.

"Ty, here I come. I'm gonna get you. Watch out!" Hal shouted, racing in hot pursuit.

The final score of the first game was Yankees 10, Tigers 7.

In the top of the eighth inning of game two, silence filled the room. Hal's shortstop was at bat, the count was 3–2, and he quickly glanced over at Tyler. The boy was curled up asleep in the corner of the couch, hugging the controller to his small frame. Smiling, Hal scooped the boy up in his arms. He quietly carried Tyler into his bedroom at the end of the hall, laid him on the bed beneath the Spider-Man comforter and kissed him lightly on the forehead. Standing in the dark doorway, he admired his son's serene face.

"He looks like an angel when he sleeps," Erin said from behind Hal. She slipped her arms around his waist and rested her chin on his shoulder.

"Yeah, he's a great kid. Every day he looks more like you, you know." Hal gently stroked his wife's soft cheek and then tucked a stray lock of her blonde hair behind her ear. "We did good with him."

"We could make another if you want," she purred, giving his chest a squeeze. Her fingers eased their way into the chest hairs sprouting out through the placket of his polo shirt. "Or we could try?"

Hal left her invitation dangling in the air. He turned and kissed Erin, extricating himself from her grasp. "Hon, got to get back to work. I know that this is a pretty crummy way to spend a Saturday night. But it'll be over soon. Really, I'm sorry."

"I know," she murmured, sadly.

He returned to the mistress awaiting him at the dining room table. But Erin invaded his thoughts. Lately, he'd found himself apologizing to her for so many things: for working late at the office, for rising at the crack of dawn to head into the office early, for taking and making calls at all hours of the day and night, for leaving his cell phone on the dinner table to monitor the constant flow of emails, for missing parents' night at school, for missing Tyler's soccer games, for not helping with their son's homework, and for being exhausted all of the time.

Additionally, he silently apologized to his wife for things she didn't even suspect: for not wanting to be home, except to spend time with Tyler; for preferring the company of his co-workers, including Lauren Hollenbeck, to her; for placing his ambitions over their relationship; and for not loving Erin the way she deserved to be loved. And most of all, for the indescribable depth of his feelings for Jessie, which tore through his flesh all the way down to his raw bones.

And the deceit. Not only for his present situation, but also for their impulsive marriage. To please his family, he'd naively convinced himself that he loved Erin, and had successfully convinced her of his love. But Hal knew all along, deep down into his core, that it wasn't so and never would be. Ever.

Hal Samuels III wasn't a bad guy. He didn't intend to act and feel the way he did, it just happened.

But he'd never apologize for creating Tyler and the joy that the boy brought into his life. Although, he did apologize, not to Erin, but to their son, for the anguished tug of guilt that he'd cheated this perfect child out of two parents who loved each other.

Hal rifled through the thick pile of documents, photographs, and affidavits, not knowing exactly what he sought. He stared at the pages until the words melted away. His hands began to tremble. Hal rose and went to the tall cherry armoire against the far wall of the dining room. He grabbed a highball glass and the bottle of Glenfiddich from the shelf and returned to his seat at the table. The bittersweet taste of the scotch burned his throat as he emptied the glass in one swift gulp. He poured another and another, guzzling the shots in rapid succession.

Snatching the file, he relocated to the den couch where the crowd mechanically cheered for the Tigers in the top of the eighth inning. He rested his heavy head against the cushions that were still warm with the scent of his son.

He thought about the complications in his life. His marriage. His work. His family. And wondered how he'd gotten here.

Hal closed his eyes as the fog descended upon him, numbing his aching brain, body, and soul.

The three adults occupying one end of the Kaplan's banquet-size table awkwardly fiddled with their teaspoons, sugar packets, and cups of coffee. Once Jeremy and Gayle's sons had fled the scene, the easy conversation had ground to a halt. A dead stop. The silence was palpable, uncomfortable, and loud, signaling that the pleasantries were over. It was time for Jeremy and Miri to get down to the business of Terrence Butterfield.

"Come on, Miri, bring your coffee. Let's go into the library." Jeremy led her across the foyer into the library. Miri's eyebrows rose in amazement as they entered the crown jewel of his money pit, the type of space not found in McMansions. The musty scent of leather emanated from the volumes stacked on the mahogany shelving that flanked the floor-to-ceiling marble fireplace. Above them, an ornate crown molding capped the ten-foot ceilings and accentuated the plaster ceiling medallions which had been restored to their original majesty. They tread across the plush oriental carpets toward a pair of leather chairs that faced a fireplace large enough to rotisserie a pig.

"As you know, I'm having a problem with our client," Miri said, settling into the well-worn seat. "It's quite distressing. I've never met anyone who's so completely resistant to my methods. You witnessed our first encounter and I was optimistic, but after our last episode I'm in a quandary."

"So where do we stand? The hearing is set for Monday and if I lose on the motion, I need to know my options." Jeremy walked to the bar built into one of the bookshelves and poured himself a tall bourbon. He offered a glass to Miri but she declined.

"You don't intend to call him at the pretrial, do you? Or even have Butterfield present?"

He shook his head. "No way. You should have seen him at the arraignment. He was completely zoned out."

"Good. He's incapable of handling any additional stress at this moment. Terrence's behavior is atypical for someone who has taken the life of another human being. He has created a world in his mind where his crime did not occur. There is no remorse since he's in complete denial of his actions. And when I probe, Terrence becomes stressed. His protective wall begins to crack. He reacts with uncontrollable violence." Miri gazed for a moment into the dark fireplace. "At present, it's difficult to say exactly what triggered the murder. Whether it was the boy or other factors. Sadly, I suspect that the Paige boy was at the wrong place at the wrong time. He unknowingly walked into the nightmare of Terrence's psychotic break from reality. Because Terrence's rage is too overwhelming, we may not be able to extract any useful information from him right now. We need to stabilize him before he can assist with his own defense. My preliminary impression is that he requires an antipsychotic, a mood stabilizer, and an antidepressant." Miri took a sip of her coffee.

Jeremy folded himself back into the armchair, crossing his long crane legs. He sipped his bourbon and, rolling it slowly around in his mouth, he considered her comments. "Miri, I know that you may want to bag the whole deal, but without sounding overly dramatic, this guy's life is at stake. From what you're telling me, we need to impress upon the court that he needs medical assistance, not punishment or rehabilitation. Terrence isn't a criminal in the traditional sense; he's damaged goods."

"I'm not considering abandoning Terrence. But I'm deeply concerned about the degree of brutality expressed through his murder of Ryan Paige. It was like a massive, cataclysmic explosion. I need to know what caused the explosion, but I need his help." Miri paused. "I appreciate your dedication to Terrence, but it is questionable as to whether he'll ever be functional in society again. There's no doubt in my mind that he requires institutionalization, but without obtaining a comprehensive diagnosis, my hands are tied. I have some initial suspicions, but I require more. You understand that."

"Hmmm." Jeremy rose and leaned one arm against the fireplace, staring at the gray ashes littering the hearth. "So. It's meds then."

"Initially. And if they fail, we must explore other methods," she said, quietly. "But we will cross that bridge later. Let's see how he reacts on the medications. In the morning, I'll write the scripts and email them to the supervising physician at the jail."

"I appreciate your concern, but I don't want you risking your personal safety again." He placed his hand on her shoulder and gave it a squeeze.

"Jerry, I survived a desert war. I'm confident that I can survive yet another psychotic patient," Miri said, her dark eyes narrowing at the joke.

CHAPTER
41

For a long moment, Jessie and her mother measured each other. Lena cocked her head and an auburn curl dangled freely across her heart-shaped face. Jessie saw herself reflected in Lena's mismatched eyes as her mother lovingly stroked Jessie's belly. Other people often commented about their resemblance, and while flattered by the compliment, Jessie always dismissed them. Yet, at moments like this, their likeness in face and stature was undeniable. She was her mother's daughter and prayed for her youthfulness, vibrancy, and happiness when she reached her mother's age. Perhaps though, not her over-protectiveness.

It was Sunday morning, and Lena folded Jessie within her arms to say goodbye. Her mother squeezed her as though she'd never be setting eyes upon Jessie again. In a voice hoarse with unshed tears, Lena said, "I don't want you lifting anything or running up and down stairs. Sit. Relax. I've left a plate of chicken in the fridge for dinner, so you shouldn't need anything."

"I promise. No weightlifting or wrestling, but I can't make any promises for the baby," Jessie said trying to lighten the mood. "Go, enjoy the rest of your Sunday."

Ed placed an arm around Lena's shoulders. He winked at Jessie as he guided his wife through the garden path toward their Prius parked in the driveway. Lena looked back longingly and waved. "Jess will call us if she needs anything," he said.

"Thanks, Dad," she called after them. "Take a shave, will you, old man?"

From the back porch, Jessie watched the car pull away, kneading her fist into the aching bow of her back. When she returned inside, the tabby scooted alongside her and made a beeline toward his food bowl set next to the fridge. Her hands snapped the backdoor latch behind them, double-checking that the lock was secure. She leaned down and stroked Bono's lean body, gently removing a small burr tangled in his thick, dark fur. A faint purr emanated from the feline.

If human life could only be this simple, she mused. Pure joy found within a bowl of kitty chow.

Jessie left Bono to finish his meal while she checked the emails she'd neglected since Thursday evening. And then she'd treat herself to a nap. A luxurious, uninterrupted, absolutely decadent mid-afternoon Sunday siesta. The sofa whispered "Jessie... Jessie" as she passed it on the way to the den, but she ignored the siren call for the time being. The wide plank floor boards brushed softly against her bare feet, their knots tickling her sensitive soles. The cat was right; simple pleasures nurture joy.

The simple pleasure of not needing to clean house was a gift that her mother had bestowed on her. Lena had not left a speck of dust behind in the den. The mahogany desktop was polished to a high gloss and the papers, magazines, and mail had been neatly organized in stacks on its surface. Jessie picked up a manila envelope embellished with Terrence's sharp, angular script. She bristled at the thought of him, the way he'd treated her and the words they'd exchanged.

Her jaw clenched at the memories, and she hurled the envelope into the trash. Reconsidering, she retrieved it and ripped it open. Inside was a flash drive attached to a handwritten note.

Jessica, my dear:

In the dead of night when I am plagued with insomnia, which is quite often these days, my mind wanders to a dark and frightening place. I try to control these thoughts but I am defenseless against the demons tearing at my soul. They possess me. I often find myself at my computer, the devil's words rushing forth from me like I am a broken spigot.

Once the words are on the page, I am drained but I can rest. I find peace.

I share these writings only with you because we understand each other, and what it is like to be haunted by events you cannot change.

Please do not think ill of me.

I remain yours always,

T

The note was dated last March around the time when she'd discovered she was expecting. For more than six months the packet had languished on her desk. Thinking back, Terrence had often asked her about his writings. Each time she'd made some lame excuse, blowing him off. She'd promised that she'd get around to it, but she never had. Between Kyle and the exhaustion of work and her pregnancy, reading Terrence's creative writing hadn't been a priority. Finally, despite her anger toward him, she had the time.

Jessie plugged the drive into her laptop and a list of files flashed on the screen. There were twenty documents dating back over a decade ago to when she'd attended high school, with the majority being generated during the past year. She opened the earliest file, a short story entitled "The Object of Desire," a heartbreaking narrative about a master and pupil relationship gone awry after the student's advances toward his mature tutor were rebuffed. The student, a tall, sulky teen, stalked the man and, unable to bear the repeated rejection, he resorted to pills and alcohol. Ultimately, the boy attempted to end his life by an overdose.

The tale disturbed her, haunted her with its dreamlike imagery of the youth's fantasies and his desperate attempts to obtain the love and acceptance of his object of desire. It unsettled her, and she pondered whether the story offered an insight into Terrence's troubled mind.

She randomly selected other entries, their subject matter growing darker and angrier. They were difficult to read, but the sinister nature of their contents compelled her to continue. Especially the chilling account of a broken engagement where the woman is poisoned, stuffed into her antique hope chest, and dumped into a secluded inlet of the Hudson River.

No, it's not possible. Terrence's fiancée, Sheryl Espinoza, had moved to California years before the story had been written. She was being silly, letting her imagination run wild. But, Terrence had a talent for the dramatic, the macabre, and—apparent now—murder.

Jessie made a mental note to locate Sheryl and decided to check out more files. She opened the most recent, a story entitled "The Boy in the Flannel Shirt." To her horror, the plot was strikingly familiar. A boy trespassing through a yard late at night. She wanted to stop, but she couldn't avert her eyes from the grotesque descriptions: "the red rivers of blood," "ripped through his flesh," "squealed in pain," "the thrill of the making him pay the ultimate consequence."

Ryan. Oh my god, Ryan. If only. If only.

If only she'd read the story sooner.

Jessie's skin crawled at the thought of the possible truths contained in Terrence's stories and that perhaps she could've prevented Ryan's senseless murder. Perhaps the district attorney had been correct; she was an accomplice to Ryan's murder and deserved to be prosecuted. The murder that everyone concluded had been a random act of violence had been premeditated.

She wondered about the victims in the other tales and whether they were fact or fiction.

Jessie needed time to reflect, digest what she'd seen and read. The vital information contained on the flash drive could dramatically impact Hal's case against Terrence. She needed to ensure that Terrence never saw his freedom again. That he never had the opportunity to ruin another life, another family, or another community.

She signed into her email account and sifted through the mail. Buried among the junk and credit score solicitations was a thread of messages from the district attorney's office:

From: Hal Samuels, ADA

Re: Butterfield

Jess:

Just giving you a heads up that Judge Hamilton scheduled the pretrial hearing for this Monday at 10 a.m. so you can expect a subpoena. You know the drill but I'll contact you with the details. Also, your father and Emory should be receiving them as well. Please take care.

Yours,

Hal

The message had been sent on Thursday night around midnight. She moved on to the next one.

From: Hal Samuels, ADA

Re: Butterfield

Jess: Heard your father was served at your home. Sorry about that. I've left several messages on your phones, but you haven't returned my calls. I'm concerned, so please contact me.

Yours,

Hal

The date was Friday afternoon, 6:15 p.m. Jessie quickly moved on to the final message sent from his personal address.

From: Hal Samuels

Re: (No Subject)

Jess:

Still haven't heard from you. If I don't hear from you soon I will stop by. PLEASE, PLEASE CALL ME.

Hal.

The date was yesterday, Saturday evening, 7:56 p.m. She prickled at his rising panic, the urgency in his tone as well as his use capital letters. Without delay, she responded.

From: Jessie Martin

Re: No Subject

Hal:

Had my parents this weekend, but you already know that. Just received your messages, sorry have been incommunicado. It wasn't intentional. Please don't worry, I'm fine and will call you this evening.

P.S. I found something that may be of interest to you.

Confused by her feelings, she pondered how to sign off. "Yours?" "Thanks for caring?" "Love?" She simply signed "Jess."

Oddly, there were no emails from her office. After Mr. McMann's visit the other day, she'd expected to hear from him. Mr. McMann had said that the firm had wanted her to return, but he'd made no effort to follow up. While she wasn't seriously considering the offer, she still liked to be chased a little. This snubbing nagged at her with a weird sensation. Some people would call it intuition, others paranoia.

Jessie typed her firm's website into the browser's search bar and the homepage popped up onto the screen, formal and intimidating. She clicked on the attorney directory and nervously scrutinized the roster. They were a mid-size group of twenty-five lawyers and she practically knew the directory by heart. Since she'd started there five years ago, her name had always been sandwiched between John Lipton's and J.R. McMann's.

Lipton. McMann. Ostrander. Spencer. Wilson.

Something wasn't right.

Suspecting the worst, she played another hunch. Jessie dialed the general office number and keyed in her extension. The line rang. Once. Twice. Three Times. Then, an automated voice announced, "The extension you are trying to reach is not a valid entry. Please enter a different extension or press zero for operator assistance." Jessie tried again with the same result. Then she tried her secretary's extension. Same recording. In desperation, she tried Josh Spencer's extension, her heart jumping at his nasally recorded greeting. She disconnected the call and for a long moment, she listened to the dial tone on the other end of the line.

Her mouth turned sandpaper dry and her tongue felt like a wooden log. Between Terrence's stories, Hal's emails, and the firm's indifference, she was frantic. She stormed out of the den into the kitchen and snapped on the burner beneath the teapot. Her arms trembled as she lowered herself into a chair at the dining table. Muscle spasms twitched downward from her elbows to her fingertips, and from her knees to her tiny sausage toes. She willed her body to relax, but anxiety penetrated every cell.

The teapot whistled. Its ear-splitting shriek jolted her, causing her to spring from her seat. Fog descended over her pregnancy brain, muddling her thoughts. She was groggy and her off-kilter center of gravity disoriented her, and she staggered across the polished tile floor. The cat screeched as his tail and paws became entangled between her legs.

Jessie feebly reached out toward the table's edge, and, misjudging the distance, her fingers slipped across the oiled butcher block surface. The heels of her swollen feet slid out from beneath her, sending her airborne like a zeppelin. She soared weightlessly toward the kitchen ceiling, then, just as rapidly, plummeted back toward earth. She instinctively wrapped her arms around her belly to protect her baby. But the hard tile floor rose up to mercilessly slam against the bony tip of her tailbone and her fleshy buttocks and thighs. A razor-sharp electrical shock buzzed up her spine toward her neck, jolting her body flat onto the cold tile. Her heart hammered against the wall of her chest attempting to escape as she gasped for breath.

CHAPTER
42

The afternoon sun beat down through the streaked windows of Hal's downtown office. He rose, quickly peeked outside, then snapped the blinds shut. A nagging hangover wrought from the prior evening's half bottle of Glenfiddich draped him like a dark shroud. The potent cocktail of Scotch whiskey and remorse dulled his edge, rendering him useless to his staff during the eleventh-hour pre-trial preparations.

Earlier this morning had been no picnic either. Erin had been malicious when she'd discovered him crashed on the couch, snuggling the empty bottle to his chest. Man, she'd been fuming.

"Suppose Tyler sees you like this? What's he supposed to think? What kind of role model are you setting for him?" Erin's stark blue eyes bulged and her ivory complexion flushed blood red. Her long blonde ponytail swayed as she jerked her head, emphasizing each question. "You stink like a distillery. Get it together, will you?"

Here it comes, he thought. *Oh man*. His head felt like a five-car collision.

"I've had about enough. We have no life. None. Zip. Zero. Do you understand? You're always working. And when you're not, you get drunk…on a Saturday night? I feel like a single mother. You're never around for Tyler or me. I never signed up for this program, Hal. Nobody is that dedicated. Not even your boss. Nobody!" Erin railed in one breath, her pitch increasing as the tirade continued. She placed her hands akimbo, shifting her wasp-waisted figure to one side. "I know you're under a great deal of pressure with the Paige case and balancing the rest of your caseload. And that Lauren is no prize to work for, but give me a break."

That last phrase slapped him to attention. Maybe he was still wasted, but she looked sexy when she was angry. "Erin, come here," he growled, reaching out for her waist. She recoiled from his pleading hands.

"You've got to be kidding me? Don't touch me. I've had enough. I'm tired of taking a back seat to your precious career. It's not like we need the money," Erin yelled. She paced back and forth, glaring at him. He got the impression that her remarks were not off the cuff. She'd practiced this speech, waiting for a moment when he was most vulnerable. Making him suffer as she'd suffered. "I'm tired of being neglected by you. I'm tired of making an effort and getting nothing in return. Sick. And. Tired. Tell me truthfully, Hal, am I wasting my time here? Are we wasting our time?"

Hal lowered his head into his hands, trying to absorb the truth of her words. He murmured, "I wish I knew."

Hal's thoughts were drawn back to the task at hand with a sharp knock on his office door.

"My, my, someone's had a rough night. Someone looks a bit green." Lauren, dressed in a designer cranberry blouse and khaki pencil skirt, leaned against the door jam. "I thought I'd stop by to see how you were progressing. Cindie said you were in here." She approached him and offered him a bottle of water. "Here, drink this."

"This case will do it to you," Hal said, seizing the bottle and twisting off the cap. He placed the bottle to his mouth, letting the contents roll down his throat.

"Hey, slow down." Lauren coyly circled her red nails upon the veneer of his desk, refusing eye contact. "I know this is last minute, but I've been mulling over whether I should take the first chair at the hearing tomorrow. It will portray the importance of this case to the court and the public."

Hal removed the bottle from his lips and stared at her. He sensed her true motives. "You mean to the media. But you know we're under a gag order so no more leaks to the press, Lauren."

"Whatever. I am the district attorney after all so what's Hamilton going to do, hold me in contempt?" Lauren rested her palms backward on the edge of the desk and leaned forward across the desk toward him. "More to the point, I think that you're taking the case too personally. It's unprofessional, especially your involvement with Ms. Martin."

"Is your mind made up?" he asked, gnashing his teeth.

"I might be persuaded otherwise."

"Oh?" Not her, too.

"Yes, I certainly could." Lauren kicked off her heels and strutted back to the office door, keeping her sights trained on him. The metallic click of the lock ignited a fuse within him, sizzling toward an explosion that he fought to control. Placing one stocking foot before the other, she stalked across the room, radiating a carnivorous sexuality. She sidled back around to his side of the desk. Her butt pressed against the edge of the desk and she ran one foot upward along the crease of his pant leg. Sharp nails encircled his left bicep, digging through his shirt into his skin. "Or perhaps you have an idea which might be more interesting than mine."

Hal grabbed her chin and pulled her beautiful face close to his, their noses grazing each other. He stared into her eyes that burned purple like the heart of a flame. His hand skimmed down her cheek toward her clavicle, then came to rest on her shoulder. He ran his tongue across his dry lips. Lauren's eyes closed and a low moan rose up from within her. He tugged her forward, murmuring in her ear. "If you want it so badly, I'll give it to you."

"Hal," Lauren sighed, pressing her hips against his.

He was repulsed by her scent of Chanel and sex and winced at the thought of further contact with her body. Her childish overtures at seduction and bribery only disgusted him, as did her demeaning herself in this manner. "You're better than this, Lauren. You know that," he whispered. "Now I'd like you to get out of my office."

Lauren stumbled backward into the tall bookcase against the wall, gaping at him in shock. A Parisian snow globe teetered to the end of a shelf and plummeted to the floor, shattering at her feet. "What—what about the case? Don't you want it?"

"Lady, it's all yours. Be my guest. Go ahead try the damn case tomorrow." Hal smirked. "Good luck."

"But—but—I can't. I don't know the details. I'm not prepared. There's no time."

"You should've thought about that before you made the play. I'm out of here," Hal said, marching out of the room without looking back.

A shrill, chaotic whistle wormed its way into Jessie's foggy brain. Prone upon the floor, she cautiously wiggled her toes and fingers. She twisted her neck from the left to the right. So far, no pain, except for her rear end. Her hands flew to her baby bump. A sharp heel pressed into her full bladder, while the other punched her fingers on their way from her navel upward toward her breasts. A warm, wet sensation trickled between her thighs and she shivered. Her hand crept downward along her belly and brushed over the moisture spreading around toward the floor. She brought her shaking hand to her nose and sniffed.

As she examined herself, the front door flew open and footsteps sprinted toward her.

"Jessie! Jessie, are you okay?" Kyle asked.

"Blood. Blood. Do you see any blood?" she implored in a half-crazed tone. "On my jeans, is there any blood?"

Kyle bent down beside her and quickly scanned her from head to toe. "No, no. I don't see any. Do you feel pain anywhere?" His voice and face were stricken with fear as he patted her arms and legs with comfortable familiarity, searching for any broken bones. "Jessie, how did this happen? I'm going to call 911. Lie still."

"No, wait a minute, please. Can you please shut off that damn kettle? I can't think straight." She swatted at the invasive arms, but Kyle resisted, continuing with his examination. When he'd finished, he rose and turned off the burner. The room was suddenly silent except for the heartbeats resounding in her temples. Jessie's shoulders grew lax. "That's better, thanks. Is there any blood, you know, in the crotch of my jeans?" she repeated anxiously, her eyes affixed to his face.

Something appeared different about him. His ruffled dark hair was close-cropped and spiked with product. His face was covered with the shadow of a groomed beard. For the past year, she'd cajoled, strongly suggested, and ultimately pleaded with him to clean up his act. And here Kyle was, groomed almost to the point of being alien. She liked the new look.

"I already told you, no, but you peed all over yourself."

She clucked her tongue. "I think I'm okay, but my tailbone hurts like crazy. Come on, help me up, please?"

Kyle slipped his arms beneath her armpits and hoisted her up slowly. "Jessie, you really have to be more careful."

"I am careful, Kyle. It was an accident. You don't honestly think I fell on purpose, do you? What're you doing here anyway?" Crisis averted, she couldn't hide her bitterness at his betrayal and lies. "I don't recall inviting you back into this house. And you said that returning was not an option."

"Lena called to tell me they'd left you alone, so I decided to drive up and check in on you. When you didn't answer the bell, I used my key and there you were lying on the kitchen floor. You can imagine what I thought."

"Well, I'm fine. See?" While Jessie had recovered from the fall, it was apparent that he hadn't. Kyle stepped closer toward her, sadness consuming his face. She retreated but she found no refuge as he pinned her against the kitchen countertop. "Please, don't. You need to leave."

"Babe, I'm so sorry. If anything happened to you or the baby I'd never forgive myself." He gathered her up in his arms and kissed her. Jessie recoiled at his touch, but her initial desire to push him away dissolved at the warmth of his touch, his rhythmic caresses to her shoulders and back. Jessie willed herself to stand still, to just enjoy being with Kyle, if only for the moment. It had been such a long time.

"Please, please forgive me. I know we can work things out," he pleaded.

In the open doorway, the shadowy figure of a man turned away and hurried down the front steps to the street. Jessie's body stiffened. Her voice squeaked, "Stop."

CHAPTER
43

Hal was fed up with Lauren's game of sexual politics. She'd been playing them for ages, but her most recent botched attempt at seduction had reached a new level of harassment. The heat of anger flushed through him as he dashed out of the office to escape and expunge his boss from his body and mind.

Let Lauren take over his case. She'd look foolish the moment she opened her mouth in court. That would teach her to mess with him.

As his Volvo's engine whined, he stared blankly at the dashboard. He didn't know where to go. Certainly not to Erin. He was drawn back to the one place, the one person who felt like home. To Jessie. She was alone and perhaps expected him after his last email. Yes, Jessie. His chest ached for one of their prolonged, deep kisses where they blended into one, making it impossible to determine where he ended and she began. Like a long time ago. Yes, she'd be glad to see him.

He revved the car's engine, watching the accelerator needle swipe across the illuminated dial. Shifting into gear, he depressed the pedal hard to the floor racing toward her. Fast.

Her front door was open. It was a sign.

His heart pounding with possibility, Hal bounded up her front steps. Yes. He'd finally admit his feelings, and she'd reciprocate by welcoming him into her arms, open wide for an embrace, one shared with the beautiful baby growing inside her.

He stopped short in the doorway. Jessie and Kyle were wrapped in an embrace, her head leaning against his shoulder.

No, he thought, *no.* She couldn't be taking that liar back.

He felt like such an idiot, a stupid, romantic idiot. In the blink of an eye, his desire dissolved into the painful realization that this couple was on the brink of becoming a family.

The front door may have been open, but the slender window of opportunity had been slammed in his face. He was too late. Hal dashed back to his car, not knowing where to go now.

He hopped into his Volvo and sped away, listening to the motor purr as he clutched the leather steering wheel. His palms grew sweaty as the weight of the crossroads revealed itself, wrenching him in a dozen different directions. He needed to gather his thoughts, to consider his options and their consequences.

He drove south on Route 9 to the golf club. Inside the men's locker room, amidst the odor of perspiration, grass, and aftershave, he grabbed the spare clothing and toiletries stowed within his locker and stuffed them into his gym bag. He returned to his car, sped north on Route 9, skidded into a U-turn at the first intersection, and pulled into the Courtyard Hotel directly across the road from the club.

"Erin, if you need me tonight I'm at the Courtyard or you can reach me on my cell," he dictated to her voicemail.

He flopped down on the bed, kicked off his loafers, and popped open the Heineken he'd ordered from room service. He sucked on the long, cold draught as ESPN broke the suffocating white noise inside the musty hotel room. He thought about his life and the spokes radiating from the hub of his complex existence: Erin, Tyler, Lauren, Jessie, his father, the Butterfield hearing, his legal career, his marriage, his goals, his desires, and his needs. The mental gears rotated throughout the indigo night, finally grinding to a halt as the gray dawn arrived.

The next morning, there was a circus-like atmosphere in the vicinity of the Dutchess County Courthouse. Situated in the heart of Poughkeepsie, the courthouse was located midway between the north and southbound legs of the arterial highway that sliced the city in half. This morning, the traffic on the northbound leg was at a complete standstill and was backed up a mile across the Mid-Hudson Bridge. Up and down Market Street, the deputy sheriffs frantically pumped their arms as they attempted to redirect traffic away from the courthouse.

Hal had never seen a traffic jam like this, and he attributed the unusual volume to the event that the media had been hyping all weekend long: the Butterfield case. He had no time for the nonsense, so to avoid the congestion, he made a sharp right turn off the highway onto a one-way side street that led him past Jessie's old office at McMann and Curtis.

Approaching Main Street from the west, Hal turned into the parking lot adjacent to the district attorney's annex. He parked his car in the designated spot and observed the police rerouting court personnel through the side entrance to the building. Curious, he wove his way around the corner to Main Street. Picketers, designating themselves as Parents For Justice, protested in front of the courthouse, blocking its entrance. Across the street, blue uniforms infiltrated the crowd that was congregating to watch the protesters chanting and waving their placards. A scowling woman screeched into a yellow bullhorn, "Protect your children. Murder one for Butterfield!" while the hollow sound of a hand drum beat in rhythm to the mantra. Additional police were stationed at the building's entrance, attempting to preserve the other business scheduled for the day.

Hal shook his head in frustration and dove back into the river of humans flowing upstream toward the building's side entrance. Desperately, he craned his neck searching for Jessie's pregnant body pressed within the crowd or her floppy straw hat bobbing in the current like a paper boat. Something. Anything. His heart leaped when he thought he spied her on the far side of the parking lot, but his eyes were playing tricks on him. It was a mirage. Disappointed, he entered the building and climbed the four flights to the DA's suite.

Inside his office, Cindie and her co-workers were leaning out of the windows, gawking at the SWAT team positioned on the rooftops across the street. He greeted his own troops, tossed his briefcase onto his desk, and peered at his assistant over his horn-rims with a *don't-you-have-anything-better-to-do* glance. Hal fastened the top button of his Oxford shirt, tightened his Windsor knot, and shrugged on the navy blazer that he stored in the closet.

Catching his drift, Cindie ushered the pack from his office. When they were alone, Cindie tugged on the sleeves of her jacket and smoothed her skirt, gathering her nerve. Cindie was several years his senior, and despite his seniority in the office, she never pussyfooted around when she had a strong opinion on a case.

"Rumor has it that Lauren's handling the first chair this morning," she said. "With all due respect, are you out of your mind? She can't handle this pre-trial. She doesn't have a clue; you know that as well as I do."

"Excuse me, Ms. Tarrico. Who can't handle what?" Lauren Hollenbeck's sharp tongue lashed like a switch at the dumbfounded assistant. Lauren turned her attention to Hal as she entered the room. "Hal, may I speak with you alone, please?"

"Lauren, we've nothing to discuss to which Cindie cannot be privy." His voice was arctic, making the temperature in the room plunge.

"Don't be insubordinate. We've confidential administrative matters to discuss. In private." The chief folded her arms across her slender body that twitched in a bundle of over-caffeinated nerves and insomnia. When he still didn't budge, Lauren remained silent for a moment, shivering as the room plummeted to absolute zero. "I've had a bad night, that's all. I didn't get much sleep. The caregiver and I were up with my father most of the night. It's nothing really," she said dismissively.

Hal studied Lauren's face. Her skin had paled to match the sickly shade of her chartreuse blouse; there were dark circles beneath her puffy eyes, visible through the layers of her foundation; and she had streaks of scarlet lipstick that bled into the tiny smoker's wrinkles that fanned from her upper lip. The cumulative effect was freakishly clownish, bordering on whorish. His stomach churned at the spectacle shuddering before him. She was a political hooker who'd lie about anything, even her dementia-ridden father.

"I'm taking over first chair this morning at the hearing," he said, fearless in his open hostility toward her. "You want to win this motion, don't you?"

Lauren stared at him with her mouth agape.

"If you're just going to stand there with nothing to contribute to this conversation, then you're wasting my time. If you'll excuse me, we've got work to do." He snapped opened his briefcase and withdrew a legal pad. Ignoring Lauren, he peppered his assistant with a list of questions. "Did you email the stipulation of facts to Kaplan as we discussed? Any response? How about the witnesses, are we good with them? What about Emory, did we nail that creep? Do you have the affidavits of service? Are the exhibits pre-marked? Have the proposed documents been forwarded to Judge Hamilton? Did you finalize the press release regarding the media blackout?"

Cindie nodded yes and no to the barrage of questions, with a yes to the final one.

"Terrific. Please give that to Lauren."

Cindie tendered a single sheet of paper to the district attorney.

"There," Hal finally directed at Lauren, "go make yourself useful."

CHAPTER
44

The bright sunlight streamed in through the bedroom windows, rousing Jessie from the first uninterrupted night of sleep in weeks. The jackhammer in her head had temporarily subsided and no heartburn greeted her this morning. She inhaled. Sweet, fresh air flowed unrestricted into her lungs.

It was going to be a great day.

Jessie entered the bathroom and studied herself in the mirror. Maybe it was her imagination, but her profile appeared dramatically different than yesterday. She cupped her breasts in her hands, and they seemed even more voluptuous. She stroked her pear-shaped silhouette, her hands coming to rest beneath the pouch above her pelvic bone. The baby seemed to be settled in lower, descending downward in preparation for delivery. From the books she'd read, the timing was about right. Thirty-four weeks. She brushed off Dr. S.'s warnings as being too conservative. She felt wonderful, bursting with energy. She was ready and raring to go.

Her father arrived shortly before ten to pick her up for court. Jessie met him outside and slipped into the passenger's seat of the Prius. She leaned over to give her father a peck on the cheek.

"Honey, you look terrific," he said. "I guess all our TLC this weekend worked. But you've got to promise me that if you get even one hiccup, we'll come right back home." From Ed's relaxed tone, it was clear that Kyle hadn't snitched on her about the accident the previous evening. Her father patted her knee. "Kiddo, nothing is more important than you and the baby. Got it?"

Jessie cheerfully agreed with his bending the house arrest rules as that had been her plan anyway. First in, first out. Unless DA Hollenbeck had other plans for her.

"I took a personal day anyway, so maybe we can grab lunch this afternoon, okay?" An impish grin crossed his face.

"Tsk, tsk," Jessie said, shaking her head. "Some fine example you're setting for your students. The principal playing hooky. Just hope that you don't get caught." She stroked the back of her hand across his clean-shaven chin. "Hey, I'm glad to see you took my advice. You clean up pretty good, old man."

"Buckle your seatbelt and let's get this show on the road," Ed said, laughing.

Exiting the elevator with her father, Jessie stepped into a dark, windowless corridor. At one end, a crowd milled around inside the vestibule of Judge Hamilton's courtroom. Huddled together at the opposite end, the Paige family insulated themselves from the other attendees. A stoic Bob shielded his family from the curious onlookers. Ryan's older sister, Brianne, cowered against her father's shoulder with her face hidden behind the same large sunglasses she'd worn at the funeral. Even from a distance, Betty embodied brittleness as though she could easily shatter into a thousand pieces. Her designer clothing hung loosely on the former regal frame, and her blonde head wobbled upon her frail shoulders. Tightly clasping each other's hands in solidarity, the Paiges were the embodiment of loss, grief, coping, and quiet strength under overwhelming circumstances.

Jessie felt ashamed at not reaching out to them after Ryan's death. Ryan had meant so much to her, but she was lost in her ability to console them. They would have ended up comforting her. And besides, with the brouhaha at McMann and her complicated history with Robbie and Terrence, she thought it best to keep her distance. Even now, she felt unsure how to express her grief to them.

Her attention drifted toward the loud clicking of boot heels hurrying up the grand staircase, and she turned toward the sound. The boots' owner, Robbie, strolled over and extended his hand in greeting to her father. She was surprised to see him since she'd believed that he'd returned to L.A., but this presented an unexpected opportunity to resolve a question brewing in her mind.

"Son, sorry about your brother," Ed said, clasping the young man's hand. "He was a great kid. Your family should be really proud of his accomplishments."

Robbie nodded politely, shifting his gaze to Jessie. He smoothed the imaginary static in his hair with his tattooed fingers. "Jessie, I thought that you'd be interested that I decided to stick around for a while and help the folks. Plus, I wanted to hear your version of what happened the night that Ryan died."

"Can we talk privately for a second?" Jessie asked.

Robbie's gaze darted away from her, distracted by a summoning from Brianne. He waved to his sister. "Sure, if you make it quick."

They excused themselves and walked toward a bench in a vacant hallway lined with conference rooms. A door slammed shut as they approached. They sat down, Jessie reflexively sliding a safe distance from him.

"This might sound strange, but I was wondering whether Terrence tutored you for the college-board exams?" she asked.

Robbie watched her, initially perplexed, but then his knees jiggled, betraying his nervousness. "That's the last thing that I thought you were going to ask me, but if you want to discuss the past, there's plenty that I can dig up that's more relevant," he said acerbically. "But, yes. He did."

"Why didn't you tell me about you and him?"

He looked her straight in the eyes, but he didn't immediately respond. The muscles in the corner of his mouth twitched in rising anger but he refused to break his penetrating stare. He sensed her discomfort and seemed to be taking pleasure in making her squirm. "There's nothing to tell you."

"If there were, this would be the appropriate time to come forward. There's no shame or judgment being passed. Whatever happened long ago when you were a kid would help convict Terrence of Ryan's death."

"He never touched me." Robbie's voice was sharp, definitive.

"I'm not making any accusations. I'm only bringing this up because it's really important."

"No, it's not. Ryan's dead and nothing's going to change that fact." Robbie's deep sorrow appeared to drain away the poison infecting his system. "Like nothing's going to change the fact that we could've had a life together. I'm not bitter about us, not anymore, but to survive this hell, I need to look forward and not look back. I suggest that you do the same." He hesitated for a second. "I know that you mean well, but my parents have been through enough, so please let it alone. And now, if you'll excuse me, my family needs me."

"I'll never forget what you did to me, Robbie, but I've made my peace with it. You should do the same with whatever Terrence did to you." She paused and rested her hand on her belly. "For Ryan's sake as well as your own."

As she watched him strut away, she finally understood the meaning of the initials in his tattoo. I-N-O. *It's not over.* These words represented the depth of his suffering and her contributions to that misery. They'd both left scars on each other but she'd risen from the ashes. Jessie hoped he understood that hiding in the shadows only served the enemy and defeated his brother's cause. He'd never find peace until he dealt with his past. She'd opened the floodgate and prayed that Robbie would do the right thing for once. For Ryan. For himself.

Kyle appeared out of thin air and joined her on the bench. He slid close and rested his arm across the back of the seat behind her. She wondered how long he'd been lurking and listening in the corridor.

"Sometimes you drive me crazy, do you know that?" Kyle asked. "I never know what you're going to do next. That's part of your mystique, and what keeps me on my toes. But you know that you shouldn't be here; you should be home resting, so I'm going to ask Ed to take you home." He wavered a moment, then asked, "This is about him, isn't it? About your old law school boyfriend, Samuels? Was I just the rebound guy?"

"What kind of ridiculous question is that Kyle? We've lived together for years, and we're having a baby together. Besides, this is really not the time nor place to have an argument."

Kyle uttered a soft tsk-tsk of disapproval. "Well, like I said, you shouldn't be here and you should go home."

"I'm not going to do anything of the sort. I'm here because like you and my dad, I received a subpoena. And as much as I hate to admit it, you were right about Terrence. He's not who I thought that he was." Her fingers patted the pocketbook where she'd stashed Terrence's flash drive.

"Maybe I'm correct about other things as well," Kyle said smugly.

"Don't go getting on your high horse. Come on, let's go testify so I can get out of here."

They found Ed where she'd abandoned him, reading a discarded Business Section of the *Times*. Except for her father, the hallway was empty. Her father gave them a suspicious sidelong look and inquired whether everything was all right. To placate Ed, she kissed Kyle, wished him good luck, and dawdled behind, waiting for Kyle to enter the courtroom first. Then, they proceeded inside.

The room hummed with conversations echoing off the high ceilings of her battlefield, the New York State Supreme Court. This was her arena. It was weird to be summoned in the context of a criminal case. The law was her life, but she doubted whether her father had ever seen the inside of the Supreme Court before. She'd always anticipated that someday Ed would watch her litigate a case, but this wasn't what she'd envisioned. Rather than being the litigator, she was a key witness in a felony murder hearing.

They proceeded toward the front row seats customarily reserved for attorneys, where she and Ed settled in for the show. From the way he was babbling on with fatherly advice, she detected his nervousness. She reached over and squeezed his moist hand.

She carefully stowed her purse beneath her chair and searched the courtroom for Hal. Terrence's USB drive was a crucial piece of evidence for the prosecution and she needed to get it to him as soon as possible.

CHAPTER
45

In a conference room on the third floor of the courthouse, Jeremy slammed the door as voices approached from down the hallway. Dr. Shtern watched over his shoulder as PI Carey Wentworth dealt a series of photographs and yellowed newspaper clippings onto the small metal conference table.

The first photo depicted a paint-peeled red barn displaying a large white sign with brown letters: "Butterfield Pottery Studio and Gallery." A man in his seventies sporting a straggly ponytail and a silver-haired woman in coveralls were pictured departing the barn. Another photo showed the couple entering a shingled cottage adjacent to the barn. The final picture showed the interior of the pottery studio: colorful ceramic plates, vases, bowls, lamp bases, and candlesticks crammed its floor-to-ceiling shelving.

"Do you mean to tell me that Butterfield's parents are hippies?" Jeremy asked.

"Actually, his father was a brilliant astrophysicist who worked for the feds until the late nineties, then he went off the grid. His mother was a biochemist with a private biotech firm in Arlington, Virginia." Wentworth cracked his gum as he spoke. "The family turned up in Esopus, right across the river from here on Route 9W. You've probably passed it a hundred times on the way to Kingston."

"And why didn't we have this information before?" Jeremy asked excitedly. "No, never mind, it's not significant at this point. Miri, what do you make of this?"

Miri, who'd been leaning against the wall listening to the conversation, joined them at the table. "Terrence's false narrative about his parents is consistent with his psychosis. He has created a world filled with delusions and to him, these thoughts are the truth. Think of it as a parallel universe. Terrence's own private universe. If you were to confront him with the reality and showed him these photographs, he would deny that these are his parents. This delusional behavior is one of the numerous symptoms of his illness. The others being paranoia, agitation, and violence, to name a few. And there is something else you should know."

"I'm afraid to ask what it is." Jeremy rested his chin upon his fist. His jaw was tense.

"The act of the murder was premeditated. Propelled by delusions, Terrence fantasized, plotted, and planned the specifics of a brutal murder for a very long time. He was like a volcano and Ryan Paige wandered into the path of the eruption."

"What do you mean?"

"I visited Terrence yesterday," she said. "I wanted one more meeting before I prescribed meds, which he does not believe he needs. Terrence boasted to me that he had published a short story detailing the killing. And that he'd followed the plot to the letter."

"Could this be another delusion? Have you seen the manuscript?" Jeremy asked.

"No." Miri let out a long, slow breath. "Terrence was extremely coherent while discussing the subject. In fact, he stated that the story was located on the hard drive of his home computer and that he had shared it with only one other person, whom he trusted implicitly. Terrence was unable to reveal who the person was because my prodding agitated him. He experienced another episode and had to be sedated." She paused for a moment, thinking. "But I was intrigued by the use of his term 'published.'"

"I don't quite understand," Jeremy said, tipping forward on the front legs of his chair.

"Terrence selects his words very carefully, with aforethought. Interestingly, he did not use the word 'authored' or 'written'. He specifically said 'published' with a certain degree of pride. This led me to consider that the work might have been disseminated electronically on the internet."

Her voice was dreamlike as she described her methodology for tracking down the short story. She'd combed the websites from Amazon to fan sites and blogs, finally locating the entry on a blog for fans of violent horror stories. "In the thriller category, there was a writer with the screen name TJButtf0075, and the storyline mimicked the one Butterfield had described to me. Look, here's the transcript." From her navy slacks pocket, she retrieved a bulging envelope and set it on the table. Jeremy opened the envelope and began reading, placing the completed pages facedown into a neat pile.

"Writing's not bad," he said, adding the final page to the stack. Jeremy scratched the balding spot at the crest of his head, wheezing with each breath. "If the prosecution finds out about this, we're done. This manuscript could undermine any possibility of a plea bargain. But on the upside, the debauchery clearly springs from one extremely perverted mind and will come in handy for our insanity defense. Are you sure that Terrence didn't say who had the other copy?"

Miri shook her head.

"Wentworth, do you think you can track the manuscript down or do I need to call Magnum, PI?"

CHAPTER
46

From the corner of his eye, Hal spied Emory strolling toward the prosecutor's table, looking fit and stylish. This annoyed him for two reasons. First, because after a fitful night on the lumpy hotel mattress, Hal looked as though he'd taken the red-eye in from LA, and second, he feared that with little provocation he might haul off and clobber Emory right there on the spot. To gather his wits, he methodically removed his files, reference materials, legal pads, pens, and computer from his briefcase and ignored his rival's final approach at the landing strip on the opposite side of the table.

Kyle waited several minutes, watching Hal's trial preparations, and then cleared his throat. "Excuse me, Samuels. I received your subpoena over the weekend and I'm more than happy to comply, but I've got a small favor to ask. Not that you owe me any favors."

Hal glanced up and flattened his wrinkled tie. "No, I don't."

"I was wondering how much flexibility you have to take a witness out of order? To accommodate a personal issue?" Kyle danced from one foot to the other as though he required a trip to the men's room.

Oh, so that's it, Hal thought with reluctant relief. *The favor is for her. No problem. Maybe he's not such a schmuck after all.*

"You're probably going to begin with Jessie, but I'm sure that she wouldn't mind if you took me first. I need to catch the eleven o'clock train into the city. You'd be doing me a real solid."

"I'll see what I can do." Hal returned to his paperwork, chewing on the inside of his cheek to quell his irritation.

"This'll really help me out. Thanks." Kyle walked away toward the gallery in Jessie's direction, seemingly clueless of her physical discomfort, and settled into a seat two rows behind her.

While Hal derived zero satisfaction from any illusory indebtedness from Emory, he did take pleasure from having Emory's fate in his hands. He was going to make him sit there all day long, maybe even for two days. Emory was going to be the very last witness he called. *Let's see how the thoughtless jerk will like that,* he thought.

He turned his attention to Jessie, whose demeanor remained calm and composed despite the commotion in the courtroom. She pulled her loose hair back away from her face and twisted it into a makeshift ponytail, the way he'd seen her do it in law school whenever she was anxious. It was her tell, a hint that she was nervous about something, like having to give testimony today. The gesture made her ears stick out, and he remembered he use to tease her about those pointy little pixie ears. Her ears would turn bright red and she'd ruffle her locks to hide them behind the curtain of reddish curls. Hal loved those rarely-on-view sexy ears, and the way that, with her hair pulled back, the spot of skin below them where her long neck met her shoulders was exposed.

It was obvious to him, as it should've been to Emory, that Jessie shouldn't be attending the hearing, but that her stubbornness and pride prevented her from asking for favors. Favors he would gladly grant her. Anything. All she had to do was ask. And even if she didn't ask, he'd grant her wishes anyway because he loved her. And he was finally acknowledging to himself just how much.

Jessie caught him staring at her and as the blush tinted her cheeks, she shook the ponytail loose. The magical ears disappeared. Hal walked the short distance to the attorney's gallery and as he drew closer, he noticed that the blush he'd mistaken for embarrassment painted her entire body with a fiery glow. Her legs crossed at the ankles and her fingers that were uneasily knitted together were bloated almost twice their normal size. Her breath labored as she huffed and puffed. Tiny droplets of perspiration glistened on her forehead. He squatted beside her chair, taking a closer read of her face, her eyes.

"Jess, are you all right?" His voice was shaky with concern.

"Honestly, I feel a bit woozy. Just nerves, I suppose," she whispered so that her father couldn't hear. She squeezed the hand he'd rested on the arm of the chair. "I'm fine, really."

"We'll get you out of here as soon as we can." He searched the watery amber and jade eyes for more clues. She was a terrible liar, but he decided not to press.

"I saw you yesterday... at the house," she said.

Hal sensed the sadness behind her words. "I just want you to be happy and if Emory makes you happy—"

"It's not what you think. You've got it all wrong. I need to explain," Jessie said.

"You don't owe me an explanation. I just want you to be happy."

"Hal, yesterday—" Jessie began but was interrupted by the approach of a stern-looking Cindie, who tapped Hal's shoulder and whispered into his ear. He gave his assistant a wan smile and nodded in acknowledgment.

"Sorry, I've gotta go. The judge has summoned counsel into chambers. I'll get you out of here as soon as I can so Emory can take you home. I promise." He hoisted himself up and stretched his achy back.

"Wait, Hal. Here, you need to see this. Terrence gave it to me months ago. I'd forgotten all about it." Jessie pressed a slender package into his hand. "It's important."

Puzzled, Hal accepted the packet and slipped it into his blazer pocket. As he followed his associate across the courtroom, the cell phone in his shirt pocket began to vibrate. Hal answered the call and heard sniffling on the other end of the line. "Erin?"

"Honey, I'm so sorry. I didn't sleep a wink last night. I didn't mean any of the things I said. I don't know what has gotten into me lately," she blurted in a nasally voice congested with tears. "Can you ever forgive me?"

J udge Perry Hamilton was adjusting the front pleats of his judge's robe when Hal and Cindie entered the chambers. Kaplan was seated at the conference table, his toes tapping on the carpet to an inaudible tune apparently spinning in his head. As a finishing touch, the judge's law clerk stood behind his boss, rolling a lint brush over the black gown.

"Gentleman, since we've agreed to the facts and I understand your respective positions, we'll forego any opening statements. So it looks like we're ready for the first pitch, am I correct?" Judge Hamilton stacked his fists on top of each other and swung an imaginary bat. He smacked his lips, imitating the crack of the wood against the leather hide of a baseball. The generous material of his robe's sleeves flapped like eagle's wings. "All the players suited up and ready to get going?"

"Yes, Your Honor," the attorneys replied.

"Has the defendant arrived from the county jail?" Hamilton asked.

"No, Your Honor," Jeremy said. "Mr. Butterfield won't be attending the hearing. My client's affidavit attached to the original motion papers is sufficient, and he wouldn't be able to add anything further at the present time. If the court requires his testimony, we could arrange for an in-camera appearance."

Kaplan was playing his cards very close to his vest.

"We'll see how things progress, Mr. Kaplan. Mr. Samuels, I'm assuming that you won't be calling the defendant as a witness. Correct?"

While Kaplan and the judge conversed, Hal's mind wandered off, his eyes mesmerized by the overhead lights reflecting off the judge's scalp.

Cindie nudged Hal gently with her elbow.

"Ah, yes. That's correct, Your Honor. We believe that our witnesses' testimony will defeat the motion," Hal said.

"We will see. Okay then gentleman, batter up. I'll be in the courtroom shortly, so Mr. Samuels, please prepare to call your first witness."

Back at the prosecutor's table, he and Cindie reviewed Lauren's witness sheet, which established the order of the witnesses and summarized their testimony. The police officers were scheduled to testify first and the Martins last.

"Well, we're going to switch things up a bit." He hesitated a second scanning the faces in the courtroom and then pointed at the list.

"Are you sure?" Cindie said. "She'll be pissed, plus reversing the order will have the cops waiting around when they should be on the streets."

"Ye of little faith. We'll dismiss them and tell them to check in with us at lunchtime. We can call them if they're needed any sooner. How does that sound?"

"Works for me." Cindie broke the news to the men in blue who were congregating in the courtroom's foyer, and Hal couldn't help but notice their appreciative glances following her retreating rump swaying inside her tight pencil skirt.

"I know," Cindie said, ignoring the gawking. "What a bunch of morons."

Hal chuckled as her face reddened.

Jeremy occupied the defense table alone. He cracked his knuckles and wished that the hearing would commence already, as he reviewed his notes, witnesses, testimonies, and exhibits one more time. He sipped the cup of coffee he'd purloined from the judge's office and screwed his face at the brew's acidic taste. He prayed that the swill was not an omen of his bitter defeat.

Behind him in the front row, Miri waited with a pad of paper tucked in her lap. Next to her, Wentworth fished around in his pocket for a package of gum and offered her a stick. The investigator popped two pieces in between his yellow teeth, snapping the wad as it churned in his mouth.

A soft rumbling caught Jeremy's attention as the crowd rose to its feet. A black mass flew up into the front podium and the booming voice of the court clerk proclaimed that court was in session: "Will all persons having business before Honorable Perry Hamilton in the matter of the *People of the State of New York versus Terrence Butterfield* kindly approach the bench."

"Gentlemen, let's get this show on the road," Hamilton said to the attorneys standing before him, eyeing each other cagily like dogs ready for a fight. "Mr. Samuels?"

"The State calls..." Hal declared on his return to the prosecutor's table, "Kyle Emory to the stand."

CHAPTER
47

Hal's elbow rested atop the wall of the witness stand, awaiting the completion of the formalities. Kyle Emory's right hand was raised to God and his left covered the cracked black leather casing of the Bible. Emory solemnly swore to the oath administered by the court stenographer, which was followed by his stating of his name and address for the record. He reconsidered his answer and amended his response. "Platt Street is my legal address, but I'm temporarily residing at the Harvard Club in New York City."

From Hal's experience, people tended to react strangely when placed inside the box. The smart became stupid, the calm became edgy, and the sharp became confused. Sometimes, they forgot their names, or their birthdates, or even their kids' names. Superficially, Kyle Emory didn't appear to be one of those guys. There was a quiet aloofness about him, but Hal caught a whiff of the fear behind the intelligence and the tailored suit.

Hal considered his strategy. He could adhere to the rules as decorum dictated or play a cat-and-mouse game or go off the grid to assert his alpha-maleness. But this hearing wasn't about his personal vendetta against Emory. Rather, he had to concentrate on the three points necessary to defeat Kaplan's motion. First, that Jessie didn't contact the police. Second, that Jessie never dispensed legal advice to Butterfield, and third, that she didn't convey any confidential information to Emory or anyone else.

And if Emory's testimony exonerated Jessie on all three points, then there would be no need for her to take the stand. The case would be won and done with one witness.

He opened his examination by establishing Emory's relationship to Jessie and asking his marital status.

"Single but engaged to be married."

"Engaged to whom, sir?"

"Jessica Martin, attorney at law," Emory replied, locating her in the gallery and slyly smiling.

Out of the corner of his eye, Hal observed Jessie fidgeting in her chair, but he found it impossible to determine whether her uneasiness sprang from Kyle's testimony, her nervousness, or physical discomfort. Meanwhile, in the witness box, her fiancé exuded an air of indifference to her suffering.

Hal wanted to make this sucker squirm. "You and she are currently estranged, is that correct?"

"Objection. As to relevance," Kaplan interjected, standing at full attention. Kyle glanced from Kaplan to Judge Hamilton, seeking instructions.

"Objection overruled. Mr. Samuels, please continue, but limit your questions regarding this topic. And I would like to advise both of you gentlemen to conserve your objections. This is not a bench or jury trial. We are trying to get at the heart of the pending motion," Judge Hamilton said and instructed Kyle to answer the question.

After the question was repeated, Kyle evasively replied, "We're presently residing apart."

Hal grinned to himself upon receiving the answer he'd suspected to be true but required on the record. As a veteran prosecutor, the golden rule was etched into his brain: never ask a witness a question to which you do not already know the answer.

"Mr. Emory, were you residing with Ms. Martin at Platt Street on the morning of August 31st?"

"Yes."

"Did your household receive a call from the defendant, Terrence Butterfield, on the morning of August 31st at approximately 1:00 a.m.?" *Down to business*, he thought. This should be a walk in the park.

"Yes. Jessie received a call on her cell phone from Mr. Butterfield at that approximate time. She told me that he said that he had killed someone. Jessie said he sounded suicidal and was threatening to kill himself with his gun."

Kaplan sprang up again like a jack-in-the-box and objected on the grounds of hearsay. The judge sighed, overruling the objection because the attorneys had stipulated to Butterfield's confession regarding the death of Ryan Paige and that Jessie's statements to

Emory were relevant to her alleged breach of the attorney-client privilege. Deflated, the objector slunk into his chair.

Hal prodded Emory for details about the night of the murder and the witness described his argument with Jessie.

"I was in favor of contacting the police, while she insisted that we immediately go to Butterfield's home," Emory said.

"Do you know whether Ms. Martin contacted the police?"

"Not to my knowledge."

He mentally checked off the first item on the list. Jessie never contacted the police about the murder. On to the next item of business—the legal advice.

Kyle testified that since Jessie was intent on helping Butterfield, he had no choice but to accompany her. They'd rushed over and arrived at Park Avenue simultaneously with the police, who'd detained them outside of the house.

"Did either you or Ms. Martin speak with the defendant while you were at his house?" Hal asked.

"No, not really. He greeted us and Jessie warned him not to speak to the police. She was standing on the front steps when she yelled it up to Butterfield, who was in his doorway."

"At any time did Ms. Martin indicate to either Mr. Butterfield or the police officers that she was acting in her capacity as an attorney on his behalf?"

"I don't recall, but her relationship with Terrence is quite complicated. He has carte blanche to call her anytime, day or night, if there's any kind of problem and frankly, he takes advantage of her. Look, they've known each other a long time and she's handled legal matters for him. Terrence was her teacher and is her father's buddy, so she would do anything for him." A muscle twitched next to Emory's nostril. "I'm a patient man and I respect her privacy, but I don't need to tell you that it's an extremely trying situation. Who knows what they discuss? What he's told her? What they're plotting together?" The openly hostile comments were left dangling in the air, the suggestion of a line of inquiry better left untouched.

"That's enough, sir, you've answered the question," Hal said sharply. His mind raced, analyzing his next move. He'd achieved his second goal, proving that Jessie hadn't advised Butterfield, but he'd been derailed by Emory's rogue remarks.

"I'm innocent of any wrongdoing, but I'm caught in the middle here." Kyle's attention swung around the courtroom as though seeking guidance from the walls and the ceiling. The man's gaze finally settled back again on Jessie. "My fiancée gets a phone call and suddenly, I'm dragged into the spotlight shining on this tragedy. I don't want any part of this, and if Jessie wants to protect Butterfield, that's her business. As far as I'm concerned, he's an intruder in my life and I'll do anything to be free of him once and for all."

"Objection," Hal shouted. "Judge, I request that the witness's remarks be stricken from the record. His statements are not responsive. Please admonish the witness to answer only the questions posed."

"Mr. Samuels, I warned you about this line of questioning. He's your witness and you opened the barn door. The testimony will stand."

Hal paced back and forth before the judge's bench, his mind searching for a way to wrangle Emory back on track. "Well, then,

Mr. Emory, you sound overly suspicious of Ms. Martin's relationship with Mr. Butterfield. As you stated, she would do anything for him, correct? Are you suggesting that the nature of their relationship is more intimate than friendship?"

A blue vein bulged on Emory's neck above shirt collar. A chink in the cool, composed armor.

"Is that the reason that you despise the defendant, Terrence Butterfield? You believe that he's having an affair with your fiancée?"

"You son-of-a-bitch! Where do you get off?" Kyle jumped to his feet, leaned across the barrier separating them, and grabbed at Hal's shirt collar. Hal stepped back beyond Kyle's reach. The witness took a swipe at him and, losing his balance, tumbled backward into the booth. The chair and Emory tipped over with a shattering crash.

The words "No, Kyle!" sprang from Jessie's lips. Hal saw her father clamping a hand on her shoulder, preventing her from entering the fracas. As the chaos broke out in the courtroom, Kaplan opened his mouth to speak but appeared to stop himself as the clamoring of the judge's gavel echoed throughout the courtroom.

"Order in the court! Order in the court! Bailiff, please see if Mr. Emory is hurt," Hamilton shouted from his throne, pounding his gavel.

Above the din, the words "Your Honor!" thundered from the rear of the courtroom.

The room turned silent and Hal's head, along with all others', snapped toward the voice. District Attorney Lauren Hollenbeck marched into the center aisle. "Excuse me, Your Honor, may I request a short recess to confer with my staff?"

"Mr. Emory, please contain yourself. This is a court of law, not some college bar. And Mr. Samuels, stop antagonizing the witness. Any further outbreaks and I'll hold you both in contempt." Judge Hamilton swiped his black wing across his brow. "Ms. Hollenbeck, we're trying to conduct a hearing. But given the situation, it might be a good time for a brief recess. Court's adjourned. Back in five minutes." The judge once again smashed his gavel and fled from the bench.

Lauren smiled warmly at his retreating back and then signaled for her team to meet her outside in the hallway. Hal and Cindie joined their boss in a remote nook beyond the earshot of the crowd who was stretching their legs. She crossed her arms and excitedly tapped the pointy toes of her high heels.

"What are you doing in there? Are you intentionally blowing our case?" Lauren asked.

"Don't you see what Emory is trying to pull? He's setting Jessie up." His forehead grew hot and damp, and his trembling arm pointed in the direction of the courtroom. "He's trying to implicate Jessica Martin in the boy's murder."

"That's a load of crap and you know it. You're airing your dirty laundry in there and if you don't stop this nonsense, I'm pulling you off this case. Once and for all. Do you hear me, Hal?"

Hal glared at her in disbelief, struggling to reduce the boiling-over temper to a simmer.

"From now on, you're on a short leash. *My* leash. Cindie, if he so much as goes off the script, I want you to shut him down. Ask the judge for a recess and then call me." Her sapphire irises glistened. "You've been warned."

After the break, Judge Hamilton rested his chin on his palms, waiting for Hal to continue. The tension in the courtroom had not dissipated; if anything, the animosity had exploded like a stadium roaring after a grand slam. Emory ground his tight jaw in a horizontal motion and his muscles tightened, ready to spring again if provoked. Hal approached the witness box, but given Lauren's warning, he reconsidered and receded to safety behind the prosecutor's table. Yet, he needed to veer slightly off the path to achieve his desired results. He leaned his tall frame against the table and a mental bell announced round two. Time to nail this sucker.

"Mr. Emory, at any time on the morning of August 31st, did you personally speak with the defendant?" Hal asked.

"Yes," Kyle said, flatly.

"I'm confused. You previously denied that you had spoken with Mr. Butterfield." Hal was growing itchy. Working from a distance wasn't his *modus operandi*. He preferred to be close, look his witnesses dead straight in the eyes.

"I said that we didn't speak after we arrived at his home. I phoned him back right after he'd called Jessie. I said that she was upset by their conversation and asked what had happened. He told me about the killing—I mean the shooting—and I urged him to contact the authorities. He agreed. Plain and simple."

Hal couldn't resist. He was drawn to the witness like a moth to a flame. He needed to read Emory's expressions, his body, to determine whether he was telling the truth. The truth that would exonerate Jessie and defeat Kaplan's motion to dismiss the charges. He rounded the table, crossed the wooden floorboards, and approached the judge's bench. "For the record, Mr. Emory, did you contact the police on the morning of August 31st?"

"Mr. Samuels, honestly, I wasn't concerned about Mr. Butterfield or any crime he committed. That wasn't my problem. My priorities were elsewhere. I had an expectant partner who was going to traipse around in the middle of the night after a murderer. What would you've done?"

"Sir, please answer the question. Did you inform the police?"

There was a long, tense silence in the courtroom, and it was so quiet that Hal could hear his pulse pounding in his ears.

"Yes, I did, and I'd do it again in a heartbeat. Around 1:15 a.m., I phoned the police and told them about Butterfield's admission of murder and suicide threats."

But when asked whether Butterfield had authorized him to make the call, Kyle waffled. "Not in so many words, but it was implicit."

The sound of whispering voices trickled through the gallery.

"Did you inform Ms. Martin of your phone calls to Butterfield or the police?" Hal asked.

"No, I did not."

Just as he'd hoped, it had been Emory, not Jessie, who'd alerted the cops of the murder. Emory's testimony exonerated Jessie of all wrongdoing and exposed the real culprit. He was pleased that he'd been the one to reveal it to her. However, knowing the pain Emory had caused her made him despise her fiancé even more.

He sneaked a peek at Jessie in the gallery. She appeared frozen, not breathing, blinking, or moving a muscle. The fringe of the shawl covering her shoulders fluttered in the breeze of the ceiling fans.

"Thank you, that's all." Hal sighed in relief. He'd rounded the bases and had slid across home plate. He pivoted away from the witness to return to his chair but halted midway. He turned an about-face toward Emory. "One final thing. Who enlisted Mr. Kaplan as Mr. Butterfield's defense counsel?"

"Jessie did."

"No further questions, Your Honor. Kaplan, your witness."

Hal wasn't one to boast, but he'd hit a home run, as the judge would put it, using a dozen simple questions and a slight detour. Unexpectedly, Emory hadn't put up a much of a fight and ultimately, he'd fessed up. And then it dawned on Hal. This wasn't about Emory's hatred for Butterfield. This was about their common denominator. The one person whom all three men would protect at all costs. He couldn't figure out why Emory had waited to come forward or why he'd forced Jessie to suffer. Unfortunately, "why" questions were beyond the scope of his examination.

Kaplan's hangdog expression telegraphed desperation and defeat. "After your conversation with Mr. Butterfield, you divulged his confidential admissions to the police without his consent or knowledge, is that correct?"

"You're twisting my words. Mr. Butterfield told me about the shooting and he agreed that the police should be informed," Emory said.

"However, your call wasn't a 911 call, was it? Pretty convenient knowing that the police station's main line wouldn't be recorded."

"Argumentative," Hal called out for good measure.

Before the judge responded to the objection, Kaplan interjected, "Withdrawn. What exact words did you speak to the police, sir? To the best of your memory, of course."

"To the best of my memory," Emory said, sarcastically, "there was some sort of problem at Mr. Butterfield's home. That he told me that he had shot someone and he was extremely distressed. He threatened to kill himself with his pistol and I urged them to use caution."

"That's it? You're sure?"

"Yes, absolutely."

"Thank you. No further questions," Kaplan said.

"Any redirect?" Judge Hamilton asked. Hal declined the offer and the judge dismissed Kyle from the witness stand. "Mr. Samuels, please call your next witness."

CHAPTER
48

J essie dabbed a tissue at the sweat trickling down the back of her neck. The lethargic ceiling fans barely stirred the air inside the stuffy courtroom. Time seemed to be standing still.

Since Ryan's murder, nothing that escaped from her fiancé's mouth had been a surprise, but the hatred, jealousy, suspicion, and disrespect spewed in open court was unforgivable. These accusations could not be redacted and would become immortalized in the records of the Dutchess County Clerk's office, like postings on Facebook and Twitter.

Perhaps naively, she'd ignored the hostility between Terrence and Kyle because they'd tolerated each other in her presence and cherished her in their own special ways. Her loyalty should've been obvious to Kyle, but his damning testimony expunged all memories of their happiness. She felt hollow inside. As she watched Kyle slink from the witness stand, Jessie slipped the engagement ring from her finger and zippered it inside her coin purse. Somehow, her soul felt lighter.

Hal was no savior either. He should have known better, permitting Kyle to run amuck like that. A case of chivalry backfiring, or was it his ambition?

Jessie was pulled from her thoughts as the round ligaments supporting her womb smarted. Her toes tingled from lost circulation. She repositioned herself to ease the discomfort and wondered when she would say her peace and go home.

"Honey, are you all right?" Ed placed a warm hand over her clammy one that was gripping the armrest. "Maybe we should go?"

She shook her head.

"Mr. Martin, you're up," Hal called. "The prosecution calls Edmund Martin to the stand."

"I'll make it quick." Ed winked and patted his daughter's hand.

She'd heard enough. Since Ed's testimony wouldn't offer any new revelations, she seized the opportunity to stretch her legs outside in the corridor. Ahead of her, Kyle sailed toward the grand staircase without a glance backward. The mere sight of him made her seethe with anger. To avoid a public confrontation, Jessie stopped and leaned against the wall, watching him descend the stairs.

It was then that Jessie observed Lauren studying a recent portrait of Judge Hamilton that hung on the opposite wall. Jessie hoped that she wouldn't be noticed, but no such luck.

"Quite a shocker, wasn't it?" Lauren said. "Kyle Emory is full of surprises."

Don't let her get to you, Jessie thought. "I don't quite catch your drift."

"Calling the police? Not mentioning it to you? Convenient?"

"I'd love to stay and chat, but I have to pee."

The DA's snide smile irked Jessie and the temptation to empty her full bladder on those fancy ivory shoes seized her. After all, she couldn't fight Mother Nature's call. Controlling the impulse, Jessie entered the ladies' room, hoping that the wicked witch wasn't in hot pursuit.

The restroom was small; two stalls, two sinks with mirrors, and barely enough room to maneuver in without being bruised by the cubicle doors. The white subway tiles covering every surface failed to disguise the cramped atmosphere of the public restroom. There were two women waiting in the queue ahead of her. A petite, olive-skinned woman in a smart camel suit smiled at Jessie and motioned for her to take her spot. The eyebrow-pierced teen umbilically attached to her cell phone was oblivious and slunk into the first available stall.

"When are you due, dear?" the older woman asked in a thick Israeli accent, gently grazing her fingertips on Jessie's belly.

"A month."

"I have two of my own," she replied longingly. "All grown and moved away."

The door of the large handicap stall creaked open and a tall, slender blonde appeared, straightening the side seams of her short denim skirt. Jessie returned the polite smile as the glamazon skimmed by, leaving a honeysuckle fragrance in her wake. The beauty approached the sink and studied her hair that glowed with an iridescent green. A purple aura caressed her skin, as it did to the lady on Jessie's left. It was strange that she hadn't noticed it before.

Suddenly, Jessie's stomach lurched as though cresting the first incline of a rollercoaster, and a thousand butterflies fluttered within her chest cavity. Beneath her feet, the tile floor undulated like a wave and her body hinged like a jackknife as she felt herself falling. Falling. Falling.

"Oh, God!" Jessie cried.

"Don't move her! Give her space. Call 911," the older woman shouted.

"Quick, somebody get help!" the blonde yelled.

Voices exploded around Jessie as blindness invaded her eyes, trapping her inside a body that arched like a twig on the verge of snapping. Her own voice, thin and squeaky, begged for assistance, but it was swallowed up by the shouts of those surrounding her. While her eyes refused vision, heightened hearing remained the only sense connecting her to the world.

"I'm a doctor. Just remain calm."

"Somebody! You, teenybopper. Go get help."

"Who, me? Forget you, lady."

"Go. Get. Help. Hurry!" Two voices shouted in chorus.

The rush of the running water, a door smashing open, and shoes slapping on the floor assaulted Jessie's ears. The heavy whooshing of breath collapsing her lungs replaced the language frozen in her constricted vocal cords.

"Let's make her comfortable. Here, place my jacket beneath her head."

"Oh, god, she's turning blue!"

Jessie's universe collapsed into a vacuum. Before losing consciousness, her last thought was that she was going to die.

"Mr. Martin, on the night in question, how did you learn about the situation at Mr. Butterfield's home?" Hal asked.

Ed tapped on the microphone, transmitting a thunderous thumping through the courtroom, and he adjusted its head to his comfort level. He cleared his throat and swallowed. "I received a call from Jessie's fiancé, Kyle Emory, around 1 a.m. He said that Jessie had received a call from Terry and they were on their way over to his house. There'd been some kind of accident. We agreed that I'd call Terry and keep him on the line until he and Jessie arrived, which I immediately did."

"What was the substance of your conversation with Mr. Butterfield?"

"I told him that Jessie had called me, and Terry confirmed that there'd been a shooting. He said that he was going to kill himself. I urged him to contact the police, but he refused and said he'd wait until Jessie arrived. I was scared out of my wits as you can imagine. My wife grabbed the phone and also briefly spoke with Terry. He repeated the story about the killing to her. She offered to come over, but he refused. Then he hung up."

"What did you do?" Hal asked.

"Well, my wife and I discussed the situation. We didn't know what to do, whether to call Jessie or the police or drive over to his home anyway. We didn't want our daughter walking into a perilous situation." He rubbed the back of his neck. "We decided that since Kyle was with Jessie, we'd wait to hear from her after she'd seen Terry."

"Mr. Martin, did you contact the police?"

"No, I didn't call the police. As I said, I only spoke with Kyle, Terry and later with Jessie, not the police."

"Mr. Martin, do you know who called the police, sir?"

"You mean besides my daughter's fiancé?" Ed craned his neck, desperately seeking his daughter. He furrowed his brow and continued. "Um ... Yes, I do."

Hal quickly spun toward the gallery, searching for the source of Ed's distraction. Jessie's chair sat empty, her pocketbook neatly stowed beneath it. How long had it been since he'd last seen her? Two minutes? Five? Ten? His mind went blank as he stared off into space.

"Mr. Samuels?" Judge Hamilton asked.

"Ah, Mr. Martin, can you please ..." Hal began mechanically. The sound of a commotion emanating from the hallway and the court attendants racing from the room interrupted his question.

"Your Honor, we request a recess," Hal blurted as he pointed his chin toward Ed. "Come on."

Neither man waited for a response and they dashed out into the hallway, only to encounter a human logjam congesting the narrow corridor, blocking the entry of the women's restroom. On the court officer's heels, they pushed their way through the crowd.

Distorted fragments of conversation floated around them, "a young woman…seizure…ladies room…paramedics…"

No, no! Hal thought. *Jessie.*

Behind him, Ed screamed his daughter's name in panic as they muscled their way toward the restroom doorway. Upon reaching the portal, a young sturdy officer blocked their path.

"It's my daughter in there. Let me through. Please," Ed pleaded.

"Sir, I can't let you in until I know the situation," the guard said.

"Please, she needs to know that I'm here."

"Chet, can you cut us some slack here?" Hal asked the guard.

"Mr. Samuels, if you want to take a look-see, go ahead. But then, right out."

"Ed, I'll be right back. Sit tight." He hated to leave Ed alone, but at least he could check on the situation and report back. The guard stepped aside, and Hal squeezed into the lavatory's foyer. He gasped at the sight of what he'd dreaded and expected. Jessie was crumbled in a mass on the white tile floor, her arms and legs twitching like leaves in a storm. She lay unconscious, and white foam festered at the corner of her mouth.

Two women bent over Jessie, tenderly stroking her drenched forehead. Hal's body hitched at the unexpected appearance of his wife, Erin, who, as yet, had failed to notice him.

CHAPTER
49

Hal recognized the woman kneeling on the floor next to Erin, pressing her fingers against Jessie's inner wrist. She was Dr. Miri Shtern, a forensic psychiatrist who was well-regarded in the legal community and among her colleagues. Over the years, her reports had defeated several of his cases, and while he hadn't understood half of the medical jargon, he'd grasped the bottom line. Based on her findings, murderers, thieves, and rapists had been found incompetent to stand trial. Dr. Shtern's appearance at the hearing meant only one thing. Jeremy Kaplan had a legal ace up his sleeve.

He couldn't dwell on that possibility right now, not while Jessie was dying.

"One-ten and steady," Dr. Shtern informed the pair of paramedics who barreled past him into the room. When they began barking orders at her, she abruptly fired back, "I'm a doctor and she's hyperventilating. Oxygen stat. We need to get her to the OR and get this baby delivered."

Hal edged back into the doorway to make room for the paramedics to go about their work. Jessie's chest heaved up and down as her breathing appeared rapid, labored, and uneven. Feelings of helplessness and guilt squeezed his own chest as he watched her body tense, her limbs contract, and her back arch as a violent seizure attacked. She let out a deep throaty cry.

He'd never witnessed a seizure before. The way Jessie's body whipped about in spasms made him worry that her spine might snap if the convulsions didn't kill her.

"Somebody help her, please," he pleaded.

"That's what we're trying to do but she's clustering," Dr. Shtern said sharply, throwing him a dirty look. "She needs an anticonvulsant. Do you have any magnesium sulfate?" Dr. Shtern asked the paramedics.

"Doctor, we can't do anything until she stops," said an EMT.

"I need all non-medical personnel to clear out of here and give us some space. Except you." Dr. Shtern pointed at Hal. "As soon as she stops, we go, understand?" She paused to regroup her thoughts, then shouted, "We need a medical history. She was in the courtroom with an older gentleman. Anyone know where he is?"

"Ed," Hal shouted, waving his hands to get Ed's attention as Erin brushed by him on her way out of the restroom. "Quick, in here."

Ed squeezed his body through the crowd and froze behind Hal, staring at Jessie writhing on the floor.

"Go on," Hal urged, "they need your help."

Ed rushed into the room and dropped to his knees, reaching out to his daughter. The doctor swatted his hand away before he could make contact. She explained that his daughter was suffering clonic seizures, the rapid contracting and relaxing of muscles, and he was observing the second round within a few minutes. More were expected. "Who's her doctor? Does she have any history of epilepsy? Any allergies or existing medical conditions?"

Dazed, Ed shook his head. "She's perfectly healthy and has no allergies."

Dr. Shtern instructed Ed to call Jessie's obstetrician and to alert him about the seizure and that they were in transit to the hospital. His gray eyes welled with tears. "Will she be okay? What about the baby?"

"Sir, please do what I ask. We need her doctor waiting at the ER and ready to go."

The paramedics set the stretcher board on the floor parallel to Jessie and eagerly waited for the cue. A minute later, Jessie's muscles relaxed and the spasm surrendered her body with the exception of her fingertips, which hammered as though tinkling the keys on a piano. Dr. Shtern signaled and Hal joined the flurry of expert hands scooping Jessie up onto the stretcher. The paramedics secured her head, neck, and body to the board, affixed the oxygen mask and inserted an IV line into her forearm. Within seconds, the medical team sprinted out of the ladies' room and down the staircase past the spectators lining the hallway.

"**O**h, Jess," Hal said, joining the convoy. Trotting alongside the stretcher, he clutched Jessie's icy hand willing her to awaken. To blink her eyes open. To recognize his face. He pressed his lips into her pale palm, praying that she sensed him through the unconsciousness possessing her.

"Mr. Samuels, I'm sorry, family only," Dr. Shtern said brusquely, prying away his grip when they reached the ambulance. Jessie's fingers trembled slightly as though bidding him farewell.

Ed and Miri Shtern hurriedly climbed aboard the ambulance behind the paramedics and the gurney. The rear doors slammed shut and the vehicle sped away.

Long after the screams of the siren merged into the sounds of the street, Hal remained on the curb, watching the traffic rush by.

There was no choice. Jessie's magnetic pull was too powerful to resist. Hal needed to follow the ambulance. Now. If he didn't go, no one would call him with news, either good or bad, and not knowing would certainly kill him. His only choice, which was no choice at all, was to be waiting at the hospital for Jessie. No matter how long it took.

Hal fished around in his slacks pocket for his car keys and swore under his breath when he remembered they were tucked inside the briefcase he'd left in the upstairs courtroom. Reentering the building, he raced up the marble staircase two steps at a time and sprinted down the corridor and into the courtroom toward the prosecutor's desk.

"Returning to the scene of the crime?" a woman's icy voice inquired.

He whipped around and discovered Erin sitting alone in the rear row of the empty gallery. Her eyes were congested and her nose was red and raw.

"I came here to apologize to you for the horrible things that I said last night, but Hal, let's be honest. We're fooling ourselves." Erin sniffled. "I think that we have to talk."

"Erin, I can't do this right now." He held up his hand to stop her, but he noticed the tears rolling down her cheeks. The grief-stricken look on her face was too much for him to bear. "You were right. I haven't treated you fairly." He paused to swallow the lump in his throat. "I know that we need to talk, but now isn't the time."

"That's the problem, Hal. It's never the right time," she said. Her eyes demanded the truth from him. He owed her that much.

He wanted to tell her that he loved her, but not enough, and not in the way he should. In his heart, he knew, and had always known, that their differences were irreconcilable. He sought independence from his family and to be successful in his own right, while she craved the wealth, the glitz, and the glamour that her family represented. But he had to go. Now was not the time.

"Erin, I'm truly sorry. We'll talk when I get home tonight. I promise."

"Hal, I'm sorry, too." Erin rose, snatched her purse, and walked out of the courtroom.

The deep sorrow broadcast by her footsteps resonated down the hallway and into his heart.

CHAPTER
50

Jeremy sipped his coffee from a mug layered with cigar soot and rolled the stiffness from his neck and shoulder blades. He was feeling the weight of his fifty-nine years, especially after his most recent conversation with Butterfield. He'd made the mistake of stopping by the jail for a visit prior to his returning to the office for lunch. He was sick and tired of revisiting the litany of complaints, of squandering the retainer, of wasting time, of miscommunications, and dealing with the lack of results. Dealing with Butterfield was like poking an angry lion with a stick.

Mo burst unannounced into his office, her arms laden with documents, and rattled off messages, instructions, reminders, and trivia at a million miles a second. His hand trembled, spattering caramel spots across his white dress shirt.

Now he'd have to go upstairs and change before returning to court this afternoon. He didn't like Gayle to see him like this.

Edgy. Frazzled. For the past several evenings, he'd avoided her by holing up in his office and crashing on the moth-eaten couch. Following their unwritten code, she dutifully delivered his meals to the basement, reminded him to eat, and warned him not to work too hard or too late. In return, he plastered on a smile. Each morning, he listened for her minivan's tires spinning on the gravel driveway and snuck upstairs to shower, shave, and change his clothes. Then, he scooted downstairs to begin the cycle over again.

He'd been married to Sheila during the Klein case, so this was Gayle's first go-round with the legal marathon of murders. To her credit, she was adapting to the de rigueur schedule, although with guarded resistance. She never asked any questions or made any demands. He knew that his grizzled appearance had detoured toward repulsiveness, but it was only temporary. And that the hermitage was nothing personal. This was his trial routine and the way he made his living.

Mo was another story. She lived for the adrenaline rush of death's aftermath. That woman could accomplish more in a week inside the pressure cooker than during a month in the humdrum daily grind of the law. Sometimes it pissed him off when he found her reading a romance novel, or worse, *People Magazine*, at her desk. But when death came a-calling, Mo was at the top of her game. And this was crunch time.

"Are you listening to me? Or am I standing here farting upwind?" Mo asked, tapping the toe of her zebra print wedges. "The judge called. The hearing's been adjourned until tomorrow morning, something about a witness's medical emergency. Sounds like an exciting morning."

"Where do I begin? The fistfight? Emory admitting he called the cops? Or that Miri went missing? Or how about Butterfield's snide comments? It's been a banner morning," Jeremy said sarcastically. His fingers pinched the front placket of his shirt, and he assessed whether the stain had penetrated through to his undershirt and if he'd have to change that, too.

"Now that you've got a moment to spare, you might want to pay a little attention to your wife," Mo said, walking across the room and neatly folding the blanket bunched up on the sofa.

Hal discovered Dr. Miri Shtern waiting outside the maternity center's operating room. Lost in her thoughts, she failed to observe his approach and her serious expression registered the severity of the situation. Given the frequency and intensity of Jessie's fits, the odds were stacked against her. He was no physician, but he was aware of the potential outcomes. Maternal mortality. Infant mortality. Severe medical complications for both Jessie and her baby. He had to prepare himself for the worst.

"Where is she?" he whispered.

"They're still working on her. An emergency C-Section. She experienced another seizure on the way to the hospital."

Hal remained silent.

"I'm sorry that I was so rude before," she said.

"Dr. Shtern, there's no need," Hal said. "The most important thing is that Jess's receiving the best possible care." His voice wavered.

"Mr. Samuels, why are you here?"

He winced at the intrusion into his privacy. Helping save Jessie's life neither entitled her to ask nor to receive a response to that question. He sighed and stared into the white fluorescent fixture overhead. "That's going to take a lifetime to explain. To her."

CHAPTER
51

In the corridor outside the hospital's surgical suite, Hal watched the stainless-steel doors, waiting for them to open. The sterile walls around him seemed to be boxing him in, and he couldn't fight his suspicion that Jessie was dead. His eyes widened in horror as the doors to the operating theater swung open and a short doctor in blood-soaked scrubs emerged. As he dragged himself past Hal and Dr. Shtern, he rubbed his massive hands over his drawn and exhausted-looking face. Presuming he was Jessie's doctor, Hal chased him down and peppered him with questions about Jessie. Initially, the doctor was resistant, but finally he uttered the two words that eased Hal's mind.

"She's alive." Officially, Jessie's condition was labeled as "critical but stable" and she was resting quietly in the ICU.

There was something about the obstetrician's apprehensiveness that had not completely reassured him. Beyond the patient-client confidentiality, he sensed that the doctor was withholding critical information. Bad news. About Jessie. About the baby. Hal needed to see Jessie for himself.

He and Dr. Shtern rode the elevator together to the second floor ICU. The unit's eerie white atmosphere presented an aura of the gates of heaven rather than of a place of healing.

Dr. Shtern gave him his space by remaining behind at the nurse's station. His heart pounded in his chest as he paused outside Jessie's cubicle, peeking inside. The vertical blinds on the large glass partitions were slanted at an angle allowing him only a sliver of a view. Jessie's eyes were shut and her face was relaxed. It was difficult to see whether she was still pregnant, but to his relief, her chest rose and fell on its own accord. Like the rest of the floor's occupants, she was fettered to the machines surrounding her. The heart monitor beeped in a slow, natural rhythm. At least she was alive.

Jessie's parents lingered at her bedside while Emory sheepishly wedged himself against the far corner. Hal bristled at the sight of the guy who'd repeatedly forfeited his right to be considered her family, friend, and lover. He should be in that room, not Emory. But he restrained himself and watched in silence. A gentle hand tapped his shoulder and he allowed Dr. Shtern to guide him away.

"It's in God's hands," she said.

It was four o'clock in the afternoon by the time Hal returned to the DA's office, and the conversation hushed the moment he opened the glass door and stepped inside. He figured that gossip about his bizarre, unexplained departure had spread with the speed of a tweet, but he ignored the odd looks and walked down the hall to his office.

"Congratulations are in order," Lauren Hollenbeck sang off key. She strutted into his office, hiked up her skirt, and wiggled her buttocks onto the corner of his oak desk.

Hal looked at her with a puzzled expression.

"The senate appointment. It's been secured. Aren't you going to congratulate me? This means big things for us."

Us? The last he remembered they weren't on speaking terms, let alone on an intimate working relationship. He decided to play along. "Great job, Lauren. You deserve this."

"Just wrap up the Paige case and we're on our way to the future."

The future. Two days ago, the future had been the furthest thing from his mind. His marriage, job, and life had been secure. Then within the last forty-eight hours, everything had capsized. As he and Erin had acknowledged, the trouble had been brewing for quite a while and nothing that had occurred had been out of the blue. For years, he'd concentrated on his career to the detriment of Erin and Tyler, assuming that his marriage was strong enough to weather the storm. Apparently not, especially when Ryan Paige's murder had thrust Jessie back into his life, making him question his true values.

This morning when he'd told Lauren to take a hike, he'd half-expected the pink slip to be waiting on his desk when he returned, but here she was dangling the carrots again. Either the woman had no self-esteem or he was an irreplaceable asset. Whichever way, choices would be made.

More irrevocable decisions.

"I can see you've got a lot on your mind. We'll talk later," Lauren said, sliding off the desk. The scarlet lips threw him a smile of complete satisfaction.

Hal picked up the phone receiver and started to dial Erin's cell phone, but he changed his mind. If he timed it perfectly, he could enter the house and pack a bag or two before Erin and Tyler returned from soccer. There was no reason to call her. One less confrontation.

He hit the intercom button and pressed Cindie's extension.

"You lucked out," Cindie said, "the hearing was adjourned until the morning. How's your friend?"

Hal reported the tenuous situation at the hospital but not the fractious one on the home front. "I've got an errand to run," he said, "so we'll get down to work in about an hour's time."

Hal solidified his plan as he drove home. He unlocked the front door of his house and entered into an unnatural silence. It was strange how one small child's presence could inhabit every corner of a house. He was going to miss that. He was going to miss a lot of things but swore that he wouldn't neglect the important stuff anymore. Soccer. Little League. Birthdays. Holidays. He'd work it out with Erin even if it killed him.

His large black suitcase and duffle bag were waiting on his side of the bed. Erin was never one for subtlety. His tee shirts and boxers were neatly folded inside the suitcase, along with an assortment of sport-shirts, jeans, and sweaters. A pile of rolled socks nested like eggs on his pillow, abandoned. Maybe she'd run out of time, or Tyler had come in with questions. He entered the walk-in closet, grabbed a half dozen pair of dress slacks and three blazers and hooked them inside the suit bag he found in the back of the closet. He selected three pairs of shoes, one each in black, brown, and cordovan leather along with his sneakers, and threw them inside the duffle alongside his workout gear.

Next was the ensuite bathroom, the one that Erin had so meticulously designed with no-expense-spared. Hal rooted around the bathroom gathering his hair products, shaver, and other toiletries. From beneath the vanity, he retrieved a fresh bar of soap and his plastic travel soap dish. He placed the soap within its new home, wadded its discarded wrapper into a small ball and lifted his arm to pitch it into the wicker wastebasket, but stopped.

At the bottom of the bin, a thin blue and white plastic stick was buried among the trash. It was a pregnancy test. He retrieved it and examined the digital display. The results were unmistakably clear.

Jeremy Kaplan was sated. He sprawled on his back, watching the afternoon shadows flutter on the ceiling, his wife curled up in the crook of his arm. Gayle pulled the bed sheets over them, protecting them against the autumn breeze gusting into the open window.

"He's going to have to plead insanity," he said.

"There's no shame in using that defense," Gayle said. "You're saving his life."

"But I was so sure. I never would've pursued this line of attack or trampled over so many people if I didn't think I'd win."

"You haven't lost." She planted a kiss on his sandpaper cheek.

"I can see the handwriting on the wall." Jeremy sighed and moved to rise from the bed.

"Jerry, just a few more minutes. We haven't seen each other in days. Relax. Five minutes. And dinner with the kids tonight. Please."

His wife was irresistible. He couldn't deny her any request because she asked for so little but gave so much that it twisted his guts. Jeremy enveloped his wife into his arms and kissed her.

They showered together and dressed. Mo's car was still parked in the driveway, so he decided to check his messages once more before dinner. As Jeremy left, Gayle started dancing around the kitchen while she prepared dinner. She warbled slightly out of tune to Bon Jovi blasting on the radio.

Jeremy opened the kitchen door and walked downstairs to the office.

"The list of additional psychiatrists is on your desk," Mo said.

He narrowed his eyes at her.

"Do you think that after all this time I don't know what's going on in that whacked-out head of yours?" she said.

"You're the best. You know that?"

"You should know the half of it." Mo laughed. Whatever the joke was, it was clearly on him.

Locating Miri was the first order of business. She'd been missing since before the lunch break and her expertise was required to vet the additional forensic psychiatrists on the neatly typed list. To cop a plea, they'd have to bolster their psychiatric evidence. To support Butterfield's affirmative defense of the lack of criminal responsibility by reason of mental disease, they'd need two more shrinks to reach the same diagnosis—criminally insane. Dr. Miri Shtern would know who best suited their needs.

The psychiatrist's cell phone rang several times before the husky voice rolled a "hallo" at him.

"We're adjourned until tomorrow," he said.

"That's not surprising, considering what happened to Ms. Martin in court today." Her voice was tight as though blaming him for the tragedy. "It's touch and go, in case you're interested."

"Poor kid. Do you think she'll pull through?" he asked, outwardly dismissing Miri's silent accusation. He'd send Jessie Martin flowers; that would make her, and him, feel better.

"As I told Mr. Samuels, it's in God's hands."

"I have a bad feeling about the motion, so I'd like to be prepared." Jeremy hated to be so crass, but he'd called her for a specific reason, not to play a blame game. "The sooner we extricate Butterfield from the penal system, the better. You agree that he's not thriving in jail and he requires medical attention, not rehabilitation. Right?" He hesitated, listening to the silence on the line. "I'd like you to take a look at a list of additional psychiatrists to add to our team."

"Jerry, I suggest you wait until the judge renders his decision before you decide to proceed down this path. However, if you insist, email the list over. I'll let you know tomorrow."

"I'm meeting with Butterfield at seven o'clock tonight. Care to join me?"

"Do I have any choice in the matter?"

Jeremy chuckled and hung up the phone.

CHAPTER
52

Each time Jeremy visited Butterfield in jail, he noticed greater evidence of the man's physical and mental deterioration. Last time, he'd observed clumps of Butterfield's hair feathering his jumpsuit like a molting chicken. The man's bony fingers nervously plucked at the scabs on his scalp, which were visible through his thinning hair. The skin along his jawline sagged and his eye sockets sank into the deep craters of his skull.

The ghoul substituted for the handsome teacher terrified Jeremy, because there was no reason for the radical transformation. Racked with guilt, his sleep had become fitful as he mulled over and over again whether his abysmal representation was responsible for Butterfield's weakening state. Jeremy felt helpless. He was doing the best he could.

This evening before Jeremy and Miri entered the cell, Bernard warned them that Butterfield had been complaining of stomach cramps. However, the on-call doctor had examined him and found nothing wrong. Standing in the cell's doorway, the stench of vomit and urine burned their noses and throats. In the far corner, a bedraggled Butterfield curled up in the fetal position, wailing in the low, guttural tone of a baying coyote.

Miri ran to Butterfield's side. "How long has Mr. Butterfield been like this?"

The guard looked embarrassed. "Doc, he wasn't like this when I checked in on him a half hour ago. I swear. I never would've left him in this condition."

The trickle of running water drew Jeremy to the steel toilet tucked in the opposite corner of the cell. Dark, murky water overflowed the rim, pooling on the floor. He pointed at the surveillance cameras mounted near the ceiling. "Aren't those cameras working? Isn't he under 24/7 suicide watch?" he shouted at Bernard. He turned toward the eyes observing from the secret control booth and said, "Hey you, up there. Get. Some. Help. Now."

Their client shuddered.

"Jerry, calm down. You're upsetting Terrence." Miri calmly instructed Bernard to alert the medical team and housekeeping. Jeremy stood aside as Miri stroked the teacher's shoulders and whispered yoga breathing exercises into his ear. "Slow and deep. In through the nose, out through the mouth. In and out." She repeated the instructions until the soft whooshing of air confirmed his compliance. Gradually, his body unfolded on the damp floor. Miri fluttered her hands above him like butterfly wings, lulling her patient into a state of deep relaxation.

In the infirmary, Miri reviewed the medical chart with the jail's physician, while Jeremy watched over their shoulders. The notes reflected that over the past few days, Butterfield had complained of abdominal cramps and diarrhea on four occasions. The symptoms were dismissed as a viral infection when the tests indicated no bacterial infections or abnormalities.

"In this place, intestinal bugs travel faster than we can keep up. We've experienced a flu-like epidemic over the past week and as you know, these things have to run their course," the on-duty doctor whined.

"So you left Mr. Butterfield untreated?" Jeremy asked.

"There's nothing physically wrong with him. What do you suggest? Move him to Mid-Hudson Regional Hospital for observation?" the doctor asked.

"Let him stay here for the night. Mr. Kaplan and I will advise you in the morning," Miri said.

Outside the jail, Miri pulled a sweater tightly around her shoulders in the chilly evening air. Jeremy lit up a smoke. After a long draw he said, "If we commit him to the psych ward for observation, that would bolster our position."

Miri was quiet, too quiet. He was receiving signals that something wasn't sitting right with her, but he couldn't quite put his finger on it.

Maybe, for the first time, they were at odds over Terrence Butterfield. As a criminal defense attorney, his goal was proving Terrence's insanity while, as a psychiatrist, hers was instituting Terrence's mental health treatment plan. He knew Miri detested the legal jargon— "insane," "mentally incompetent,"—viewing them as catchphrases, throw away words, meaningless and devoid of medical substance. Clearly, the legal terminology meant one thing to him and another to her. In his mind, the issue was black and white. Terrence was either crazy or he wasn't. In psychiatry, there were symptoms, theories, diagnosis, and treatment. Gradations of black and white, shades of gray.

Hogwash.

He appreciated that if Terrence were to receive proper psychiatric treatment, Miri must provide irrefutable medical testimony to meet the legal threshold: that he lacked criminal responsibility; that he didn't understand the nature of the hostile, grisly acts he committed; and that he didn't comprehend that the brutal murder of Ryan Paige was wrong. In other words, that Terrence experienced a psychotic episode during his rampage against Ryan, losing all contact with reality at that time.

She'd exhaustively explained to him the possible triggers for Terrence's behavior: Asperger's, a corticosteroid-induced psychosis stemming from asthma inhaler abuse, opioids, alcoholism, or bipolar disorder. But she'd said the more time she'd spent with him, the more she became unconvinced. His recurring moodiness, delusions, and paranoia suggested a deeper emotional disorder, especially after he'd attacked her in the lounge.

Jeremy assessed Miri as she paced on the sidewalk. He truly believed that she'd completed the preliminary draft of her diagnosis and had locked it in her office desk drawer. So far, she'd resisted his pestering her for the report. Maybe he'd made a mistake in giving Miri carte blanche to select the two colleagues to corroborate her findings. She'd made her decision quickly, having told him earlier that she'd chosen Doctors Benedict Carlton and Roberta Peck. Perhaps she wanted to wait until they'd completed their independent analysis.

Jeremy didn't care about the reason for Miri's delay or her mind games. He was running out of time and patience. Terrence's life was hanging in the balance, and he prayed that her diagnosis was worth the wait. Without Miri's cooperation, he was lost, and so was Terrence.

CHAPTER
53

Jessie stirred and opened her eyes. The room was pitch black except for the slices of moonlight shining through the unfamiliar window. Because of its brightness, she thought it must be a full moon. Groggy with sedation, she rolled over onto her side, closed her eyes, and slipped back into sleep.

When she awoke early the next morning, her hand flew to her belly. She winced at the tenderness beneath the wide gauze bandage. Although still a bit dopey, she possessed enough clarity to realize that her baby was gone. She recalled that something terrible had happened, but she couldn't quite fill in the details. She'd been at the courthouse with her Dad, and Kyle had testified. She'd been furious with Kyle and had gone to the bathroom. After that she drew a blank.

She glanced over at Kyle, who was asleep in the large recliner next to her bed. Despite their recent rift, his presence was comforting. Yet, she hoped that his vigil wasn't a bad sign. He could certainly tell her what had occurred in the restroom, but from her present condition it must have been serious. Her stomach lurched with fear that something terrible had happened to her baby.

Frantic, she pressed the call button on her bed.

Before a nurse could respond to her call, Dr. S. entered the room for his morning rounds. Kyle startled awake as she started talking to the doctor.

Jessie swallowed hard, fighting back the tears. "Where's my baby?"

"Your baby's in the neonatal intensive care unit, but you were in quite a state when they brought you in," Dr. S. said.

Although she felt somewhat relieved, she had a million questions to ask him.

"Can you please tell me—"

"I'll address all of your concerns, but please let me explain," Dr. S. said, launching into a monologue.

The momentary reassurance that she'd felt melted into horror when the doctor described her traumatic arrival at the hospital. She'd been thrashing about in another seizure, and, notwithstanding the administration of anticonvulsant medications, she'd experienced an additional half-dozen episodes. Eventually, they'd stabilized her enough to allow for a cesarean delivery. When her convulsions subsided after the delivery, she had still risked slipping into a coma. So, for several hours, she'd been closely monitored in the maternity ICU before being transferred to her private room. The culprit of her problems had been severe eclampsia, a potentially fatal pregnancy complication that manifested itself not only in seizures, but also in heart, artery, and liver dysfunction.

"Eclampsia was nearly impossible to diagnose since its symptoms were masked by your other pregnancy symptoms like high blood pressure and previa placenta, and you had no genetic predisposition for eclampsia," Dr. S. said.

While the condition explained her symptoms, she couldn't believe that an undiagnosed disease had almost stolen her life. But Dr. S. still hadn't revealed any details about her baby.

"I don't care about me; I'm alive. What about my baby?"

She clasped Kyle's hand as Dr. S. continued. "My dear, you've given birth to a three-pound, nine-ounce baby girl. Your daughter's lungs were underdeveloped, but that is to be expected given her premature birth at thirty-four weeks. Otherwise, she's a fighter, like you." His jack o'lantern smile spread across his face. "Your daughter is thriving nicely in the NICU."

Jessie was comforted to know that her baby was alive, but she grew alarmed at the thought of her daughter struggling to breathe air into her premature body. She opened her mouth to speak, but Kyle squeezed her hand, indicating that she should let the doctor finish.

"With your pregnancy behind you, you and your baby will be fine, but you'll both have to remain in the hospital for observation. The neonatologist will bring you up to speed on your daughter's progress."

Dr. S. was reassuring, but she kept replaying his diagnosis in her mind: eclampsia, seizures, coma, NICU. Her life seemed so out of control. The only cure to ease Jessie's mind was to see, touch, and hold her newborn.

"I want to see her now," she insisted.

"I visited her last night and she's perfect and lovely, just like you. Here look." Kyle showed her his phone's wallpaper.

Jessie's eyes and cheeks grew wet as she saw her daughter for the first time. Her baby looked like a fragile porcelain doll that would shatter if she were touched. Inside a flannel-lined incubator, the baby's eyes were closed, and she looked peaceful, but Jessie's heart broke at the sight of the monitor wires and blue breathing tube covering her daughter's face.

"I know you're worried, but she's fine, really. She's being watched like a hawk and they're taking good care of her," Kyle said, "Let's wait to hear from her doc."

"You must rest," Dr. S. said, handing her a tissue. "You need to flush the medications from your system before you can see her. You must be patient and give your baby time to develop properly."

She heard what he'd prescribed, but the excitement was intoxicating. It was like it was her own birthday, and she couldn't wait to cradle the most precious gift in the world.

The next evening, an on-duty nurse helped Jessie into a wheelchair and rolled her down the hall to the NICU. The hallway was short, but to Jessie it felt like a journey around the world. When the nurse finally placed her baby, Lily, into her arms for the first time, she felt grateful. Not only for Lily, but for her life, too. The maternity nurses had told her that she'd been lucky. After the birth, she'd teetered on the fine line between life and death, and there had been a great deal of concern over her condition. Under

Dr. S.'s vigilant care, she'd rallied, and here she was holding Lily. As Jessie fondled the baby's miniature hands and feet, her life came into focus. The world assumed a new meaning. The path of her life became clear. Who would remain and who would be left behind.

Over the next four days, Jessie shuttled down the hall between the NICU and her room on the maternity wing. Her hospital room became an embarrassment of well-wishes, jam-packed with flowers and presents from her relatives, friends, McMann and Curtis, and even Jeremy Kaplan. The most surprising baby gift had arrived in the form of a two-foot tall stuffed giraffe. Attached to its furry neck was a note: "Jessie, congratulations. She's lucky to have such a cool mom. The best always, Robbie."

On discharge day, her bag was packed and she was ready to go home. Kyle conveniently begged off as the chore didn't involve Lily, only his ex-fiancée. To avoid friction, she'd asked him to clear the rest of his belongings from their house by the time she got home. The proud grandparents, Ed and Lena, jumped at the chance to bring her home from the hospital, but instead, she accepted Hal's offer. She couldn't resist a handsome man bearing a pink and white balloon bouquet and Belgian chocolates.

Jessie was thrilled to be discharged from the hospital, but she was anxious, and a little depressed that her daughter would be left behind. Dr. Yu, the neonatologist, had indicated that it would be at least another month before Lily was ready to leave. Jessie would have to tough it out, commuting the ten minutes between her home and the hospital. At least that would give her time to complete the nursery preparations left unfinished by Lily's hasty arrival.

CHAPTER
54

Jeremy checked the Lawyer's Diary on his desk and swore out loud. It had been a week since he'd last seen Miri at the jail, and he hadn't heard a peep from her. He was still waiting for her report as well as dreading the impending issuance of Judge Hamilton's decision. The pre-trial hearing had been reconvened the morning following their last meeting, and after hearing the damning testimony of the arresting cops, Jeremy had grown more certain and more desperate that they'd have to pursue the insanity plea.

Mo stuck her head into his office, interrupting his brooding. "Dr. Shtern called. She'll be here at two. Does that work?"

"About time," he snarled, popping an antacid into his mouth.

When Jeremy welcomed Miri into his office, she was all business. She wore a white lab coat with her name embroidered over her heart and her dark hair was pulled away from her face. It was a bit off-putting since he was used to seeing her in civilian clothes, not those she wore at the psych clinic.

They proceeded to the library, and Jeremy shut the door behind them.

"Please take a seat," he said, and she joined him at the conference table. Her fingers gripped a white envelope he assumed contained the final forensic evaluation that would determine the future of Terrence Butterfield.

"Jerry, before I present my findings," Miri said, "I'd like to share some personal observations, strictly off the record." Her words were rushed, and seemed almost apologetic.

Her comment worried him. The report's results must not meet the legal criteria to establish criminal insanity if she was prefacing her remarks with "off the record."

"From the first moment I entered Terrence's cell, I felt assaulted by two individuals inhabiting the same corpus and competing for dominance over his flesh and blood. One intelligent and wickedly charming, the other conniving and dangerous. Angel and devil. Jekyll and Hyde. Frankenstein and monster." She paused. "I have never witnessed such extreme personal turbulence, and frankly, I was concerned that he would take his own life, especially after his initial suicide attempt. But as we began to work together, my opinion changed."

It was obvious to Jeremy that on some level, she truly liked Butterfield, or at least she liked the challenge he presented. But that was her problem. He didn't like the guy, but Butterfield was entitled to his best efforts in representing him under the law.

"I wanted you to know that in reaching my conclusion, I applied a multidimensional approach to my diagnosis. I considered my clinical observations of Terrence, his medical and psychiatric histories, the DA files and police reports, his financial and employment records, and my forensic evaluation. As requested, my report makes a determination as to whether Terrence lacked the capacity to appreciate the nature of his actions at the time of the murder and whether his conduct was wrong."

Miri wasn't giving up her verdict in any short order. With each passing minute, a knot grew tighter and tighter in Jeremy's stomach, until he felt he couldn't breathe. He willed himself to relax by focusing on Miri's detailed attention to their client. After all, Judge Hamilton would analyze not only her conclusion, but the methodology employed in reaching that result. There must be absolutely no doubt, procedurally or substantively, in the judge's mind that Butterfield lacked the criminal responsibility for the death of Ryan Paige. Jeremy's defense of Butterfield's incompetency to stand trial, as well as his life, depended on it.

"I believe that this is what you require of me, is it not?" Her dark eyes sparkled. "Terrence has been an extremely complex and challenging case and I wanted to thank you for including me on your team. I hope that we can work together again in the future." She slid the envelope across the table and he greedily accepted it.

Jeremy was aware of the sudden dryness in his mouth, of the drumming in his chest and the rough texture of the envelope in his hands as he tore open the slim package and extracted the report. His eyes skipped over the summaries of the patient's background and his impressions of himself to the section upon which everything, his case, Terrence's life, hinged—the last paragraphs.

When Mr. Butterfield speaks about the murder, it is as if he is discussing someone other than himself and assumes no responsibility for his actions. He is in denial about his responsibility for the death of Ryan Paige. He is delusional, presenting himself as completely opposite from how he perceives and feels about himself and his place in society. He strives for achievement but feels wholly inadequate to attain such accomplishments. He goes to great effort to present a veneer of normalcy to the world, but when the veneer begins to slip away, the brutality of his unconscious motivations and wishes, and possibly suicide, take precedence. His grasp on reality becomes increasingly unstable. On the night of August 31st, his internal conflicts reached a crisis point, and he became unaware of his actions. These perverse desires led him to commit the vile acts upon Ryan Paige.

The diagnosis: schizoaffective disorder and psychosis. Depersonalization disorder. These conditions had remained undiagnosed for a decade, because Terrence Butterfield had suppressed any outward symptoms. However, during the past year, he became more aware of his violent tendencies and became depressed and suicidal. As the stresses in his life increased, it became more and more difficult for him to mask his mental illness, feelings of anger, and inadequacy.

As he read the bottom line, a warm glow radiated throughout his body as though he'd hit a grand slam right out of the freaking park, as Judge Hamilton would say.

Due to the violent nature of the crime, the patient's lack of understanding the nature and consequence of his conduct and that his conduct was wrong, and his unpredictability in future times of stress, the undersigned considers the patient to be suffering from dangerous mental disorders, requiring continuous in-patient treatment and services inside a secure psychiatric hospital.

Signed,

Miri Shtern, M.D.

Included in the packet were the reports of Miri's colleagues, Doctors Carlton and Peck, concurring with the diagnosis. Armed with this forensic ammunition, he could crush the district attorney's office. They'd have no choice but to discuss a plea bargain. The expression on Hollenbeck's face would be priceless.

"From your smile, I trust that you're pleased with my diagnosis," she said.

"Miri, I knew I could count on you."

"I'll hope that you'll smile when you get my bill."

"Maybe this will save Terrence's life, so it's worth it's weight in gold."

Somehow, Jeremy didn't think that Butterfield would mind. But who knew how the narcissistic, stubborn, crazy teacher would react?

CHAPTER
55

Hal logged off his computer and was looking forward to leaving the office at the end of the long day. The intercom buzzed, halting him as he gathered up his paperwork. It was his secretary, who said that Judge Hamilton's chambers had called. The decision on the motion to dismiss was ready. He closed his eyes and sighed. This was it. Everything rode on this pre-trial decision. His case against Butterfield, Jessie's career, and maybe even his own.

He dashed next door to the courthouse and collected the papers from the judge's clerk. The afternoon was warm and sunny and he sat down on the courthouse steps. He licked his parched lips as he flipped to the last page to read the final words.

MOTION DENIED.

"Yeah! All right." He pumped his fist in the air. The prosecution had prevailed. The motion to dismiss the murder charges had been denied. The case would proceed to trial.

In fact, Judge Hamilton's decision covered all the bases, making Kaplan's appeal impossible. Although Hal had never doubted it for a second, the judge had ruled that Jessie hadn't breached the attorney-client privilege owed to Butterfield because one had never existed. It was irrelevant whether he'd contacted her as a friend or as an attorney. Butterfield had never retained her to represent him, so she'd been free to relate the bizarre, upsetting midnight call to Emory and her father. Finally, Hamilton ruled that although Emory and Ed Martin had learned about the killing from Jessie, Butterfield had confessed his crime to each of them when they'd spoken with him on the telephone. At that point, they'd been free to take whatever steps they'd thought were advisable. Emory had done just that. He'd contacted the police.

With this shut out, his team was on track to a slam-dunk at the trial with Butterfield's admission of guilt. Thanks to Jessie's flash drive, they could establish Butterfield's premeditation of the killing. Their case would be further buttressed by the abuse allegations against Butterfield made by the older brother, Robbie, stemming from when the teacher had tutored the kid in high school. Life without parole would be guaranteed.

Hal should've been pleased by the way the puzzle pieces were fitting together, but he felt a sense of foreboding. His victories were never this easy.

The judge had scheduled a conference for nine o'clock the first thing the next morning.

Hal appeared at Judge Hamilton's chambers with a cup of coffee in hand. A sense of impending doom filled him as soon as he saw Kaplan's smug expression.

"Here you go, Samuels," Kaplan said, handing him a manila envelope. "Read it and weep."

Hal tore it open and scanned the contents. His chest tightened. Kaplan had outwitted him with reports from three psychiatrists who attested to Butterfield's mental incapacity. There had been *no mens rea*. In other words, Butterfield had no criminal intention to commit murder. According to the experts, his admission wasn't what it appeared to be. When the killer had used the words, "I think I killed someone," it indicated that he'd lacked the presence of mind to know that he'd shot, killed, and maimed Ryan Paige. The experts argued that Butterfield's mind was not in concert with his actions. In other words, the defendant had been out of his mind at the time of the murder.

"What a crock," Hal said. He didn't buy into a single syllable of the psychiatric mumbo-jumbo. Butterfield was educated, conniving, and manipulative. Kaplan was even smarter. The killer and his lawyer had outplayed him. That was all there was to it.

"Sometimes you win, sometimes you lose, and sometimes your client's just plain crazy," Kaplan said, shrugging.

Judge Hamilton proved to be of no assistance. "The defense has pitched a perfect game, Mr. Samuels. We can't proceed to try a man who's not mentally responsible for his crime. Not without a run to the appellate division and court of appeals."

At that moment, he hated the judge's inane baseball metaphors almost as much as he hated Jeremy Kaplan.

When he returned from court, Lauren was brandishing a copy of the psych reports. Her mouth was twisted as though she'd eaten a sour grape.

"Hal, call Kaplan. Have him submit an order of commitment for Butterfield as soon as possible so we'll be rid of this case." He opened his mouth to argue that their office obtain their own psych evaluations, but she held up her hand. "I know what you're going to say, but our psych experts would agree with their findings. Let's wrap this up and we can move on to more pressing issues."

There was no use fighting with his boss. He knew when to fold 'em and this was one of those situations. Like wisps of a cloud, his landmark case had evaporated. Reduced to the equivalent of a traffic violation. The worst part was going to be breaking the news to Bob and Betty Paige. They'd feel cheated, knowing that their son's murderer had been committed to a hospital, albeit a high-security facility, instead of a high-security prison. He detested being the messenger of this travesty of justice and defeat.

CHAPTER
56

Jeremy Kaplan carefully drafted the final order in the matter of the *People of the State of New York Against Terrence Butterfield.* As negotiated with the district attorney, the order committed Butterfield to the custody of the New York State Mental Health Commission, in exchange for his client's acquittal from all responsibility in the death of Ryan Paige on the grounds of mental illness.

The use of the word "acquittal" in the court order was a bit archaic and would shock the citizens of Poughkeepsie, maybe even the nation. His neighbors would take the word's meaning at face value; Butterfield had been set free without being found guilty of murder. They'd be enraged, disappointed even, but that was the law. Crazy people cannot be held accountable for their crimes. The community should be grateful that Butterfield was being locked away. They should be grateful to Jeremy for making it happen.

Jeremy suspected that the media would have a field day. Terrence Butterfield, the once-beloved high school teacher, had gotten away with bloody murder. The press would minimize the unanimous conclusion of the three psychiatrists that Butterfield suffered from several dangerous mental disorders. They'd harp on the fact that Butterfield had escaped the ultimate punishment, imprisonment without parole. Rather, he'd be confined to a mental institution; in this case, the Mid-Hudson Psychiatric Forensic Center in New Hampton, New York. Snide comments would suggest that Butterfield's new residence at the plush campus was designed to expedite his rapid recovery from psychiatric illness. Sooner or later, he'd be back on the streets, back in their community.

They'd paint this as another OJ situation. The injustice resulting from the prosecution's incompetence would sell their newspapers and magazines like hotcakes.

But Jeremy didn't view the case that way. Butterfield's acquittal and commitment to a psych hospital had nothing to do with justice or punishment. He knew, the DA knew, everyone knew that his client was culpable for the death of Ryan Paige, but the law had been on his side. Sure, he felt terrible that a kid had been intentionally and brutally murdered, but he had simply done his job.

He'd lost the battle to dismiss the murder charges, but he'd won the war to rehabilitate Butterfield's life. However, ahead lay the greatest obstacle. It was imperative for psychotic Terrence

Butterfield to buy in. To admit that he was crazy, even though it was obvious to the rest of the universe that the guy possessed a carton of loose screws. Jeremy anticipated a battle, but he was mistaken.

Butterfield was already seated in the jail's conference room when Jeremy and Miri arrived. Butterfield's appearance was neat and tidy. Clean-shaven. Not a hair out of place. He relaxed in the chair, his long legs crossed at the knee, as though he was at home watching a ballgame.

"Jeremy, Dr. Shtern. To what do I owe this visit?" Butterfield asked in a sarcastically cheery voice.

Their approach was two-pronged. Miri explained her medical conclusions and Jeremy outlined the terms of the plea arrangement as compared with their chances of success after a jury trial. Which was nil.

"I have to admit that I'm pleasantly surprised. I didn't know what to expect with the both of you walking in here with such sour pusses," Butterfield said. "Of course I'll accept the plea. You've done me a great service, recognizing that one isolated incident shouldn't mar the rest of my life. After all, I was, I *am,* an excellent educator, held in the highest regard by my peers and the New York State PTA. After the completion of my treatment, which will no doubt be wildly successful, I'll be able to resume my life. Perhaps teach again." A smirk played upon his lips and gold flecks danced like fire in his irises. "But now that I'm acquitted, it's truly amazing how exhilarated freedom makes you feel. Giddy, almost. Thanks to you, my sins have been washed away forever."

Butterfield pressed his palms against the table's edge and folded his chest forward toward them. "Thank you, Dr. Shtern, Jeremy. Thank you both, sincerely. Or maybe I should thank God for the baptismal? The resurrection? Please excuse the ecclesiastical references. Mind you, I'm not a religious man, but God has forgiven me. How else can you explain that he has given me liberty?" He gestured his chained hands toward the heavens.

Jeremy remained calm, but Miri's features hardened.

"Or, Dr. Shtern, have you cured me?" Butterfield's chin rested on the tips of his pointer fingers and he wagged his head in mock disbelief. "Come now, Doctor. Don't you believe in medical miracles? Do you doubt your skills? Correct me if I'm wrong, Dr. Shtern, but isn't medicine a game of skill, not one of chance?" He paused. "In your honorable opinion, what does it take to get away with murder? Skill or chance?"

Jeremy didn't want to tangle with Terrence although his smugness irked him. At this point, it made no difference to him whether Butterfield was innocent or guilty. Sane or nuts. He'd been amply compensated to represent his client to the best of his ability, and he'd accomplished that goal. Perhaps too well. If Miri wanted to get mind-melted by Butterfield, that was her prerogative.

With Butterfield's consent to the deal and the signing of the order by Judge Hamilton, his client's fate was released from his hands and placed into those of the State of New York. No jury trial, no endless appeals. He doubted whether he'd ever hear from Terrence Butterfield again. Good riddance to bad rubbish.

In the few short weeks after the resolution of the Butterfield case, Jeremy benefited from a remarkable payday. The quote from P.T. Barnum proved true: "I don't care what you say about me, just spell my name right." That's Kaplan, with a K. The office phone rang off the hook. The *New York Times*. *SuperLawyers.com*. Some guy from *Vanity Fair*. They all wanted to discuss the murderous teacher from Poughkeepsie. His legal mojo was back.

Mo sat across from him, sipping on a diet cola and reviewing the new retainers. Jeremy slumped in his large leather chair, examining his newest acquisition, a box of 1966 limited edition Cohibas. He raised one from the wooden crate, delicately removed the commemorative band as if from a woman's finger, and inhaled its spicy aroma. The robust flavor would be well worth the sixty bucks he'd shelled out for the pleasure of the vintage Cuban smoke.

"Let's pack up the Butterfield files and put them in storage. I can't stand looking at them another minute." He snipped the tip off of the cigar's nipple and his mouth watered in anticipation.

"Yeah, yeah, I will. I've been swamped," Mo said. "It seems like every criminal between Yonkers and Albany has harkened at your cellar doorstep. And they're some real goodies, like the councilman who allegedly took bribes on the town hall's expansion project and, my favorite, the art dealer who pilfered her ex-husband's artwork and made a fortune from the sales. Where do you find these people?"

"They find me, remember? At least there's no blood on their hands," Jeremy said as a shiver traveled down his spine. He twirled the cigar in his fingers. "Think we need some help around here? A paralegal maybe or an associate?"

Mo peered at him over the reading glasses propped on her nose. "Only if you want to see Gayle and the boys again."

"Did I hear someone mention my name?" His wife entered the sanctuary and placed a wooden tray carrying his lunch on the credenza against the wall. "How's your appetite?" she said suggestively.

"Come here." Jeremy beckoned to her while slyly concealing the contraband inside his desk drawer.

Gayle sidled over and he slipped his arm around her waist. She bent and brushed her lips against his crown and then raked her fingers through the fine springs of his hair. "Jerry, you need a haircut... and nice cigars. Cubans?"

He shrugged like a kid caught with his hands in the cookie jar and flattened out the curls she had sent tumbling across his eyes. "Isn't she the greatest wife ever? I don't deserve her."

"You're right, you don't. So hire someone to help you, otherwise, you'll be nagged to death by your work wife and your real wife. Right, Mo?" Gayle winked at her co-conspirator.

"She's right, you know. Between the two of us, you don't stand a chance." Mo gathered up the signed correspondences from her boss's desk.

"Okay, draft an advertisement. I'll review it in the morning."

Mo made no indication she was listening as she left, but he knew she was.

"And hold all my calls," Jeremy yelled before he kicked the door closed.

CHAPTER
57

Hal couldn't shake his disappointment. All day, he sulked around in a pissed-off state as though life was an elephant squatting on his head. The Butterfield case hadn't been resolved to his satisfaction, although the rest of the office, especially Lauren, basked in the glory of the conviction. To Hal, the plea fell short of a conviction. It was an *acquittal*. Butterfield was scot-free of the murder charge and double jeopardy prevented the homicidal maniac from being retried for the murder of Ryan Paige. The killer would be institutionalized, treated for his mental deficiencies, and then, who knew?

Later in the afternoon, Lauren trotted into his office. "May I?" she asked, planting herself on the sofa. Her bearing was strangely reserved and respectful.

He narrowed his eyes and nodded.

"You can't let this case get to you. It's one of a thousand you'll prosecute unless you come work for me in Albany." Her red lips curled into a coy smile. "I've received the senate nomination and I'd like you to run my staff there. However, if you'd prefer to fill my slot here, I'll understand." Lauren paused as though waiting for a show of appreciation. "Take the weekend and let me know on Monday."

When he remained silent, she rose and left.

He leaned back in his office chair and scanned the panorama along Market Street. The marquee of the Bardavon Theater, the cupola of the post office, the Fountain Plaza at City Hall, and the storefronts came into sharp focus. He felt no elation about Lauren's offer. Defeat had siphoned all of his energy, and his joints ached in anticipation of a predicted thunderstorm. He didn't want to think about Lauren or the office right now. All he wanted to do was go home.

Hal grabbed his briefcase and left for the weekend.

The strangeness of the Fox Hill condo hadn't worn off, even after a month of Hal's living there. The silence, the space, and the solitude welcomed him home whenever he inserted the key into the front door lock. Yet, Hal didn't question his good karma in snatching up this three-bedroom place all for himself. He'd previewed several apartments advertised in the *Journal* and they had all been dumps. Moldy bathrooms. Peeling paint. Close to the office but overlooking the arterial highway or the Metro North train tracks. Then, out of the blue, his golf buddy Eric Winston offered him the use of the place while Eric was on a six-month assignment with IBM in Singapore.

Hal had jumped at the offer because the condo was right out of the pages of *GQ*. Brazilian cherry floors. Honed marble kitchen countertops with top-of-the-line stainless appliances. Floor-to-ceiling rear windows that overlooked a pond. State of the art home theater. Italian marble bathrooms.

The slick digs were like a perplexing new skin, a different identity. He felt like a cliché. Hal Samuels III, a late thirty-something soon-to-be divorced man shacking up in a groovy bachelor pad. The only thing missing was the Porsche 911 Carrera Cabriolet. And lots of young chicks, but scoring wasn't his style. Monogamy was his style.

Hal changed out of his work clothes into his faded jeans and a Coldplay T-shirt. He sunk into the soft leather couch and propped his bare feet up on the ottoman. He folded his hands behind his head and leaned back. The masculine odor of rawhide and beer filled his nostrils as he closed his eyes.

He thought about Erin. Her indifference aggravated him. Whenever he saw her, she remained polite, distant, and frozen in her model's figure. There had been no signs of a pregnancy. It was early anyway, or was it? Only she knew how far along she was and he was afraid to ask.

The stink of suspicion teased his imagination. Dishonesty? Infidelity? Had another guy been the real reason she'd agreed to separate? Or had there been a miscarriage or a false pregnancy? Had the pregnancy test even been Erin's? He had a right to know. She was still his wife. He stopped himself, catching a whiff of the crazies hovering over him like a dark cloud and decided to let life settle out a bit. Eventually, the truth would be revealed.

For the most part, he'd enjoyed the seven years he'd been married to Erin. When Jessie had unexpectedly tumbled back into his life, the blinders had been ripped off. Like Lady Justice's scales, he weighed a life filled with obligation versus love. There'd been no choice.

Jessie. Yeah, he'd stop by to see her later. Jessie was presently keeping him at arm's length, but she appeared to be receptive to his attention. She'd yet to admit that she loved him, but he'd read the devotion in her mossy eyes, her soft voice, and her smile. He wasn't worried; he understood. He was willing to wait until she was ready to share the lifetime he offered.

Hal rose from the couch, opened the Sub-Zero fridge and was rudely reminded of the absence of any food or substance in the fridge. It would be impossible to whip up a meal from French's mustard, a quart of milk, and a pair of apples rotting on the glass shelf. Maybe he'd call for a calzone or steamed dumplings. Maybe he'd become the next District Attorney or maybe he'd be Chief of Staff for State Senator Lauren Hollenbeck. Hal studied the take-out menus taped to the refrigerator door. The possibilities were endless.

CHAPTER
58

Jessie checked and double-checked the infant car seat, making sure that it was properly secured into the rear seat of her Jeep, facing backward. According to the manual, she'd installed it correctly, but she was nervous anyway. Lily was coming home from the hospital today. During the past month, the scrawny three-pound and nine-ounce preemie had blossomed into a roly-poly five pounder, who was alert and smiled euphorically at the world.

When Dr. Yu discharged Lily from her care, the news had stirred up a mixture of emotions inside Jessie—happiness, relief, gratitude, anxiety, and fear. Leaving her baby behind in the NICU had been stressful. She'd spent nearly every waking hour by Lily's side. More than once, the nurses had ordered her to go home. Moms require rest, too, especially after such an ordeal, they'd delicately urged. Starting today, the doctors, nurses, incubators, and

NICU were reflections in Jessie's rearview mirror. The nursery lay ahead on the bright horizon.

Her mother leaned over her shoulder, performing a final inspection on the car seat. "Are you sure that you don't want me to come with you to the hospital?"

"Mom, Kyle said that he'd meet me there."

"Well, all right, but this is my first grandchild," Lena said, clearly miffed.

"Mom, I'll really need your help when Lily's home. Somebody's got to show me the ropes." Her mother smiled, apparently satisfied with the compliment on her motherly abilities.

True to his word, Kyle was waiting on the curb outside the hospital's main entrance. They hadn't seen each other in almost a month. During the strain of the past few months, his visits to Poughkeepsie had become scarce. Before Jessie's discharge from the hospital, he'd moved most of his belongings from the house. The only visible remnants of their relationship were the skis, guitars, and a few cartons of books he'd left in the basement.

Kyle offered to carry the infant carrier upstairs to the NICU and grabbed its handle. "It's about time that we brought her to our own home." He blushed as he realized his error, but she let the comment pass. She was in a hurry to see Lily.

Inside a clear plastic bassinet, Lily Martin Emory lay bundled in a pink flannel blanket. A matching stocking cap covered her furry black hair and elfin ears. On discharge days, the neonatal nurses dressed the baby girls like this as their way of saying goodbye. During Lily's month in the NICU, Jessie had witnessed dozens of teary discharges and had been jealous. Yet, it struck Jessie that the nurses' attachment to her and Lily registered deeper, stronger, so she anticipated that the farewells would be heart-wrenching. She hugged the team who'd cared for her daughter, thanking them for their support and expertise.

"Don't worry. I've got her," Kyle said, grasping the carrier's handle with both hands. Jessie wiped away her tears as they entered the elevator and bid the NICU goodbye. Unaware, Lily sucked on her pacifier. It bobbed up and down in between her rosebud lips.

Outside, a chilly breeze had kicked up so Jessie tucked an extra blanket over the carrier as she locked Lily into the car seat.

Kyle checked his watch as though he had someplace more important to be. "Okay, go ahead. I'll drive," he said, slipping into the driver's seat. "You can sit in back with her."

"Thank you," she whispered. She snuggled up next to Lily in the back seat while Kyle drove home at what seemed to be five miles per hour. When they finally reached home, she unlocked the car seat and Kyle gently carried Lily inside.

"I see you've finished the nursery," Kyle whispered as they carried Lily into her new bedroom. Three walls were painted soft pink while bright pink, white, and lime green stripes accented the wall behind the crib. Framed letters spelling LILY hung from ribbons on the wall. Pink gingham curtains festooned the two large casement windows, highlighting the white crib, changing table, rocking chair, and armoire. Rays of light streamed through the crystal chandelier, sparkling across the ceiling like stars in the sky.

"I had some help," she said noncommittally.

Last week, while Jessie and her father had been interpreting the crib's instructions, the doorbell had rung. When she'd opened the door, Hal had stood on the front porch, clutching a bouquet of stargazer lilies. He'd seen them and thought of her, he'd said. It was late October, almost Halloween, and these flowers were rare, out of season. Butterflies fluttered inside her at the sight of the warm, broad smile she recalled from their NYU days. Without being asked, he rescued Ed from his chore, and her father excused himself under the guise of making coffee.

"I think deep down he likes you," she whispered.

"I certainly hope so. I'm planning to stick around for a while." Hal's arms embraced her waist and he pulled her close. "Maybe forever."

She gave him a long, inviting kiss. His lips nibbled at the spot on her neck just below her ear. "Hold on. That's all you get for now."

"Not so fast, Jess. Have I told you how thankful I'm that you're alive and healthy? And that I'm sorry for putting you and Lily in danger over, well, you know?" A flicker of guilt shadowed his handsome face. "I realize that we're taking it slow, but have I told you how much I love you?"

Right that very second she could have responded that she loved him because it was true. Jessie had always loved him. In her mind and heart, she was joyfully announcing it, but it was too soon for her to speak the words. During the past several months, too much had happened to abandon all reason and be swallowed up in him. She wanted to take it slow the second time around. "Not today, but it's nice for a girl to hear."

He feigned a wounded expression at her refusal to return the declaration. She laughed and wiggled her way free. "Harold Samuels III, get working will you?"

"That's what I'm trying to do, missy, but you're distracting me."

Jessie felt Kyle's eyes on her as she delicately peeled off Lily's sweater so as not to disturb the baby asleep in her crib. Outwardly, they looked like a picture-perfect family, but sadness hung over Jessie like the mobile of farm animals dancing over Lily's bed.

"She has your beautiful dark hair," Jessie said softly, standing next to him as they admired their child.

"And your nose." His voice was barely audible. He smiled and his eyes were wet with tears.

She hoped that they were happy tears, filled with the future joys they'd share watching Lily grow, and not tears for what they'd lost. Jessie cupped her hand over the one he rested on the crib's railing and gave it a squeeze. For a few moments longer, they watched their daughter coo and suck on an imaginary teat. Then, they tiptoed from the room and down the stairs to the front hallway.

"I've got to go," Kyle said, his voice choked. "Taxi's waiting."

"Kyle, despite everything, I'll always be grateful to you for Lily." It was the truth spoken from her heart.

"Me, too, babe. Me, too." He planted a polite, dry kiss on her cheek, opened the front door, and walked toward the cab. "Text me if she needs anything."

Kyle wasn't such a bad guy. He'd meant well taking the job in Brooklyn, but his betrayals had broken her trust. They'd never shared the deep connection in their souls that would make them sacrifice everything for one another. And she'd never felt an attraction to him that had shaken her to the core. He wasn't Hal Samuels.

Jessie leaned against the doorjamb, folded her arms across her breasts, and watched him drive away. They were bound together by the blood and love of their child, and she wanted them to remain friends. She wondered if he'd really meant what he'd said about being grateful and being there for Lily. She hoped that with Lily home from the hospital, Kyle would be true to his words. Only time would tell.

One thing was certain, even if Kyle turned out to be unreliable, she could handle this single motherhood gig by herself. And the law thing, too. She'd decided that the chapter with McMann and Curtis had ended, and even though she hadn't yet informed them, that would come in due time. When she was ready. At present, other priorities demanded her attention.

In the far recesses of her mind, Jessie was toying with the idea of hanging up her own shingle. It wouldn't be easy, but thanks to Terrence, she'd gained both criminal defense and prosecution experience, even if it had been to save her own skin.

She'd start over, fresh, without her former teacher and mentor. Terrence Butterfield would not bother her again as long as he remained incarcerated in a high-security state psychiatric hospital across the river. Hopefully, the authorities had the good sense to throw away the key.

As for the rest of her life, which would include Hal, she'd savor each minute, each hour, each day.

Her cell phone buzzed on the foyer table. She ran to answer it before it woke the baby.

"Hello, Jessica," Terrence said.

THE END

ACKNOWLEDGEMENTS

I have been researching and writing this book for a long time, and I owe a debt of gratitude to many people who've contributed to my novel's creation.

When I needed technical assistance, I was lucky to be able to call on old friends to pick their brains. I'd like to thank Retired Sergeant Edward Cox of the Town of Poughkeepsie Police Department for educating me on the proper police procedures and weapons used throughout the book. My dear friends, Drs. Rajan and Nalaini Sriskandarajah graciously shared their knowledge with me so that I could accurately portray Jessie's and Terrence's medical issues. Rajan is an obstetrician–gynecologist extraordinaire with a soft voice and immeasurable humanity, and Nalaini helped me delve into the demented mind of our killer.

Over the years, I've been fortunate to attend classes instructed by Steve Berry, who taught me about story structure and POV, David Morrell, who helped me discover my first line and Rick Moody, who taught me to appreciate sentence fragments and the green under-scoring in Word. And special thanks to my wonderful writing teacher and story coach, Laurie Sanders, for helping me delve into deep POV in her Yellow Highlighter Classes.

Jane Rosenman edited the very first draft of the manuscript, when the book didn't even have a title. Jane deserves credit for helping me wrangle an unruly mess into the story you are reading.

I would be remiss if I didn't mention the terrific writing programs that I've attended such as Thrillerfest, NYU Summer Writing Intensive Program and the now-defunct Backspace Writers Conference. They provided the knowledge and confidence that I needed to be set on the path to publication. Also, thanks to my friends at the Hudson Valley Fiction Writers Workshop, for sustaining my project of a safe space for writers to share their works.

This book would not be in print if it weren't for Jason King, Holli Anderson, James Wymore, and Beth Buck of Immortal Works and I am so grateful to them for publishing my book. It's hard to believe that it all started with #PitMad. Special thanks goes to my amazing editor, Lindsay Flanagan for gently guiding me through the editing process and allowing my own voice to shine through. Everyone at Immortal Works has been wonderful and supportive, and I'm lucky to be part of their publishing family.

I'd like to thank Maureen O'Donnell Esposito Cohen Cockburn for allowing me to borrow Mo, and for all the laughs we've shared in my law practice and as best pals.

My parents deserve infinite and loving thanks for supporting my dream to become an attorney. I hope I've proved them proud.

Most importantly, I want to express my love and gratitude to my husband, Mike, our sons Max and Ben, and my daughter-in-law, Aleigha, for believing in me and encouraging me to continue to write, even when I was ready to burn the manuscript. They taught me never to give up.

Finally, thank you, dear reader. I hope you've enjoyed the exploits of Jessie, Hal, Jeremy and Terrence. Crime doesn't take a holiday and neither do my characters, so they'll be back.

ABOUT THE
AUTHOR

Jodé Millman is the author of the best-selling *Seats: New York* Theatre guidebooks. Her debut novel, *The Midnight Call*, was short-listed for the Clue Award and was designated as "Best Police Procedural" by Chantireviews.com. She is an attorney, blogs about publishing law, and is the co-host and co-producer of the popular podcast *Backstage with the Bardavon* (available on iTunes, Spotify and GooglePlay). Jodé lives with her family in the Hudson Valley, where she is at work on her next novel. Visit her at www.jodesusanmillman.com or on Facebook @JodeSusanMillmanAuthor.

DID YOU ENJOY THIS BOOK?

TELL JODÉ!

Post a REVIEW at
https://www.amazon.com/Midnight-Call-Jod%C3%A9-Millman-ebook/dp/B07PXGWZ26

Visit jodesusanmillman.com for more information and opportunities:

- Contact Jodé
- Find out about Author Events
- Watch Book Trailers
- Enter Contests
- Read Jodé's Blog
- Sign up for the Newsletter

Follow Jodé on  @JodeSusanMillmanAuthor
@jodemillmanauthor

This has been an
Immortal Production

CPSIA information can be obtained
at www.ICGtesting.com
Printed in the USA
LVHW030751210919
631813LV00007B/82